# THE
# NEW
# GOTHIC

A Collection of Contemporary Gothic Fiction

Edited by
## Bradford Morrow

## Patrick McGrath

Vintage Books
A Division of Random House, Inc.
New York

FIRST VINTAGE BOOKS EDITION, OCTOBER 1992

Portions of this work have been previously published in *Conjunctions*.

Grateful acknowledgment is made to the following for permission to reprint previously published and unpublished material:

KATHY ACKER: "J" by Kathy Acker. Copyright © 1991 by Kathy Acker. Reprinted by permission of Kathy Acker.

HARMONY BOOKS, A DIVISION OF CROWN PUBLISHERS: Excerpt from *London Fields* by Martin Amis. Copyright © 1989 by Martin Amis. Reprinted by permission of Harmony Books, a division of Crown Publishers.

JOHN HAWKINS & ASSOCIATES: "Why Don't You Come Live With Me It's Time" from *Tikkun* by Joyce Carol Oates. Copyright © 1990 by Joyce Carol Oates. Reprinted by permission of John Hawkins & Associates, Inc.

MARTIN SECKER AND WARBURG LIMITED: Excerpt from *Blood* by Janice Galloway. Copyright © 1991 by Janice Galloway. Reprinted by permission of Martin Secker and Warburg Limited.

Library of Congress Cataloging-in-Publication Data
The New Gothic: a collection of contemporary Gothic fiction / edited
  by Bradford Morrow, Patrick McGrath. —1st Vintage books ed.
     p. cm.
  Originally published: New York: Random House, © 1991.
  ISBN 0-679-73075-3
   1. Horror tales, American.  2. Gothic revival (Literature)
 3. Horror tales, English.  I. Morrow, Bradford, 1951–
II. McGrath, Patrick, 1950–
[PS648.H6N38  1992]
813' .0872908–dc20      92-50089
               CIP

*Manufactured in the United States of America*
10  9  8  7  6  5  4  3  2

# Acknowledgments

The editors would like to express their thanks to Susan Bell and Robin Desser for the sound advice and generous assistance they gave us during the preparation of this book.

# Contents

Gothic fiction, in its earliest days, was known by the props and settings it employed, by its *furniture*. Dark forests and dripping cellars, ruined abbeys riddled with secret passages, clanking chains, skeletons, thunderstorms, and moonlight—from such materials did the first gothicists frame their tales. It's not until the 1830s and '40s, with Edgar Allan Poe, that the gothic begins to shift the emphasis away from all this gloomy hardware and become increasingly fascinated with the *psyche* of the gothic personality. With this shift a fresh vein of gothic ore is opened, and in Poe's work we encounter minds and souls haunted by the urge to transgress and do evil, crippled with distortions of perception and moral sense, and obsessed with death and morbidity. With Poe the gothic turns inward, and starts rigorously to explore extreme states of psychological disturbance.

Poe recognized how the furniture of the genre could be spliced together with the sensibility. Roderick Usher's mind is as much a reflection of his house as his house is a reflection of his mind. When the one fissures, the other fissures also—"and the deep and dank tarn at my feet closed sullenly and silently over the fragments of the *'House of Usher.'*" In such a tale climate, landscape, architecture, genealogy, and psychology seem to bleed into one another until it is impossible to distinguish a figure from its metaphors. The coalescence of all these elements sets in motion a process of regression, decay, a collapsing back into a state of primal unity—a death, in other words; and this, finally, is what the gothic has always addressed, though it has often hedged and skirted, avoided the thing itself and become preoccupied with side effects and repercussions. Where Poe recognized the possibilities of fusion between the historical elements that defined the genre, and his own motivations as a writer to plumb more subtly the geography of madness and the depths of spiritual derangement, the new gothicist would take as a starting place the concern with interior entropy—spiritual and emotional breakdown—and address the exterior furniture of the genre from a contemporary vantage. Night remains as dark as it ever was, but the streets we walk, the houses we live in could not be more different.

The gothic tradition is a fascinating one. Several factors conspired in its birth, among them the aesthetic theory that the Horrid and the Terrible were legitimate sources of the Sublime. Another influence was the cult of Nature, which came to full flower in de Sade, who himself considered the tale of terror a product of revolutionary upheaval: in 1800 he wrote, "there was nobody left who had not experienced more misfortunes in four or five years than could be depicted in a century by literature's most famous novelists: it was necessary to call upon hell to arouse interest." Finally, there was a long-standing appetite for the gentle melancholy of ruins, an appetite that now acquired rather sinister undertones.

Horace Walpole is credited with the first gothic novel, *The Castle of Otranto* of 1765, but the best of the first wave is Matthew Lewis's *The Monk,* which energetically tracks the spiritual collapse of Ambrosio, a bad priest, his rape of a lovely maiden in the crepuscular vaults of a church, and his eventual damnation. On its publication in 1796 it caused an uproar. Lewis (aged twenty) and his publisher were indicted, and *The Monk* was expurgated. Thus did the gothic in its very infancy display its subversive inclinations.

Subterranean passages, vaults, dungeons, cellars—these are all staples of the early gothicists. Such chthonic, claustrophic spaces they were! Each was a vivid analogue of the tomb, and each provided a site of inversion, where terror and unreason subverted consensus and rationality, where passion was transformed into disgust, love turned to hatred and good engendered evil. The architecture of *The Monk* supplies a fine example, for there the house of God is mirrored, with a ghastly perfect symmetry, by the desolate vaults directly beneath it, in which Ambrosio foully besmirches the honor of the virgin. Then, as now, the gothic clearly delighted in moving to the dark term of any opposition it encountered. Inversion was its basic structural principle.

The nineteenth century witnessed a glorious efflorescence of gothic writing. *Wuthering Heights* is perhaps the finest example, articulating as it does the terrible possibility of a passion so intense as to transcend the biological barrier that separates the living from the dead. The vampire, who makes a first literary appearance in about 1800, is also biologically anomalous, being a creature distinguished by his or her inability to rot, as well as possessing a perverse and predatory sexuality. In much of Poe's best work that same theme recurs, an obsessive fascination with necrophilia, arguably the most radical of the transgressions. (We even find a gothic moment in what is considered one of the crowning glories of nineteenth-century realism, George Eliot's *Middlemarch*, in the character of Mr. Casaubon, black-clad, dusty scholar of the world's myths, and a figure of death, whose one small triumph is briefly to ensnare the heroine Dorothea in his moribund and ghoulish work.) But it is Poe who stands central to the tradition, reaching backward into the eighteenth century for his crumbling fungoid castles and clammy vaults, and forward into the twentieth with his demented drunks, his paranoids and neurotics, blazing a trail through the darkness that the greatest of his followers, the psychologist Freud, would explore in the creation of some of the most inspired tales in the genre, the chillingly macabre "case studies."

We stand at the end of a century whose history has been stained perhaps like no other by the blacker urges of human nature. The prospect of apocalypse—through human science rather than divine intervention—has redefined the contemporary psyche. The consolation that Western souls once found in religion has faded; Faustus no longer faces a Mephistopheles from divinity's antithetic underworld, nor is Ambrosio doomed to Christianity's eternal hell. Now hell is decidedly on earth, located within the vaults and chambers of our own minds.

That the gothicists of the past created an artistic vision intended to reveal bleaker facets of the human soul is a given; that such an impulse is very much alive in contemporary British and American fiction is the assumption that underpins this anthology of stories and excerpts from novels. Though no longer shackled to the conventional props of the genre, the themes that fuel these pieces—horror, madness, monstrosity, death, disease, terror, evil, and weird sexuality—strongly manifest the gothic sensibility. Were Poe to come upon this collection he might perhaps be bewildered by the various accents and settings of the work, but he would certainly recognize and applaud the spirit animating them. This is the new gothic.

—Bradford Morrow and Patrick McGrath
New York City, January 1991

# THE
# NEW
# GOTHIC

# Ovando

## JAMAICA KINCAID

A knock at the door.

It is Frey Nicolas de Ovando. I was surprised. I was not expecting him. But then on reflecting, I could see that though I was not expecting him, he was bound to come. Somebody was bound to come. On reflecting, I could see that while I sat I thought, Someone will come to me; if no one comes to me, then I will go to someone. There was that knock at the door. It was Ovando then. Immediately I was struck by his suffering. Not a shred of flesh was left on his bones; he was a complete skeleton except for his brain, which remained, and was growing smaller by the millennium. He stank. Immediately I was struck by his innocence: for he had made himself a body from plates of steel, and it was stained with shades of red, blood in various stages of decay, and he thought I would not know the difference. He carried with him the following things: bibles, cathedrals, museums (for he was already an established collector), libraries (banks, really, in which he stored the contents of his diminishing brain), the contents of a drawing room. "Ovando," I said, "Ovando," and I smiled at him and threw my arms open to embrace this stinky relic of a person. Many people have said that this was my first big mistake, and I always say, How could it be a mistake to show sympathy, to show trust, to show affection to another human being, on first meeting? How can my action, then, with its foundation fixed in love, be judged a mistake? For I loved him then, not the way I would love my mother, or my child, but with that more general and spontaneous kind of love that I feel when I see any human being. As I shall show you, my first actions should not have been rewarded as they were. But wait here a minute and I shall show you what happened next.

With a wave of my hand I threw the door open and said, "Come in." I did this with great exaggeration, for it was unnecessary. You see, he was already inside. And so too when I

said, "Sit down, make yourself at home, in fact think of this as
your new home," not only was he already sitting down but he
said, "Yes, this is the new home I have been looking for, and
I already like it so much that I have sent for my relatives in
Spain, Portugal, France, England, Germany, Italy, Belgium,
and The Netherlands. I know that they will like it here as
much as I do, for they are just like me, we have met the same
fate in the world." So many things at once seemed wrong to
me that it was hard to know where to begin. I could not see
his eyes; they were shut. Any number of things could explain
this, I thought: perhaps he was blind, perhaps all his deeds so
far had left him in a permanent state of inner bliss. And as for
the relatives! Imagine whole countries populated by people
with not a shred of flesh left on their bones, complete skeletons
inside bodies made from plates of steel, people who had lost the
ability to actually speak and could only make pronouncements,
their brains growing smaller by the millennium, their bodies
covered with blood in various shades of decay; whole countries
of people coming to visit me even though I had not invited
them, whole countries of people sitting down in my house
without asking my permission!

The most confusing thing was that he had used the word
*fate*. I gathered then that mere reasoning him out of his plans
would not work. ("Ovando, look, let us be reasonable. All of
your words and deeds toward me so far have been incredibly
unjust. Already, just in the first few moments of our meeting,
you have done me irreparable harm. Stop now, let me show to
you the grave errors you have made." "Really, there is nothing
I can do about this. A power outside and beyond me has
predetermined these unalterable events. All of my actions have
been made for me in eternity. All of my actions are divine.")

I could have brought a stop to what was an invasion to me,
a discovery to him; after all, I too knew of divinities and

eternities and unalterable events. But I looked closely at him. He was horrible on a scale I did not even know existed before. I sat at his feet and helped him take off his shoes.

For a very long time Ovando believed the world to be round. It suited him to believe that, for from his point of view he could see only horror and misery and disease and famine and poverty and nothingness. If the earth were round, thought Ovando, he could go away, far away from his immediate surroundings, far away beyond the horizon, which would prove not to be a ledge over which he would fall into a sea of blackness. For a while, then, a round earth spun on its axis in Ovando's mind's eye. At first this world was small and bare and chalk-white, like a full moon in an early evening sky; it spun around and around, growing into perfection and permanence until finally, awake or asleep, alone or in a procession, in silence or in battle, Ovando carried this round, bare, chalk-white world. Then, after a few hundred years of this, Ovando filled his earth with seas, across the seas he placed lands, the lands were covered with mountains and rivers, and the mountains and rivers hid enormous treasures. When Ovando's imagination brought forth the round earth and then the seas and then the land and then the mountains and then the rivers, he acted with great calm. But in imagining the treasures he grew agitated, and then he fainted. He took this to be a sign from his various divinities, for all visionaries take as a sign of affirmation a momentary loss of contact with the ordinariness of daily life.

"Ah, then," said Ovando, as he entered a small room. He sat at a desk and proceeded to fill countless volumes with his meditations on the spheres, divine assertions, liberation from bonds spiritual and physical, and phlebotomy. To say that his meditations were nothing more than explanations and justifications for his future actions might seem unfair, for after all is it not so that all human beings are, from moment to moment, vulnerable to overwhelming self-love? When Ovando emerged from this small room, his eyes were half-shut. The lights had burnt out many, many years earlier, but he had continued his work of filling up the volumes in the half dark, and not once did he get to sleep. In his hands now he carried a large piece of paper, a piece of paper that was as large as a front lawn, and on this piece of paper Ovando had rendered flat the imagined contents of his world. Oh what an ugly thing to see, for the lands and the seas were painted in the vile colors of precious stones just ripped from their muddy home! It looked like the effort of schoolchildren. It looked like a fragile object that had been dropped on a hard surface and its pieces first swept up in a dustpan and then gently but haphazardly placed on a ta-bletop. It looked like sadness itself, for it was a map. Ovando spread his map out before him. Using the forefinger of his left hand, he traced on his map a line. Months later his finger came to a stop. It was at a point not too far from where he had started. Removing his finger from his map, he let out a long, satisfying breath, and then he looked up. At that moment the world broke.

From where I sit the world looks flat. I look out to the horizon. The world ends in a sharp, flat, clear line where the seas and the sky are joined. I look out on my world. I accept it in its flatness. I am not tempted to transgress its boundaries. My world bears me no ill; on the contrary, my world bears me only goodness. I accept the goodness that my world bears me. My world with its goodness is not a burden; on the contrary, I find grace and light and comfort in my world. I find the things I need in my world. And yet—; for all hearts contain within them an eternal yearning, a yearning for a peace that is not death, a yearning for an answer to a question that cannot quite be asked. My heart is no exception and so my world is not infinite. To the stranger's eye (Ovando's) my world is a paradise. To the stranger's eye (Ovando's) everything in my world appears as if it were made anew each night as I sleep, by gods in their heavenly chambers. The climate in which I live is unchanging and kind; it does not exhaust me with extremes of hot and cold. I have by now lost interest in knowing the exact number of trees that bear me food; so, too, in the number that bear me only flowers, and in the ones that bloom only at nights and only when the moon is in its full phase.

I sit in the morning sun. I idly rub my toe against the earth beneath me, and a large vein of gold is revealed to me. I walk in the warm evening air. I stumble over the glittering stones that are scattered in my path. What can I do with all that I am surrounded by? I can fashion for myself bracelets, necklaces, crowns. I can make kingdoms, I can make civilizations, I can lay waste. But I can see the destruction of my body, and I can see the destruction of my soul. Then in my flat world I am blessed with a certain vision. I see the end in everything around me. I see its beginnings, I see its ends. I see the way things will always be. For me then, all discovery results in contemplation. I see a thing I have never seen before, I place it in the palm of my hand; eventually I see the many purposes to which it can be put, eventually I see all its many purposes brought to an end, eventually I see it die. I replace the thing I have never seen before in the exact place in which I found it. Again let me say: I see an object, I see its myriad uses good and bad, I see it rise up to great heights. I see it hold sway, the foundations of vast enterprises are laid in it, I see it reduced again to its humble origins, a thing I can hold in my hand. In the many things I have held in my hand, from time to time I see my own humanity: I can hold religious beliefs, I can extol a moral value, I can prevent myself from entering the dungheap that is history. My world is flat. I accept this. Its borders are finite. I accept this. The flatness of my world is kind to me.

. . .

"My Sheer Might!" said Ovando loudly and then fell silent. Those three words rushed out of his mouth and vanished into the silence of things so completely that Ovando did not believe that he had said them. He had spent many years in preparation for this moment, the moment in which these words could be said. The moment in which the words could be said was the moment in which the words would be true. And so for a long time Ovando stood in front of a mirror, more in the stance of a child at play than an actor in preparation for a great part, and he tried to say the words "My Sheer Might!" At first he could only see the words glowing in the darkness inside his head. Then the words burned in a cool, soft way, an indication that they were at the beginning of their life span. In the meantime—that is, during the time Ovando stood in front of the mirror, a mirror, by the way, that reflected nothing but his own image—my own world in its flatness heaved up and down in the way of something alternately freezing and thawing out. I looked at my world: its usually serene and pleasing contours began to change before my eyes. The roots of trees were forced out of the ground. The grasses were ablaze with a fire that I did not know how to put out. The streams dried up, and the riverbeds became barren tracks. The birds all hovered overhead and blotted out the light of the sun. The unwinged creatures stood up and cried into the charged air, but their own sounds disturbed them so that they then lay down and buried their heads in their stomachs. I said, "What is it? Who is it?" and then without speech I observed this frightening wonder, waiting for the moment when my world would return to the way it had always been, waiting for the moment when I would doubt that what I saw before me had really taken place. Ovando said again, "My Sheer Might!" and this time the words did not vanish into the silence of things. This time the words became like a poisonous cloud of vapor, and they spread out, swallowing up everything in their path. In that moment the mirror into which Ovando looked, the mirror which reflected only Ovando, broke into thirteen pieces in some places, into six hundred and sixty-six pieces in other places, and in still other places into different numbers of pieces, and in all of these places the breaking of the mirror signified woe. In that moment, I, my world, and everything in it became Ovando's thralls.

One morning, Ovando arose from his bed. Assisted by people he had forcibly placed in various stages of social and spiritual degradation, he prepared a document, which, when read to me, would reveal to me my real predicament. He had by this time grown an enormous tail, which he would cause to flail about in the air whenever he was amused. What amused him was predictable: the endless suffering he could cause whenever he wished. He had also grown horns on either side of his head, and from these he hung various instruments of torture; his tongue he made forked. The document that he had prepared for me was only six inches long and six inches wide, but it was made from the pulp of one hundred and ten trees and these trees had taken ten millennia to reach the exquisite state of beauty in which Ovando found them: their trunks were smooth, and so thick that two arms wrapped around them would just meet, and they glowed ruby red in the sunlight. At the very top the leaves and branches formed globes of yellow and green that also glowed in the sun; they perfumed the air but not pervasively, not enough that one could become accustomed to it. These trees Ovando had ordered cut down so that only stumps remained, and boiled and pounded and dried, and the process repeated again and again until they were reduced to something that measured six inches by six inches. Holding it up to the light, he said, "Do you see?" and I understood him to mean not only that he could reduce these precious trees to something held between the tips of two of his fingers but that he also held in his hands the millennia in which the trees grew to maturity, their origins, their ancestry, and everything that they had ever, ever been, and so too he held me. Then on this paper Ovando wrote that he dishonored me, that he had a right to do so for I came from nothing, that since I came from nothing I could not now exist in something, and so my existence was now rooted in nothing, and though I seemed to live and needed the things necessary to the living such as food and water and air, I was dead; and so though I might seem present, in reality I was absent. This document consisted of hundreds of articles and each of them confirmed my dishonor, each of them confirmed my death, each of them confirmed my nothingness. I listened to him carefully, his voice the sound of metal rapidly corroding. At the end of this I stood up and made an extremely long and incoherent speech, so shocked I was at the brutality of tone and language of Ovando's document, so unused to such cruelty, such barbarism, such harshness. In my long and incoherent speech, which I delivered in a heartfelt and sorrowful and earnest way (for should I not be touched by my own pain, should I not be moved on seeing a picture of myself humbled by a power over which I had no desire to triumph, a power I wished would stay out of my way?), I tried to point out to Ovando that since the ideas of Honor, Death, and Nothingness were not within my view and so held no meaning for me, he could not really rob me of anything; since these ideas constituted some of his deepest beliefs it was himself then that he dishonored, it was himself then that he made dead, it was himself then that he consigned to nothingness. But Ovando could not hear me, for by that time his head had taken the shape of a groundworm, which has no ears.

Ovando has conquered the ages and placed them in medallions he wears around his neck, his waist, his wrists, and his ankles. After consulting for a long time the one he wears around his left wrist, Ovando said, "I shall raise the curtain, and my relatives shall now make their appearance." Of course, such a thing as Ovando's curtain was invisible to me. Ovando made an enormous flourish with his hands and, as if a curtain really had been parted, there suddenly, in what used to be an empty space, now stood a covered floating vessel. Ovando smiled at me, his face splitting with pleasure and conceit. Ovando's relatives arranged themselves into pairs of male and female and then began to leave their covered floating vessel. As they did so they announced in loud voices, as if it were a curse, the names of the places from which they had come: Spain, France, England, Belgium, The Netherlands, Germany, Portugal, Italy. As they entered the earth they kissed the ground, not as a sign of affection but rather as a sign of possession. They looked around and at last they saw me. In unison, like a clap of thunder, they all said, "Mine!" Ovando, seeing the danger in this, said, "Draw lots," but the people who drew my head really wanted my legs, and the people who drew my arms wanted my insides, and so on and so on until they fell on each other with a ferociousness that I could not have imagined possible. This battle now lasted for hundreds and hundreds of years, at the end of which time they should have exterminated themselves, but wherever their blood was spilt new versions of themselves grew up. It was in this way that they multiplied, by spilling blood over the earth itself.

Ovando speaks his own name. He says, "Ovando!" His name then gently leaves his lips in a long sigh, a delicious parting. Saying his name, Ovando runs his hands through his hair; saying his name, Ovando caresses his face; saying his name, Ovando gently passes his hands down his own back, through the crevices of his private parts, gently unmatting the tightly curled hair that grows in thick sworls and covers completely his child-sized penis; saying his name, Ovando gently runs his hands down one leg and up the other, across his chest, stopping to pinch sharply first one flattened breast and then the other; then raising his hands to his nostrils, he inhales deeply, and then bringing his hands to his mouth he kisses and sucks them until he feels content. His desire for his own mortal self fulfilled, he falls into a state of bliss, into a deep, deep sleep.

Ovando then lived constantly in night; but it was not a quiet night, a night that bore a soft sleep in which dreams of a long-ago-lived enchanted childhood occurred; it was not the sort of night that the day angrily interrupts, jealous of the union between the sleeper and the borderless, soft tapestry of blackness; and it was not a night of nature, which is to say the progression from the day to the opposite of day; it was not the night of just after sunset or the night of just before the sun rises. Ovando lived in the thickest part of the night, the deepest part of the night, the part of the night where all suffering dwells, including death; the part of the night in which the weight of the world is made visible and eternal terror is confirmed. In this night, Ovando's body was covered with sores (sores, not wounds, for the hand that inflicts wounds may be an unjust hand and injustice calls forth pity); he lay on a bed of broken glass bottles (not nails).

Who will judge Ovando? Who can judge Ovando? A true and just sentence would be imbued with love for Ovando. The sentence must bear within it sympathy and identification, for only if the judge resides in Ovando and Ovando resides in the judge can an everlasting judgment be passed. Ovando cannot pass judgment on himself, for, as is to be expected, he loves himself beyond measure. Such a love is a worm asleep in every heart, and must never be awakened; such a love lies like kindling in every heart, and must never be lit. A charge against Ovando, then, is that he loved himself so that all other selves and all other things became nothing to him. I became nothing to Ovando. My relatives became nothing to Ovando. Everything that could trace its lineage through me became nothing to Ovando. And so it came to be that Ovando loved nothing, lived in nothing and died in just that way. I cannot judge Ovando. I have exhausted myself laying out before him his transgressions. I am exhausted from shielding myself so that his sins do not obsess and so possess me.

# Horrorday

MARTIN
AMIS

The first three events—light, sound, and impact—were all but instantaneous. First, the eye opened to the scalding bulb of the foundered standard lamp; next, the rushing report of some lofted cherrybomb or megabanger; and then the brisk descent of the crammed glass ashtray. This ashtray had been teetering for hours on the shelf above the bed: now it was dislodged—by the frenzied physics of everyday life. It fell at the usual rate of acceleration: thirty-two feet per second per second: thirty-two feet per second squared. And it flipped in mid-air. So Keith copped the lot. Impact, crushed butts, a shovelful of ash—right in the kisser. Right in the mush. This was the fifth of November. This was horrorday.

Keith spat and struggled and thrashed himself to his feet. She was gone. Where? With his eyes bobbing and rolling in their sockets, he focused on the horrorclock. *No.* He swore through a dry cloud of horrordust. In the spent tempest of the bedroom he sought out his clothes. When he pitched himself toward the toilet he barked a horrortoe on the bed's brass stanchion. Tearfully he mollified his incensed bladder. In the mirror Keith's reflection started getting dressed. A split horrornail kept snagging in the blur of fabrics, all of them synthetic: made by horrorman. On the wall Keith's shadow straightened and dived headlong from the room. He paused in the passage and roughly freed a segment of his scrotum, nastily snared in the seized teeth of his horrorzip.

Out onto the street he stumbled. He made for the car—for the heavy Cavalier. Builders' dust and builders' orange sand formed an orange mist at the level of his eyes, his agent-orange vision, which was itself engrained with motionless impurities, like a windscreen splattered with dead insects. In a ditch, in a bunker full of pipes and cables, a workman was giving his drill a horrid kneetrembler, louder than an act of God. Like me, myself, last night, with her. Underfoot the pavement crackled with horrorgrit. It went crackling right into the roots of Keith's horrorteeth.

The car *looked* funny. Keith scrunched up the parking tickets. Then he froze. The front window on the passenger side had been stove in! Keith's body throbbed from the sudden wound. He went round and unlocked and opened the door—and felt the horrorslide and horrortrickle of the crushed glass. The welded stereo had been scrabbled at, its dials torn off, but . . . Keith's library of darts tapes! It was okay: intact, entire. They hadn't stooped that low. For a while he stared at the faulty burglar alarm he had recently stolen. Without thinking he reached down and with his right hand brushed from the seat the jeweled horrorglass.

Fresh catastrophe: the stained tip of his middle finger had been sweetly pierced by the horrorshard. No pain: only mental anguish. A fat dome or bulb of horrorblood now pulsed above the yellow rind. It started dripping. On the car floor he found a crumpled pin-up with which he rudely dressed his damaged darting digit. And the digital on the dash—what was the horrortime?—remained garbled, made nonsense of, by the rays of the low sun, which had surely never been lower (he was on his way now), bouncing at bus height over the spines of traffic. Through the open window the sound of passing cars came like the zip and sniff of a boxer's feints and punches. Ten-twenty. His appointment with Mrs. Ovens had been scheduled for 9:15. But there were always queues. As he drove, motes of the shattered glass, quarks of glassdust, seemed to tickle his scalp like particles of horrorlight.

He arrived at the tricky junction on the Great Western Road: familiar horrorspot, with zebra-crossing, bus station, and humpbacked bridge over the canal, all complicating access. Fifteen minutes later, he was still there. Timing their runs to split-second perfection, the launched horrorcars, the bowling horrorlorries successively denied the heavy Cavalier. Whenever a gap appeared, so would some contrary vehicle, seeming to pounce or spring into position. Either that, or, as Keith inched forward, the Underground station would emit a resolute trainload onto the crossing before him. Keith pounded his fists on the steering-wheel's artificial leopard skin. At his rear he sensed the climbing volume of thwarted hurry: how it groaned and squirmed . . . In his face he felt the low sun like a lamp bent for interrogation. Now the road cleared but as Keith revved and shuddered, and yearned forward, another watch of horrorsouls bobbed onto the zebra—the passing faces of the horrorsouls.

Finally he churned his way through with his bloodied hand on the horn. And into what? Driving was like a test film or a dramatization of the Highway Code, whatever *that* used to be, with every turn and furlong offering multiple choice, backing learner, swearing cyclist, peeking perambulator. Richly sectioned with doubleparkers and skip-collectors and clamp-removers, the roads became a kiddy-book of excavators, macadam-layers, streetlamp-changers, white-line painters, mobile libraries, armed-personnel-carriers, steamrollers, bulldozers, tanks, ditch-diggers, drain cleaners. For an extended period he was wedged behind a leaf-disposal truck. From its rear a vacuum tube slurped up the sear broomed roadside pyramids. He watched the suck, the feathery flip; sex reentered his head and found no room there. Everything he had ever done to womankind he had done again ten times last night, with her. The whipped dance of the moistened leaves. Defoliated, deflowered, stripped of leaves and flowers, with trees sharp-lined like old human faces, and wringing their bare hands, London could still drown in all its horrorleaves.

At the civic building, at 10:55, a stroke of good fortune—or motoring knowhow. The back street was double, tripleparked,

parked out, with cars parked beside, athwart, on top of. But as usual nobody had dared block the old dairy exit (which Keith knew to be disused)—or so it seemed, when he peered into the dusty fire of his rear window. Keith backed in smartly. This was horrorday, however. Therefore, a horrorbike was waiting there, leaning on its stick, and Keith heard the eager horror-crunch. Worse, when Keith crept out to disensnare his bumper, the horrorbike's own horrorbiker formidably appeared—one of that breed of men, giant miracles of facial hair and weight problem, who love the wind of the open road, and love the horrorbikes they straddle there. He hoisted Keith onto the boot of the Cavalier, and banged his head on it for a while, and then direly raised a gauntleted horrorfist. Keith whimpered his way out of that one, offering up a stolen credit card in earnest of his false address. He went and parked about three miles away and tearfully sprinted back through the fuming jams and the incredible crowds of the horrormany.

Guy Clinch was heading toward London at twice the speed of sound, one of half a dozen passengers on the hurled dart of the Concorde. He had missed the earlier flight by ten minutes and had spent three hours trying to sleep, in a kind of capsule hotel at Kennedy, before taking off, smoothly but dramatically, in the still center of Hurricane Lulu. Now he was in another capsule, his eyes rinsed by the coldly beautiful blue of the troposphere. Through his porthole Guy could also see both sun and moon, the former discreetly filtered by the treated plastic. Because of the elevation and velocity of this particular observer, the two bodies seemed to be moving toward each other with uncelestial haste. Below, the turning planet fell through its curve of spacetime, innocent (though much traduced) in its blond fur coat. Beyond, inanely vast, the inanity of space.

Two glamorous, multilingual stewardesses exhaustively pampered him; he had recently relished a plateful of scrambled eggs and smoked salmon; and he was reading *Love*. Even so, Guy happened to be in dramatic discomfort. Bending to refill his cup with the excellent coffee (a mixed roast, he would guess), one of his stewardesses had noticed the odd tilt of the meal tray: she had given it a careful nudge and then, suddenly, leaned on it quite hard with the full weight of her shoulder. When Guy reopened his eyes, probably about ninety seconds later, he was confronted by the frown of the cabin steward, solicitously crouched in the aisle. The stewardess was hanging back with the knuckle of her forefinger pressed against her teeth. Guy apologized to them and eventually they went away. But the pain went nowhere.

The last chapter of *Love* was called "Concerning Fiascos": " 'The whole realm of love is full of tragic stories,' said Madame de Sévigné, relating her son's misfortunes with the celebrated Champmeslé. Montaigne handles so scabrous a subject with great aplomb." Guy finished the chapter, wonderingly, and then flipped through the copious appendices. It would be a relief to be done with *Love*: this famished sampling of erotic thought would never ease his hunger pains. *Concerning Courts of Love.* Guy smiled modestly as he thought of that last telephone call and the delightful carnality he seemed to have awakened in her. "The plea of marriage is not a legitimate defense against love." No doubt she would meet him halfway up the stairs, with all that color in her face. "A lover shall, on the death of the other lover, remain unattached for two years." As they kissed, he would place both palms on the back of her thighs, beneath what might well be that black cashmere dress with the buttons, and almost lift her whole body onto him. "Success too easily won soon strips love of its charm; obstacles enhance its value. Every lover grows pale at the sight of the beloved." As they moved through the sitting-room her breath would be sweet and hot (and *hers*: everything would be *hers*); teardrops, too, perhaps, rather deliciously. "Suspicion and the jealousy which derives from it aggravate the condition called love." It didn't matter what happened in the bedroom and in a way one feared for the loss of individuality (in the blinding rapture and so on); yet how strange her face would look from that angle, when, as she had laughingly promised, she knelt to remove his trousers and undershorts. "A person in love is unremittingly and uninterruptedly occupied with the image of the beloved." So brown, so close together. "Nothing forbids a woman to be loved by two men . . ."

Guy put *Love* aside and took up the second book, *The Light of Many Suns*. For a moment he vaguely wondered what Keith was up to; but then his eyes fell on Nicola's inscription, over which he had already done some puzzling:

> Thou art the grave where buried love doth live,
> Hung with the trophies of my lovers gone,
> Who all their parts of me to thee did give,
> That due of many now is thine alone:
>   Their images I loved I view in thee,
>   And thou—all they—hast all the all of me.

One of the Sonnets, of course (and Guy knew the Sonnets tolerably well); a complete sestet. How did it . . . ? Ah yes: Thy bosom . . . Thy bosom is endeared with all the hearts . . . Rather a knotty one, this. Addressed by the man to the woman. The past lovers aren't just "gone": they're dead. But people died earlier in those days. Wish I had a copy. And there reigns Love, and all Love's loving parts. Absolutely fascinating.

"That leaves four hundred," said Mrs. Ovens, "for the nose."
"Nose? What nose? There weren't no *nose*."

"Same incident, Keith."

"That was an earhole."

"You can't *fracture* an ear, Keith. And we're coming to that.
The torn ear."

"Bitten," said Keith firmly. "Bitten."

"Which reminds me: the tooth'll be twelve-fifty."

"Twelve-fifty! Blimey . . . Gone up again, has it?"

"The seven-fifty's for a molar. This is an incisor. Canines are
seventeen twenty-five."

"Jesus. I mean, I'm just a working *man.*"

"It's what the law considers fair, Keith."

"Capitalism innit," said Keith. "Just bloodsuckers as such."
He sighed longsufferingly.

"And then there's the split tongue."

Keith now raised a dissenting forefinger. "When there was
all this," he said carefully, "I, *I* was hospitalized on thirteen
occasions. Sustaining permanent injury to me chest. We don't
hear nothing about that. No danger."

"Yes, but what were you *doing* at the time, Keith?"

"Trying, in my own way, to establish a small business. Escape the poverty trap. That's it. Go on. Laugh."

"The split tongue, Keith."

"Jesus."

In the end Keith agreed to up his weekly payment from £5
to £6.50. On top of that, to show good will, he committed
himself to forty-eight hours of community service. Consisting
as it did of stealing odds and ends from very old people, community service was nowhere near as bad as it sounded. Community service, in Keith's judgment, had been much maligned.
But on a day such as this a man's thoughts should surely be
with his darts. Not haggling here with some old hippie about
the price of horrornose, of horrortooth, of horrortongue.

Keith drove to the garage in Rifle Lane. Fortunately Fucker
was on shift.

"Who did *this* fucker?" asked Fucker. "It'll be a rough job. But you'll have security."

Gratefully Keith relaxed on a winded carseat in the back room. He read the ripped mags: nude skirt. Peace at last. Beside him in a large cardboard box an even larger cat lay dying. Cruelly cramped, it struggled and sneezed and sighed. It began weeping rhythmically. Keith was used to noise, incessant and unwelcome noise. Most of his life was played out to a sound-track of sadistic decibelage. Noise, noise—noise on the brink of bearability. He was used to unwelcome nearnesses, also, to stinging proximities; but did the bald cat's sneezes really have to bubble and dampen the very thigh of his trouserleg? It wept in rhythm. Sounds almost like . . . The nude birds in the book. Nothing on Nick. She'd show them. He closed his eyes and saw himself naked and twanging back and forth with incomprehensible violence and speed, as if in controlled preparation for spaceflight. There she was, just a G-spot in a G-string. And there was Keith in his G-suit, ready to take on gravity . . . A new noise, a new nearness, a new order of alarm: Keith was staring at the horrorcat.

"Gone, has she? It's a rough job," said Fucker.

They stood there inspecting the Cavalier's warped windowframe, the mauled glass, smothered in fingerprints.

"But you've got security."

"Appreciate it."

And Keith bent into his pocket and parted with the money: endlessly, horrornote after horrornote.

With the low sun like a prickly sweater gently pressed into his unshaven face, Keith drove to the Black Cross, for his breakfast. The backslaps and the fagsmoke, the lagers and the Scotch eggs, did not combine well. A pork pie, Keith decided, was what he really fancied. Then you feel twice the price. Shakespeare staggered over and fiercely tousled Keith's hair for at least a minute. When he had stopped doing that, Keith looked down at the bar: a new soft-fallen mask of dandruff now salted his food, and melted into the lager's horrorhead. At that moment his teeth lanced a spectacular impurity among the knotted gristle inside his mouth. Keith, who took his chances and ate a great many pork pies, was no stranger to impurity; but he had never encountered anything so throatfloodingly gangrenous as this. Without interrupting the conversation he was having with somebody else, Pongo handed him the bottle of green mouthwash kept under the bar, and Keith loped off to the Gents. Half an hour later, when the tortured gagging had subsided, to the relief of everyone in the building, Keith returned and drank the complimentary Scotches and dabbed at his eyes with a piece of newspaper tenderly torn by Pongo from his own tabloid. Keith nodded as he studied the pork-pie wrapping: the eat-by date was placed well into the next millennium. He had a few more Scotches and was cheering up enough to make a start on telling the lads about his night with Nick. His stomach still bubbled and spat, still noisily ruing that horrorpie.

When everything began to go dark.

"Look!"

Through the stained glass they stared, or some of them did, as in perfect parallax the two white balls conjoined like something unanswerable under the microscope, and the moon began to burn like a little sun.

"It's eclipse . . . Eclipse! . . . What fucking clips? . . . Fucking power-cut . . . It's the fucking eclipse . . . Put the fucking lights on . . . Eclipse, innit . . . It's the fucking eclipse . . ."

Keith turned away, in horror. To his left a dartsman waited at the dimmed oché with his arrows, head dropped in a martyrdom of impatience. Someone pitched a coin onto the counter. It clattered on its rim, noisily, like a cold car just before it fires.

And the coin went on wobbling, clattering, faster, tighter. That was him last night, himself, twirling to the very end of his band . . . Shivering Shakespeare stood ten feet away with his face between the double doors of the Black Cross. Today was the day when, in Shakespeare's scheme of things, he was due to lead his chosen people to the mountains of Eritrea: the promised land. As he looked round the Black Cross that morning, though, it didn't look terribly likely . . . Outside, he had sensed the cold, the eclipse wind, the silenced pigeons. Four hundred miles across, the point of a dark cone of shadow a quarter of a million miles long was heading toward him at two thousand miles per hour. Next came the presentiment of change, like the arrival of weatherfront or thunderhead, with the light glimmering—but getting fierier. Then a shade being drawn across the sky. Totality. Shakespeare was crying. He knew that something awful had to happen, when horrorday was horrornight, when horrorsun was horrormoon.

Up above also (if anybody had been able to find her), and looking her very best in the sudden twilight, proudly shone Venus, daughter of Jupiter, wife of Vulcan, lover of Mars, and never brighter than when the darkness of totality played across the earth.

Where was Nicola Six?

Nobody knew.

*The Light of Many Suns* turned out to be a war memoir: rather remarkable in its way. Guy finished his *faisan à la mode de champagne* and shamefacedly went on drinking the claret, which he suspected would have a restaurant price of about three times the minimum weekly wage. Group Captain Leonard Cheshire, VC, OM, DSO, DFC, the author, a Catholic and obviously a good egg, was one of the two British observers of the atom-bombing of Hiroshima.

Guy looked out of the porthole. The "second contact," or the first moment of full eclipse, had occurred twenty minutes earlier. The pilot of the Concorde, an eclipse-enthusiast and member of the Thousand Second Club, had announced his intention of staying within the eastward-moving umbra until he began his descent over Ireland. Thus totality was lasting far longer than its terrestrial three minutes. When it came, Guy had tensed, as if for an impact. Or he had tried to. But he realized then that he couldn't get any tenser than he was already. Just as his phallus couldn't get any harder. At the moment that the moon's shape fully covered the sun, then with fantastic simultaneity the solar corona bathed the circumference with unforgettable fire. Guy was amazed, harrowed, by the tightness of the fit. Surely only the divinely privileged observer would be blessed with this full-true billiards shot, straight, dead straight, for ninety million miles. Perhaps that was the necessary condition of planetary life: your sun must fit your moon. The umbra began to overtake the plane; the pilot came on again and with emotion commanded his few passengers to admire the "diamond-ring" effect of the "third contact," when the leading slice of the sun re-emerged. Yes, yes, yes: just like a sparkler on its band. Like a ring for her, perhaps. Heavenly engagement.

The descent began. Guy picked up *The Light of Many Suns*. On page forty-six he dropped the book to the floor. He reached for his paper bag and opened it in front of his mouth. He waited. Perhaps there was an explanation. Perhaps, after all, it was something quite innocent . . .

*Enola Gay* was the plane that flew the mission to Hiroshima. The pilot named the aircraft after his mother. He was once her little boy.

But Little Boy was the name of the atom bomb. It killed 50,000 people in 120 seconds.

· · ·

Keith stood on her stoop, fumbling weepily with his great ring
of keys—Keith's keys, his gaoler's keys, keys for Debbee,
Trish, and Analiese, keys for flat, for car, for go-down and
lock-up. But keys for Nicola? He rang the bell again; he tried
all the keys again. Now Keith was close to panic, to cursing,
rattling panic. He wanted to see her very badly, not for the act
of love and hate, which, to his surprise, and so far as he could
tell, he wanted never to perform again with anybody. No: he
wanted her for her belief in him, because she was the other
world, and if she said that Keith was real then the other world
would say it too. But hang on. Suppose she's under a bus
somewhere? His darts boots, his darts strides, his darts shirt, his
very—! Keith clapped a hand to his horrorchest. Then his
knees gave with relief. All is not lost. His darts pouch remained
in its rightful place, in the pocket closest to his heart. He
buzzed the buzzer again; he tried all the keys again. Throughout he was aware of eyes on his back. Today, even the dead-
end street was crowded, and sharply charged in voice and
gesture: a sense of population shift. Keith turned. A lone policeman was watching him from the pavement, motionless
against the plunging figures beyond. Just a kid. In a uniform.
Fucking tithead. Keith was fairly confident that the policeman
wouldn't try nothing here, or he'd get lynched. But now he
was coming forward, his shoulders interestedly inclined, and—
okay—maybe it didn't look too good, unkempt Keith crooked
over his keys. So he did a great mime of casually patting his
pockets, then swiveled, shaking his head. He sauntered down
the path and, with a bit of the old insouciance (the Scotches
and supplementary *pornos* were about their work), hopped
into the heavy Cavalier. Keith started off with an unintended
bound, just missing an unattended pram, and monitoring in his
rearview mirror the shape of the tapering horrorfilth.

With the low sun playfully tickling the hairs in his nostrils, Keith drove to Windsor House. Nick'd show up later: call her from there. And, besides, he wanted to see how Clive was doing. The radio worked all right. As he drove home he listened irritatedly to the news, the dissolution of the Crisis, the improving condition of the president's wife, the delegations leaving simultaneously for Paris and Prague (not a summit: more like twin peaks), and wondered if this explained the pronounced congestion he encountered in Ladbroke Grove. He doubleparked outside Maharajah Wines. On the way to the lift his gait changed from its accustomed boxy shuffle to the sudden dance of a paddler entering a cold sea. His right foot, deep in horrorturd. Luckily, on the other hand, the lift was working, more or less. It came all the way down in answer to his punched summons. But it didn't get very far up. Sitting on the floor, waiting the twenty minutes for the next power surge, Keith took a matchstick to the slender grids of his tarnished sole. One mercy: the dog responsible for such a dropping was by now almost certainly dead. His thoughts were all with horrordog and horrorcat as, after a sickening drop, he shuddered his way tormentedly upward, wedged in the pungent horrorlift.

On the narrow walkstrip Keith attacked the lock, which was often recalcitrant. But today was horrorday. He stared down at the single gnarled key. On the outer mat were four horrorletters: two horrorbills, a horrorsummons, and a horrororder of distraint. Keith had had enough with all this locks and keys: he took a step back and detonated himself against the door. Normally it would have given like a dunked biscuit. But the devices Keith himself had sometimes deployed were evidently in place: the bars and braces used by him to keep out bailiffs, bad-debt buyers, repo men, cheated horror*cheats*.

"Kath," he said in a low voice.

He flinched at the misted glass. A warning shape moved away, then reappeared, like a figure glimpsed in church.

"I saw you," it whispered.

"Fuck off," coaxed Keith. "What? When? Come on, darling."

"On the telly."

". . . That weren't nothing. Just for the telly like. Load of nonsense. *For* the telly."

"You told the world," she said. "On the telly."

And Keith had no answer.

Even the old Metrocab coming in from Heathrow had its own slant about forms of torture. For one thing, the vibration, the cauldron-bubble beneath the seat, appeared to whet the pain in Guy's groin, assuming that any kind of increase was possible down there. But it was stranger than that. The driver treated his cab as a peasant might treat his horse or ass, with numb and proprietorial cruelty. The bursts of acceleration were like long-toothed, lip-flapping exhalations; then came the looping whinny of the brakes. It was diversion of a kind to listen to the grades of neigh and whinny, of anger and submission, that the driver thrashed out of his livelihood, the black machine.

As he paid, a passing child tossed a jumping-jack in through the window, and paused to watch it raise hell in the back of a cab—its headbanging ecstasy of entrapment.

"Bombfire night," said the driver, listlessly.

Guy walked on down the dead-end street; he had called her from the airport, without success; he didn't expect her to be home. Nor was she. He let himself in at the front door and climbed the stairs. The second key opened up an olfactory world that Guy remembered from his schooldays: duckboards and lockers, the lavatory where the smokers went. He saw the dartboard, the pewter tankard engraved to him, to Keith. Next door, through the thin passage, he saw the ruin of the bed, the upended ashtray on the pillow and its droppings on the sheets. Scattered about the floor were shiny puddles of exotic underwear. He saw the three empty brandy bottles, the hookah pipe. On the chair, as if laid out ready for school, brocaded trousers and the red shirt saying, KEITH TALENT—THE FINISHER.

Next door again he found an envelope marked *Guy*, unprominently displayed among the fashion and darts magazines on her crowded bureau. The note said: "Gone to the darts." There was a pass or ticket attached. The telephone rang. He waited before picking it up.

"Where the fuck a you been?" said a voice Guy knew well.

". . . Guy here."

". . . Oh, hello, mate. I uh, I had some stuff I was picking up. She there is she?"

"No, she's not here."

"Know when she be back?"

"No, I don't know."

"Minge," said Keith indulgently. "Never around when you want them. Always there when you don't. I couldn't, I couldn't pop— Nah. Yeah well cheers."

Guy waited.

"Okay. See you later then, pal." He added monotonously, "Yeah well she said you'd want to be there. As my virtual sponsor. Helping with the funding like."

"No doubt."

"Onna darts."

No joy there then, thought Keith. He can't be feeling too brill neither. Either. But this is it, *it*, success in this life always going to the guy who . . . The dartboard in Keith's garage looked on as he finished his *porno*, removed his clothes, and, jogging lightly on the cold floor, washed himself, horribly, in the hor-

rorsink. Keith's lifestyle. Skeptically he connected the electric
kettle he had recently stolen. It hummed faultily for several
seconds, and Keith's hopes soared. But then the machine gave
a scorching fizz and pooped the blackened plug from its hor-
rorrear. He shaved in lukewarm water before the mirror's acne.
Next, with the jellied shampoo, colder still, his horrorhair. He
donned his number-three darting shirt, so damp and creased.
It said: KEITH TALENT—THE PICKOFF KING. He dried his hair
with some old horrorrag.

A sudden orange cockroach rushed past and Keith stamped
on it, urbanely, out of grooved urban habit. But the glazed and
tendriled body of the cockroach, even as it collapsed inward,
sent Keith a reminder that his foot was unshod, unsocked. Just
a horrorfoot. Keith yanked his whole leg up with a senile yodel
of disgust. So he was still capable of disgust; and he didn't go
all the way through with that skillful stomp of his. The look
he gave the half-crushed roach might even have been mistaken
for appalled concern. The vermin lay there, half-turned; its
various appendages were all moving at different speeds—but
none of them were human speeds. Me, myself, only hours ago,
thought Keith, with intense lassitude . . . He put on his left
shoe. After many unsatisfactory minutes with a scrubbing-
brush, he put on his right shoe. Reckon I get there early, in
good time. Soak up the atmosphere. He got to his feet. Blimey.
You just decide you're going to enjoy every minute of it.
Wouldn't miss it for the world. Never ask about . . . He zipped
up his windcheater. Relax, few drinks. Take the opportunity
of using the celebrity practice boards. And generally compose
myself, Tony. It's fortunate, Ned, that I seem to respond to the
big occasion. On his way out he took a last look at the hate-
filled face of the flickering horrorroach.

Guy had gone home.

Or he had gone to Lansdowne Crescent. His housekeys

were still in his pocket, but manners—and caution—demanded that he ring the bell. Through the half-glass door and its steel curlicues a redoubtable figure loomed. Guy thought it might be Doris—the one who couldn't climb stairs. Because of her knees. The one who feared and hated all stairs.

The door opened. It was Lizzyboo. He couldn't help staring. And he couldn't help thinking of the helium blimp he had seen that day, effortfully hovering over Terminal Four.

"Isn't it wonderful? Isn't it *wonderful.*"

She said this joyfully. And as Guy listened he clearly saw the other Lizzyboo, the one he had loved for a month, the one he had kissed and touched among the trembling porcelain. The other Lizzyboo was still there all right, hiding within; and now it was safe to come out.

"Everything's okay again."

Of course this was neither here nor there to Guy, because she only meant the planet. "How's Hope? How's the boy?"

"You'd better go on up."

He went on up. As he turned the corner of the stairs he was disquieted by the sight of a silhouette in the passage, near the bedroom door. Something about the waiting shape was admonitory, ritualized, ecclesiastical. As he approached he saw that it was a little boy, in full armor.

"Who is it?" came a voice. "Darling?"

Guy was about to frame a grateful reply. But the little boy answered sooner. "A man," he said.

"What man?"

". . . Daddy."

Marmaduke stepped aside, with some formality, and Guy entered the room. The little boy followed, and then moved quietly past his father to the side of the bed, where Hope lay, on her barge of pillows.

"Where is everyone?" said Guy, for the house was eerily staffless.

"All gone. There's no need. He's different now."

"What happened?"

"It was quite sudden. The day after."

As they spoke, Marmaduke was undressing, or unbuckling himself. He laid down sword, dagger, pike, and shield, neatly, on the chair. He freed his breastplate. Finger by finger he loosened his gauntlets.

"And you?" said Guy.

Her face expressed, in terms of time and distance, the kind of journey he would have to undertake if he were ever to return. It was a long journey. Perhaps even the earth wasn't big enough to contain it . . . One by one Marmaduke removed his shin-guards, then the little chainmail slippers. Next, his authentic-looking tights were meticulously unpeeled.

"No nappy!" said Guy.

Marmaduke stood there in his underpants. These too he stepped out of. He climbed into bed. "Mummy?"

"Yes, darling?"

"Mummy? Don't love Daddy."

"I won't. I certainly won't."

"Good."

". . . Byebye, Daddy."

Guy came out into the fading afternoon. He looked at the pass or ticket she had left for him and wondered how he would ever kill all that time. Bent with his bag, he stood by the garden gate. He looked up. Already the sky was dotted with firebursts, rocket-trails: its proxy war. Soon, all over London, a thousand, a million guys would be burning, burning.

It's weird: you pull the sunguard down and it don't—the sun's still there, like Hawaii. Keith motored to the studio, which was very convenient, being amongst the refurbished warehouses down the the old canal. Once there, he availed himself, as instructed, of the private carpark. A janitor came hurdling out from behind the dustbins and told Keith, in no uncertain terms, to park elsewhere. On Keith producing ID, the janitor huddled over his faulty walkie-talkie. Keith listened to denial, to horrorfizz and horrorsquawk, and endless denial. When the clearance eventually came through Keith sniffed and realigned his jacket, and decisively shoved the car door shut with the flat of his hand. The window on the passenger side exploded outward. Firmly the janitor brought him dustpan and horror-brush.

Celebrity practice boards? *What* fucking celebrity practice boards? He was taken through the canteen and into a stockroom that happened to have a dartboard in it. Incredibly the sun sought him out even here. What was the sun made of? Coal? Oxyacetylene? Glo-logs? What was the matter with it? Why didn't it go away? Why didn't it go *out?* No: it went on funneling its heat into his exhaustedly hooded eyes. He blinked into the numbered orb of the board, itself like a low sun, the vortex of all his hopes and dreams. His head bowed in its horrorglare. With the purple pouch in his hand (how very worn and soiled it looked) Keith paced out the distance, turned, sniffed, coughed, and straightened himself. The sun vanished. The first dart was flying through the horrornight.

---

Excerpt from *London Fields*

# Newton

JEANETTE
WINTERSON

This is the story of Tom.

This is the story of Tom and his neighbors.

This is the story of Tom and his neighbors and his neighbor's garden.

This is the story of Tom.

"All my neighbors are classical physicists," said Tom. "Their laws of motion are predetermined. They rise at seven and leave for work at eight. The women take coffee at ten. If you see a soul on the street between one and two, it can only be the doctor, it can only be the undertaker, it can only be the stranger.

"I am the stranger," said Tom.

"What's the first law of thermodynamics?" said Tom. "You can't transfer heat from a colder to a hotter. I've never had any warmth from my neighbors, so I'd say that was true. Here in Newton we don't talk much. That is, my neighbors talk all the time, they swap gossip but I never have any, although sometimes I am some.

"What's the second law of thermodynamics?" said Tom. "Everything tends toward the condition of entropy. That is, the energy's still there, somewhere, but for all useful purposes it's lost. Take a look at my neighbors here in Newton and you'll see what I mean."

My neighbor has a garden full of plastic flowers. It's easy, she says, and so nice. When her husband died, she had him laminated and he stands outside now, his hands on his hips, carefully watching the sky.

"What's the matter Tom?" she says, her head bobbing along the fence like a duck in a shooting parlor. "Why don't you get married? Y'know, in my day, nobody had any trouble finding someone, we just did it and made the best of it. There were no screwballs then."

"What, none?"

She bobs faster and gathers an armful of underwear from the washing line. I know she wants me to stare at it, she wants to prove I'm a screwball. After all, if it's me, it's not her, it's not the others. You only get one per block. She wheels around, ready to bob back up the other way, knickers pop from every pore.

"Tom, we were glad to be normal. In those days it was something to be proud of."

Tom the screwball. Here I am with my papercovered foreign editions and my corduroy trousers. ("You got something against Levi's?" he said before he was laminated.) All the men around here wear Levi's; denims or chinos. The only stylistic difference is whether you pack your stomach inside or outside the waistband.

They think I must be homosexual. I wouldn't mind. I wouldn't mind what I was if only I were something.

"What do you want to be when you grow up?" said my mother, a long time ago, many times a long time ago.

"A fireman, an astronaut, a spy, a train driver, a hard hat, an inventor, a deep-sea diver, and a doctor and a nurse."

What do you want to be when you grow up? I ask myself in the mirror most days.

"Myself, I want to be myself."

And who's that Tom?

Into the clockwork universe, a baby boy. Heard that story before? Maybe it's why all men like to think that they're Jesus.

Every few seconds another clutch of redeemers gets born and the exhausted mother bending over her bloody child won't know if he's Karl Marx or Charles Manson. Interestingly, the one time he was Jesus, she did know, but then she had friends in high places. For the rest of us, it's swagger or perish, that's what I hate about being a man.

I do contemplate some awful crime. Some evil thing to leave my mark. Evil and awful because it's easier than being awesome and good. You need a lot of imagination to be good. I can slide along all right, like the rest of the little sperm that made it, but to live and die obscure in Newton, tick-tock till my last breath?

There's a knock at the screen door. I hide my Camus in the fridge and peer toward the frosted glass. Of course I can't see anything. They never tell you that when you buy frosted glass.

Tom? Tom? RAP RAP.

It's my neighbor. I shuffle to the door and open it. There she is, her hair coiled on her head like a wreath on a war memorial. She's all in pink.

"I'm not interrupting you am I Tom?" she says, her eyes shoving past me into the kitchen.

"I was reading."

"That's what I thought. I said to myself, Tom will be reading. He won't be doing anything. I'll ask him to help me out. You know how difficult it is for a woman to manage alone. Since my husband was laminated I haven't had it easy Tom."

She smells of woman; warm, perfumed. I mustn't act like a screwball. I'll offer her coffee. I do. She's pleased. She's here because she wants me to help her old mother into the house. That's a nice Boy Scout thing to do. It's very normal, very nice, and I want to do it.

. . .

Shouldn't we go now? We shouldn't keep her waiting?

"She's had a long journey, she's in no hurry. To tell you the truth, I'm the one who's exhausted. You make the coffee and then we'll help her in."

I don't love my next-door neighbor but still my hand trembles over the spoon. They've made me feel odd and outside for so long that in their eyes the simplest things look strange.

How does a normal person make coffee?

And what is it about me that worries them so much anyway? I'm clean. I have a job.

"Tom, tell me, is it a modern thing to keep your books in the refrigerator?"

In cheap crime novels, you often read *"He spun round."* It always makes me laugh to imagine a human being so animated, but when she asked me that, I did, I spun. One second my whole being was facing the sink and the next I was facing her, and she was facing me holding my copy of Camus.

"I was just getting the milk out Tom. K Mew. Who is Albert K Mew?"

"He's a Frenchman. A French writer. I don't know how he came to be in the fridge."

She repeats my words slowly as though I had just told her a universal truth. "You don't know how he came to be in the fridge?"

I shrug and smile to try and disarm her. "It's a big fridge. Don't you often find things in the fridge that you had forgotten about?"

"No Tom. I have cheese at the top and then beer and bacon and underneath that I put my weekend chicken and in the containers at the bottom I have salad things and eggs. Those

are the rules. It was the same when my husband was alive and
it's the same now."

I am beginning to regard her with a new respect. The Grim
Reaper came to call. He took her husband from his bed but left
the weekend chicken on the shelf.

O death, where is thy sting?

My neighbor, still holding my Camus, leans forward confi-
dentially, her arms resting on the table. She looks intimate, soft.
"Tom, have you ever thought that you might need Help?" She
says help with a capital letter, like a doorstep evangelist.

"If you mean the fridge, anyone can make a mistake."

"Tom, I'm going to be tough with you. You know what
your problem is? You read too many geniuses. Now I don't
know if Mr. K Mew is a genius but the other day I saw you
with Picasso's notebooks. You were reading them in the main
square in front of everyone. Children were coming out of
school and you were reading them. Miss Fin at the library tells
me that all you ever order are works of genius. She's got no
record of you ever having taken out a sea story. Now that's
unhealthy. Why is it unhealthy? Because you yourself are not
a genius. If you were, we would have found out by now, you'd
have painted something, or written something. You don't even
have a typewriter. So you're ordinary, like the rest of us, and
ordinary people need to live ordinary lives. What's the point
of dreaming about Montmartre when you're here, at number
nine Tranquil Gardens?"

She sat back, satisfied. I thought she'd finished but she was
fixing her mouth for another round.

"I tell you this Tom, if you're not a genius, you gotta be

ordinary or you go down the other side and end up a screwball."

"Shall we get your mother?" I said.

Outside, my neighbor walked ahead toward a closed van parked in front of her house. I'd seen her mother a couple of years previously, but I couldn't see her now.

"She's in the back Tom. Come around the back."

My neighbor flung open the doors of the hired van and certainly there was her mother, sitting upright in the wheelchair that had been her home and car. She was smiling a terrible plasticky smile, her teeth perfect like a cheetah's. She had been laminated.

"Haven't they done a wonderful job? She's even better than Doug and he was pretty advanced at the time. I wish she could see herself, she'd be so proud."

"Are those her own teeth?"

"They are now Tom."

"Where are you going to put her?"

"In the garden. She loved flowers."

Slowly, slowly, we heaved her mother down from the van and wheeled her over the pavement to the house. It was afternoon coffee time by then and a lot of neighbors came to pay their respects. They were so respectful that we were outside for an hour talking plastic. My neighbor gets an incentive voucher for every successful lamination she introduces and she reckons that if Newton goes on seeing it her way, she'll have 75 percent of her own preservation money before she dies.

"I've seen you hanging around the cemetery Tom. It's not hygienic."

What does she think I am? A ghoul? I've told her before that my mother's buried there but she just shakes her head and says "Young married couples need the land Tom. Until we learn to stop dying we have to live with the consequences. There's no room for the dead unless you respect them as ornamental."

I have tried to tell her that if we stop dying, all the cemeteries in the world will never provide enough land for the bulging aging population. She doesn't listen, she just looks dreamy and thinks about the married couples.

Newton is jammed with married couples. We need one-way streets just to let the singles through. I hate going shopping in Newton. I hate trying to weave my way between the crocodiles filing up Main Street two by two like the ark has just landed. His 'n' Hers, complacent shoulder blades and battered baby buggies and the DIY shops are full of Him and the supermarkets are full of Her. Don't they know that too much role playing is bad for your health? Imagine being a wife and saying "Honey, have you got time to fix the toilet?" Imagine being a husband and not knowing how to clean the toilet when she's left you.

And do they know why they're married? No, they just do it, the way they do everything else in Newton. Tick-tock says the clock.

"Tom, thank you Tom," she says when her mother is settled so sweetly beside the duck pond. The ducks are bath-time yellow with chirpy red beaks and their pond has real water. I've never been in my neighbor's garden before. It's very quiet, no rustling in the undergrowth, no birds yammering away. She tells me that peace is what the country is about.

"If you were a genius Tom, you'd be able to work here. The silence. The air. I have a unit you know. It filters all the air entering the garden."

It's autumn and there are a few plastic leaves scattered on the Astroturf. My neighbor has a shed at the bottom of the garden.

It's made of wood, although I can hardly believe this. I wonder if she's noticed. Inside are her stocks for the changing of the seasons. She's told me before that a garden has to have variety and in her old-fashioned Aladdin's cave are the reassuring copies of nature. Tulips, red and white hanging meekly upside down by their stems. Daffodils tied in bright bunches are jumbled with loose camellia blooms waiting to be fixed on the all-year-round tree. She's even got a row of squirrels clutching identical nuts.

"I'll be putting those out soon, along with the creeper."

She has Virginia creeper cascading her house. It's still green. This is the burnt and blazing version.

"Mine's already turning," I tell her.

"I don't like leaves Tom, you can't depend on them to fall where they should or to turn when they should. Nature doesn't care about you and me, she just goes ahead and does what she likes when she likes and that's why we have to regulate her. If we don't, it's volcanoes, forest fires, floods, and death and the bodies scattered anywhere, just like leaves."

Like leaves. Just like leaves, just a little, like them a little where they fall and nobody turns them over to see what's written on the other side. Like that. Like the simple text that can be read or not, that lies under your feet, read or not. That falls and stays red, rain and wind, though nobody scoops it up to take it home. Life has fallen at your feet and you kicked her away and she bled on your shoes and when you came home your mother said, "Look at you covered in leaves."

You were covered in leaves. You peeled them off one by one exposing the raw skin beneath. All those leavings. And when what was to fall had fallen, you picked it up to read what was written on the other side. It made no sense to you, you screwed it into your pocket where it burned like a live coal. Tell me

why they all left one by one in single file. Didn't they like you?
Didn't they, like you, need a heart that was a book with no last
page? Turn the leaves.

"The leaves are turning," said Tom.

She asked me back to supper as a thank you, and I thought I
should go because that's what normal people do; eat with their
neighbors, even if it's boring and the food's horrible.

I found a tie and wore it.

"Tom, come in, what a lovely surprise."

She must mean what a lovely surprise for me, how can she
be surprised, she's been cooking all afternoon. Once inside the
dining room, I do know she means me. I know that because
the entire population of Newton is already seated at a table that
begins crammed up against the Capodimonte display cabinet
and extends . . . and extends through a jagged hole in the side
of the house and on out toward the bus station.

"I think you know everyone Tom," says my neighbor.

"Sit, here, by me, in Doug's place. You know, you're about
his height."

Do I know everyone? It's hard to say since I can't see everyone. Beyond the hole, all is lost.

"Tom, take a plate. We're having chicken cooked in bacon
strips and stuffed with hard-boiled eggs. There's a salad I made
and plenty of cheese and if you want beer it's in the fridge."

She drifts away from me, her dress clinging to her like a
drowned man. Nobody looks up from their plates. They're all
eating chicken, denims or chinos, must be three or four hundred fowl on the table, half a dozen eggs per arse. I'm still
going over the roasting details when one of them explodes,
BAM, and pelts my neighbor's neighbor with six solid hand

grenades. One of her arms flies off but luckily for her not the one she needs for her fork. Nobody notices. I want to say something. I want to do something. I am about to say and do something when my neighbor herself returns carrying a covered silver dish.

"It's for you Tom," she says, and the table falls silent.

Already on my feet, I am able to lift the lid with some dignity.

"Thank you. It's very nice. I see it's a chicken."

"It's your chicken Tom."

She's telling the truth. Poking out of the neck of the chicken I can see my copy of *L'Étranger* by Albert Camus. It hasn't been shredded, so I can take it out and look at it. When I look at it I see that there are no words left on any of the pages. The pages are blank.

"We wanted to help you Tom." Her eyes are full of tears. "Not just me, all of us." A helping hand for Tom.

Slowly the table starts to clap, faster and louder. The table shakes, the dishes roll from side to side like the drunken tableware in a sea story. This is a sea story. The captain and the crew have gone mad and I am the only passenger. Reeling, I run from the dining room to the kitchen, slam the door on the din behind me. I am panting but here is peace. Hygienic enameled peace.

Tom slid down the door and cried.

Time passed. In Newton it always does and everyone knows how long it takes for time to pass and so nobody gets confused. Tom didn't know how much time had passed. He woke from an aching sleep and put his fist through the frosted glass in the kitchen door. He went home and took his big coat and filled the pockets with books and the books seemed like live coals to

him. He walked away from Newton, but he did once look back
and what he saw was a table stretching out past the bend in the
road and on past the streets and houses, through the streets and
houses, joining them together in an orgy of matching cutlery.
World without end.

But now, says Tom, the hills are ripe and the water leaps at my
throat when I shave.

Tick-tock says the clock in Newton.

Banquo
and the
Black
Banana:
The
Fierceness
of the
Delight
of the
Horror

PAUL WEST

*. . . out of this our cloud upon the precipice's edge, there
grows into palpability, a shape, far more terrible than any
genius or any demon of a tale, and yet it is but a
thought, although a fearful one, and one which chills the
very marrow of our bones with the fierceness of the delight
of its horror. . . . it involves that one most ghastly and
loathsome of all the most ghastly and loathsome images of
death and suffering which have ever presented themselves
to our imagination—for this very cause do we now the
most vividly desire it.*

*—Edgar Allan Poe,*
*"The Imp of the*
*Perverse"*

## THE FIERCENESS

What bloody man is that? See how he has butchered himself to bits? Did you know that, ever after, you would know
him only as a man slashed and crimson, eyes dangling either
side of his nose, his carelessly outstuck tongue cut off, his lips
sliced into loops? Would you know him, this unhistorical man,
as the authorities describe him? Whose bloody man is that? Do
you say this as you watch him, now and latterly one of the
*Wehrmacht* walking home to a Germany that no longer exists?
Do you understand? Do you fathom it? Did you realize that I,
being mythical, a Holinshed convenience, fathered kings but
was none? Do you understand that, although my progeny has
been vast, my own life, a series of knots tied in a pig's umbilical,
has been nothing but little sidlings into and out of the lamplight? Did you know that I have always been either a murdered
man or one that didn't matter? Am I me? Or many others?
Have I always been among the beaten, the downcast, the de-

moted? Ha, am I no more than a little sidling, akin to a spider-
ling, a pawn situated in dusty corners, in old wounds full of
flies, in the anus of a rotting wildebeest? Do you wonder that
I ask questions all the time? All other modes have been denied
me, haven't they? Is nothing certain, then? Can't you tell? You
knew me once, didn't you, as the ghost at the banquet, alarm-
ing him only, the general? Do you recall? How can you forget?
Am I he? Am I none other? Do you see how I never pause for
an answer, but answer everything myself? Have you concluded, then, that there is nothing to be known? Because I was
only a figment, am I never to be known, husbanding my few
lines like some insane Norman farmer? Have I even learned to
ask questions about my questions? I have, haven't I? Who are
you anyway, eavesdropping on a butchered phantom? Will
you go away? Did you say no? Must I therefore go on talking
about the general in his kilt with his enormous ballocks bruising his sporran? Shouldn't he have worn his ballocks on the
outside and tucked the sporran between his legs, high up
among the fuse wire and the suppurating truncheon? Didn't
you know the general had syphilis? And that we wanted to see
him rotting like an old goose? Did it worry her? Didn't she
always worry? Have you ever known anyone worry that
much, especially after touching the beastly thing for him,
bringing him to his climax, and then laving her hands all night
in a basin made of painted clay? Did you know she never
touched herself? Will you all forgive if I hand over some real
information? You will? Shall I go on? Will you believe me if
I tell you the real lowdown? Would you credit it that, at some
risk of monotony, I had to do duty for the following ill-fated
denizens of this world? Have you heard of

Sophie Scholl (beheaded)
Count Ciano (shot in the back)

Sir Roger Casement (hanged)
Klaus von Stauffenberg (shot in the front)
William Francis Kemmler (electrocuted)
the orangutan that preceded Kemmler (charred)
Eugene Victor (a thousand cuts)
Emi Brunner (strangled—Austrian method)
Henry McCracken (gassed)
Half-Hanged Smith?

Did you know that I was always the attendant ghost? I had no lines, did I, but many facial expressions, many twists and writhes? Have I been useful? Whose phantom am I now? Would you know me in the street? Nay, but would you scream and flee? I am Lethe's proxy, am I not, a rentable death's-head doomed to float in and out of history? Will you join me, sirs, ladies, for another sortie? Am I not worth making real for twenty minutes? Once, had I not a lovely glossy quiff and a mouth that shone and curved like tomato? Am I not ripe? And, and, and? Have you ever gone *and, and, and?* What do you do after it? Especially if it's all said and done and, after your last *and*, there's nothing to come, as there never is, is there? Can you imagine the penultimate *and*, after which there's the last *and*, and, well, after that, not so much a lack of *and*s as a surreptitious creeping recognition that it's no good justifying an *and* simply because you can put another *and* after it? I mean, don't I, that life has no right to be a sequence of unfollowed *and*s, it being understood that an *and* after an *and* doesn't add up to a hill of beans? And therefore isn't worth saying, as I said? Did you see them shoving balloons up my throat into the vestibule of the brain? No? That's what it felt like, don't you know? While I wait, they torture me, see? It hurts, but, more than it hurts it intensifies loneliness, telling me that I was never historical but crystallized out of ectoplasm, get it? Don't you see that I came to roost out of blood steam, and stayed, like a leech of conscience? Would you not have done the same? Unwanted yet reintroduced, dispatched yet everlastingly put upon, wouldn't you bitch about it? Be pissed, peeved, swacko-bollocked out of your shithead gourd? What? Am I raving? No, my Saps, don't you know an argot of the dead when you hear one? I'm a priceless baboon, aren't I? What were you asking, late, about blood steam? Didn't you know it was the exhalation of the blood stream? Are you duffers all? Must I speak in Esperanto to get through to you? Do you not see the wobbling of my chops? Am I not the throttler of daydreams? Am I what you would like to meet in the dark, the light, the half-light, the dawn, the dusk, the hovering mauve cloud from your father's corncob pipe? If you were dying, would you ask for me? No, but, don't you see, it's me you'd get, planting myself on your face to blot out the last few gasps? Do I not even allow a death-rattle? I do not, do I? I cough magma into your heart, and you know what magma does, don't you? It keeps you from being stoical; you knew that long ago, surely? Don't you think, though, that instead of planting *me* in a toilet's gob they could have given life to some geraniums, even a delicate and pudendal hibiscus we kept gentling with our tongues? What am I doing perched above the soil in the basin, as if my head were going to take its first shit after five hundred years? Who holds me up to dry? Who holds me over it, as far as possible, so the ancient farts will waft the other way, exterminating Papua? Can this be true? Pah, I'm unheld, aren't I? I'm wedged afloat, I'm floating wedged, am I not? I'm like the full moon of June, coming up low and leering along the horizon like a dinner gong busted loose to reflect the fiery furnace, yeah? Didn't they say *yea* in the old days, and then they added breath in the form of *h* to it? Dare I say yeah? Would you *yea* me if I *yeah*ed you? You knew, did you not, that when called upon to give artificial resuscitation I just suck the air right out of you? I kneel, don't you know, and press my mouth where it belongs in that hoax of passion? Then I do the wrong thing, unhinging all I lean upon, don't you remember? And, when I was young, I did vice versa, blowing air into all the girls I kissed until they exploded, don't you you remember, ducky? Why should you vulgarly assume I was saving and slaying, slaying and saving, at the nether porthole? Sucking the offal out, blowing the trumps back? No, don't you see that the other way was better, more susceptible of melodramatic treatment in the yellow press of the time? You'll get used to me, won't you, before I have to off you? Unless something riper comes along—what'd you call that? A change of tune? Or tack? A call to the colors, even, for which we have all yearned, haven't we, falling over ourselves to be constitutionally useful? Have you heard anything on the grapevine? Are the wires a-hum with good news coming my way? Am I to have a change of heart? What was the worst, though? Do I have to remember? Wasn't it taking the children of Macduff for a walk, after the atrocity, the butchering, in some august uncontaminated dimension where only the dead walked? Well, what was wrong with that? I tripped over something warm, and it was Macduff's briar pipe left on the field of battle, just like something in the Western desert in World War II, see? What's that, Banquie, they asked, and I squeezed their hands hard to get them ready for the awful truth, and then I saw that in each hand I had only a severed arm with no child attached even as the voices out of nowhere's cauldron went on asking What's that, Banquie? Even worse, would you believe it, was the time, much later, I had to stand in for Admiral Canaris, the head of German Intelligence (I mean the department, not the nation's brainpower as a whole)? At Flossenberg that morning, they made him pay, didn't they? Out they hauled him: remember?

Naked as a babe, noosed, then the ladder removed from beneath him, only a little stepladder, remember? He dangled awhile, and then they got him down, right? Then they hanged him again and got him down again, can you imagine it? It went on for twenty minutes until the blessed time when they did not let him down, did not loosen the noose, and then, wouldn't you know it, they burned him and his ashes floated on the wind into the cells? I was present, you see don't you, in my capacity as horror's ventriloquial doll? Did I suffer what he suffered? Did I also look on as some of the dying claim to have done? Did I do both? Would I lie to you? What on earth or elsewhere could I hope to gain? Did you know that beneath him there accumulated a little mound of his droppings and that, after each strangling and release, the fierce guard dogs were allowed to race in toward the stepladder and gobble up the remains? Have you ever heard the phrase "a shit-eating grin"? Well, you have now, haven't you? Do you begin to have the faintest idea of the role enforced upon me of participating spectator, proxy ghoul, neither Canaris nor not him, neither hanged nor let down, neither burned nor left intact? What had I done? Had I merely sneered at the weird sisters, chaffing them about any knack for reading the future precisely? Was it that? Was I, through empathy, indistinguishable from the poor souls whose ends I monitored? If so, my karma's a canker, isn't it? Do I learn from experience, then? Do I ever? Nothing at all? Can you imagine no progress in all the centuries? Am I omitting the crucified on purpose, then? No, I just haven't got to them, have I, I'm swamped with cadavers, all of them loved ones? Will you hear me out?

THE DELIGHT

Behold my most favorite island, Elba or Catalina, but it is only a shower stall in which, still legless, I cower, shielded by antiradiation drapes, the sound of the pouring water that of those British movies in which the mikes are in the wrong place and, because the actors are mumbling anyway (as they always do), you hear only the spurt of diphthongs. I hear voices in the downpour, but they tell me little I do not already know. For a wild moment I thought I was making a speech, an address, and my hearers were interrupting to heckle or to praise. But it was only the water saying You're all right, they've given you a decent job at long last. No more gore. I don't know about that; as well believe the human race has given up violence. It's just that I somehow unearth myself from the dry toilet next door and roll, blood vessels dragging and tangling, the foot or two to the shower stall, somehow bundling myself over its tinny lintel. The water is always on and therefore goes cold quite often. In fact, the toilet is part of the same bathroom in which the stall is. En suite, as we say. I presume I was lifted here, transported; I don't recall, overwhelmed as I was at the time by the lifting of the embargo requiring nonstop questions. I am allowed to make

paragraphs, paragiraffes, just like
this.

Not that I write or type, but I imagine a typography of voice full of little pauses, indents, half drops, and the heroic-sounding page break, in which the heart etcetera. Unprepossessing as I may be, I am a comptroller of sorts. At a given moment, the curtains part and my team of sturdy Japanese and Hawaiians snap to attention before me as I peer at them with naked-feeling frontal lobes. They are the instructors, a Gestapo who police the people not doomed to living in shower stalls. It having been discovered long ago that, with so few trees left, our beloved planet was choking on its own carbon dioxide, on which in the proper way of things trees feed, converting it into oxygen—surely one of the Almighty's niftiest bits of reciprocal chemistry. How I exactly got the idea across, mumbling and blurting as I do, my vowels full of blood, my consonants mired in catarrh that slides from my sinuses into the back of my throat, I have no idea; but I did, after some days of labor, and my proposal was so simple, so bald, it bowled them over.

All we have to do, I intimated to them (and I addressed them as one who has been buffeted about in all the crimps and bloodbaths of history) is breathe less. All we need to do is hold our breath, taking only two breaths where ordinarily we would take three. Whatever the ratio of new to old would have to be, it was bound to help us. But how to manage it? I then proposed that we gather up all the divers on the planet and have them instruct and demonstrate such arts as deep inhaling, transferring breath to the mind, needing less air, going down deep to prove the pudding—after all, if you have learned to hold your breath, what better test than to go to sixty-feet depth? In so proposing, and bringing about, a new regime (The New Pneu), I also inadvertently brought into being a whole new range of human facial expressions, ranging from the suffocated to the ice-bland quiet of the beta-blocked, from passing-out purple to guru trance. After a year, quite a number of people were going about holding their breath as if it were quite literally something to proffer to others. There was less talk too, though less explosive "letting-of-the-breath-out" than you might think. The art was to let it puff narrowly away from you like a sigh. The divers were past masters of course, able to hold breath for five minutes, lying doggo on the bottom among sponges and necklaces. Up here, even in the shower stall, things were more difficult. After a minute, I felt as if there were a ferret in my chest scampering madly to get out, and I was only pretend-breathing, having no lungs, although there was a period between Agincourt and Waterloo when I had two spongy sacs dangling beneath my severed head, just for show, not for receipt of air, rather like the empty scrotum patched to the back of my neck—a nether scalp. I could imagine how the gaspers felt, and the divers too, the former always trying to achieve the sleek petrifaction of the Hawaiians and the Japanese, their gaze of glass.

That was years ago. I regret to say that humans became too fond of holding their breath, were always trying to outdo the divers (Bizet?), so there began to be thousands of deaths from asphyxia: children dying in class while teachers died, trying to teach with their mouths clenched tight, their airways shut down for the afternoon. That sounds wrong; it's the lack of practice. I mean with their noses blocked, not with their airlines grounded. You can have too much of a good thing. Then I suspected the whole thing was a hoax invented by those who, heedless of the choking planet, just wanted to reduce the population. Knowing the grisly end we would come to, they had naturally thought of me: good old Banquo, atrocity's familiar, blood's henchman, unable to die, but endowed with ghoulish adaptability, able to invade and transcend any physique, state of mind, any afterlife even, in the end destined by weird sisters, or the power that told even the Greek gods what to do, to perform an auto-da-fé on the last human remaining. Then to be found by some alien form and duplicated throughout the galaxy as the one surviving life-form, having his progeny as it were sideways: cloned, copycat perfect. The instant this sublime plan began to declare itself to me in the squalid downpour of the shower stall, I began to shudder with delight. To have been spurned and denied so long, to have been fobbed off as a groveling nothing, to have been made into a peripathetic death's-head, these were minor trials in view of my reward.

The thing now, I thought, was to make the whole population even better breath-holders, to off them even faster. The divers themselves were no problem since they always had a suicidal (dare I say kamikaze) element in their makeup, not their cosmetics. I am still out of practice, especially at being non-interrogative. No, the target was asphyxia for all, self-induced, and fostered in the popular imagination by pleas to breathe ever deeper without breathing out. Dizziness was in. Blackouts ousted rock music. People encouraged one another, rather like the Japanese soldiers who turned into lemmings on the lips of cliffs, to remember how Captain Oates walked out from his tent into the blizzard on Captain Scott's doomed expedition to the South Pole. I saw now what General Macbeth had been after, laying waste all before him: needing a clear space in which to work, though I doubted if even the hags had intended him for galactic emigration as the last sample of his kind. You could tell, however, he wanted to be the only one of himself, so to speak, which I already was. He wanted to be a being that had none of the characteristics of others, as I think the long-lost Mary McCarthy essay had pointed out, calling him a Babbitt and such things. No, Macbeth wanted to be an avatar, not a bourgeois, whereas I owed nothing to anyone save those big brass talking heads in the early Elizabethan plays. I was catching up with the general, that was clear, and I had achieved greater sway over the Sapiens than he. Mouthing uncouthly, and punctuating my barbaric turns of speech with spike-shaped hemorrhages, I nonetheless over the years made the planet silent. People even swallowed their own death rattles, anxious not to blight a tree; but the real problem was the cloud of carbon dioxide that sealed us in, rising away from the trees (of which there were not many anyway). As for me, did I breathe? Did Benny Goodman hire his brother to play the drums in the band or send him out to starve? I breathed shallow, taking tiny metaphysical breaths mostly water vapor anyway, or its mental equivalent. I waited as the planet quietened and the dead stayed where they fell as the exertion of gravedigging, and lugging corpses about, made folk gasp for breath. It was for this that I had been kept waiting all those centuries. I did not have to be nice, clever, or polite. All I had to do was hunker down in my shower stall, by which I mean squat on the stump of my brain stem, and ogle the sow bugs as they inched along by the lintel, sometimes climbing it to look at my vertical Ganges. Banquo, I told myself, they are dying like flies out there: choking, croaking, swallowing their tongues. Alas, I thought, as death claimed its millions, to have been privy to all minds and hearts without making use of them—many of them anyway. Mine was the plight of the symptomatic anthologist, able to dip into lives and hearts, use them, but without ever making a generalization for which I would be remembered. Though by whom?

You see, then, how Banquo has barbered himself to bits, maybe because the general (Macbeth or Patton, who cares?) says it's all very well to prate about the usefulness and high-mindedness of the pearl and sponge divers. The oceans are so crammed with oil, he rants, that nobody can find anything ever again—pearls, sponges, mines. These divers, he claims, are lucky to have a job, so it's just as well the planet is swathed in $CO_2$. I wish I'd been among them in the old days, when someone tossed a crucifix or a Buddha into the waves and down they went to search. The winner climbed the tallest mast and set a bouquet on its top. It was all exercise, but they had enormous lungs, a slowly beating heart. The one in charge of them, the commendatore of ocean divers, needs no such thing;

his heart can beat as it wants, as if someone were to ask a youth what he does for a living and he answers, "I work as a mechanic in a mirage." Lovely answer, that, making life on Earth almost tolerable, better than watching millions walking around with their breath held, eyeing the heavens for the first signs of yellow: fur or scum. The art (or torture) of conversation has gone, like running, all playing of musical instruments. Oral sex is a help, though, and nowadays children are encouraged to place plastic bags over their heads. People watch a diving movie in which the father stepped backward off the reef into octopus land, and he got the bends on the way up, which killed him. A rival family had stolen his pearls and sponges at gunpoint anyway. There were never, it seems, enough movies honoring divers, at least not of the kind that lull the watchers. There are no telephones, of course, but retired divers—gimpy and stunted—walk from place to place with messages in a cleft conch. It's a slower life, much slower than being in that play about the general, forever wondering how many children Lady M. had. In the play, you see, you can get excited without breathing, and there is all that peacock language to keep you warm.

So I live two lives, administering divers who cannot bear to look at me, and sitting in place at the banquet with a look of comatose ruefulness, or like a pretty prospecting snail, his twin pipettes at the ready, to scare the general until the end of time. Call me a bureaucratic ghost, wishing my last utterance in the play had been *It will be rain tonight*, which has about it a mellow obviousness, instead of all that stuff, short as it was, about treachery, fly, fly, fly, revenge and slavery. You can tell I wanted out right after *They set upon Banquo*. What a pity the eminent addict Tom De Quincey, famous for an essay on mere knocking, had not addressed himself instead to Banquo's ghost. Too late now to coerce him with the threat of ten-minute breath-holds brought about with clamps and plugs. Once it was the method of execution; now it's the staff of life. What's your pleasure, my pretty ones, my pretty chickens? Shall I stay and drill the divers to drill the populace to cut down on the carbon dioxide? Or would you have me sequestered again inside the drama? Off goes the general to play golf on the Scottish fairways, where his wife is buried, especially the course at what was formerly Birnam Wood. Myself, blood-boltered in perpetuity, I sometimes think of aping the divers by holding my breath and diving down into the oil to see what I can come up with, at last breaking clear of the sea's surface, just a punished face bleeding black, my entrails bled white, my destiny dead long ago, before there were suns to set. Imagine.

Imagine my fragments lying by the roadside, scattered by a speeding Rolls-Royce. Would you Humpty-Dumpty me? Envy, as I have done, cows' heads sitting on butchers' slabs or those of sheep grinning avidly with blood seeping from the velvet muzzle they kiss with. I too am only a vagrant incarnation. Imagine fleeing from me in dank cellars, abandoned stables, or ruined factories in which huge cobwebbed saws swing gently above you, never to spin or rend again. Call me the destroyer of delight. My head is a big book-burning, my loins are a guttering candle. My heart halts each time that taste of blame and ashes invades my mouth from below, bringing the lovely mucous continuum to a halt. It was I, see, who chopped down Birnam Wood.

Verily then. Amen. Ahem. As it were. Heavens. Bear with me. To begin with, then. I'm getting there. I have my lapses, when my mind becomes something a hawk dropped or a salmon bone spat out by a grizzly. I'm almost there, o golden ptarmigan, o saliva-decked slug. Half a mo'. What's all this here? Lord love us. Oh my. Cripes. Ah. It begins to come. I thought it would never. Banquo. Banquet. Banquotha. It is as

if, late at night, you have strolled outside to leave a letter in the
mailbox, raise the red flag to catch the mailman's eye, and, as
you lower the door from its clip, a fanged octopus hits you in
the face and a roar flows outward after it.

## THE HORROR

Is all my gossamer turning to silicon? Why do I feel so ener-
gized, gliding forward, at a dead sardine's pace, yes, but stray-
ing from my hitherto assigned throne? No more water
cascading? No peat left beneath me? Is that the water coming
back, plus a chime of heavy chains within it? Is that peat I smell
again, even if leavened with a barely concealed aroma of feces
being neutralized? Do I whiff Japan? What can I be gliding on,
down this interminable erector set of a tunnel? Into an ante-
room structured from gigantic, organic-looking ribs? How can
I see? Dangling where they are, can my eyes still work? Have
they been switched on for me like landing lights? Is it truly me
lurching and skidding through this rib cage of a refectory? Are
they saying *Here comes the ghost?* What can have solidified
under me, what piece of me, to make a skid or a castor? Is any
of this happening, or do I live by illusion? How can you have
another incarnation when your life has been nothing else but
incarnations? I mean, why bother? Who takes the trouble to
enforce another role on a death's-head whose trailing tripes
have befouled many a mile of linoleum? Will they let me off
if I slip and fall, terrorizing none perhaps, but demonstrably
ungainly? I'm a dab hand with an adverb, aren't I now? Is this
the future? Is this my destiny? Am I here to be a horror, to
*represent* it as if it were some politician's constituency? Or is
it something even worse? Am I here to be merely useful? Are
we going to Mars at last? Am I the one appointed to pollute

the skies of Mars? They're too cold, don't you know? Didn't you know that, to warm them up to make them habitable, and all the atmosphere that goes with them, we have to warm them up with filth, as here at home? Didn't you know they'll tell you anything down here, just to get you up there? No, wrong wasn't I? Even up here, don't you know, they'll tell you anything just to keep you in the spaceship? But how jump out? Is there a way? Is there a way for useful fellows such as me? Do any of you know? Is this the one place, traveling as fast as light, from which there is no exit? What I glide along upon, connected to them only by sudden-stiffened ganglia thin as stair rods, are these my kidneys? Were they? Or my testicles unsheathed, unpursed? Hardened for the use? There must be two, for symmetry, mustn't there? I totter, see? Will you do my looking for me and peer, kind folks, 'neath my kilt? Scots talk, especially when pleading, has a minty sound, has it not? Could I, the Scottish ghost from the bad-luck Scottish play, be walking on a double sporran? What urges my hideousness lumbering forward? Where do I go? I hear them shrieking as I approach; do you? When I reach them, don't you know, I'll butt my silicon head into their chests and smash all before me. 'Tis my role, wouldn't you know it? Would you not conclude I've been assigned a haunting? Are we en route to Orion, to Tom De Quincey's hideous nebula? Can they all be awake or are some of them still asleep in transparent pods? Am I sent to them to test them? Have they been told it will be long and clinical, all of it, a life among plastic and the almost lyrical metallurgical radiance of the main structure? Do they know that, as well as traveling several times a normal lifetime, so as to arrive (and return) refreshed, they will also have to put up with me? Have they any idea, or have their magnificent know-itall abacuses, who or what I am, that my used-up head blazes yellow and red like a freshly exposed beef in the abattoir? Are they ready for underslung eyes, the little brittle brogues my kidneys or balls have become? The landing gear made of what feels like celery lacquered with airplane dope? Are they ready for horror, for being devoured at the rate of one a month (I smell hundreds, all breeding)? Do they know my role, even as it grows within my skull like a manchineel tree, is to keep them up to scratch, that I remain untainted by napalm, flamethrowers, bombs, acid, or even hostile ideas? Do they know they have a hideous traveling companion, versatile, relentless, insatiable, fathered by Shakespeare upon Mary Shelley? Or was it another monster, Stoker's, whose name eludes me? Wasn't it someone such? There is no end, is there? You go on, don't you? It's karma, isn't it, good old karma at work again? When they want you, do you have to go, heaving your unlovely carcass from its fetid squat over the toilet's mouth, the business bowl, taking a last painful shower among the hot morse of the indoor rain? No goofing off, is there, in this teratologist's Almanac de Gotha? Am I deluded, or does each assignment better its predecessor? No more divers? For lack of me and my management skills, will Earth and its -lings smother now? Am I to blame? No, I'm like a sleeping bird wakened to song by a saxophone coming from the late party at the country club, see? I have a thistledown voice, wouldn't you concede? Am I not at a loss, as the phrase goes, in both senses? I don't know what to do, except come up with some means of choosing my first victim in the boundless ribbed halls of the space cruiser (dank and gray like an old fort a child plays with), but I must keep on asking questions, mustn't I? At a loss means also being present at a bereavement too, doesn't it? Is that my former self? Is its grave, are its graves, as wide and orange-peel-flavored as space? Will I ever run out of lives? Somewhere I'll find you, won't I? Will it help if I make it as quick as I can? Do all damage in the first strike, from behind? And stalk the rest like the flayed remnant I am, gliding on pipe cleaners of bone marrow? One day I will know what I am made of, won't I, my fellow travelers, my angel accomplices? Bear with me, will you, please, until I improve? Or just fade away, like an old soldja? Believe it or not, in your carnal swoon, you have heard the last confession of a ghost. Just watch for me in the darkest tunnels of the spaceship. I'm on duty again, bound to afflict you sooner or later, whoever you are or used to be, with the fierceness of the delight of the horror.

# Freniere

ANNE
RICE

"But, let me describe New Orleans, as it was then, and as it was to become, so you can understand how simple our lives were. There was no city in America like New Orleans. It was filled not only with the French and Spanish of all classes who had formed in part its peculiar aristocracy, but later with immigrants of all kinds, the Irish and the German in particular. Then there were not only the black slaves, yet unhomogenized and fantastical in their different tribal garb and manners, but the great growing class of the free people of color, those marvellous people of our mixed blood and that of the islands, who produced a magnificent and unique caste of craftsmen, artists, poets, and renowned feminine beauty. And then there were the Indians, who covered the levee on summer days selling herbs and crafted wares. And drifting through all, through this medley of languages and colors, were the people of the port, the sailors of ships, who came in great waves to spend their money in the cabarets, to buy for the night the beautiful women both dark and light, to dine on the best of Spanish and French cooking and drink the imported wines of the world. Then add to these, within years after my transformation, the Americans, who built the city up river from the old French Quarter with magnificent Grecian houses which gleamed in the moonlight like temples. And, of course, the planters, always the planters, coming to town with their families in shining landaus to buy evening gowns and silver and gems, to crowd the narrow streets on the way to the old French Opera House and the Théâtre d'Orléans and the St. Louis Cathedral, from whose open doors came the chants of High Mass over the crowds of the Place d'Armes on Sundays, over the noise and bickering of the French Market, over the silent, ghostly drift of the ships along the raised waters of the Mississippi, which flowed against the levee above the ground of New Orleans itself, so that the ships appeared to float against the sky.

"This was New Orleans, a magical and magnificent place to live. In which a vampire, richly dressed and gracefully walking through the pools of light of one gas lamp after another might attract no more notice in the evening than hundreds of other exotic creatures—if he attracted any at all, if anyone stopped to whisper behind a fan, 'That man . . . how pale, how he gleams . . . how he moves. It's not natural!' A city in which a vampire might be gone before the words had even passed the lips, seeking out the alleys in which he could see like a cat, the darkened bars in which sailors slept with their heads on the table, great high-ceilinged hotel rooms where a lone figure might sit, her feet upon an embroidered cushion, her legs covered with a lace counterpane, her head bent under the tarnished light of a single candle, never seeing the great shadow move across the plaster flowers of the ceiling, never seeing the long white finger reached to press the fragile flame.

"Remarkable, if for nothing else, because of this, that all of those men and women who stayed for any reason left behind them some monument, some structure of marble and brick and stone that still stands; so that even when the gas lamps went out and the planes came in and the office buildings crowded the blocks of Canal Street, something irreducible of beauty and romance remained; not in every street perhaps, but in so many that the landscape is for me the landscape of those times always, and walking now in the starlit streets of the Quarter or the Garden District I am in those times again. I suppose that is the nature of the monument. Be it a small house or a mansion of Corinthian columns and wrought-iron lace. The monument does not say that this or that man walked here. No, that what he felt in one time in one spot continues. The moon that rose over New Orleans then still rises. As long as the monuments stand, it still rises. The feeling, at least here . . . and there . . . it remains the same."

The vampire appeared sad. He sighed, as if he doubted what he had just said. "What was it?" he asked suddenly as if he were slightly tired. "Yes, money. Lestat and I had to make money. And I was telling you that he could steal. But it was investment afterwards that mattered. What we accumulated we must use. But I go ahead of myself. I killed animals. But I'll get to that in a moment. Lestat killed humans all the time, sometimes two or three a night, sometimes more. He would drink from one just enough to satisfy a momentary thirst, and then go on to another. The better the human, as he would say in his vulgar way, the more he liked it. A fresh young girl, that was his favorite food the first of the evening; but the triumphant kill for Lestat was a young man. A young man around your age would have appealed to him in particular."

"Me?" the boy whispered. He had leaned forward on his elbows to peer into the vampire's eyes, and now he drew up.

"Yes," the vampire went on, as if he hadn't observed the boy's change of expression. "You see, they represented the greatest loss to Lestat, because they stood on the threshold of the maximum possibility of life. Of course, Lestat didn't understand this himself. I came to understand it. Lestat understood nothing.

"I shall give you a perfect example of what Lestat liked. Up the river from us was the Freniere plantation, a magnificent spread of land which had great hopes of making a fortune in sugar, just shortly after the refining process had been invented. I presume you know sugar was refined in Louisiana. There is something perfect and ironic about it, this land which I loved producing refined sugar. I mean this more unhappily than I think you know. This refined sugar is a poison. It was like the essence of life in New Orleans, so sweet that it can be fatal, so richly enticing that all other values are forgotten. . . . But as I was saying up river from us lived the Frenieres, a great old

French family which had produced in this generation five young women and one young man. Now, three of the young women were destined not to marry, but two were young enough still and all depended upon the young man. He was to manage the plantation as I had done for my mother and sister; he was to negotiate marriages, to put together dowries when the entire fortune of the place rode precariously on the next year's sugar crop; he was to bargain, fight, and keep at a distance the entire material world for the world of Freniere. Lestat decided he wanted him. And when fate alone nearly cheated Lestat, he went wild. He risked his own life to get the Freniere boy, who had become involved in a duel. He had insulted a young Spanish Creole at a ball. The whole thing was nothing, really; but like most young Creoles this one was willing to die for nothing. They were both willing to die for nothing. The Freniere household was in an uproar. You must understand, Lestat knew this perfectly. Both of us had hunted the Freniere plantation, Lestat for slaves and chicken thieves and me for animals."

"You were killing *only* animals?"

"Yes. But I'll come to that later, as I said. We both knew the plantation, and I had indulged in one of the greatest pleasures of a vampire, that of watching people unbeknownst to them. I knew the Freniere sisters as I knew the magnificent rose trees around my brother's oratory. They were a unique group of women. Each in her own way was as smart as the brother; and one of them, I shall call her Babette, was not only as smart as her brother, but far wiser. Yet none had been educated to care for the plantation; none understood even the simplest facts about its financial state. All were totally dependent upon young Freniere, and all knew it. And so, larded with their love for him, their passionate belief that he hung the moon and that any conjugal love they might ever know would only be a pale reflection of their love for him, larded with this was a desperation as strong as the will to survive. If Freniere died in the duel, the plantation would collapse. Its fragile economy, a life of splendor based on the perennial mortgaging of the next year's crop, was in his hands alone. So you can imagine the panic and misery in the Freniere household the night that the son went to town to fight the appointed duel. And now picture Lestat, gnashing his teeth like a comic-opera devil because he was not going to kill the young Freniere."

"You mean then . . . that you *felt* for the Freniere women?"

"I felt for them totally," said the vampire. "Their position was agonizing. And I felt for the boy. That night he locked himself in his father's study and made a will. He knew full well that if he fell under the rapier at four A.M. the next morning, his family would fall with him. He deplored his situation and yet could do nothing to help it. To run out on the duel would not only mean social ruin for him, but would probably have been impossible. The other young man would have pursued him until he was forced to fight. When he left the plantation at midnight, he was staring into the face of death itself with the character of a man who, having only one path to follow, has resolved to follow it with perfect courage. He would either kill the Spanish boy or die; it was unpredictable, despite all his skill. His face reflected a depth of feeling and wisdom I'd never seen on the face of any of Lestat's struggling victims. I had my first battle with Lestat then and there. I'd prevented him from killing the boy for months, and now he meant to kill him before the Spanish boy could.

"We were on horseback, racing after the young Freniere towards New Orleans, Lestat bent on overtaking him, I bent on overtaking Lestat. Well, the duel, as I told you, was scheduled for four A.M. On the edge of the swamp just beyond the city's northern gate. And arriving there just shortly before four, we had precious little time to return to Pointe du Lac, which meant our own lives were in danger. I was incensed at Lestat as never before, and he was determined to get the boy. 'Give him his chance!' I was insisting, getting hold of Lestat before he could approach the boy. It was midwinter, bitter-cold and damp in the swamps, one volley of icy rain after another sweeping the clearing where the duel was to be fought. Of course, I did not fear these elements in the sense that you might; they did not numb me, nor threaten me with mortal shivering or illness. But vampires feel cold as acutely as humans, and the blood of the kill is often the rich, sensual alleviation of that cold. But what concerned me that morning was not the pain I felt, but the excellent cover of darkness these elements provided, which made Freniere extremely vulnerable to Lestat's attack. All he need do would be step away from his two friends towards the swamp and Lestat might take him. And so I physically grappled with Lestat. I held him."

"But towards all this you had detachment, distance?"

"Hmmm . . ." the vampire sighed. "Yes. I had it, and with it a supremely resolute anger. To glut himself upon the life of an entire family was to me Lestat's supreme act of utter contempt and disregard for all he should have seen with a vampire's depth. So I held him in the dark, where he spit at me and cursed at me; and young Freniere took his rapier from his friend and second and went out on the slick, wet grass to meet his opponent. There was a brief conversation, then the duel commenced. In moments, it was over. Freniere had mortally wounded the other boy with a swift thrust to the chest. And he knelt in the grass, bleeding, dying, shouting something unintelligible at Freniere. The victor simply stood there. Everyone could see there was no sweetness in the victory. Freniere looked on death as if it were an abomination. His companions advanced with their lanterns, urging him to come away as soon as possible and leave the dying man to his friends. Meantime, the wounded one would allow no one to touch him. And then, as Freniere's group turned to go, the three of them walking heavily towards their horses, the man on the ground drew a pistol. Perhaps I alone could see this in the powerful dark. But, in any event, I shouted to Freniere as I ran towards the gun. And this was all that Lestat needed. While I was lost in my clumsiness, distracting Freniere and going for the gun itself, Lestat, with his years of experience and superior speed, grabbed the young man and spirited him into the cypresses. I doubt his friends even knew what had happened. The pistol had gone off, the wounded man had collapsed, and I was tearing through the near-frozen marshes shouting for Lestat.

"Then I saw him. Freniere lay sprawled over the knobbed roots of a cypress, his boots deep in the murky water, and Lestat was still bent over him, one hand on the hand of Freniere that still held the foil. I went to pull Lestat off, and that right hand swung at me with such lightning speed I did not see it, did not know it had struck me until I found myself in the water also; and, of course, by the time I recovered, Freniere was dead. I saw him as he lay there, his eyes closed, his lips utterly still as if he were just sleeping. 'Damn you!' I began cursing Lestat. And then I started, for the body of Freniere had begun to slip down into the marsh. The water rose over his face and covered him completely. Lestat was jubilant; he reminded me tersely that we had less than an hour to get back to Pointe du Lac, and he swore revenge on me. 'If I didn't like the life of a Southern planter, I'd finish you tonight. I know a way,' he threatened me. 'I ought to drive your horse into the swamps. You'd have to dig yourself a hole and smother!' He rode off.

"Even over all these years, I feel that anger for him like a white-hot liquid filling my veins. I saw then what being a vampire meant to him."

"He was just a killer," the boy said, his voice reflecting some of the vampire's emotion. "No regard for anything."

"No. Being a vampire for him meant revenge. Revenge against life itself. Every time he took a life it was revenge. It was no wonder, then, that he appreciated nothing. The nuances of vampire existence weren't even available to him because he was focused with a maniacal vengeance upon the mortal life he'd left. Consumed with hatred, he looked back. Consumed with envy, nothing pleased him unless he could take it from others; and once having it, he grew cold and dissatisfied, not loving the thing for itself; and so he went after something else. Vengeance, blind and sterile and contemptible.

"But I've spoken to you about the Freniere sisters. It was almost half past five when I reached their plantation. Dawn would come shortly after six, but I was almost home. I slipped onto the upper gallery of their house and saw them all gathered in the parlor; they had never even dressed for bed. The candles burnt low, and they sat already as mourners, waiting for the word. They were all dressed in black, as was their at-home custom, and in the dark the black shapes of their dresses massed together with their raven hair, so that in the glow of the candles their faces appeared as five soft, shimmering apparitions, each uniquely sad, each uniquely courageous. Babette's face alone appeared resolute. It was as if she had already made up her mind to take the burdens of Freniere if her brother died, and she had that same expression on her face now which had been on her brother's when he mounted to leave for the duel. What lay ahead of her was nearly impossible. What lay ahead was the final death of which Lestat was guilty. So I did something then which caused me great risk. I made myself known to her. I did this by playing the light. As you can see, my face is very white and has a smooth, highly reflective surface, rather like that of polished marble."

"Yes," the boy nodded, and appeared flustered. "It's very
. . . beautiful, actually," said the boy. "I wonder if . . . but what
happened?"

"You wonder if I was a handsome man when I was alive,"
said the vampire. The boy nodded. "I was. Nothing structur-
ally is changed in me. Only I never knew that I was handsome.
Life whirled about me a wind of petty concerns, as I've said.
I gazed at nothing, not even a mirror . . . especially not a mirror
. . . with a free eye. But this is what happened. I stepped near
to the pane of glass and let the light touch my face. And this
I did at a moment when Babette's eyes were turned towards
the panes. Then I appropriately vanished.

"Within seconds all the sisters knew a 'strange creature' had
been seen, a ghostlike creature, and the two slave maids stead-
fastly refused to investigate. I waited out these moments impa-
tiently for just that which I wanted to happen: Babette finally
took a candelabrum from a side table, lit the candles and,
scorning everyone's fear, ventured out onto the cold gallery
alone to see what was there, her sisters hovering in the door
like great, black birds, one of them crying that the brother was
dead and she had indeed seen his ghost. Of course, you must
understand that Babette, being as strong as she was, never once
attributed what she saw to imagination or to ghosts. I let her
come the length of the dark gallery before I spoke to her, and
even then I let her see only the vague outline of my body beside
one of the columns. 'Tell your sisters to go back,' I whispered
to her. 'I come to tell you of your brother. Do as I say.' She
was still for an instant, and then she turned to me and strained
to see me in the dark. 'I have only a little time. I would not
harm you for the world,' I said. And she obeyed. Saying it was
nothing, she told them to shut the door, and they obeyed as
people obey who not only need a leader but are desperate for
one. Then I stepped into the light of Babette's candles."

The boy's eyes were wide. He put his hand to his lips. "Did you look to her . . . as you do to me?" he asked.

"You ask that with such innocence," said the vampire. "Yes, I suppose I certainly did. Only, by candlelight I always had a less supernatural appearance. And I made no pretense with her of being an ordinary creature. 'I have only minutes,' I told her at once. 'But what I have to tell you is of the greatest importance. Your brother fought bravely and won the duel—but wait. You must know now, he is dead. Death was proverbial with him, the thief in the night about which all his goodness or courage could do nothing. But this is not the principal thing which I came to tell you. It is this. You can rule the plantation and you can save it. All that is required is that you let no one convince you otherwise. You must assume his position despite any outcry, any talk of convention, any talk of propriety or common sense. You must listen to nothing. The same land is here now that was here yesterday morning when your brother slept above. Nothing is changed. You must take his place. If you do not, the land is lost and the family is lost. You will be five women on a small pension doomed to live but half or less of what life could give you. Learn what you must know. Stop at nothing until you have the answers. And take my visitation to you to be your courage whenever you waver. You must take the reins of your own life. Your brother is dead.'

"I could see by her face that she had heard every word. She would have questioned me had there been time, but she believed me when I said there was not. Then I used all my skill to leave her so swiftly I appeared to vanish. From the garden I saw her face above in the glow of her candles. I saw her search the dark for me, turning around and around. And then I saw her make the Sign of the Cross and walk back to her sisters within."

The vampire smiled. "There was absolutely no talk on the

river coast of any strange apparition to Babette Freniere, but after the first mourning and sad talk of the women left all alone, she became the scandal of the neighborhood because she chose to run the plantation on her own. She managed an immense dowry for her younger sister, and was married herself in another year. And Lestat and I almost never exchanged words."

Excerpt from *Interview with the Vampire*

# Blood

JANICE
GALLOWAY

He put his knee up on her chest getting ready to pull, tilting the pliers. Sorry, he said. Sorry. She couldn't see his face. The pores on the backs of his fingers sprouted hairs, single black wires curling onto the bleached skin of the wrist, the veins showing through. She saw an artery move under the surface as he slackened the grip momentarily, catching his breath; his cheeks a kind of mauve color, twisting at something inside her mouth. The bones in his hand were bruising her lip. And that sound of the gum tugging back from what he was doing, the jaw creaking. Her jaw. If you closed your eyes it made you feel dizzy, imagining it, and this through the four jags of anesthetic, that needle as big as a power drill. Better to keep her eyes open, trying to focus past the blur of knuckles to the cracked ceiling. She was trying to see a pattern, make the lines into something she could recognize, when her mouth started to do something she hadn't given it permission for. A kind of suction. There was a moment of nothing while he steadied his hand, as if she had only imagined the give. She heard herself swallow and stop breathing. Then her spine lifting, arching from the seat, the gum parting with a sound like uprooting potatoes, a coolness in her mouth and he was holding something up in the metal clamp; great bloody lump of it, white trying to surface through the red. He was pleased.

There you go eh? Never seen one like that before. The root of the problem ha ha.

All his fillings showed when he laughed, holding the thing out, wanting her to look. Blood made a pool under her tongue, lapping at the back of her throat and she had to keep the head back instead. Her lips were too numb to trust: it would have run down the front of her blazer.

Rinse, he said. Cough and spit.

When she sat up he was holding the tooth out on a tissue, roots like a yellow clawhammer at the end, one point wrapping the other.

See the twist? Unusual to see something like that. Little twist in the roots.

*88* 　Like a deformed parsnip. And there was a bit of flesh, a piece of gum or something nipped off between the crossed tips of bone.

Little rascal, he said.

Her mouth was filling up, she turned to the metal basin before he started singing again. *She's leaving now cos I just heard the slamming of the door* then humming. He didn't really know the words. She spat dark red and thick into the basin. When she resurfaced, he was looking at her and wiping his hands on something like a dishtowel.

Expect it'll bleed for a while, bound to be messy after that bother. Just take your time getting up. Take your time there. No rush.

She had slid to the edge of the chair, dunting the hooks and probes with having to hold on. The metal noise made her teeth sore. Her stomach felt terrible and she had to sit still, waiting to see straight.

Fine in a minute, he said. Wee walk in the fresh air. Wee walk back to school.

He finished wiping his hands and grinned, holding something out. A hard thing inside tissue. The tooth.

You made it, you have it haha. There you go. How's the jaw?

She nodded, and pointed to her mouth. This almost audible sound of a tank filling, a rising tide over the edges of the tongue.

Bleed for a while like I say. Don't worry though. Redheads always bleed worse than other folk. Haha. Sandra'll get you something: stop you making a mess of yourself.

Sandra was already away. He turned to rearrange the instruments she had knocked out of their neat arrangement on the green cloth.

Redheads, see. *Don't take your love to town.*

Maybe it was a joke. She tried to smile back till the blood started silting again. He walked over to the window as Sandra came back with a white pad in her hand. The pad had gauze over the top, very thick with a blue stripe down one side. Loops. A sanitary towel. The dentist was still turned away, looking out of the window and wiping his specs and talking. It took a minute to realize he was talking to her. It should stop in about an hour or so he was saying. Maybe three at the outside. Sandra pushed the pad out for her to take. If not by six o'clock let him know and they could give her a shot of something ok? Looking out the whole time. She tried to listen, tucking the loops at the ends of the towel in where they wouldn't be obvious, blushing when she put it up to her mouth. It was impossible to tell if they were being serious or not. The dentist turned back, grinning at the spectacles he was holding between his hands.

Sandra given you a wee special there. Least said haha. Redheads eh? *Oh Rooooobeee,* not looking, wiping the same lens over and over with a cloth.

The fresh air was good. Two deep lungfuls before she wrapped her scarf round the white pad at her mouth and walked. The best way from the surgery was past the flats with bay windows and gardens. Some had trees, crocuses, and bits of cane. Better than up by the building site, full of those shouting men. One of them always shouted things, whistled loud enough to make the whole street turn and look. Bad enough at the best of times. Today would have been awful. This way was longer but prettier and there was nothing to stop her taking her time. She had permission. No need to worry about getting there for some particular ring of some particular bell. Permission made all the difference. The smell of bacon rolls at the café fetched her nose coffee and chocolate. They spoiled when they reached her mouth, heaped up with sanitary towel and the blood still coming. Her tongue wormed toward the soft place, the dip where the tooth had been, then back between tongue root and the backs of her teeth. Thick fluid. A man was crossing the road, a greyhound on a thin lead, a woman with a pram coming past the phone box. Besides, girls didn't spit in the street. School wasn't that far though, not if she walked fast. She clutched the tooth tight in her pocket and walked, head down. The pram was there before she expected it; sudden metal spokes too near her shoes before she looked up, eyes and nose over the white rim of gauze. The woman not even noticing but keeping on, plowing up the road while she waited at the curb with her eyes on the gutter, trying hard not to swallow. Six streets and a park to go. Six streets.

The school had no gate, just a gap in the wall with pillars on either side that led into the playground. The blacked-out window was the staff room; the others showed occasional heads, some white faces watching. The music block was nearest. Quarter to twelve. It would be possible to wait in the practice rooms till the dinner bell in fifteen minutes and not shift till the afternoon. She was in no mood, though, not even for that. Not even for the music. It wouldn't be possible to play well. But there was no point in going home either because everything would have to be explained in triplicate when the mother got in and she never believed you anyway. It was all impossible. The pad round her mouth was slimy already, the wet going cold farther at the far sides. She could go over and ask Mrs. McNiven for another towel and just go anyway, have a lie-down or something but that meant going over to the other block, all the way across the playground again and the faces looking out knowing where you were going because it was the only time senior girls went there. And this thing round her mouth. Her stomach felt terrible too. She suddenly wanted to be in the music rooms, soothing herself with music. Something peaceful. Going there made her feel better just because of where it was. Not like at home. You could just go and play to your heart's content. That would be nice now, right now this minute, going up there and playing something: the Mozart she'd been working on, something fresh and clean. Turning, letting the glass door close, she felt her throat thicken, closing over with film. And that fullness that said the blood was still coming. A sigh into the towel stung her eyes. The girls' toilets were on the next landing.

Yellow. The light, the sheen off the mirrors. It was always horrible coming here. She could usually manage to get through the days without having to, waiting till she got home and drinking nothing. Most of the girls did the same, even just to avoid the felt-tip drawings on the girls' door—mostly things like split melons only they weren't. All that pretending you couldn't see them on the way in and what went with them, GIRLS ARE A BUNCH OF CUNTS still visible under the diagonal scores of the cleaners' Vim. Impossible to argue against so you made out it wasn't there, swanning past the word CUNTS though it radiated like a black sun all the way from the other end of the corridor. Terrible. And inside, the yellow lights always on, nearly all the mirrors with cracks or warps. Her own face reflected yellow over the nearside row of sinks. She clamped her mouth tight and reached for the towel loops. Its peeling away made her mouth suddenly cold. In her hand, the pad had creased up the center, ridged where it had settled between her lips and smeared with crimson on the one side. Not as bad as she had thought, but the idea of putting it back wasn't good. She wrapped it in three paper towels instead and stuffed it to the bottom of the wire bin under the rest, bits of paper and God knows what, then leaned over the sinks, rubbing at the numbness in her jaw, rinsing out. Big, red drips when she tried to open her mouth. And something else. She watched the slow tail of red on the white enamel, concentrating. Something slithered in her stomach, a slow dullness that made it difficult to straighten up again. Then a twinge in her back, a recognizable contraction. That's what the sweating was, then, the churning in her gut. It wasn't just not feeling well with the swallowing and imagining things. Christ. It wasn't supposed to be due for a week yet. She'd have to use that horrible toilet paper and it would get sore and slip about all day. Better that than asking Mrs. McNiven for two towels, though, anything was better than asking Mrs. McNiven. The cold tap spat water along the length of one blazer arm. She was turning it the wrong way. For a frightening moment, she couldn't think how to turn it off then managed, breathing out, tilting forward. It would be good to get out of here, get to something fresh and clean, Mozart and the white room upstairs. She would patch something together and just pretend she wasn't bleeding so much, wash her hands and be fit for things. The white keys. She pressed her forehead against the cool concrete of the facing wall, swallowing. The taste of blood like copper in her mouth, lips pressed tight.

The smallest practice room was free. The best one: the rosewood piano and the soundproofing made it feel warm. There was no one in either of the other two except the student who taught cello. She didn't know his name, just what he did. He never spoke. Just sat in there all the time waiting for pupils, playing or looking out of the window. Anything to avoid catching sight of people. Mr. Gregg said he was afraid of the girls and who could blame him haha. She'd never understood

the joke too well but it seemed to be right enough. He sometimes didn't even answer the door if you knocked or made out
he couldn't see you when he went by you on the stairs. It was
possible to count yourself alone, then, if he was the only one
here. It was possible to relax. She sat on the piano stool,
hunched over her stomach, rocking. C-major triad. This piano
had a nice tone, brittle and light. The other two made a fatter,
fuzzier noise altogether. This one was leaner, right for the
Mozart anyway. Descending chromatic scale with the right
hand. The left moved in the blazer pocket, ready to surface,
tipping something soft. Crushed tissue, something hard in the
middle. The tooth. She had almost forgotten about the tooth.
Her back straightened to bring it out, unfold the bits of tissue
to hold it up to the light. It had a ridge about a third of the way
down, where the glaze of enamel stopped. Below it, the roots
were huge, matte like suede. The twist was huge, still bloody
where they crossed. Whatever it was they had pulled out with
them, the piece of skin, had disappeared. Hard to accept her
body had grown this thing. Ivory. She smiled and laid it aside
on the wood slat at the top of the keyboard, like a misplaced
piece of inlay. It didn't match. The keys were whiter.

Just past the hour already. In four minutes the bell would go
and the noise would start: people coming in to stake claims on
the rooms, staring in through the glass panels on the door.
Arpeggios bounced from next door. The student would be
warming up for somebody's lesson, waiting. She turned back
to the keys, sighing. Her mouth was filling up again, her head
thumping. Fingers looking yellow when she stretched them
out, reaching for chords. Her stomach contracted. But if she
could just concentrate, forget her body and let the notes come,
it wouldn't matter. You could get past things that way, pretend
they weren't there. She leaned toward the keyboard, trying to

be something else: a piece of music. Mozart, the recent practice. Feeling for the clear, clean lines. Listening. She ignored the pain in her stomach, the pressure of paper towels at her thighs, and watched the keys, the pressure of her fingers that buried or released them. And watching, listening to Mozart, she let the music get louder, and the door opened, the abrupt tearing sound of the doorseals seizing her stomach like a fist. The student was suddenly there and smiling to cover the knot on his forehead where the fear showed, smiling fit to bust, saying, Don't stop, it's lovely; Haydn isn't it? and she opened her mouth not able to stop, opened her mouth to say Mozart. It's Mozart—before she remembered.

Welling up behind the lower teeth, across her lips as she tilted forward to keep it off her clothes. Spilling over the white keys and dripping onto the clean tile floor. She saw his face change, the glance flick to the claw roots in the tissue before he shut the door hard, not knowing what else to do. And the bell rang, the steady howl of it as the outer doors gave, footfalls in the corridor gathering like an avalanche. They would be here before she could do anything, sitting dumb on the piano stool, not able to move, not able to breathe, at this blood streaking over the keys, silting the action. The howl of the bell. This unstoppable redness seeping through the fingers at her open mouth.

# Didn't
## She
## Know

---

SCOTT
BRADFIELD

Alison Parrott was the sort of woman who appealed to old men. "I never ask them for anything," Alison told her landlady, Mrs. Flanders, one sunny afternoon in Canoga Park. "But then they give me stuff anyway. Nice stuff, usually; sometimes even pretty expensive-looking stuff. Stuff they don't need, but stuff they're too fond of to ever throw away." Rattly ostentatious bracelets and watches, countertop kitchen appliances, book-club editions of forgotten lurid best-sellers, sun-stained draperies, and discontinued grooming supplies. "Most of their wives died many years ago, and they tell me many sad stories about them. I'm really surprised, for example, just how many elderly women have died in motel bathrooms and public laundromats. You'd be surprised, Mrs. Flanders. There's been quite a few of them, actually." Mrs. Flanders, meanwhile, sniffed suspiciously at the dusty, vaguely ominous gifts and cards that gathered daily in Alison's studio apartment like errant premonitions. A few months later, Alison purchased her own condo in the San Gabriel Mountains. She leased a silver Mazda RX-7 and disdained fast-food. She continued working as a waitress at the Glendale Coco's, but she no longer worked nights or weekends. She never saw Mrs. Flanders again.

Usually they arrived in the early morning, about the same time as the newspapers. They sat at the counter beside the cash register and requested buttered toast, coffee, sweet rolls, English muffins, tea with lemon, foil-wrapped after-dinner mints and repeated directions to the restroom. Alison, meanwhile, provided them many easy, complimentary attentions. Bright smiles, unsolicited refills, additional units of jelly and jam; occasionally she even unfastened a liberal button of her striped uniform blouse. Sometimes the old men sat there for hours, patting their thin hair in place and humming distantly while they pretended not to look at her. They seemed strangely collapsed and inconspicuous inside their faded slacks, iron-stained shirts and loosening, inelastic white wool socks. They said things like, "Very good coffee, Alison." "Always surrounded by your boyfriends—aren't you, Alison?" "I really must be going—but okay. Just fill it halfway, Alison. And then I really must be going."

Whenever Alison's young men dropped by for coffee, they and the old men grew moody and indecorous with one another. The old men didn't approve of Alison's young men, who often wore heavy leather tool belts, T-shirts and Levi's, and displayed their muscular chests and tattooed biceps while they smoked cigarettes and scratched their lean, sunburnt stomachs. "If only you could see how silly you look," Alison admonished her young men whenever they grew excessively curt or impolite. "Being jealous about some sweet old man who hardly has any real friends left alive in the whole wide world, and who just happens to leave me a really nice tip every once in a while. I get off at three, honey, but I won't be able to meet you until at least half past eight. Old Mr. Saunders is at St. Vincent's again for another of his hernia operations, and I promised I'd drop by in case he needed anything."

Hospitals were echoing, angular white places where incoherent elderly women perambulated about with the aid of aluminum walkers, and everything smelled faintly of chemistry and soiled cotton. Middle-aged nurses hurried from room to room transporting bright, color-coded dosages of medication in tiny corrugated paper cups. Black orderlies parked their empty gurneys against bare beige walls in order to smoke their generic menthol cigarettes and watch Alison walk by. Alison always wore bright wool skirts, glossy lipsticks, and sheer silk blouses. Even the high harsh fluorescents could not imperil her cautiously-rouged complexion. Alison liked the high ceilings, and the sense of close, distantly articulated corridors enclosing and defining the thick spaces all around her. Most of all, though, Alison liked the sound of her own heels clacking across the antiseptically swabbed gray linoleum floors, and the sight of her reflection gliding imperturbably across the round surfaces of chrome wheelchairs and meal trays like some sort of transistorized ghost.

"Of course you'll be up and around again in no time," Alison assured Mr. Saunders. "In fact, if I do say so myself, you're starting to look one hell of a lot better already—and I'm not just saying that to make you feel good. You're definitely look-ing a whole lot better than you did the last time I came to visit." Mr. Saunders lay motionless beneath his excessively starched sheets and didn't say anything, his cheeks deflated and sallow, his gummy mouth wide open and long-deprived of teeth. He breathed stiffly and with visible effort. In fact, Alison was beginning to think that breathing was probably the only visible effort Mr. Saunders was capable of making anymore.

"I think you'll have to admit, Mr. Saunders," Alison said, "that life can be a very special experience indeed. As long as there is life, there is hope—isn't that how the old saying goes? If they can put men on the moon, then I certainly don't see why they can't cure some silly little intestinal disorder like you've been experiencing lately—and I don't care *what* those overpriced doctors say about your colon. Mr. Saunders? Did you want to rest? Am I talking your ears off? Am I boring you half-silly?" Alison took Mr. Saunders's hand in her lap. The hand was faintly and placidly warm, like the tiny engine of a portable cassette player. Alison held Mr. Saunders's hand in her lap for nearly ten minutes before she left, but Mr. Saunders never seemed to notice.

The funerals were always held at sparsely attended veteran's and welfare cemeteries. Often military guns were fired, and

American flags folded atop the clean caskets before they were deposited into deep, rectangular pits—in order to keep the patriotic old men warm, Alison liked to reassure herself. Down there in the deep somatic earth, the old men recovered warmth again; they regained the ancient communities of families and loved ones they had lost to wars, disease, and time, communicating with one another through intricate, resonant folds in the planet's subcrustal blankets and mantle. Perhaps, down there, they enjoyed spectacular transformations. Their frayed parched skin and muscles burst forth new wings and shiny, segmented bodies. They burrowed passages and wide regressive chambers, long ornate halls decorated with gold and bronze medallions, elaborate tapestries and muted brocade carpets. They gathered together in the dark buzzing colonies of their past and discussed remote details of their lives while the earth reminded them of generalities far more ancient. The beat and the hum, the spin and the heat.

After the ceremonies concluded, Alison was ritually approached by other, even more attentive old men. These old men wore ill-fitting military uniforms and bright deployments of citation and medal. It was as if every funeral articulated Alison with some secret network of old age and dark assignation. "Well, sure. I don't see why not," Alison told them, applying rouge to her cheeks with a bright flashing compact, watching herself take a breath mint with her flat red tongue. "I don't see how one little drink could hurt anybody. And of course, as you well know, Mr. Saunders always told me so many nice things about you."

Mr. O'Connor and Mr. Cherboninski, Mr. Jones and Mr. Reilly. Eventually Alison purchased a four-bedroom modular-style home in Pasadena, as well as an isolated and fully winterized cabin at Lake Arrowhead. She sublet her condo to graduate students from Caltech and, occasionally, even to some of her own young men. Young men were very difficult, peripatetic sorts of people who were always leaving and being replaced by other, even younger men. All day they brooded alone in their hot rooms, preparing themselves sullen meals of canned and frozen food. They gazed at Alison with a formal obtuseness. Their brains were thick, imprecise objects that did not grasp things so much as obtrude clumsily against them. The young men always told Alison to return home quickly. But then, whenever Alison did return home, they greeted her with resentment and hard looks.

"These days, young men are filled with terrible anger," Alison told her only true, abiding friends, those faded and absently remembering old men. "It's as if youth were a sort of fury, something rapacious and excessive, blundering and unprofound. Young men never do anything constructive, and all they ever think about all day long is making love to young women. Young men aren't content to be planted into the warm earth. They don't want to make themselves plentiful or productive in any way. They want to take beauty, and keep it, and hurt it because young men are eternally doomed to love only their own youth. Until, that is, they don't have it anymore."

In July Alison was taken to court by Mr. Reilly's estranged widow, Madeline, as well as Madeline's two grim and mercenary foster children, Dwayne and Jeannette. "Roger Reilly and I enjoyed nearly forty-four years of happy marriage," Madeline Reilly told the courtroom, "until *Miss* Parrott came along one day and ruined *everything*. Suddenly, Roger began to spend an inordinate amount of time in the bathroom. He began combing his hair with some sort of slick, greasy substance. He made frequent unscheduled trips to Walgreen's and Long's Drugs, where he purchased unusual creams and ointments, vitamins and skin conditioners. One day while I was baking I nearly dropped all my cookies when Roger returned home wearing some fruity men's cologne. I should have seen it coming. I should have suspected something was up. It wasn't until two weeks after he died that I learned about the will."

Mrs. Reilly's voice grew increasingly dry and severe. Alison, meanwhile, paid many polite covert attentions to individual members of the jury with her eyes. She exposed one knee and a lustrous glimmer of nylon; then, with a barely perceptible flourish, she crossed it over her other knee. On the final day of the trial, the judge requested a private counsel with Alison in his office. The judge had beautiful white hair, a Thunderbird Classic convertible, and a large, generally unfrequented home in Glendale. Eventually Alison began visiting the judge's house every Thursday afternoon, whenever the judge's wife was away working for one of her local school charities.

"It's not like I don't understand Mrs. Reilly's point of view," Alison told the judge one warm autumn evening many weeks after the trial's conclusion. "Just because I don't happen to agree with someone doesn't mean I can't understand their point of view. But that also doesn't mean I can just disregard Mr. Reilly's last wishes, either." While Alison talked, the judge liked to hold her hand and dream of remote, gliding airplanes and beautiful young women.

Although Alison considered herself a happy and firmly centered individual, some nights she started suddenly awake in her bed. She sat up in the dark bedroom and felt the breathing weight of the young man beside her, entangled by her silk sheets, enveloped by the translated warmth of her body in the blankets. Her bedroom, her house. Alison would get quietly out of bed and pull on her blue cashmere robe. The young man would sigh and turn over in his dreams of her. As Alison moved alone into the dark house she felt herself verging upon vast unlabeled places. She felt a quick thin rush of vertigo. Gravity seemed to shift. Alison sensed the heavy white gaze of the moon in the garden. Methodical spiders spun shining nets out there and swung from invisible threads. In the trees birds gathered sticks and brushy moss and bugs, and in the earth strange blind creatures burrowed and tugged and crawled. We build and build, Alison thought. We build houses, estates, families, empires, even notions about the way worlds work. We build and build, and then we all grow old and die anyway.

Earlier that day in Whittier Alison had visited her friend Mr. Peabody, whose brain, heart, and lungs were attached to a battery of humming, discordant machines with round, radar-like screens and formidable steel paneling. Mr. Peabody had not died exactly, but he was not altogether very well. For the rest of his life, Mr. Peabody would have to lie alone in his expensive room, embraced by the steel musculature of technology, infused with the glowing and often perilous blood of strangers. Alison had worn her low-cut, slim-waisted green silk Halston blouse when she visited Mr. Peabody that afternoon. The green silk Halston blouse had always been Mr. Peabody's favorite.

"They all think I was just friends with Mr. Peabody because I wanted his money," Alison said out loud. Her young man continued to sleep, breathing noisily in a way that Alison always found comforting. He was very curled and very tan, and Alison liked to examine his strong back while he slept. "But no matter what anybody says, I'll always miss Mr. Peabody very much. We used to play chess together all the time, and he never once let me win on purpose. Baby? Are you awake?"

The young man stretched in his sleep, anemone-like, as if slowly unsprung at Alison's indelicate touch.

Alison touched him again.

"Come here, baby," Alison said. "Come over to this side of the bed where it's warm."

It was as if Alison could feel old age gathering in the world like heat or information. Old men rang her at home and on the cellular phone in her car. They left messages on her answering machine, cards and flowers on her porch. They mailed her money orders and savings certificates, stock options and government bonds. Alison's doorbell was always buzzing, and immaculately uniformed delivery personnel presented her with outrageous kiss-o-grams, personalized birthday ballads, pungent roses, and elaborately packaged European chocolates. Gift-wrapped boxes arrived bearing stereos and diamonds, kittens and puppies. "They're all such sweethearts," Alison said, pale and deflated on her leather-upholstered sofa, the mountains of pink-chiffon tissue paper and coiled ribbons lying collapsed around her like flushed, napping children after a sugar high. A new Guatemalan wool sweater lay draped across Alison's perfect white knees. "I don't know how to thank them sometimes. I don't even know what to say."

The old men suffered debilitating strokes and hemorrhages, senile dementia and gout, neglect and bad dreams. "Have you ever thought of buying a VCR?" Alison asked Mr. Stanford, who always called well past midnight. Mr. Stanford had outlived two wives and three middle-aged children. He never slept more than one or two hours each night, and often awoke to find himself somnambulating along Lankershim Boulevard, or sitting alone in bright all-night laundromats as far away as Sepulveda. "There's a lot of good movies available on VCR these days—even many forgotten classics from the thirties and forties." Alison was holding a cold damp cloth against her forehead. She was drinking Seagrams and 7, and two of her cigarettes smoldered in a glazed ceramic ashtray like a sort of unraveling helical clock. She sat on the deeply cushioned sofa amidst the wide, empty room like a shipwreck survivor on a raft, leaning into the luminous telephone, tugging aimlessly at her new haircut. "I know it's boring, Mr. Stanford," she said. "I know it's lonely. I know you can't sleep. I really do understand, Mr. Stanford. I really, really do."

Alison stopped answering the phone and opening her mail. Every day she sat outside on the sunny back porch drinking tall, icy glasses of mineral water with lime, eating fresh fruit salads, and listening to baroque music on her portable CD system. She wore sunscreens, sunglasses, and Vitamin E lotions. She did deep knee bends, leg-lifts, tummy-tensers, and facial aerobics, examining herself in the full-length Cinerama-style dressing-room mirror about two hundred times each day. In January, she purchased an exercycle; in the spring, she radon-proofed her basement. Every night she made love with the young men until dawn when they fell asleep without her, and then she would wander alone out to the back patio where she gazed at the far, Spanish-style redbrick roofs and leafy, fading verandas of the San Fernando Valley. Everything seemed perfectly immaculate and disingenuous at night. Automobiles raced along Van Nuys Boulevard, disguising the race and beat of Alison's own young heart. "Who wants to live forever, anyway?" Alison asked herself, sipping Gordon's gin and smoking clove cigarettes. "That would be really boring. You'd run out of new things to do. You'd have worn all the nice clothes already. You'd have taken all the best vacations."

Alison could feel youth being methodically extracted from her body like the thin smooth exudated thread of a silkworm. The sleepless old men lurked outside her house at night, pacing in the dry dark street, looking very obvious and unalert in the backseats of their Yellow Cabs. Mr. Brenly and Mr. Chin, Mr.

Sampson and Mr. Gray. Sometimes they ventured up the long cement path to her door and rang the bell, or knocked gently a few times. Meanwhile, Alison stood invisibly behind her wide tinted patio window, watching them. She drank icy gin and tonics; she smoked harsh, acrid, and overpriced marijuana. "Why don't you just give them a good kick in the butt," Alison's young men suggested, squeezing rubber wrist developers, or pumping hard black iron weights as they stood behind her in the dark living room. They wore tight silk gym trunks and bright tank-top T-shirts. "I'll bet that's one clear message they'd comprehend *muy* pronto, sweetheart. A good swift kick in the raggedy old derriere sometime." Alison took another hit from the joint and felt the fuzzy comprehension lift high into her chest, throat, and boney face. It was filling her skull and sinuses now. Now her eyes were swimming in the damp sweet mystery of it.

Eventually the old men went away again in their cabs. The young men unclenched their exercise equipment and shrugged their way into the kitchen for glasses of mineral water and light beer. "If I were an old geezer like that, I'd be too embarrassed to go around hassling some sweet young thing that didn't want to be hassled," the young men muttered into their sparkling Perrier, tearing celery from crisp stalks. Then they spread peanut butter, chives, and sour cream on the celery with a blunt, flat knife. "And if I couldn't live with it, man, like I'd just go off quietly and cut my own throat, you know? I'd jump out a twelve-story window—no parachute. I'd fire a teflon bullet point-blank right into the old brain-basket—that's what *I'd* do, sweetheart. Believe you goddamn me. You wouldn't catch *me* hanging around for one goddamn minute where *I* wasn't wanted. And that's for *damn* sure."

Even at night while she slept, Alison could feel the old men going away from her. They were departing on trains and buses

and planes. They were hiring private cars and drivers, or gliding across misty foreign rivers, channels, and oceans on hissing
hovercraft and wide slow exorbitant luxury liners. Usually
they took care to shave and comb their hair first. They wore
their best pressed white shirts and unsnagged smooth cotton
trousers. They listened to their favorite records on the phono-
graph, and thumbed through old leather-bound photo albums
before replacing them on high, dusty shelves in neglected closets and outdoor storage sheds. Then they latched all the doors
and windows in their memento-cluttered rooms and houses.
They never carried more than a single piece of hand luggage,
or perhaps a few spare shorts and socks in roughened brown
paper shopping bags. The old men were going away, and
Alison knew she would never see any of them ever again.

Alison attended their funerals incognito now. She wore long
black dresses and hats and ominous-looking black satin veils.
She sat anonymously in the back row while the old men
watched their compatriots being lowered into the warm earth.
Sometimes the mournful old men glanced quickly and surreptitiously at Alison over their shoulders. They fidgeted on their
clumsy metal folding chairs, or coughed awkwardly into their
red, arthritic fists. Most of the time, though, they worked very
hard not to look in Alison's direction at all. Sometimes it was
because they didn't recognize her. Sometimes it was because
they did.

As the old men went away, the young men grew angrier and
angrier. They slammed doors and cupboards, they smashed
plates and windows and clocks. They drove Alison's cars out
on the freeway at night and crashed them, and returned home
smelling of petrol, gin, and imprecation. They made abrupt,
sore love to Alison in the middle of the night, usually while she
was still half-asleep, and when they left her now they took
things. Money from her wallet, credit cards, checks; jewelry,

stereo equipment, cameras, and linen. Often at night Alison could hear the young men rummaging through the house while she pretended to sleep. They knocked over lamps, they collided with the abrupt edges of tables and sofas, they overturned bookshelves and glass-paneled cabinets and stuffed chairs. "The bitch," they muttered in the dark, as if they could actually smell the old men still lurking somewhere in the fabric of Alison's life. "The lying little bitch," they said. "It's around here somewhere. There's more. It's here. There's more around here somewhere."

In the mornings they were gone, and Alison tried to make amends. She replaced unbroken dishes on their shelves, and soothed the scratched furniture with conditioners, waxes, and polishes. "You can't hate a young man just because he's angry," Alison said out loud to herself in the large, echoing kitchen. She was sweeping motes and shards of brilliant crystal into a tidy aluminum dustpan. "Young men live at a different pitch, a different frequency from young women. Sometimes I think young men must be the loneliest people on the face of the earth. Other times, though, I think the loneliest people on the face of the earth have got to be young women."

The old men were almost gone now, and already Alison was beginning to miss them. She could remember the way they breathed, and their white fingers trembling against the rims of regulation-size Coco's coffee cups. She remembered the linty, crumpled bills and excessive pools of change they left behind, the smell of lanolin and Vaseline, and the way they watched her when they thought she wasn't watching them. Some nights she would drive out to the San Fernando Valley, or down Highway 1 to Retirement Village, and coast slowly past their untended ranch-style homes, which were filled with watery silence and ripe, abandoned equity. Sometimes she would pull over for a little while and gaze at the dry, unraveling yards, the alert Real Estate signs, the dark glimmering windows from which all the curtains had been removed. Once the old men were gone, they could never come back, and this thought filled Alison with both a sense of profound sadness, and a thin hormonal rush of visceral relief.

Alison couldn't even sleep at night anymore, the cold was so bright and unremitting. It penetrated walls, insulation, clothing, doors. It radiated from televisions, kitchen appliances, porcelain bathroom tiles, the flat moon and glittering, inalienable stars. Down there in the dirt and the earth, the old men whispered. "Alison," they whispered. "Was it something we said? Was it the way we looked at you, or was it the way we always tried to touch your hair?" Alison couldn't explain. She turned over and over again, unable to sleep. "It wasn't you," Alison tried to tell them. "It's something wrong with *me*. I don't even know how to explain it. But it was never anything at all the matter with *you*." Sometimes she felt as haunted by the old men now as she did when they were still alive.

Meanwhile, outside her home, the young men arrived drunk and unscheduled, confronting one another in one another's stray clothing. They cursed and battled across the yards and driveways, overturning birdbaths and garbage cans, mailboxes and concrete lawn ornaments, pounding at one another's hard chests and faces and stomachs until neighbors called the police. There was all this noise and clatter in the world, Alison thought, feeling the cold center of her heart where the old men whispered. All this roil and struggle, and nowhere to just lie down, relax for a minute, and hear yourself think. The cold in Alison's body was like a recollection, a river, a simple animal notion of the heart. It circulated in Alison's blood like plasma. It brought a strange caress to the rubbery, secret interior of veins and arteries. "You fuck!" the young men cursed each other outside. "You stupid fuck! Who're *you* calling a stupid fuck, you stupid fuck!"

"I like boys," Alison told the old men, the only men she had ever known who listened. "The trouble is, I've never been able to tell whether boys liked me or not. I mean, sometimes they can be quite sweet, really. But other times it's like, well, I don't know. It's like I'm everything they don't want. It's like I'm everything about the world that they don't love, and that doesn't love them." Every morning Alison sat among the ruins of her living room, drinking instant coffee and trying to explain. Throughout her house the young men had ripped the upholstery from sofas and chairs, uprooted the pile carpet with chopping knives and fireplace implements, and torn all the framed landscapes and photographs from the walls. "It's sort of the same way I felt about you," she told the old men, and at this point she often started to cry. "It's sort of the exact same way I treated you. Though I didn't mean it. Because I didn't *mean* to treat you that bad. I just didn't know I was doing it at the time."

At night, in her bed, Alison lay quiet and listened for sounds from the driveway, the garden steps, the porch. The young men were stealthy and compact. They slammed their car doors and cursed. They were here. It was tonight. They wanted it now. They wanted everything tonight.

They kicked cans in the street. Sometimes they howled like wild dogs and threw their bottles at passing cars that honked back at them, as if they were engaged in a primitive debate. Then they let themselves in Alison's front door with their key. Alison usually knew his name before he was halfway down the hall. Bobby, she thought. Or Reggie, or Stan. Down there in the dark earth, the old men continued to whisper, as if they didn't know they could never return. "They don't love you," the old men said. "Only we really love you, Alison. And just look what you did to us in return."

Now the young man was prowling through the office, the guest room, the closets, the bath. Lights were snapping on and off, blankets and mattresses being whipped from beds, lamps crashing insensibly to the floor. Then the young man was in the hallway again. Then, covered with darkness, the young man was standing in Alison's bedroom again.

"It's okay, baby," Alison said. She was clutching her blankets and sheets in her cold hands. Everything she touched these days was cold. "Just relax, baby. Don't be mad at me."

She could feel the heat and steam of him expanding in the room, lost, dark, limbic, and round. She could feel the ridged scars along the spine of his forearm, his bruised lip, the tiny weblike cracks in his face and his skull. She could feel his hot fists clenching, unclenching. The young man wanted more. He wanted more, but no matter how many times she tried, Alison couldn't seem to explain.

"They're all gone," Alison whispered. "All buried and dead. Did you hear me? They're all gone, sweetheart. Why don't you come lie down with me and get warm."

This was night and recollection all at once, Alison thought. The young man moved closer, the darkness sliding across him like a sort of film. The young man kept moving closer. This happened to Alison night after night after night. Suddenly, Alison's world was filled with nothing but young men.

"It should've been you," the young man said, coming closer, not starting to reach out for her just yet. "You bitch. It should have been you. It should have been you."

# Regulus
# and
# Maximus

JOHN
HAWKES

Deception and despair, those twin handmaidens of desire, appeared in the little Abbey of Rochefort as slowly as lichen creeps across a stone or any of the four seasons changes in the eye of a child. The novices fell first—a sudden turn, a gesture suddenly furtive though it went unseen—and then the monks themselves succumbed. The sun shone, birds darted about in the rain, the little Abbey of Rochefort appeared unchanged. Who could have known that the dreaded hand of desire, as fragile as the hand of a dying girl, more potent than the slow infection sapping her life, was feeling its way into the sweetness of this religious place? After all, it was generally accepted that there were no purer men than those of this particular band of barefooted Basilians, no world safer from temptation than theirs. But it was not so. The smallest, most tranquilly situated, and most admired monastery of the entire brotherhood of religious houses was doomed. Not one of its twenty-three inmates—five novices and eighteen monks, including Regulus the abbot—was safe from contamination. And this at the very time when the little Abbey of Rochefort was in the fullest bloom that was its life.

Even then, at the time of this tale, not every man was caught in the fervor. Not every man, even then, had a taste for prayer in caves or that silence known only in cell and cloister. Yet once in the deepest reaches of history, though not so long ago by the large reckoning, there was no stopping the exodus of men young and old from cities, towns, hamlets, all equally inspired into flight and ordeal, all equally driven in search of the Second World, as it was called, on earth. Hardly a man was left in the ordinary walks of life, marriages dissolved in a breath, horses were abandoned in the midst of shoeing by farriers inexplicably swept off on the tides of zealousness, whole deserts were overrun with fifteen thousand hooded men at a time. Men who wanted to be alone among the living sought the company of others equally desperate to be alone. They wandered and they crowded together. Never was the community of isolated souls so vast. Monks were everywhere, there was not an empty cave to be found by even the sweetest-eyed of all those aspiring to be St. Benedict.

Monks were persecuted, saints appeared. Monasteries sprang up in green forests, hung from cliffs like nests woven by wasps, became as permanent as bridges, as numerous as all the towns and cities initially threatened with depletion. But the world of ordinary folk survived after all, even as monasticism spread from country to country, age to age, suffered dissention, heresy, excesses of self-mortification, became a chaos of mystical teachings, evolved into rules, charters, administrations, and brought about, in a word, the heyday of religious power.

And the result of these centuries that had consolidated the forms and practices of pure spirit? The result of the assemblage of these uncountable havens for the pure of heart? These penitential places promising the soul's freedom? These workstations of unearthly effort? Why, the Abbey of Rochefort, of course, which emerged above all the rest like the perfect pearl of spray that tops those few mighty waves that consume us in the longest curves of time sent rolling from the seas to heaven. The perfection, then, of monasteries. Such, in its proper time, was the smallest abbey of them all. Rochefort.

As follows.

On a wet night in early spring, in the largest monastery of the more than two thousand then extant, at Chrodegang, that famous place of religious overindulgence, the monks were having their annual patronal feast, all seven hundred of them seated together at hand-hewn tables and already intoxicated in the broadest sense on wine from Chrodegang's own vineyards and cellars and produce from its own barns and fields. The immense hall was alight with candles, platters of guinea fowl and spring lamb, whole silvery fish with eyes popping in amazement at such proceedings, great plates of the thinnest and greenest shoots of new asparagus, forty pheasants stuffed with river trout and red berries, tureens of soup and bowls of steaming potatoes and bricks of butter as large as the loaves of bread fresh from the ovens, and thick dishes piled high with savory heaps of kidneys as small as black olives or the droppings of goats and similarly colored, when cooked, since they were in fact the kidneys of infant rabbits—all this steamy sumptuousness lay half-eaten, carved and gouged, spilled and slopped onto the surfaces of greasy wood up and down the lengths of the tables. The faces of the monks were dripping, their cheeks and eyes were red, they ate and drank, broke silence, soared on the wings of laughter at the height of extravagance for which Chrodegang had become famous as the tavern of God's houses. Wooden spoons and silver spoons banged and clattered, spilled wine flowed across the greasy wood, innumerable icons glittered and winked from niches in the rock walls, ranks and islands of fat candles sputtered and danced, two choirs of young boys in robes sang and competed with the roar and racket of seven hundred monks enjoying this yearly ravishment of natural life by which, thanks to its abbot, the immense Chrodegang had earned its reputation as the underworld of canonical squalor. And the abbot's name? The notorious Bonum, of course, thanks to whom the first sin, that of eating, was no match for the stuffing of stomachs that went on at Chrodegang in the midst of the general decay that he inspired.

But did all seven hundred of Bonum's monks indulge themselves? Were all seduced by the yearly patronal feast and the lesser daily meals that prepared for it? Did all seven hundred succumb to the debacle? Were they, down to the last misguided soul, grotesque exaggerations of the typically fat and florid monk of the middle ages? Not quite all.

In fact there were only six hundred and ninety-three such monks under Bonum's sway. Seven, among the youngest, were thin, including Regulus and Varro and five other full-fledged monks who were hardly more than boys.

This night, with the spring rain falling and the choirs singing and the monks gorging themselves, Regulus and Varro and their five still-younger confreres refused to eat. They were thin, they were frowning, they were hungry but not for mere food and drink. Sated shadows leapt to the high rude beams, sacred music fell to the purposes of entertainment, Bonum shouted to his chefs, the grinding of the monks' teeth filled the hall, the gold of religious art was bright. Yet thin Regulus neither ate nor drank. Like thin Varro, he waited. The five youngest of the thin monks watched their leaders, for such in fact were Regulus and Varro despite their youth. They had a plan.

The smoke of roasting flesh and sizzling fat burned the eye, aroused the nose, while the acrid smell of the inordinately intoxicating wine, new as it was, inspired still more the appetite for food. The choirs of little sweating boys sang on, the sounding of a clear bell went unheard. Regulus was the first to rise. He slipped away. In bold stealth Varro did the same. One by one the remaining five thin monks followed Varro and Regulus into the sudden purity of the spring rain.

Off they fled.

None of these seven, who were fleeing for nothing less than their spiritual lives, had any knowledge of the compass or of theories of celestial navigation. In fact they had scant knowledge of anything except Latin, theology, monastic history, liturgical teachings, the rudiments of farming. Beyond the walls of the monastery they had gone only as far as the fields tilled by the monks of Chrodegang for more than nine centuries. So they did not know what direction they had taken in the wet darkness of that spring night or where their flight would end. But having worked in the fields and vineyards surrounding the religious bastion which, so far, was all they had known of existence, and having bent their backs to hoe and plow, and having helped carry Bonum's religious treasures large and small into the massive labyrinthine monastery, the seven young monks were strong and wiry, while providence had given them innocence and the strength to deplore the secular indulgence that Bonum, for two decades, had brought to Chrodegang like swill to swine.

So Varro and Regulus, who was in the lead, and the other five sped through the night at the ferocious pace set by Regulus. They ran in silence, as fast as their thin legs could carry them, and soon beneath their soft white hooded robes they were as wet as the rain-drenched terrain they crossed. It grew light; first one and then another tripped and fell, regained his bare feet, raced on with hardly a lost moment. They ran as if driven by the worst possible pangs of fear and guilt, furtively, never once pausing for breath or rest, seven men so frantic to escape some unseen hand that they might have been the worst of wrongdoers instead of the only still-uncorrupted and devoted young men in all of Bonum's seven hundred. Early that first morning, while all around them the gray light rose from the surface of the wild hardly inhabited earth itself, small rabbits began to appear as Regulus entered this clearing or that, and day-old birds, silently chirping, toppled from their nests high overhead at the mere approach of the running monks. For several hours there was nothing but the creaking of branches, the slippage of virgin water between smooth stones, the sound of grasses bending, the pattering of swift but tortured feet. Then Regulus heard something. Without the slightest slowing of his knee-high stride or the slightest loss of confidence in the security of their journey's end, about which he knew nothing, or any slackening of the urgency that fueled his flight, still Regulus listened, puzzled, despite his desperation and distraction, at the sound which was both fragile and light-hearted, familiar yet unfamiliar too. And all at once he understood that the free-floating sound, strangely pleasing yet strangely inappropriate to their flight, was coming from none other than himself. How long he had heard it he could not tell. But hear it he did, and in the instant realized that, depending on one's point of view, he himself was the culprit responsible for producing the jaunty sound or was the guileless source of it. His lips were puckered. The breath he expelled in running was being diverted into this lively sound. Yes, Regulus was whistling. The leader was whistling like any small boy on a cowpath or any young man out for a stroll of a spring morning. Varro and the other five were amused, despite themselves. Regulus was shocked at first and then, for the time it took to climb from one fresh note to the next, the disembodied sound coming from his own unconsciously puckered lips, he took pleasure in the whistling he had not practiced since the time of his youth before he had entered what even then he had thought would be the rigorous serenity of Chrodegang. For a moment he gave way to this natural profane expression of good feeling in the very midst of their desperate flight from the disease of secularism behind monastic walls, then fell again to silence like the others, intent on nothing more than speed, distance, disappearance, delivery.

On they went and traveled for a full fifteen days and fourteen nights, though they themselves lost track of time and exertion, for the most part running at the fleetest pace of helpless animals pursued through a forest, pausing only for the occasional berry or to sleep huddled beneath banks of green ferns. In single file, skirts of their heavy white wool robes pulled high, bent double, faces concealed inside their hoods, thus they raced on, a long line of seven bony young fellows that shot across half-tilled fields or scrambled up the faces of cliffs or clawed their way through thickets, plunged without hesitation into fetid swamps, swam streams and then steamed violently in friendly bursts of sunlight. They lay down to rest and then for no apparent reason started up again in full flight, Regulus trusting the silent voice that urged him on, Varro and the others trusting Regulus. Dogs barked, owls hooted, the occasional peasant waved from the distance; once a young girl alone in a field dropped and spilled two buckets of warm milk at the sudden sight of a string of seven monks bent double with bare legs flashing across the far corner of the field blanketed in new green shoots. She was one of the few country folk who saw the pathetic bloodied footprints that the thin monks left behind.

Finally on the eve of the fourteenth night, without knowing how long or far they had run or had still to go, they fell together in a heap, exhausted, unable to run another step. The rain came down. Naked except for torn and soiled and sodden scapulas and cowls, the monks lost themselves to sleep, oblivious of the wind that rose, the roar of crashing branches. How, thought Regulus, as he too lost consciousness and became inert in the dark night, how could they ever rise and run again? How long the torment? How far the end of the journey? Or must they run forever, outcasts in a world of monks?

Up shot Regulus, or thus it seemed, as good as on his feet, or so he thought, starting awake as usual, light in head and body both, timorous, determined, already spurting across the next field at the silent sound of the alarmed insistent voice inside his head. Like a deer, Regulus, like a deer, it cried, and he felt himself shooting upright and hitching up the skirts of his robe and drawing the sinister hood more closely still about his anxious face—he would not be recognized, not he—and striking off into the dawn light. Already, he thought, he was hopping bushes, outdistancing the invisible dogs howling and nipping at his bloodied heels. But it was not so.

Poor Regulus lay sprawled on his back as he had fallen the night before. He could not move. He could not open his eyes though he knew that the clearest and warmest and most benevolent of suns was shining full in his face this dawn in spring. He groaned. His joints, he thought, had surely been dried out and ground to painful dust by long uncountable days of running. And as he lay there he heard Varro moaning and the other five as well. None of them could move let alone leap to his feet, they too were weighted down by pain.

But their situation was not as hopeless as it appeared. Regulus waited, listening to the soft dismal sounds of his companions and giving in to the terrible weight of his frail body. He turned his face more gently up to the sun, he breathed in the scent of a small plant flowering not far from his head. He opened his eyes, he squinted into orange light, without moving his parched lips he smiled. And lying there, following with a faint interest the little pangs of pain that darted down ligaments, raced up tendons, leapt like flashes of light from knee to thigh to forearm to collarbone and back to hip, beginning to distinguish this sharp ache from that one, slowly Regulus regained his strength, his courage, his conviction. If they could not run at least they could walk. Slowly. So at last, and holding his breath, he rolled over. He heard the others doing the same. He managed to climb to his hands and knees. A new pain began to shriek aloud in his hip. He ignored it. He heard the voiceless sounds of men moving in pain. He became conscious of a sharp pebble burrowing into his kneecap. He ignored it.

Blindly he felt the young sun rising and opened his eyes. And at last he forced himself to his feet, stood up, swayed, though the soles of his feet cried out for relief, and stood there hunching over, hands at his sides, head hanging. All around him the others were doing the same, moving, untangling themselves, amidst groans and sighs and sudden muffled exclamations were rising and staggering together in the sunlight.

Then suddenly, without intending to do so, Regulus extended his right arm, his right hand, the forefinger of that bony hand, and Varro, joined by the other five, looked in the direction in which Regulus was pointing. If they had not been monks they might have cheered at the sight. They glanced about, finding themselves at the edge of a wood on the lip of a gentle rise that overlooked a shallow valley. Again following the eye and hand of Regulus, they looked down at what lay full in the sunlight on the floor of the peacefully sloping valley. A ruin. A heap of toppled stones and fallen walls oddly orange in color, shining in the morning dew, bedecked in cracks and crevices with wild flowers in their first bloom. The valley was like the bowl of a green spoon, the ruin was as bright and pleasing as the trickle of fresh springwater bubbling up from the earth at its center. But here was no ordinary ruin, as Regulus and his men knew at once, not the ruin of mere farm or hamlet, rude bridge or viaduct, but instead the ruin of precisely what the seven momentarily weakened monks meant to build—a monastery. Yes, they had somehow come upon the very spot where in ancient times the monastery they meant to raise had stood. And stand again it surely would.

So limping and hobbling, Regulus and Varro and the others descended the grassy incline into the valley toward the ruin. They would run no more. And though the seven thin monks were thinner than ever, still they had survived their journey, had come to its end, had lost not a single member of their band.

Regulus picked his way carefully. Down they went. The moaning ceased. The scattering of rocks and walls drew near. They saw rather than heard the hidden spring. And did they hear the chanting of monks long dead? The ringing of a bell long gone? The clanking sounds of industrious monks who had left behind hardly a sign of their labors? They did. All this and more. But first they discovered the source of the orange color they had seen from above at the edge of the wood. Snails. On blackened stones oblong and square they were packed together, a great community of fat slimy limpid snails naturally yellowish orange in color intensified by the tranquil deepening rays of the morning sun. Thousands of bright snails sliding infinitesimally against each other and blanketing in translucent life the abandoned stones of the past. And what could the snails be except a further sign of good fortune? An example of that divine simplicity appropriate to the pleasure of children and religious men alike? So thought Regulus and smiled as did the rest.

The silence of the place was musical. The snail-covered remnants of the ruined monastery revealed not so much the symmetry of former structures or signs of the sacking that had destroyed them as it did the shape of the monastery yet to come. The past was already inspiring the future, the future was already atoning for the savagery that had attacked the past.

And now? Now, thought Regulus, coming suddenly to his senses, sobered, free of momentary reveries of relief and pleasure, now they had only to work, to perform the arduous menial tasks that would transform the ruin before them into the little Abbey of Rochefort—its name came then and there to Regulus—which, though already standing in the mind's eye, had yet to stand in this providential place, occupied, functioning, existing as undeniably as had that monastery of old whose former shape and shadow were now attested to by nothing more than rubble. Yes, thought Regulus again, staring at the undulating orange snails, now they had only to do the work they were ordained to do.

But how?

Time and events sometimes run exactly parallel. Things happen twice. And not only twice but simultaneously. On a given day in separate countries two men looking alike may well be hanged for the same crime. Or two black horses may die of colic on the same night at the same hour in equally decrepit barns on equally impoverished farms a hundred kilometers apart. A battle fought between the armies of two small stubborn states may be duplicated man for man, horse for horse, day for day by two other hostile states as small and stubborn as the first. Duplication of actors, action, scene, and time of action is not as rare as we think. So it was with the seven young monks who fled from Chrodegang on one now familiar night in spring. That is, unbeknownst to Regulus and Varro and their followers, seven other young monks were taking flight at the same hour and on the same dark night from a monastery second in size only to Chrodegang and quite as infamous as Chrodegang, though for opposite reasons. Unlike Chrodegang, whose evils were those of pleasure, the Abbey of Sallust—it could be no other—was known far and wide as the religious house of pain. Self-indulgence was the key to Chrodegang, self-mortification to Sallust. The sin of eating lay at the heart of the one, starvation at the heart of the other. Decay due to unbounded license, darkness due to the tyranny of denial— thus these two great monasteries, like their abbots Bonum and Brugus, were alike yet opposite. Bonum taught that grace could not thrive except in a climate of satiety, Brugus that only monks who lived by punishment were pure.

Candles, sacred music, the patronal feast, prayers said aloud at meals, talking or whispering, the simplest flower placed on the altar—all were forbidden at Sallust. There was not a work of religious art in the place, not even the crucifix itself hung in the chapel. Gloom and worse than gloom prevailed. No monk who had vowed to spend his eternity of days at Sallust was ever seen again beyond its walls, no visitor was allowed within. Even the cloister, where only weeds and thistles grew in what should have been a garden, was denied the inhabitants of Sallust except on one brief afternoon each month. And these poor penitents gladly allowed themselves to be wakened after only three hours of sleep a night—no more or less—and gladly existed on one cold meal a day which they ate standing up, of course, in the dark refectory. They could neither read nor perform good works for the world beyond Sallust. Their lot was to suffer and suffer they did year in, year out, unflagging in their self-mortification, unwearying of all the forms of pain and deprivation that they inflicted on themselves and their fellows. Their cries and groans rang out day and night. Bathing or washing of any kind, even in cold water, was never allowed. No prison or military regiment was ever as ominous as this monastery that rose like an island of smoke-blackened rock in a fallow field bordered by a forest of dead trees. No place of pestilence was more feared and shunned than this brooding monument to the pious mind. It was from this fortress of perfidy that Maximus and Orvio and five other still younger monks fled at last, and on the very night that Regulus led the flight from Chrodegang.

Regulus and his followers were young and thin, Maximus and his were young and gaunt. Maximus and his followers had suffered in a way that Regulus and his had not. Yet it must not be assumed that Maximus and the others had revolted from the rule of Brugus merely to escape pain or in search of relief not only from the affront inflicted night and day on their souls but also from that inflicted on their skins, on their vitals, on the whole of the pitiful remnants of their persons. Not at all. Maximus and the others had lived by pain, had welcomed it, had grown used to it, had savored it as did the remaining five hundred and ninety-three hollow-eyed self-mortifiers under the sway of Brugus. There was no physical agony that Maximus, Orvio, and their five young prematurely aged companions could not endure. No, Maximus and his little band fled at last from Sallust for the same reason that Regulus and his followers fled Chrodegang—to right the balance, to destroy excess, that single mightiest obstacle to the pure love that was the right and obligation of any devoted soul.

So Maximus, like Regulus, made his plan, chose his moment, left Sallust forever at the hour of the single meal when it was easiest to slip away unseen from among all the other monks of the place packed upright in the darkness while slurping their cold bowls of gruel.

Maximus proved nearly as fast a runner as Regulus, despite his emaciation, and was prompted on by the same silent voice that spoke to Regulus and, as ignorant as Regulus of compasses and the other myriad instruments and ideas of the familiar world, nonetheless ran as directly as did Regulus toward the gentle valley where lay the ruin, though of course Maximus was running in exactly the opposite direction from that taken by Regulus.

It rained, it stormed, Maximus ran on like a wounded deer, flowers sprang open in his path, a peasant girl dropped two buckets of warm milk at the sight of Maximus and the others bounding across a far corner of a field of lavender plants beginning to bloom. The same but different berries that nourished Regulus and his followers nourished Maximus and his, spiders suspended in silken webs watched intently the progress of the monks from Sallust, the fourteenth night arrived and Maximus and his men, unwearied, far from the exhaustion that had overtaken Regulus and Varro and theirs, kept running. His pace had been slower than that of Regulus, he had farther to go in the amount of time which, unbeknownst to him, had been allotted to his journey. So on the morning of the fifteenth day Maximus burst out of the trees at the crest of the valley exactly opposite the seven monks of Chrodegang already congregated at the peaceful ruin set aglow by the soft dawn light and orange snails.

Sunrise. End of the journey. A surprised meeting.

Excerpt from *Monks in Shadow*

# The
# Fish
# Keeper

YANNICK
MURPHY

When my mother said that the Salvation Army was marching through her house, coming to take her away, we took her away. The children and John go to visit her, they go late in the day when there are people up and down the street, I know because I lean out the window and watch the people.

Joshey is twelve years old but only now as tall as some little thing, some tadpole, and bald from the treatments they say he takes. He comes slinking down the street, breaking off car antennas. I almost yell down to him to stop, but I don't want him looking up here at me, and, besides, this child won't be with us much longer and it is not our car he is fooling with.

I make the tuna-in-the-blanket dish for them when they come back from seeing my mother. I like the idea of tucking all that loose flaky tuna into the blanket of dough I've made, then I turn down the sides of the blanket so it looks just like a loaf of bread and not some cookbook surprise.

At night my Matthew cries out for me. I can hear him because his window is open and I'm leaning out of mine so his voice comes from his window, into the street and then up to me. I don't go down to see him because he only cries out once and besides, it is from the street that I hear him crying out and maybe it really isn't Matthew crying out for me but some other kid, that dying Joshey kid crying out for his mother instead.

At times my mother called me some kind of witch because in my eye I've got what looks like a black pie slice. When I was little I went down in our basement where the floors are dirt and in this city there are not many houses left like this, and I looked at pictures of some others of us, my mother's mother, her mother's mother, women I didn't know, but none of them had this thing in their eye the way I have this thing in my eye, or maybe the pictures were just too old, with the earth of this city covering them up and clouding all the women's faces.

• • •

I take my dogs out early when the streets are quiet and you can hear water slapping up against pier pilings at the river. The last time I was at the river I was so young. Then the river was clean and I swam in it. An uncle took me there and held down a hand to me to pull me up out of the water when I was done with my swim and my body was shaking from the cold. My Rebecca hates this story because she says now the river is just a sea of rubbers shed off from men the whores get down there.

John is not home again. I am watching the coffee table we have that has the fish tank for its base. My Jack Dempsey feeds like a shark and chases out angels and convicts. I think about how if the fish don't like me looking at them with the pie slice in my eye, then they have nowhere to go, just around and around, and I sit on my couch in my living room and I watch them all I want. "Who has the food?" I say and shake their can of fish food in the air in circles above their water world.

When I am out with the dogs, I never see anyone, like I said. It's just the sound of the water coming at me from down the street.

I look at John, ask him if he's seen the extra fish tank. I've got to separate this Jack Dempsey from the others. He's eating all their food, even the green terrors' food. I ask John if he hasn't seen the extra fish tank in the bathroom closet, and then I ask him to go look down there to see if it isn't hidden back behind some junk. There is a stack of magazines John has in there where on the pages the tits of the women are scratched.

"Your mother doesn't talk about the Salvation Army anymore," John says. "She begs to be told of the nurse's vision, 'S'il vous plait' she says to the nurse, 'Tell me the dream,' and the nurse says, 'Dios mío, cariño, I know not what you are talking about.'"

· · ·

"My baby was bit by a rat," the mother tells me from down below. "This happened in her sleep. Can you hear me?" she says, with a cupped hand above her eyes to shade, "it happened in her sleep—how was I to know, we were all asleep," the mother says, "it was the middle of the night. Rat poison's out," she says, "it's all over, they put it in here," she says, "in each one of these trees," and she points to the squares of earth on our block with trees growing out of them and ankle-high metal fences around them to keep the earth in. "Rat playgrounds," she calls them, and pets her baby's head.

Leaning out, I see my mother walking down the street wearing her leopard robe and heading for our door. From the pocket of her leopard robe she pulls out her set of keys, and when I go to the stairs I can hear her walking up them. Before she can get to the top of them, I go down to her and take her to the bathroom where she sits on the side of the tub and says how cold it is. My mother closes her leopard robe tighter around her. With her hair not brushed for what must be many days, it looks like the fuzzy hair on the head of a baby monkey. I take my mother upstairs and sit her down on the couch, where we watch the Jack Dempsey off by himself in his own tank swimming around, headed for corners as if by way of them he will hit upon a door. I let my mother feed the green terrors and the angels, and the convicts, but I am the one to feed the Jack Dempsey.

Before my mother goes away again, I wrap up slices of the tuna blanket and put them into the pocket of her leopard robe. Looking out of the window down at her on the street, I see that I did not brush her hair and that she has no shoes on her feet.

Even though it is so dirty and teeming with rubbers, little Joshey has taken a dive into the river. "He's yellow," his mother says up to me. "That disease from dirty water, I told him what it is but he thinks it's called Joshness instead. The kid thinks he is a disease. What else could happen to my boy?" the mother says.

One of my dogs eats the rat poison off the street. The Jack Dempsey is floating on his back, rolling over every once in a while like a fat man in the water. I go into the bathroom and sit on the tub. But it is too cold so I go downstairs into the basement we have that still has a dirt floor.

Up above it becomes so loud. I can hear them walking across the floor, the children in their rooms. My mother was right—it sounds like some kind of army marching through this house.

Then I go to the river and jump in and think of all the people there could be to come and tell me that now I have to get out.

# A
# Dead
# Summer

LYNNE
TILLMAN

The coffin was never opened. The soul, she recited to herself, selects its own society. . . . They wheeled the dark wood casket down the aisle of the church. It came to a halt next to her. The priest said that her friend had prepared for this day since his baptism thirty-two years earlier. He was returning to God. She touched the side of the coffin furtively, then it moved past her. People congregated on the street in front of the church. The coffin disappeared into a gray hearse. She thought, Where will it go, where will he go? Another friend, known for his dark humor, whispered, "Elizabeth, he's out of here." She smiled then and walked with friends to his mother's apartment where everyone drank and talked of other things than death. His mother was brave, but every once in a while Elizabeth caught her staring into space, a helpless frightened expression on her face. Or Elizabeth found her staring at a photograph of him when he was a child, a healthy delighted child with no trace of disease, not even the idea of disease, touching the image. That perfect past would never allow a death like his, Elizabeth thought.

It was a hot summer, the summer of the ticker-tape parade for Nelson Mandela. Elizabeth had trouble waking up. Perhaps it was because the city's heat, with its ever-present malodorousness, lingered like a sullen fog in the streets. She slept deeply, as if drugged, and gave her nights over to a dealer who meted them out for days.

I am on a tour in a mansion, where I decide to curate an exhibition of images of women in mental hospitals. On the tour a man and a woman, who live in the building, become attracted to me and follow me. I cannot understand their attraction but it is extreme, even obscene. The man begins to lean on me. The two fight over me. It is supposed to be about me but it has nothing to do with me. I run away from them but they are rapacious, desperate. They tell me they are sex-starved and lonely. The woman beseeches me, Please love me. Love me. I need you. I will die without you.

Elizabeth's dreams had always been vivid. She wrote them down every morning and filled notebook after notebook. At the new year she reread the old year's dreams. It was her diary, a veritable autobiography. But lately her dreams seemed too real. They were like movies she would never have made. When asleep Elizabeth felt invaded. During the day she stayed at home as much as she could. She turned down jobs—Elizabeth worked as a film editor—and hoped to pass the summer on what she had saved all year. Elizabeth thought the lonely woman in her dream looked like someone she knew.

The streets slithered with discontent and malcontents, unhappy creatures desperate for painkilling potions and numbing smoke. Arguments erupted, sudden and sharp, under an intense sun that irritated skins of all colors. Elizabeth avoided groups of young men who hung out in doorways and whose apathetic expressions could only hide something much worse than she could feel. She avoided seventeen-year-old Debbie, out of jail again, her scarred coffee-colored arms and thin face a kind of flag of the hidden nation. Elizabeth felt too white. She walked quickly past Benny, Prince, and their girlfriends, who never had names, and handed them quarters without saying anything. She bought milk and *The New York Times*. She turned first to the obituary page. She wondered if the good die young, or the young die good, or even if it is good to die. She read that Castro "accused President Bush of having a 'sick obsession' with Cuba. 'Neither asleep nor awake can Bush forget about Cuba.'"

I am in the country. The time is the early part of the nineteenth century. A train comes to a cottage in the mountains where a group of people are living. They may be revolutionaries. The women are waiting for men, who alight from the cars of the train. They are sickly, though, and need help walking. Now it is the twentieth century. I watch a woman leap through an open window. She is followed by a man, who calls her name. I am just about to hear her name. I strain to hear it.

The telephone rang harshly in the nearly empty room. It broke into the dream. The sound made her cringe. Were they Cuban revolutionaries? Who was the woman leaping through the window? She supposed it was herself and she buried her head under the pillow and burrowed farther beneath the covers. It was the way Elizabeth wanted to be buried when she was a child—with a blanket and a pillow, with her arms under the covers so that evil spirits wouldn't pull at her when she was gone, dragging her down and down, to hell. She had begged her father: Daddy, please bury me with my blanket and pillow. Though she was only five, she was obsessed with death. He reassured her as best he could. He promised he would bury her just the way she wanted. But he was dead. She placed her friend's picture next to her father's. The machine answered the telephone but she didn't return the call.

Her boyfriend grew tired of her moodiness. His lackluster treatment of her was now an indication of great perversity. She could not speak of it to anyone. He told her she was inconsolable. It didn't seem important what happened between them, anyway. And how could she explain what she let him do to her? His sadism not only mirrored her masochism but was also perfect in its reflection of her inner world, which was already a mirror to the outer one. She considered that he might be the devil. He was too good-looking. The TV news reported that the funeral of a Vietnamese man, a member of Born to Kill who'd been assassinated at the age of twenty-one, was interrupted by machine-gun fire from Chinese gang members who

shot into the crowd of mourners. Some of the mourners fired
back.

I am feeding worms. They are growing larger and larger. I
realize that they are living creatures and if I continue to feed
them, more will be born and grow. A man appears and sings,
The worms crawl in, the worms crawl out. They eat your guts
and spit them out. I want to laugh, but I realize that this may
happen at any moment. I scream. The man, she decided, was
telling her that not all life is worthwhile.

The Mets were doing better, but with so many new players on
the team, she didn't have the same relationship to them. Her
dead friend had loved the Mets too. Sometimes she watched a
game just for him, as if he could use her as a medium. She was
sure his spirit was hovering near her, especially at those times.
But she did not speak of this to her boyfriend who was talking
about breaking up. That night she let him gag her. She didn't
have anything to say anyway, not anything worthwhile. She
read that the Ku Klux Klan had marched in Palm Beach.

I am a young black child. I am in a school bus driven by an
angry white man. He is obviously a racist. He may want to kill
me. We are trying to cross the Brooklyn Bridge. But the bridge
is being reconstructed. The bus careens across the bridge,
going much too fast. I am afraid we will crash. I'm afraid I'll
never get to school.

Her boyfriend finally broke up with her. She felt nothing.
Friends tried to be sympathetic, but she knew they didn't really
understand. There was a sheet of glass between her and them.
She didn't return their calls. She watched TV and cut out
articles from the newspaper. The stench in the streets nau-

seated her and she ate less and less. She stopped washing the dishes and wore dirty clothes. Elizabeth turned her underpants inside out and wore them twice and knew no one would notice. Her mother, when she was alive, had never been one of those mothers who said, "Always wear clean underpants, because what if you get hit by a bus." Elizabeth didn't expect to get hit by a bus, though she knew that death could come at any time. On a talk show she heard a man in a wheelchair say that the difference between health and sickness was negligible, that sick people know sickness is just the other side of wellness. In the hot apartment a cold shiver pierced her body. Her skin seemed too thin to be a protective covering.

I see my friend. He is dying. He is lying on a bed, thin and stiff. He dies in front of me. I am helpless. I know he is dead but somehow he is not dead. He sits up and walks. He walks grimly and is looking for something, someone. But you are dead, I say to him. Still he continues to walk, and then I see he is carrying the corpse of a woman. She is thinner than he is. She has thin scraggly hair. It falls onto her face, which is a sick greenish color. She is truly dead. He is dragging her beside him. He is like the grim reaper. But you are dead, I say to him again. His hands reach out for me. He cannot rest. He cannot sleep. I must help him. I run to find his mother. I must find her so that she can let her son die. Let him rest. I bang on a heavy wooden door but no one hears.

On her occasional walks around the neighborhood Elizabeth first noticed, and then became fascinated by, an older woman, a blond woman in her fifties, who walked with a limp and spoke with a German accent. She looked poor but proud. The woman's fat old dog struggled to keep up with his limping mistress. Elizabeth began to follow her, because she felt the

German woman, whom she named Ursula, had an answer. The older woman's singularity and dignity amazed her. It meant survival at any cost.

Ursula went into a neighborhood bar at about five P.M. every day. Her dog accompanied her, first panting and then lying still at the base of the barstool. Ursula's feet didn't touch the floor. Her gray cotton sweater hung loosely over her breasts. Her straight linen skirt, always clean but worn, hiked up to reveal well-developed thighs that age had not yet rendered to itself. Elizabeth took a seat at the bar and tried not to stare. She wanted to listen to the woman's stories as if she weren't. But the woman talked little and when she did, she spoke in hushed tones to the bartender or other customers whom she favored with her attention. Elizabeth wrote about Ursula in the notebook reserved for dreams.

She wanted to be the woman's friend. She was obsessed with the idea of making contact with her and learning her secrets. But Elizabeth couldn't relate to people as she once had. She didn't feel entirely alone as she knew she was receiving messages in her dreams that she couldn't possibly convey to anyone else. Though only thirty-two, she felt terribly old, as if her life were already over. The German woman, who was many years older, seemed not to need friends. Elizabeth never saw Ursula with anyone but her dog.

Ursula strolled the streets as if she wasn't looking for anything in particular. She seemed to lack nothing. She bought the newspaper and carried home cups of take-out coffee. Sometimes she talked to neighbors or shopkeepers, but Elizabeth could tell that Ursula kept a distance between herself and them. From across the street she watched Ursula approach the door to her building, turn the key in the lock, open the door, and enter, glancing behind her in case someone was about to mug her. Ursula always waited patiently for her fat dog to follow her in. Then the door slammed shut and Ursula disappeared. Elizabeth could picture Ursula in her apartment, reading the newspaper, looking out the window, or watching TV.

She decided that Ursula was fearless in the face of life and death, not at all like Elizabeth herself who lately feared stray bullets. Some had already taken the lives of several small children while they slept in cars or in their beds, in the supposed safety of their homes. Elizabeth went to the bar at five P.M. every day. She waited for Ursula and ordered a scotch and soda, which was Ursula's drink. Elizabeth liked the bar—its anonymity, that no one expected anything from her, that she could watch TV and sit for hours and hours without saying a word. She went home with a bellicose old man who bought her drinks and touched her thigh. She hated his smell and his body but she felt sorry for him. When he fell asleep she got out of bed and walked home.

I am about to have sex with a very young man. He may be old too. We are in a bedroom. I am very excited. I am afraid someone will walk in. I go into a dark hallway. My mother, who's dead, is standing there. Her decrepit body is barely hidden by a diaphanous black nightgown. She is shriveled and skeletal. She is bent over. She is angry. She screams at me.

Elizabeth decided to approach the German woman, to make conversation with her. She rehearsed the conversation as she walked along the streets. "I have noticed you for some time. You seem wise. I'm sure your life has been very interesting." The young guys she'd been afraid of looked less deadly. They were just selling grass, maybe crack. She was fairly certain they weren't carrying guns, but if they were, they probably wouldn't want to shoot her. She wasn't anyone for them to worry about. Now she smiled at them because she wanted them never to fear her. She wouldn't ever call the police. Florida's electric chair, she read, might malfunction, so some executions were being held up while they tested it. If she were given the choice, she'd choose an injection and die in her sleep. Her friend had told her that he wasn't afraid to die. Late at night she thought of that as she watched movie after movie. She didn't want to fall asleep. She didn't want to dream. If life were so fragile, she might easily drift away in her sleep. But finally she did fall asleep.

I am with my mother. She looks like Ursula. We start to have a fight about politics. My mother makes many right-wing statements. She thinks the poor don't want to work and that's why they're poor. She is for the death penalty. How can you be for death, I ask. Death stands nearby. He takes my hand and I strike my mother. She dies. I can't believe that I've killed her but there is nothing I can do. I am sentenced to death. But I am not allowed to have an injection. The judge says my crime is so heinous, I must suffer.

Elizabeth didn't remember the dream completely. She thought her father may have been in it too. What if he were the judge? And she didn't hear the telephone ring. It was perhaps the first time in her adult life that, when she tried, she couldn't invoke her unconscious life adequately. It took many cups of coffee to wake her. She dressed carefully. Today she would approach Ursula in the bar. At five she walked over there but Ursula wasn't in her regular seat. The bartender poured Elizabeth a scotch and soda, and she felt that he knew her in a special way. She waited for Ursula. Men who were also regulars talked with her. She spoke to them in hushed tones.

Elizabeth looked down at her feet and thought she saw Ursula's dog. He was brushing against her leg. She looked down several times because the dog's fur tickled her. After her third scotch, even though the bar was air-conditioned, her cotton sweater and skirt stuck to her body. She was sweating and wiped her forehead again and again. She was restless waiting for Ursula. The dog licked her ankle. He licked and licked. Elizabeth laughed out loud. At least she thought she did, but when she looked around the bar, no one seemed to have noticed her. That's why she liked it there.

# Why Don't You Come Live With Me It's Time

JOYCE
CAROL
OATES

The other day, it was a sunswept windy March morning, I saw my grandmother staring at me, those deep-socketed eyes, that translucent skin, a youngish woman with very dark hair as I hadn't quite remembered her who had died while I was in college, years ago, in 1966. Then I saw, of course it was virtually in the same instant I saw the face was my own, my own eyes in that face floating there not in a mirror but in a metallic mirrored surface, teeth bared in a startled smile and seeing my face that was not my face I laughed, I think that was the sound.

You're an insomniac, you tell yourself: there are profound truths revealed only to the insomniac by night like those phosphorescent minerals veined and glimmering in the dark but coarse and ordinary otherwise, you have to examine such minerals in the absence of light to discover their beauty: you tell yourself.

Maybe because I was having so much trouble sleeping at the time, twelve or thirteen years old, no one would have called the problem insomnia, that sounds too clinical, too adult and anyway they'd said "You can sleep if you try" and I'd overheard "She just wants attention—you know what she's like" and I was hurt and angry but hopeful too wanting to ask, But what am I like, are you the ones to tell me?

In fact, Grandmother had insomnia too—"suffered from insomnia" was the somber expression—but no one made the connection between her and me. Our family was that way: worrying that one weakness might find justification in another and things would slip out of containment and control.

In fact, I'd had trouble sleeping since early childhood but I had not understood that anything was wrong. Not secrecy nor even a desire to please my parents made me pretend to sleep, I thought it was what you do, I thought when Mother put me to bed I had to shut my eyes so she could leave and that was the way of releasing her though immediately afterward when I was alone my eyes opened wide and sleepless. Sometimes it was day, sometimes night. Often by night I could see, I could discern the murky shapes of objects, familiar objects that had lost their names by night as by night lying motionless with no one to observe me it seemed I had no name and my body was shapeless and undefined. The crucial thing was to lie motionless, scarcely breathing, until at last—it might be minutes or it might be hours, if there were noises in the house or out on the street (we lived on a busy street for most of my childhood in Hammond) it would be hours—a dark pool of warm water would begin to lap gently over my feet, eventually it would cover my legs, my chest, my face . . . what adults called "sleep" this most elusive and strange and mysterious of experiences, a cloudy transparency of ever-shifting hues and textures surrounding tense islands of wakefulness so during the course of a night I would sleep, and wake, and sleep, and wake, a dozen times, as the water lapped over my face and retreated from it, this seemed altogether natural, it was altogether desirable, for when I slept another kind of sleep, heavily, deeply, plunged into a substance not water and not a transparency but an oozy lightless muck, when I plunged down into that sleep and managed to wake from it shivering and sweating with a pounding heart and a pounding head as if my brain trapped inside my skull (but "brain" and "skull" were not concepts I would have known, at that time) had been racing feverishly like a small machine gone berserk it was to a sense of total helplessness and an exhaustion so profound it felt like death: sheer nonexistence, oblivion: and I did not know, nor do I know now, decades later, which sleep is preferable, which sleep is normal, how is one defined by sleep, from where in fact does "sleep" arise.

When I was older, a teenager, with a room at a little distance
from my parents' bedroom, I would often, those sleepless
nights, simply turn on my bedside lamp and read, I'd read until
dawn and day and the resumption of daytime routine in a state
of complete concentration, or sometimes I'd switch on the
radio close beside my bed, I was cautious of course to keep the
volume low, low and secret and I'd listen fascinated to stations
as far away as Pittsburgh, Toronto, Cleveland, there was a
hillbilly station broadcasting out of Cleveland, country-and-
western music I would never have listened to by day. One by
one I got to know intimately the announcers' voices along the
continuum of the glowing dial, hard to believe those strangers
didn't know *me*. But sometimes my room left me short of
breath, it was fresh air I craved, hurriedly I'd dress pulling on
clothes over my pajamas, and even in rainy or cold weather I
went outside leaving the house by the kitchen door so quietly
in such stealth no one ever heard, not once did one of them
hear *I will do it: because I want to do it* sleeping their heavy sleep
that was like the sleep of molluscs, eyeless. And outside: in the
night: the surprise of the street transformed by the lateness of
the hour, the emptiness, the silence: I'd walk to the end of our
driveway staring, listening, my heart beating hard. *So this is—
what it is!* The ordinary sights were made strange, the side-
walks, the street lights, the neighboring houses. Yet the fact
had no consciousness of itself except through *me*.

For that has been one of the principles of my life.

And if here and there along the block a window glowed
from within (another insomniac?), or if a lone car passed in the
street casting its headlights before it, or a train sounded in the
distance, or, high overhead, an airplane passed winking and
glittering with lights, what happiness swelled my lungs, what
gratitude, what conviction, I was utterly alone for the moment,
and invisible, which is identical with being alone.

· · ·

*Come by anytime dear, no need to call first* my grandmother said often, *Come by after school, anytime, please!* I tried not to hear the pleading in her voice, tried not to see the soft hurt in her eyes, and the hope.

Grandmother was a "widow": her husband, my step-grandfather had died of cancer of the liver when I was five years old.

Grandmother had beautiful eyes. Deep-set, dark, intelligent, alert. And her hair was a lovely silvery-gray, not coarse like others' hair but fine-spun, silky.

Mother said, "In your grandmother's eyes you can do no wrong." She spoke as if amused but I understood the accusation.

Because Grandmother loved me best of the grandchildren, yes and she loved me best of all the family, I basked in her love as in the warmth of a private sun. Grandmother loved me without qualification and without criticism which angered my parents since they understood that so fierce a love made me impervious to their more modulated love, not only impervious but indifferent to the threat of its being withdrawn . . . which is the only true power parents have over their children. Isn't it?

We visited Grandmother often, especially now she was alone. She visited us. Sundays, holidays, birthdays. And I would bicycle across the river to her house once or twice a week, or drop in after school, Grandmother encouraged me to bring my friends but I was too shy, I never stayed long, her happiness in my presence made me uneasy. Always she would prepare one of my favorite dishes, hot oatmeal with cream and brown sugar, apple cobbler, brownies, fudge, lemon custard tarts . . . and I sat and ate as she watched, and, eating, I felt hunger, the hunger was in my mouth. To remember those foods brings the hunger back now, the sudden rush of it, the pain. In my mouth.

At home Mother would ask, "Did you spoil your appetite again?"

The river that separated us was the Cassadaga, flowing from east to west, to Lake Ontario, through the small city of Hammond, New York.

After I left, aged eighteen, I only returned to Hammond as a visitor. Now everyone is dead, I never go back.

The bridge that connected us was the Ferry Street bridge, the bridge we crossed hundreds of times. Grandmother lived south of the river (six blocks south, two blocks west), we lived north of the river (three blocks north, one and a half block east), we were about three miles apart. The Ferry Street bridge, built in 1919, was one of those long narrow spiky nightmare bridges, my childhood was filled with such bridges, this one thirty feet above the Cassadaga, with high arches, steep ramps on both sides, six concrete supports, rusted iron grillwork, and neoclassical ornamentation of the kind associated with Chicago Commercial architecture, which was the architectural style of Hammond generally.

The Ferry Street bridge. Sometimes in high winds you could feel the bridge sway, I lowered my eyes when my father drove us over, he'd joke as the plank floor rattled and beneath the rattling sound there came something deeper and more sinister, the vibrating hum of the river itself, a murmur, a secret caress against the soles of our feet, our buttocks, and between our legs so it was an enormous relief when the car had passed safely over the bridge and descended the ramp to land. The Ferry Street bridge was almost too narrow for two ordinary-sized automobiles to pass but only once was my father forced to stop about a quarter of the way out, a gravel truck was bearing down upon us and the driver gave no sign of slowing down so my father braked the car, threw it hurriedly into reverse and backed up red-faced the way we'd come and after that the Ferry Street bridge was no joke to him, any more than it was to his passengers.

The other day, that sunny gusty day when I saw Grandmother's face in the mirror, I mean the metallic mirrored surface downtown, I mean the face that had seemed to be Grandmother's face but was not, I began to think of the Ferry Street bridge and since then I haven't slept well seeing the bridge in my mind's eye the way you do when you're insomniac, the images that should be in dreams are loosed and set careening through the day like lethal bubbles in the blood. I had not known how I'd memorized that bridge, and I'd forgotten why.

The time I am thinking of, I was twelve or thirteen years old, I know I was that age because the Ferry Street bridge was closed for repairs then and it was over the Ferry Street bridge I went, to see Grandmother. I don't remember if it was a conscious decision or if I'd just started walking, not knowing where I was going, or why. It was three o'clock in the morning. No one knew where I was. Beyond the barricade and the DETOUR—BRIDGE OUT signs, the moon so bright it lit my way like a manic face.

A number of times I'd watched with trepidation certain of the neighborhood boys inch their way out across the steel beams of the skeletal bridge, walking with arms extended for balance, so I knew it could be done without mishap, I knew I could do it if only I had the courage, and it seemed to me I had sufficient courage, now was the time to prove it. Below the river rushed past slightly higher than usual, it was October, there had been a good deal of rain, but tonight the sky was clear, stars like icy pinpricks, and that bright glaring moon illuminating my way for me so I thought *I will do it* already climbing up onto what would be the new floor of the bridge

when at last it was completed: not planks but a more modern
sort of iron mesh, not yet laid into place. But the steel beams
were about ten inches wide and there was a grid of them, four
beams spanning the river and (I would count them as I crossed,
I would never forget that count) fourteen narrower beams at
perpendicular angles with the others, and about three feet
below these beams there was a complex crisscrossing of cables
you might define as a net of sorts if you wanted to think in such
terms, a safety net, there was no danger really *I will do it because
I want to do it, because there is no one to stop me.*

And on the other side, Grandmother's house. And even if
its windows were darkened, even if I did no more than stand
looking quietly at it, and then come back home, never telling
anyone what I'd done, even so I would have proved something
*Because there is no one to stop me* which has been one of the
principles of my life. To regret that principle is to regret my
entire life.

I climbed up onto one of the beams, trembling with excitement. But how cold it was!—I'd come out without my gloves.

And how loud the river below, the roaring like a kind of
jeering applause; and it smelled too, of something brackish and
metallic. I knew not to glance down at it, steadying myself as
a quick wind picked up, teasing tears into my eyes, I was
thinking *There is no turning back: never* but instructing myself
too that the beam was perfectly safe if I was careful for had I
not seen boys walking across without slipping? didn't the
workmen walk across too, many times a day? I decided not to
stand, though—I was afraid to stand—I remained squatting on
my haunches, gripping the edge of the beam with both hands,
inching forward in this awkward way, hunched over, right
foot, and then left foot, and then right foot, and then left foot:
passing the first of the perpendicular beams, and the second,

and the third, and the fourth: and so in this clumsy and painful fashion forcing myself to continue until my thigh muscles ached so badly I had to stop and I made the mistake which even in that instant I knew was a mistake of glancing down: seeing the river thirty feet below: the way it was flowing so swiftly and with such power, and seeming rage, ropy sinuous coils of churning water, foam-flecked, terrible, and its flow exactly perpendicular to the direction in which I was moving.

"Oh no. Oh no. Oh no."

A wave of sharp cold terror shot up into me as if into my very bowels, piercing me between the legs rising from the river itself, and I could not move, I squatted there on the beam unable to move, all the strength drained out of my muscles and I was paralyzed knowing *You're going to die: of course, die* even as with another part of my mind (there is always this other part of my mind) I was thinking with an almost teacherly logic that the beam *was* safe, it was wide enough, and flat enough, and not damp or icy or greasy yes certainly it *was* safe: if this were land, for instance in our backyard, if for instance my father had set down a plank flat in the grass, a plank no more than half the width of the beam couldn't I, Claire, have walked that plank without the slightest tremor of fear? boldly? even gracefully? even blindfolded? without a moment's hesitation? not the flicker of an eyelid, not the most minute leap of a pulse?— *You know you aren't going to die: don't be silly* but it must have been five minutes before I could force myself to move again, my numbed right leg easing forward, my aching foot, I forced my eyes upward too and fixed them resolutely on the opposite shore, or what I took on faith to be the opposite shore, a confusion of sawhorses and barrels and equipment now only fitfully illuminated by the moon.

But I got there, I got to where I meant to go without for a moment exactly remembering why.

*Now the worst of it's done: for now.*

Grandmother's house, what's called a bungalow, plain stucco, one-story, built close to the curb, seemed closer to the river than I'd expected, maybe I was running, desperate to get there, hearing the sound of the angry rushing water that was like many hundreds of murmurous voices, and the streets surprised me with their emptiness—so many vacant lots, murky transparencies of space where buildings had once stood—and a city bus passed silently, lit gaily from within, yet nearly empty too, only the driver and a single (male) passenger sitting erect and motionless as mannequins, and I shrank panicked into the shadows so they would not see me: maybe I would be arrested: a girl of my age on the street at such an hour, alone, with deep-set frightened eyes, a pale face, guilty mouth, zip-up corduroy jacket and jeans over her pajamas, disheveled as a runaway. But the bus passed, turned a corner, and vanished. And there was Grandmother's house, not darkened as I'd expected but lighted, and from the sidewalk staring I could see Grandmother inside, or a figure I took to be Grandmother, but why was she awake at such an hour, how remarkable that she should be awake as if awaiting me, and I remembered then—how instanteously these thoughts came to me, eerie as tiny bubbles that, bursting, yielded riches of a sort that would require a considerable expenditure of time to relate though their duration was in fact hardly more than an instant!—I remembered having heard the family speak of Grandmother's sometimes strange behavior, worrisome behavior in a woman of her age, or of any age, the problem was her insomnia unless insomnia was not cause but consequence of a malady of the soul, so it would be reported to my father, her son, that she'd been seen walking at night in neighborhoods unsafe for solitary women, she'd been seen at a midnight showing of a film in downtown Hammond, and even when my step-grandfather was alive (he worked on a lake freighter, he was often gone) she might spend time in local taverns, not drinking heavily, but drinking, and this was behavior that might lead to trouble, or so the family worried, though there was never any specific trouble so far as anyone knew, and Grandmother smoked too, smoked on the street which "looks cheap," my mother said, my mother too smoked but never on the street, the family liked to tell and retell the story of a cousin of my father's coming to Hammond on a Greyhound bus, arriving at the station at about six in the morning, and there in the waiting room was my grandmother in her old fox-fur coat sitting there with a book in her lap, a cigarette in one hand, just sitting there placidly and with no mind for the two or three others, distinctly odd near-derelict men, in the room with her, just sitting there reading her book (Grandmother was always reading, poetry, biographies of great men like Lincoln, Mozart, Julius Caesar, Jesus of Nazareth) and my father's cousin came in, saw her, said, "Aunt Tina, what on earth are you doing here?" and Grandmother had looked up calmly, and said, "Why not?—it's for waiting isn't it?"

Another strange thing Grandmother had done, it had nothing to do with her insomnia that I could see unless all our strangenesses, as they are judged in others' eyes, are morbidly related, was arranging for her husband's body to be cremated: not buried in a cemetery plot, but cremated: which means burnt to mere ash: which means annihilation: and though cremation had evidently been my step-grandfather's wish it had seemed to the family that Grandmother had complied with it too readily, and so immediately following her husband's death that no one had a chance to dissuade her. "What a thing," my mother said, shivering, "to do to your own husband!"

I was thinking of this now seeing through one of the windows a man's figure, a man talking with Grandmother in her kitchen, it seemed to me that perhaps my step-grandfather had not yet died, thus was not yet cremated, and some of the disagreement might be resolved, but I must have already knocked at the door since Grandmother was there opening it, at first she stared at me as if scarcely recognizing me then she laughed, she said, "What are *you* doing here?" and I tried to explain but could not: the words failed to come: my teeth were chattering with cold and fright and the words failed to come but Grandmother led me inside, she was taller than I remembered, and younger, her hair dark, wavy, falling to her shoulders, and her mouth red with lipstick, she laughed leading me into the kitchen where a man, a stranger, was waiting, "Harry this is my granddaughter Claire," Grandmother said, and the man stepped forward regarding me with interest, yet speaking of me as if I were somehow not present, "She's your granddaughter?" "She is." "I didn't know you had a granddaughter." "You don't know lots of things."

And Grandmother laughed at us both, who gazed in perplexity and doubt at each other. Laughing, she threw her head back like a young girl, or a man, and bared her strong white teeth.

I was then led to sit at the kitchen table, in my usual place, Grandmother went to the stove to prepare something for me and I sat quietly, not frightened now, yet not quite at ease though I understood I was safe now, Grandmother would take care of me now and nothing could happen, I saw that the familiar kitchen had been altered, it was very brightly lit, almost blindingly lit, yet deeply shadowed in the corners, the rear wall where the sink should have been dissolved into what would have been the backyard but I had a quick flash of the backyard where there were flower and vegetable beds, Grandmother loved to work in the yard, she brought flowers and vegetables in the summer wherever she visited, the most beautiful of her flowers were peonies, big gorgeous crimson peonies, and the thought of the peonies was confused with the smell of the oatmeal Grandmother was stirring on the stove for me to eat, oatmeal was the first food of my childhood: the first food I can remember: but Grandmother made it her own way, her special way stirring in brown sugar, cream, a spoonful of dark honey, so just thinking of it I felt my mouth water violently, almost it hurt, the saliva flooded so and I was embarrassed that a trickle ran down my chin and I couldn't seem to wipe it off and Grandmother's friend Harry was watching me: but finally I managed to wipe it off on my fingers: and Harry smiled.

The thought came to me, not a new thought but one I'd had for years, but now it came with unusual force, like the saliva flooding my mouth, that when my parents died I would come live with Grandmother—of course: I would come live with Grandmother: and Grandmother at the stove stirring my oatmeal in a pan must have heard my thoughts for she said, "—Claire why don't you come live with me it's time isn't it?" and I said, "Oh yes," and Grandmother didn't seem to have heard for she repeated her question, turning now to look at me, to smile, her eyes shining and her mouth so amazingly red, two delicate spots of rouge on her cheeks so my heart caught seeing how beautiful she was, as young as my mother, or younger, and she laughed saying, "—Claire why don't you come live with me it's time isn't it?" and again I said, "Oh yes Grandmother," nodding and blinking tears from my eyes, they were tears of infinite happiness, and relief, "—oh Grandmother, *yes.*"

Grandmother's friend Harry was a navy radio operator, he said, or had been, he wore no uniform and he was no age I could have guessed, with silvery-glinting hair in a crewcut, muscular shoulders and arms, but maybe his voice was familiar? maybe I'd heard him over the radio? Grandmother was urging him to tell me about the universe, distinctly she said those odd words "Why don't you tell Claire about the universe," and Harry stared at me frowning and said, "Tell Claire what about the universe?" and Grandmother laughed and said, "Oh—anything!" and Harry said, shrugging, "Hell—I don't know," then raising his voice, regarding me with a look of compassion, "—the universe goes back a long way, I guess. Ten billion years? Twenty billion? Is there a difference? They say it got started with an explosion and in a second, well really a fraction of a second a tiny bit of tightness got flung out, it's flying out right now, expanding,"—he drew his hands, broad stubby hands, dramatically apart—"and most of it is emptiness I guess, whatever 'emptiness' is. It's still expanding, all the pieces flying out, there's a billion galaxies like ours, or maybe a billion billion galaxies like ours, but don't worry it goes on forever even when we die—" but at this Grandmother turned sharply, sensing my reaction, she said, "Oh dear don't tell the child *that*, don't frighten poor little Claire with *that*."

"You told me to tell her about the—"

"Oh just *stop*."

Quickly Grandmother came to hug me, settled me into my chair as if I were a much smaller child sitting there at the kitchen table, my feet not touching the floor; and there was my special bowl, the bowl Grandmother kept for me, sparkling yellow with lambs running around the rim, yes and my special spoon too, a beautiful silver spoon with the initial *C* engraved on it which Grandmother kept polished so I understood I was safe, nothing could harm me, Grandmother would not let anything happen to me so long as I was there. She poured my oatmeal into my dish, she was saying, "—It's true we must all die one day, darling, but not just yet, you know, not tonight, you've just come to visit haven't you dear? and maybe you'll stay? maybe you won't ever leave? *now it's time?*"

The words *it's time* rang with a faint echo.

I can hear them now: *it's time: time.*

Grandmother's arms were shapely and attractive, her skin pale and smooth and delicately translucent as a candled egg, and I saw that she was wearing several rings, the wedding band that I knew but others, sparkling with light, and there so thin were my arms beside hers, my hands that seemed so small, sparrow-sized, and my wrists so bony, and it came over me, the horror of it, that meat and bone should define my presence in the universe: the point of entry in the universe that was *me* that was *me* that was *me:* and no other: yet of a fragile materiality that any fire could consume. "Oh Grandmother—I'm so afraid!" I whimpered, seeing how I would be burned to ash, and Grandmother comforted me, and settled me more securely into the chair, pressed my pretty little spoon between my fingers and said, "Darling don't think of such things, just *eat.* Grandmother made this for *you.*"

I was eating the hot oatmeal which was a little too hot, but creamy as I loved it, I was terribly hungry eating like an infant at the breast so blindly my head bowed and eyes nearly shut brimming with tears and Grandmother asked *is it good? is it good?* she'd spooned in some dark honey too *is it good?* and I nodded mutely, I could taste grains of brown sugar that hadn't melted into the oatmeal, stark as bits of glass, and I realized they were in fact bits of glass, some of them large as grape pits, and I didn't want to hurt Grandmother's feelings but I was fearful of swallowing the glass so as I ate I managed to sift the bits through the chewed oatmeal until I could maneuver it into the side of my mouth into a little space between my lower right gum and the inside of my cheek and Grandmother was watching asking *is it good?* and I said, "Oh yes," half choking and swallowing, "—oh *yes.*"

A while later when neither Grandmother nor Harry was

watching I spat out the glass fragments into my hand but I never knew absolutely, I don't know even now: if they were glass and not for instance grains of sand or fragments of egg- shell or even bits of brown sugar crystalized into such a form not even boiling oatmeal could dissolve it.

I was leaving Grandmother's house, it was later, time to leave, Grandmother said, "But aren't you going to stay?" and I said, "No Grandmother I can't," and Grandmother said, "I thought you were going to stay dear," and I said, "No Grandmother I can't," and Grandmother said, "But why?" and I said, "I just can't," and Grandmother said, laughing so her laughter was edged with annoyance, "Yes but *why?*" Grandmother's friend Harry had disappeared from the kitchen, there was no one in the kitchen but Grandmother and me, but we were in the street too, and the roaring of the river was close by, so Grandmother hugged me a final time and gave me a little push saying, "Well—goodnight Claire," and I said apologetically, "Good- night, Grandmother," wondering if I should ask her not to say anything to my parents about this visit in the middle of the night, and she was backing away, her dark somber gaze fixed upon me half in reproach, "Next time you visit Grandmother you'll stay—won't you? Forever?" and I said, "Yes Grand- mother," though I was very frightened and as soon as I was out of Grandmother's sight I began to run.

At first I had a hard time finding the Ferry Street bridge. Though I could hear the river close by—I can always hear the river close by.

Eventually, I found the bridge again. I know I found the bridge, otherwise how did I get home? That night?

The
Dead
Queen

ROBERT
COOVER

The old Queen had a grin on her face when we buried her in the mountain, and I knew then that it was she who had composed this scene, as all before, she who had led us, revelers and initiates, to this cold and windy grave site, hers the design, ours the enactment, and I felt like the first man, destined to rise and fall, rise and fall, to the end of time. My father saw this, perhaps I was trembling, and as though to comfort me, said: no, it was a mere grimace, the contortions of pain, she had suffered greatly after all, torture often exposes the diabolic in the face of man, she was an ordinary woman, beautiful it is true, and shrewd, but she had risen above her merits, and falling, had lost her reason to rancor. We can learn even from the wretched, my son; her poor death and poorer life teach us to temper ambition with humility, and to ignore reflections as one ignores mortality. But I did not believe him, I could see for myself, did not even entirely trust him, this man who thought power a localized convention, magic a popular word for concealment, for though it made him a successful King, decisive and respected, the old Queen's grin mocked such simple faith and I was not consoled.

My young bride, her cheeks made rosy by the mountain air, smiled benignly through the last rites, just as she had laughed with open glee at her stepmother's terrible entertainment at our wedding feast the night before, her cheeks flushed then with wine. I tried to read her outrageous cheerfulness, tried to understand the merriment that such an awesome execution had provoked. At times, she seemed utterly heartless, this child, become the very evil she'd been saved from. Had all our watchfulness been in vain, had that good and simple soul been envenomed after all, was it she who'd invited her old tormenter to the ball, commissioned the iron slippers, drawn her vindictively into that ghastly dance? Or did she simply laugh as the righteous must to see the wicked fall? Perhaps her own release

from death had quickened her heart, such that mere continuance now made her a little giddy. Or had she, absent, learned
something of hell? How could I know? I could vouch for her
hymen from this side, but worried that it had been probed from
within. How she'd squealed to see the old Queen's flailing
limbs, how she'd applauded the ringing of those flaming iron
clogs against the marble floors! Yet, it was almost as though she
were ignorant of the pain, of any cause or malice, ignorant of
consequences—like a happy child at the circus, unaware of any
skills or risks. Once, the poor woman had stumbled and
sprawled, her skirts heaped up around her ears, and this had
sprung a jubilant roar of laughter from the banqueters, but
Snow White had only smiled expectantly, then clapped gaily
as the guards set the dying Queen on her burning feet again.
Now, as I stood there on the mountainside, watching my
bride's black locks flow in the wintry wind and her young
breasts fill with the rare air, she suddenly turned toward me,
and seeing me stare so intensely, smiled happily and squeezed
my hand. No, I thought, she's suffered no losses, in fact that's
just the trouble, that hymen can never be broken, not even by
me, not in a thousand nights, this is her gift and essence, and
because of it, she can see neither fore nor aft, doesn't even
know there is a mirror on the wall. Perhaps it was this that had
made the old Queen hate her so.

If hate was the word. Perhaps she'd loved her. Or more
likely, she'd had no feelings toward her at all. She'd found her
unconscious and so useful. Did Snow White really believe she
was the fairest in the land? Perhaps she did, she had a gift for
the absurd. And thereby her stepmother had hatched a plot,
and the rest, as my father would say, is history. What a cruel
irony, those red-hot shoes! For it wasn't that sort of an itch that
had driven the old Queen—what she had lusted for was a part
in the story, immortality, her place in guarded time. To be the

forgotten stepmother of a forgotten Princess was not enough. It was the mirror that had fucked her, fucked us all. And did she foresee those very boots, the dance, that last obscenity? No doubt. Or something much like them. Just as she foresaw the Hunter's duplicity, the Dwarfs' ancient hunger, my own weakness for romance. Even our names were lost, she'd transformed us into colors, simple proclivities, our faces were forever fixed and they weren't even our own!

I was made dizzy by these speculations. I felt the mountain would tip and spill us all to hell or worse. I clutched for my bride's hand, grabbed the nose of a Dwarf instead. He sneezed loudly. The mourners ducked their heads and tittered. Snow White withdrew a lace kerchief from her sleeve and helped the Dwarf to blow his nose. My father frowned. I held my breath and stared at the dead Queen, masked to hide her eyes, which to what my father called a morbid imagination might seem to be winking, one open, the other squeezed shut. I thought: we've all been reduced to jesters, fools; tragedy she reserved for herself alone. This seemed true, but so profoundly true, it seemed false. I kept my feet apart and tried to think about the Queen's crimes. She had commissioned a child's death and eaten what she'd hoped was its heart. She'd reduced a Princess to a menial of menials, then attacked her body with laces, her mind with a comb, her soul with an apple. And, I thought, poisoned us all with pattern.

In the end, in spite of everything, she'd been accepted as part of the family, spared the outcast's shame, shrouded simply in black and granted her rings and diadems. Only her feet had been left naked, terribly naked: stripped even of their nails and skin. They were raw and blistery, shriveling now and seeming to ooze. Her feet had become one with the glowing iron shoes, of course, the moment we'd forced them on her—what was her wild dance, after all, but a desperate effort to jump out of her own skin? She had not succeeded, but ultimately, once she had died and the shoes had cooled, this final freedom had been more or less granted her, there being no other way to get her feet out of the shoes except to peel them out. I had suggested—naively, it seemed—that the shoes be left on her, buried with her, and had been told that the feet of the wicked were past number, but the Blacksmith's art was rare and sacred. As my Princess and I groped about in our bridal chamber, fumbling darkly toward some new disclosure, I had wondered: do such things happen at all weddings? We could hear them in the scullery, scraping the shoes out with picks and knives and rinsing them in acid.

What a night, our wedding night! A pity the old Queen had arrived so late, died so soon, missed our dedicated fulfillment of her comic design—or perhaps this, too, was part of her tragedy, the final touch to a life shaped by denial. Of course, it could be argued that she had courted reversals, much as a hero makes his own wars, that she had invented, then pursued the impossible, in order to push the possible beyond her reach, and thus had died, as so many have believed, of vanity, but never mind, the fact is, she was her own consummation, and we, in effect, had carried out—were still carrying out—our own ludicrous performances without an audience. Who could not laugh at us?

My sweetheart and I had sealed our commitment at high noon. My father had raised a cup to our good fortune, issued a stern proclamation against peddlers, bestowed happiness and property upon us and all our progeny, and the party had begun. Whole herds had been slaughtered for our tables. The vineyards of seven principalities had filled our casks. We had danced, sung, clung to one another, drunk, laughed, cheered, chanted the sun down. Bards had pilgrimaged from far and wide, come with their alien tongues to celebrate our union with pageants, prayers, and sacrifices. Not soon, they'd said, would this feast be forgotten. We'd exchanged epigrams and gallantries, whooped the old Queen through her death dance, toasted the fairies and offered them our firstborn. The Dwarfs had recited an ode in praise of clumsiness, though they'd forgotten some of the words and had got into a fight over which of them had dislodged the apple from Snow White's throat, pushing each other into soup bowls and out of windows. They'd thrown cakes and pies at each other for awhile, then had spilled wine on everybody, played tug-of-war with the Queen's carcass, regaled us with ribald mimes of regicide and witch-baiting, and finally had climaxed it all by buggering each other in a circle around Snow White, while singing their gold-digging song. Snow White had kissed them all fondly afterwards, helped them up with their breeches, brushed the crumbs from their beards, and I'd wondered then about my own mother, who was she?—and where was Snow White's father? Whose party was this? Why was I so sober? Suddenly I'd found myself, minutes before midnight, troubled by many things: the true meaning of my bride's name, her taste for luxury and collapse, the compulsions that had led me to the mountain, the birdshit on the glass coffin when I'd found her. Who *were* all these people, and why did things happen as though they were necessary? Oh, I'd reveled and worshipped with the rest of the party right to the twelfth stroke, but I couldn't help thinking: we've been too rash, we're being overtaken by something terrible, and who's to help us now the old Queen's dead?

The hole in the mountain was dug. The Dwarfs stepped back to admire their handiwork, tripped over their own beards, and fell in a big heap. They scrambled clumsily to their feet, clouting each other with their picks and shovels, wound up bowling one another over like duckpins and went tumbling in a roly-poly landslide down the mountain, grunting and groaning all the way. While we waited for them to return, I wondered: why are we burying her in the mountain? We no longer believe in underworlds nor place hope in moldering Kings, still we stuff them back into the earth's navel, as though anticipating some future interest, much as we stuff our treasures in crypts, our fiats in archives. Well, perhaps it had been her dying wish, I'm not told everything, her final vanity. Perhaps she had wanted to bring us back to this mountain, where her creation by my chance passage had been accomplished, to confront us with our own insignificance, our complaisant transience, the knowledge that it was ended, the rest would be forgotten, our fates were not sealed, merely eclipsed. She had eaten Snow White's heart in order to randomize her attentions, deprive her of her center, and now, like her victim and the bite of poisoned apple, she had vomited the heart up whole and undigested—but like the piece of apple, it could never be restored to its old function, it had its own life now, it would create its own circumambience, and we would be as remote from this magic as those of a hundred generations hence. Of course . . . it wasn't Snow White's heart she ate, no, it was the heart of a boar, I was getting carried away, I was forgetting things. She'd sent that child of seven into the woods with a restless lech, and he'd brought her back a boar's heart, as though to say he repented of his irrational life and wished to die. But then, perhaps that had been what she'd wanted, perhaps she had ordered the boar's heart, or known anyway that would be the Hunter's instinct, or perhaps there had been no Hunter at all, perhaps it had been that master of disguises, the old Queen herself, it was possible, it was all possible. I was overswept by confusion and apprehension. I felt like I'd felt that morning, when I'd awakened, spent, to find no blood on the nuptial linens.

The wedding party had ended at midnight. A glass slipper had been ceremoniously smashed on the last stroke of the hour, and the nine of us—Snow White and I and, at her insistence, my new brethren the seven Dwarfs—had paraded to the bridal chamber. I had been too unsettled to argue, had walked down the torchlit corridors through the music and applause as though in a trance, for I had fallen, moments before, into an untimely sobriety, had suddenly, as it were, become myself for the first time all day, indeed for the first time in my life, and at the expense of all I'd held real, my Princeship, my famous disenchantments, my bride, my songs, my family, had felt for a few frantic moments like a sun inside myself, about to be exposed and extinguished in a frozen void named Snow White. This man I'd called my father, I'd realized, was a perfect stranger, this palace a playhouse, these revelers the mocking eyes of a dying demiurge! Perhaps all bridegrooms suffer this. Though I'd carried my cock out proudly, as all Princes must, I'd not recognized it as my own when the citizenry in the corridors had knelt to honor it—not a mere ornament of office, I'd told myself, but the officer itself, I its loyal and dispensable retinue. Someone, as I'd passed, had bit it: I had recorded the pain like an awakened clerk, then had resigned my post and become a wandering peddler of antiquarian novelties.

But once inside the nuptial chamber, the door clicking shut behind me, Snow White cuddling sleepily on my shoulder, the Dwarfs flinging off their clothes and fighting over the chamber pot, I'd returned from my extravagant vagrancy, cock and ceremony had become all mine again, and for some reason I hadn't felt all that grateful. Maybe, I'd thought, maybe I'm a little drunker than I think. I could not have hoped for a more opulent setting: the bed a deep heap of silken eiderdowns, the floors covered with the luxuriant skins of mountain goats, mirrors on all the walls, perfume burning in golden censers, flasks of wine and bowls of fruit on the marble tables, lutes and pipes scattered decorously about: in the morning, I'd vowed, I shall arise before daybreak and compose a new song for my bride to remember this night by. Gently then, sequentially, as though being watched and judged, as though preparing the verses for my song, I'd embraced and commenced to disrobe her. I'd thought: I should be more excited than this. The Dwarfs had seemed to pay us no attention, but I'd begun to resent them: if I failed, they'd pay! One of them had got his foot stuck in the chamber pot and was clumping about in a rage. Another had seemed to be humping a goatskin. I'd nuzzled in Snow White's black tresses, kissed her white throat, whence she'd vomited the fateful apple, and wondered: why hadn't I been allowed to disenchant her with a kiss like everybody else?

Her nimble hands had unfastened my sashes and buckles with ease, stroked my back, teased my buttocks and balls, but my own fingers had got tangled in her laces. The Dwarfs had come to the rescue, and so had made me feel a fool again. Leave me alone! I'd cried. I can do it by myself! I'd realized then that Snow White had both her arms around my neck and the finger up my ass certainly wasn't my own. I'd gazed into the mirrors to see, for the first time, Snow White's paradigmatic beauty, but instead it had been the old Queen I'd seen there, flailing about madly in her red-hot shoes. Maybe it had been the drinking, all the shocks, or some new trick of my brethren, or else the scraping of the shoes in the scullery that had made me imagine it, but whatever, I had panicked, had gone lurching about drunkenly, shaking off Dwarfs, shrouding all the mirrors with whatever had come to hand, smashing not a few of them, feeling the eyes close, the grimaces fade, the room darken: This night is *mine!* I'd cried, and covered the last of them.

We'd been plunged into night—I'd never known a dark so

deep, nor felt so much alone. Snow White? Snow White! I'd
heard her answer, thought I'd heard her, it was as though she'd
called my name—I'd lunged forward, banged my knee on a
marble table, cut my foot on broken glass. Snow White! I'd
heard whispering, giggling, soft sighs. Come on, what're you
doing? I've cut myself! Light a candle! I'd stumbled over someone's foot, run my elbow through a lute. I'd lain there thinking: forget it, the state I'm in, I might as well wait until
morning, why has my father let me suffer such debasement, it
must be yet another of his moral lessons on the sources of a
King's majesty. The strange sensation had come to me suddenly that this bride I now pursued did not even exist, was just
something in *me,* locked and frozen, waiting to be released,
something lying dormant, like an accumulation of ancestral
visions and vagaries seeking corporeity—but then I'd heard
her struggling, gasping, whimpering. *Help me! please—!* Those
Dwarfs! I'd leaped up and charged into a bedpost. *I'm coming!*
Those goddamn dirty Dwarfs! Ever since the day of Snow
White's disenchantment, when I'd embraced them as brothers,
I'd had uneasy suspicions about them I couldn't quite allow
myself to admit, but now they'd burst explosively to the surface, in the dark I'd been able to see what I couldn't see in full
daylight, from the first night she'd shared their seven beds, just
a child, to the unspeakable things they were doing with her
now beneath the eiderdowns, even their famous rescues had
been nothing more than excuses to strip her, play with her,
how many years had the old witch let them keep her? *Leave
her alone! You hear?* I'd chased her voice, but the Dwarfs had
kept shifting her about. They worked underground, it was
easy for them, they were used to the dark. I'd kept pushing
toward her muted voice, scrambling over goatskins and fea-
therbedding, under bed and tables, through broken glass and
squashed fruit, into closets, cracking my head on pillars and

doorjambs, backing my bare nates into a hot oil lamp, recently extinguished. I'd tried to light it, but all the oil had been spilled: in fact, I was sitting in it.

But never mind, I'd begun to enjoy this, I was glad to have it out in the open, I could beat those Dwarfs at their own game, yes, I'd got a real sweat up, and an appetite, too: whatever those freaks could do, I could do better! I'd brushed up against a couple beards, grabbed them and knocked the heads together: *Hah!* There'd been the popping sound of something breaking, like a fruit bowl. I'd laughed aloud, crawled toward Snow White's soft cries over their bodies: they'd felt like goatskins. The spirit had begun to wax powerful within me, my foaming steed was rampant, my noble lance at the ready. Hardly before I'd realized I'd begun, I'd found myself plunging away in her wet and eager body, the piercing of her formidable hymen already just a memory, her sweet cry of pain mere history, as now she, panting, breathed my name: Charming! Charming! *Oh dear dear Charming!* She'd seemed to have a thousand hands, a mouth everywhere at once, a glowing furnace between her thrashing thighs, I'd sucked at her heaving breasts, groped in her leaping buttocks, we'd slithered and slid over and under one another, rolling about in the eiderdowns, thrice around the world we'd gone in a bucking frenzy of love and lubricity, seven times we'd died in each other, and as at last, in a state of delicious annihilation, I'd lost consciousness, my fading thoughts had been: those damned Dwarfs are all right after all, hey, they're all right. . . .

And we'd awakened at dawn, alone, clasped in each other's arms, the bed unmussed and unbloodied, her hymen intact.

The Dwarfs had returned from their roll down the mountain, patched and bandaged and singing a lament for the death of the unconscious, and we prepared to enter the old Queen in her tomb. I gazed at her in the glass coffin, the coffin that had once contained my wife, and thought: if she wakes, she will stare at the glass and discover there her own absence. I was beginning to appreciate her subtlety, and so assumed that this, too, had been part of her artifice, a lingering hope for her own liberation, she'd used the mirror as a door, tried to. This was her Great Work, this her use of a Princess with hair as black as ebony, a skin as white as snow, lips as red as blood, this her use of miners of gold! Of course, there were difficulties in such a perfect view of things, she was dead, for example, but one revelation was leading to another, and it came to me suddenly that maybe the old Queen had loved me, had died for *me*! I, too, was too prone to linger at still pools, listen to the flattery of soothsayers, organize my life and others' by threes and sevens—it was as if she'd lived this exemplary life, died this tragic death, to lead me away from the merely visible to vision, from the image to the imaged, from reflections to the projecting miracle itself, the heart, the pure snow white . . . !

One of the Dwarfs had been hopping about frantically, and now Snow White took him over behind a bush, but if this was meant to distract me, it did not succeed. The old Queen had me now, everything had fallen into place, I knew now the force that had driven her, that had freed me, freed us all, that we might live happily ever after, though we didn't deserve it, weren't even aware of how it had happened, yes, I knew her cause, knew her name—I wrenched open the coffin, threw myself upon her and kissed her lips.

If I'd expected something, it did not occur. She did not return my kiss, did not even cease grinning. She stank and her blue mouth was cold and rubbery as a dead squid. I'd been wrong about her, wrong about everything. . . .

The others had fallen back in horror and dismay. Snow White had fainted. Someone was vomiting. My father's eyes were full of tears and anger.

Though nauseated, I pitched forward and kissed her again, this time more out of pride and affection, than hope. I thought: it would've helped if the old clown had died with her mouth shut.

They tore me away from her body. It tumbled out of the coffin and, limbs awry, obstinately grinning, skidded a few feet down the mountainside. The flesh tore, but did not bleed. The mask fell away from her open eye, now milky white.

Please! I pleaded, though I no longer even hoped I was right. Let me try once more! Maybe a third time—!

Guards restrained me. My father turned his back. The Dwarfs were reviving Snow White by fanning her skirts. The Queen's corpse was dumped hastily back into the coffin and quickly interred, everyone holding his nose. The last thing I saw were her skinned feet. I turned and walked down the mountain.

Thinking: If this is the price of beauty, it's too high. I was glad she was dead.

# The
# Merchant
# of
# Shadows

ANGELA
CARTER

I killed the car. And at once provoked such sudden, resonant quiet as if, when I switched off the ignition, I myself brought into being the shimmering late-afternoon hush, the ripening sun, the very Pacific that, way below, at the foot of the cliff, shattered its foamy peripheries with the sound of a thousand distant cinema organs.

I'd never get used to California. After three years, still the enchanted visitor. However frequently I had been disappointed, I still couldn't help it, I still tingled with expectation, still always thought that something wonderful might happen.

Call me the Innocent Abroad.

All the same, you can take the boy out of London but you can't take London out of the boy. You will find my grasp of the local lingo enthusiastic but shaky. I call gas "petrol," and so on. I don't intend to go native, I'm not here for good, I'm here upon a pilgrimage. I have hied me, like a holy palmer, from the disheveled capital of a foggy, three-cornered island on the other side of the world where the light is only good for watercolorists to this place where, to wax metaphysical about it, Light was made Flesh.

I am a student of Light and Illusion. That is, of cinema. When first I clapped my eyes on that HOLLYWOOD sign back in the city now five hours hard drive distant, I thought I'd glimpsed the Holy Grail.

And now, as if it were the most everyday thing in the world, I was on my way to meet a legend. A living legend, who roosted on this lonely clifftop like a forlorn seabird.

I was parked in a graveled lot where the rough track I'd painfully negotiated since I left the minor road that brought me from the freeway terminated. I shared the parking lot with a small, red, crap-caked Toyota truck that, some time ago, had seen better days. There was straw in the back. Funny kind of transportation for a legend. But I knew she was in there, behind the gated wall in front of me, and I needed a little time alone with the ocean before the tryst began. I climbed out of the car and crept close to the edge of the precipice.

The ocean shushed and tittered like an audience when the lights dim before the main feature.

The first time I saw the Pacific, I'd had a vision of sea gods, but not the ones *I* knew, oh no. Not even Botticelli's prime 36B-cup blonde ever came in on *this* surf. My entire European mythology capsized under the crash of waves Britannia never ruled and then I knew that the denizens of these deeps are *sui generis* and belong to no mythology but their weird own. They have the strangest eyes, lenses on stalks that go flicker, flicker, and give you the truth twenty-four times a second. Their torsos luminesce in every shade of technicolor but have no depth, no substance, no dimensionality. Beings from a wholly strange pantheon. Beautiful—but alien.

Aliens were somewhat on my mind, however, perhaps because I was somewhat alienated myself, in LA, but also due to the obsession of my roommate. While I researched my thesis, I was rooming back there in the city in an apartment over a New Age bookshop-cum–health-food restaurant with a science fiction freak I'd met at a much earlier stage of studenthood during the chance intimacy of the mutual runs in Barcelona. Now he and I subsisted on brown rice courtesy of the Japanese waitress from downstairs, with whom we were both on, ahem, intimate terms, and he was always talking about aliens. He thought most of the people you met on the streets were aliens cunningly simulating human beings. He thought the Venusians were behind it.

He said he had tested Hiroko's reality quotient sufficiently and *she* was clear but I guessed from his look he wasn't too sure about me. That shared diarrhea in the Plaza Real was proving a shaky bond. I stayed out of the place as much as possible. I kept my head down at school all day and tried to manifest humanity as well as I knew how whenever I came home for a snack, a shower, and, if I got the chance, one of Hiroko's courteous if curiously impersonal embraces. Now my host showed signs of getting into leather. Would it soon be time to move?

It must be the light that sends them crazy, that white light now refracting from the sibilant Pacific, the precious light that, when it is distilled, becomes the movies. *Ars Magna Lucis et Umbrae*, the Great Art of Light and Shade, as Athanias Kircher put it, he who tinkered with magic lanterns four centuries ago in the gothic north.

And from that gothic north had come the object of the quest that brought me to this luminous hilltop—a long-dead Teutonic illusionist who'd played with light and shade as well as any. You know him as Hank Mann, that "dark genius of the screen," the director with "the occult touch," that neglected giant, etc etc etc.

But stay, you may ask, how can a dead man, no matter how occult his touch, be the object of a quest?

Aha! In that clifftop house he'd left the woman part of whose legend was, she was his widow.

He had been her ultimate husband. First (silent movies) she'd hitched up with an acrobatic cowboy and, when a pinto threw him, she'd joined a soi-disant Viennese tenor for a season of kitschissimo musicals during early sound. Hank Mann turned her into an icon after he rescued her off a cardboard crag where he'd come upon her, yodeling. When Mann passed on, she shut up marital shop entirely, and her screen presence acquired the frozen majesty of one appreciating, if somewhat belatedly, the joys of abstinence. She never did another on-screen love scene, either.

If you are a true buff, you know that he was born Heinrich

von Mannheim. One or two titles in two or three catalogues survive from his early days at UFA, plus a handful of scratched, faded stills.

My correspondence with his relict, conducted through somebody who pp'd for her in an illegible scrawl, finally produced this invitation. I'd been half-stunned with joy. I was, you understand, writing my thesis about Mannheim. He had become my pet, my hobby, my obsession.

But you must understand that I was prevaricating out of pure nerves. For she was far, far more than a Hollywood widow; she was the Star of Stars, no less, the greatest of them all . . . dubbed by *Time* magazine the "Spirit of the Cinema" when, on her eightieth birthday, she graced its cover for the seventh time, with a smile like open day in a porcelain factory and a white lace mantilla on the curls that time had bleached with its inexorable peroxide. And had she not invited little me, me! to call for a chat, a drink, at this ambiguous hour, martini time, the blue hour, when you fold up the day and put it away and shake out the exciting night?

Only surely she was well past the expectation of exciting times. She had become what Hiroko's people call a "living national treasure." Decade after ageless decade, movie after movie, "the greatest star in heaven." That was the promo. She'd no especial magic, either. She was no Gish, nor Brooks, nor Dietrich, nor Garbo, who all share the same gift, the ability to reveal otherness. She *did* have a certain touch-me-not thing that made her a natural for *film noir* in the forties. Otherwise, she possessed only the extraordinary durability of her presence, as if continually incarnated afresh with the passage of time due to some occult operation of the Great Art of Light and Shade.

One odd thing. As Svengali, Hank Mann had achieved a posthumous success. Although it was he who had brushed her with stardust (she'd been a mere "leading player" up till then), her career acquired that touch of the fabulous only after he adjourned to the great cutting room in the sky.

There was a scent of jasmine blowing over the wall from an invisible garden. I deeply ingested breath. I checked out my briefcase: notebook, recorder, tapes. I checked that the recorder contained tape. I was nervous as hell. And then there was nothing for it but, briefcase in hand, to summon the guts to stride up to her gate.

It was an iron gate with a sheet of zinc behind the wrought squiggles so you couldn't see through and, when I reached up to ring the bell, this gate creaked open of its own accord to let me in and then swung to behind me with a disconcerting, definitive clang. So there I was.

A plane broke the darkening dish of sky that sealed up again behind it. Inside the garden, it was very quiet. Nobody came to meet me.

A flight of rough-cut stone steps led up to a pool surrounded by clumps of sweet-smelling weeds. I recognized lavender. A tree or two dropped late summer leaves on scummy water and, when I saw that pool, I couldn't help it, I started to shiver, I'll tell you why in a minute. That untended pool, in which a pair of dark glasses with one cracked lens rested on an emerald carpet of algae, along with an empty gin bottle.

On the terrace, a couple of rusty, white-enameled chairs, a lopsided table. Then, fringed by a clump of cryptomeria, the house von Mannheim caused to be erected for his bride.

That house made the Bauhaus look baroque. An austere cube of pure glass, it exhibited the geometry of transparency at its most severe. Yet, just at that moment, it took all the red light of the setting sun into itself and flashed like a ruby slipper. I knew the wall of the vast glittering lounge gaped open to admit me, and only me, but I thought, well, if nobody has any objections, I'll just stick around on the terrace for a while, keep well away from that glass box that looks like nothing so much as the coffin for a classical modernist Snow White, let the lady come out to me.

No sound but the deep, distant bass of the sea; a gull or two; pines, hushing one another.

So I waited. And waited. And I found myself wondering just what it was the scent of jasmine reminded me of, in order to take my mind off what I knew damn well the swimming pool reminded me of—*Sunset Boulevard,* of course. And I knew damn well, of course I knew, that this was indeed the very pool in which my man Hank Mann succumbed back in 1940, so very long ago, when not even I, nor my blessed mother, yet, was around to so much as piss upon the floor.

I waited until I found myself growing impatient. How does one invoke the Spirit of Cinema? Burn a little offering of popcorn and old fan magazines? Offer a libation of Lysol mixed with grape soda?

I found myself vengefully asserting that I knew one or two things about her old man that perhaps she never knew herself. For example, his grandmother's maiden name (Ernst). I knew he entered UFA and swept the cutting-room floor. I talked to the son he left behind in Germany shortly after conceiving him. Nice old buffer, early sixties, retired bank clerk, prisoner of war in Norfolk, England, 1942–1946, perfect English, never so much as met his father, no bitterness. Brought up exclusively by the first Frau von Mannheim, actress. He showed me a still. Kohled eyes, expressionist cheekbones, star of Mannheim's UFA one-reeler of *The Fall of the House of Usher,* now lost. Frau von Mannheim, victim of the Dresden fire raid. H'm. Her son expressed no bitterness at that, either, and I felt ashamed until he told me she'd ended up the official mistress of a fairly nasty Nazi. Then I felt better.

I'd actually got to meet the second Mrs. Mann, now a retired office cleaner and full-time lush in downtown LA. Once a starlet; lack of exposure terminated her career. Once a call girl. Age terminated her career. The years had dealt hardly with her. Vaguely, she recalled him, a man she once married. She'd had a hangover, he moved into her apartment. She'd still had a hangover. Then he moved out. *God,* she'd had a hangover. They divorced and she married somebody else, whose name escaped her. She accepted ten bucks off me with the negligent grace of habitual custom. I couldn't think why he'd married her and she couldn't remember.

Anyway, after I'd donated ten bucks and packed up my tape recorder, she, as if now I'd paid she felt she owed, started to rummage around amongst the cardboard boxes—shoe boxes, wine crates—with which her one-room competency was mostly furnished. Things tipped and slithered everywhere, satin dancing slippers, old hats, artificial flowers; spilled face powder rose up in clouds and out of the clouds, she, wheezing with triumph, emerged with a photograph.

Nothing so quaint as out-of-date porn. It was an artfully posed spanking pic. I knew him at once, with his odd, soft, pale, malleable face, the blond, slicked-down hair, the mustache, in spite of the gym slip, suspenders, and black silk stockings; he sprawled athwart the knee of the second Mrs. Mann, who sported a long-line leather bra and splendid boots. Hand raised ready to smack his exposed botty, she turned upon the camera a toothy smile. She'd been quite pretty, in a spit-curled way. She said I could have the snap for a couple of hundred dollars but I was on a tight budget and thought it wouldn't add much to the history of film.

Foresightfully, von Mannheim had left Germany in good time, but he started over in Hollywood at the bottom (forgive the double entendre). His ascent, however, was brisk. Assistant art director, assistant director, director.

The masterpiece of Mann's Hollywood period is, of course,

*Paracelsus* (1937), with Charles Laughton. Laughton's great bulk swims into pools of scalding light out of greater or lesser shoals of darkness like a vast monster of the deep, a great, black whale. The movie haunts you like a bad dream. Mann did not try to give you a sense of the past; instead, *Paracelsus* looks as if it had been made in the middle ages—the gargoyle faces, bodies warped with ague, gaunt with famine, a claustrophobic sense of a limited world, of chronic, cramped unfreedom.

The Spirit of Cinema cameos in *Paracelsus* as the Gnostic goddess of wisdom, Sophia, in a kind of Rosicrucian sabbat scene. They were married, by then. Mann wanted his new bride nude for this sabbat, which caused a stir at the time and eventually he was forced to shoot only her disembodied face, floating above suggestive shadow. Suggestive, indeed; from his piece of sleight of hand sprang two myths, one easily discredited by aficionados of the rest of her *oeuvre,* that she had the biggest knockers in the business, the other, less easily dismissed, that she was thickly covered with body hair from the sternum to the knee. Even Mann's ex-assistant director believed the latter. "Furry as a spider," he characterized her. "And just as damn lethal." I'd smuggled a half pint of Jack Daniel's into his geriatric ward; he waxed virulent, he warned me to take a snakebite kit to the interview.

*Paracelsus* was, needless to say, one of the greatest box-office disasters in the history of the movies. Plans were shelved for his long-dreamed-of *Faust,* with the Spirit either as Gretchen or as Mephistopheles, or as Gretchen doubling *with* Mephistopheles, depending on what he said in different interviews. Mann was forced to perpetrate a hack job, a wallowing melo with the Spirit as twins, a good girl in a blond wig and a bad girl in a black one, from which his career never recovered and her own survival was truly miraculous.

Shortly after this notorious stinker was released to universal jeers, he did the *A Star Is Born* bit, although he walked, not into the sea, but into the very swimming pool, that one over there, in which his relict now disposes of her glassware.

As for the Spirit, she found a new director, was rumored to have undergone a little, a very little plastic surgery, and, the next year, won her first Oscar. From that time on, she was unstoppable, though she always carried her tragedy with her, like a permanent widow's veil, giving her the spooky allure of a born-again *princesse lointaine.*

Who liked to keep her guests waiting.

In my nervous ennui, I cast my eyes round and round the terrace until I came upon something passing strange in the moist earth of a flower bed.

Moist, therefore freshly watered, though not by whatever it was had left such amazing spoor behind it. No big-game hunter, I, but I could have sworn that, impressed on the soil, as if in fresh concrete outside Grauman's Chinese Theatre, was the print, unless the tiger lilies left it, of a large, clawed paw.

Did you know a lion's mane grows gray with age? I didn't. But the geriatric feline that now emerged from a clump of something odorous beneath the cryptomeria had snow all over his hairy eaves. He appeared as taken aback to see me as I was to bump into him. Our eyes locked. Face like a boxer with a broken nose. Then he tilted his enormous head to one side, opened his mouth—God, his breath was foul—and roared like the last movement of Beethoven's Ninth. With a modest blow of a single paw, he could have batted me arse over tip off the cliff halfway to Hawaii. I wouldn't say it was much comfort to see he'd had his teeth pulled out.

"Aw, come on, Pussy, he don't want to be gummed to death," said a cracked, harsh, aged, only residually female voice. "Go fetch Mama, now, there's a good boy."

The lion grumbled a little in his throat but trotted off into the house with the most touching obedience and I took breath, again—I noticed I'd somehow managed not to for some little time—and sank into one of the white metal terrace chairs. My poor heart was going pit-a-pat, I can tell you, but the personage who had at last appeared from somewhere in the darkening compound neither apologized for nor expressed concern about my nasty shock. She stood there, arms akimbo, surveying me with a satirical, piercing, blue eye.

Except for the jarring circumstance that in one hand she held a stainless-steel, many-branched candlestick of awesomely chaste design, she looked like a superannuated lumberjack: plaid shirt, blue jeans, workboots, butch leather belt with a giant silver skull and crossbones for a buckle, coarse, cropped, gray hair escaping from a red bandana tied Indian-style around her head. Her skin was wrinkled in pinpricks like the surface of Parmesan cheese and a putty gray in color.

"You the one that's come about the thesis?" she queried. Her diction was pure hillbilly.

I burbled in the affirmative.

"He's come about the thesis," she repeated to herself sardonically and discomforted me still further by again cackling to herself.

But now an ear-splitting roar announced action was about to commence. This Ma, or Pa, Kettle person set down her candlestick on the terrace table, briskly struck a match on the seat of her pants, and applied the flame to the wicks, dissipating the gathering twilight as She rolled out the door. Rolled. She sat in a chrome and ivory leather wheelchair as if upon a portable throne. Her right hand rested negligently on the lion's mane. She was a sight to see.

How long had she spent dressing up for the interview? Hours. Days. Weeks. She had on a white satin, bias-cut, lace-trimmed negligee circa 1935, her skin had that sugar almond,

one hundred percent Max Factor look, and she wore what I
assumed was a wig due to the unnatural precision of the snowy
curls. Only she'd gone too far with the wig, it gave her a
Medusa look. Her mouth looked funny because her lips had
disappeared with age so all that was left was a painted-in red
trapezoid.

But she didn't look her age, at all, at all—oh, no; she looked
a good ten or fifteen years younger, though I doubt the vision
of a sexy septuagenarian was the one for which she'd striven
as she decked herself out. Impressive, though. Impressive as
hell.

And you knew at once this was the face that launched a
thousand ships. Not because anything lovely was still smoldering away in those old bones; she'd, as it were, transcended
beauty. But something in the way she held her head, some
imperious arrogance, demanded that you look at her and keep
on looking.

At once I went into automatic, I assumed the stance of
gigolo. I picked up her hand, kissed it, said: *"Enchanté,"*
bowed. Had I not been wearing sneakers, I'd have clicked my
heels. The Spirit appeared pleased but not surprised by this but
she couldn't smile for fear of cracking her makeup. She whispered me a throaty greeting, eyeing me in a very peculiar way,
a way that made the look in the lion's eye seem positively
vegetarian.

It freaked me. She freaked me. It was her *star quality.* So
*that's* what they mean! I thought. I'd never before, nor am I
likely to again, encountered such psychic force as streamed out
of that frail little old lady in her antique lingerie and her
wheelchair. And, yes, there was something undeniably erotic
about it, although she was old as the hills; it was as though she
got the most extraordinary sexual charge from being looked at
and this charge bounced back on the looker, as though some

mechanism inside herself converted your regard into sexual energy. I wondered, not quite terrified, if I was for it, know what I mean.

And all the time I kept thinking, it kept running through my head: "The phantom is up from the cellars again!"

Night certainly brought out the scent of jasmine.

Her faded voice meant you had to crouch to hear her, so her cachou-flavored breath stung your cheek, and you could tell she loved to make you crouch.

"My sister," she husked, gesturing toward the lumberjack lady who was watching this performance of domination and submission with her thumbs stuck in her belt and an expression of unrelieved cynicism on her face. Her sister. God.

The lion rubbed its head against my leg, making me jump, and she pummeled its graying mane.

"And this—oh! you'll have seen him a thousand times; more exposure than any of us. Allow me to introduce Leo, formerly of MGM."

The old beast cocked its head from side to side and roared again, in unmistakable fashion, as if to identify itself. Mickey Mouse does her chauffeuring. Every morning, she takes a ride on Trigger.

"*Ars gratia artis,*" she reminded me, as if guessing my thoughts. "Where could he go, poor creature, when they retired him? Nobody would touch a fallen star. So he came right here, to live with mama, didn't you darling."

"Drinkies!" announced Sister, magnificently clattering a welcome, bottle-laden trolley.

After the third poolside martini, which was gin at which a lemon briefly sneered, I judged it high time to broach the subject of Hank Mann. It was pitch dark by then, a few stars burning, night sounds, sea sounds, the creak of those metal chairs that seemed to have been designed, probably on purpose, by the butch sister, to break your balls. But it was difficult to get a word in. The Spirit was briskly checking out my knowledge of screen history.

"No, the art director certainly was *not* Ben Carré, how absurd to think that! . . . My goodness me, young man, Wallace Reid was dead and buried by then, and good riddance to bad rubbish. . . . Edith Head? Edith Head design Nancy Carroll's patent-leather evening dress? Who put that into your noddle?"

Now and then the lion sandpapered the back of my hand with its tongue, as if to show sympathy. The butch sister put away gin by the tumblerful, two to my one, and creaked resonantly from time to time, like an old door.

"No, no, no, young man! Laughton certainly was *not* addicted to self-abuse!"

And out of the dark it came to me that the dreamy perfume of jasmine issued from no flowering shrub but, instead, right out of the opening sequence of *Double Indemnity,* do you remember? And I suffered a ghastly sense of incipient humiliation, of impending erotic doom, so that I shivered, and Sister, alert and either comforting or complicitous, sloshed another half pint of gin into my glass.

Then Sister belched and announced: "Gonna take a leak."

Evidently equipped with night vision, she rolled off into the gloaming from whence, after a pause, came the tinkle of running water. She'd gone back to Nature as far as toilet training was concerned, cut out the frills and so on. The raunchy sound of Sister making pipi brought me down to earth again. I clutched my tumbler, for the sake of holding something solid.

"About thish time," I said, "you met Hank Mann."

Night and candlelight turned the red mouth black, but her satin dress shone like water with plankton in it.

"Heinrich," she corrected with a click of orthodontics; and then, or so it seemed, fell directly into a trance for, all at once, she fixed her gaze on the middle distance and said no more.

I thankfully took advantage of her lapse of attention to pour my gin down the side of my chair, trusting that by the morrow it would be indistinguishable from lion piss. Sister, clanking her death's-head belt buckle as she readjusted her clothing, came back to us and juggled ice and lemon slices as if nothing untoward was taking place. Then, in a perfectly normal, even conversational tone, the Spirit said: "White kisses, red kisses. And coke in a golden casket on top of the baby grand. Those were the days."

Sister t'sked, possibly with irritation.

"Reckon you've had a skinful," said Sister. "Reckon you deserve a stiff whupping."

That roused the Spirit somewhat, who chuckled and lunged at the gin which, fortunately, stood within her reach. She poured a fresh drink down the hatch in a matter of seconds, then made a vague gesture with her left hand, inadvertently biffing the lion in the ear. The lion had dozed off and grumbled like an empty stomach to have his peace disturbed.

"They wore away her face by looking at it too much. So we made her a new one."

"Hee haw, hee haw," said Sister. She was not braying but laughing.

The Spirit propped herself on the arm of her wheelchair and pierced me with a look. Something told me we had gone over some kind of edge. Nancy Carroll's evening dress, indeed. Enough of that nonsense. Now we were on a different plane.

"I used to think of prayer wheels," she informed me. "Night after night, prayer wheels ceaselessly turning in the darkened cathedrals, those domed and gilded palaces of the Faith, the Majestics, the Rialtos, the Alhambras, those grottoes of the miraculous in which the creatures of the dream came out to walk within the sight of men. And the wheels spun out those subtle threads of light that wove the liturgies of that reverential age, the last great age of religion. While the wonderful people out there in the dark, the congregation of the faithful, the company of the blessed, they leant forward, they aspired up-ward, they imbibed the transmission of divine light.

"Now, the priest is he who prints the anagrams of desire upon the stock; but whom does he project upon the universe? Another? Or himself?"

All this was somewhat more than I'd bargained for. I fought with the gin fumes reeling in my head, I needed all my wits about me. Moment by moment, she became more gnomic. Surreptitiously, I fumbled with my briefcase. I wanted to get that tape recorder spooling away, didn't I; why, it might have been Mannheim talking.

"Is he the one who interprets the spirit or does the spirit speak through him? Or is he only, all the time, nothing but the merchant of shadows?

"Hic," she interrupted herself.

Then Sister, whose vision was not one whit impaired by time or liquor, extended her trousered leg in one succinct and noiseless movement and kicked my briefcase clear into the pool, where it dropped with a liquid plop.

In spite of the element of poetic justice in it, that my file on von Mannheim should suffer the same fate as he, I must admit that now I fell into a great fear. I even thought they might have lured me here to murder me, this siren of the cinema and her weird acolyte. Remember, they had made me quite drunk; it was a moonless night and I was far from home; and I was trapped helpless among these beings who could exist only in California, where the light made movies and madness. And one of them had just arbitrarily drowned the poor little tools of my parasitic trade, leaving me naked and at their mercy. The kindly lion shook himself awake and licked my hand again, perhaps to reassure me, but I wasn't expecting it and jumped half out of my skin.

The Spirit broke into speech, again. "She is only in semire-tirement, you know. She still spends three hours every morn-ing looking through the scripts that almost break the mailman's back as he staggers beneath them up to her clifftop retreat. Age does not wither her; we've made quite sure of that, young man. She still irradiates the dark, for did we not discover the true secret of immortality together? How to exist almost and only in the eye of the beholder, like a genuine miracle?"

I cannot say it comforted me to theorize this lady was, to some degree, possessed, and so was perfectly within her rights to refer to herself in the third person in that ventriloqual, insubstantial voice that scratched the ear as smoke scratches the back of the throat. But by whom or what possessed? I felt very close to the perturbed spirit of Heinrich von Mannheim and the metaphysics of the Great Art of Light and Shade, I can tell you. And speaking of the author of the latter—Athanias Kircher, author, besides, of *Spectacula Paradoxa Rerum* (1624), "The Universal Theater of Paradoxes."

Her eyelids were drooping now, and as they closed her mouth fell open, but she spoke no more.

The Sister broke the silence as if it were wind.

"That's about the long and short of it, young man," she said. "Got enough for your thesis?"

She heaved herself up with a sigh so huge that, horrors! it blew out all the candles and then, worse and worse! she left me alone with the Spirit. But nothing more transpired because the Spirit seemed to have passed, if not on, then out, flat out in her wheelchair, and the inner light that brought out the shine on her satin dress was extinguished, too. I saw nothing, until a set of floods concealed in the pines around us came on and every-thing was visible as common daylight, the old lady, the drows-ing lion, the depleted drinks trolley, the slices of lemon ground into the terrace by my nervous feet, the little plants pushing up between the cracks in the paving, the black water of the swimming pool in which my over-excited, suddenly light-wounded senses hallucinated a corpse.

Which at last resolved itself, as I peered, headachy and blinking, into my own briefcase, opened, spilling out a floating debris of papers and tape boxes. I poured myself another gin, to steady my nerves. Sister appeared again, right behind my shoulder, making me jog my elbow so gin soaked my jeans. Her Indian headband had knocked rakishly askew, giving her a piratical air. In close-up, her bones, clearly visible under her ruined skin, reminded me of somebody else's, but I was too chilled, drunk, and miserable to care whose they might be. She was cackling to herself, again.

"We hates y'all with the tape recorders," she said. "Reckon us folks thinks you is dancin' on our graves."

She aimed a foot at the brake on the Spirit's wheelchair and briskly pushed it and its unconscious contents into the house. The lion woke up, yawned like the opening of the San Andreas Fault, and padded after. The sliding door slid to. After a moment, a set of concealing crimson curtains swished along the entire length of the glass wall and that was that. I half-expected to see THE END come up on the curtains but then the lights went off and I was in the dark.

Unwilling to negotiate the crazy steps down to the gate, I reached sightlessly for the gin and sucked it until I fell into a troubled slumber.

And I awoke me on the cold hillside.

Well, not exactly. I woke up to find myself tucked into the back seat of my own VW, parked on the cliff beside the Toyota truck in the gray hour before dawn, my frontal lobes and all my joints a-twang with pain. I didn't even try the gate of the house. I got out of the car, shook myself, got back in again, and headed straight home. After a while, on the perilous road to the freeway, I saw in the driving mirror a vehicle approaching me from behind. It was the red Toyota truck. Sister, of course, at the wheel.

She overtook me at illicit speed, blasting the horn joyously, waving with one hand, her face split in a toothless grin. When I saw that smile, even though the teeth were missing, I knew who she reminded me of—of a girl in a dirndl on a cardboard alp, smiling because at last she saw approaching her the man who would release her . . . If I hadn't, in the interests of scholarship, sat yawning through that dire operetta in the viewing booth, I would never have so much as guessed.

She must have hated the movies. Hated them. She had the lion in back. They looked as if they were enjoying the ride. Probably Leo had smiled for the cameras once too often, too. They parked at the place where the cliff road ended and waited there, quite courteously, until I was safely embarked among the heavy morning traffic, out of their lives.

How had they found a corpse to substitute for von Mannheim? A corpse was never the most difficult thing to come by in Southern California, I suppose. I wondered if, after all those years, they finally decided to let me in on the masquerade. And, if so, why.

Perhaps, having constructed this masterpiece of subterfuge, von Mannheim couldn't bear to die without leaving some little hint, somewhere, of how, having made her, he then *became* her, became a better she than she herself had ever been, and wanted to share with his last little acolyte, myself, the secret of his greatest hit. But, more likely, he simply couldn't resist turning himself into the Spirit one last time, couldn't let down his public . . . for they weren't to know I'd seen a picture of him in a frock, already, were they, although in those days, he still wore a mustache. And that clinched it, in my own mind, when I remembered the first Mrs. Mann's spanking picture, although this conviction did not make me any the less ill at ease.

In the health-food restaurant, Hiroko slapped the carrot juic-
er with a filthy cloth and fed me brown rice and chilled bean
curd with chopped onion and ginger on top, pursing her lips
with distaste; she herself ate only Kentucky fried chicken.
Business was slack in the midafternoon and I wanted her to
come upstairs with me for a while, to remind me there was
more to flesh than light and illusion, but she shook her head.

"Boring," she said, offensively. After a while she added,
though in no conciliatory tone, "Not just you. Everything.
California. I've seen this movie. I'm going home."

"I thought you said you felt like an enemy alien at home,
Hiroko."

She shrugged, staring through her midnight bangs at the
white sunlight outside.

"Better the devil you know," she said.

I realized I was just a wild oat to her, a footnote to her trip,
and, although she had been just the same to me, all the same
I grew glum to realize how peripheral I was, and suddenly
wanted to go home, too, and longed for rain, again, and television, that secular medium.

The
Road
to
Nadĕja

BRADFORD
MORROW

I knew I loved Lydia when I stole her ring. How she cherished that pretty object, cameo of a stag carved in bloodstone and set in gold. The stag's haunches had been rubbed to white—she always worried the face of the stone with those nervous fingers of hers. I wondered how many other fingers down the centuries had fondly touched that talisman, as I hid it in a small leather pouch and pulled the drawstrings tight. Then I thought, *Listen, ring, nobody owns you now.*

How Lydia cried! I was so harsh with the concierge at the seaside hotel, threatened to call the authorities, demanded that the maid be brought in so I could question her myself. Yes, I was enraged, my heart was burning, while next to it in the breast pocket of my jacket the ring raced and pulsed, like a little eel chasing its phosphorescent tail in the surf beyond our window.

This has always been the way with me. I take things. And the unhappiness Lydia felt for weeks after the disappearance of her ring made for some of the most exquisite joy I have ever known. She wept, she needed me; I consoled her. It was the crowning gesture of a short courtship, my theft, and was purifying for her. I never made the mistake of offering to get her another ring. That would have been crass. Nor did I patronize her with the sermon that toyed at my tongue, pled to be spoken as we made our way from Italy to Spain, the sermon about renunciation. Whenever a few days passed without any mention about the theft I did allow myself subtly to reintroduce it into our conversation. "I wonder if we ought to hire somebody to look around the hotel where you lost your ring, and see if that maid is wearing it." Lydia thought this was a wonderful idea, and when I was sure she approved, watching the light of hope come back into her pale green eyes I hesitated, brushed my hand over my lips, and shook my head no. "Why torture ourselves about it?"

. . .

Lydia's ring was not, of course, my first theft. Far from it. Indeed, the pouch in which I kept it was once the property of my grandfather. He used to keep his old fob watch in it, and though it had been the watch that motivated my theft—silver with a face white as a full moon—I liked the pouch as well. It has served as a faithful hiding place for other little objects over the years.

My activities as a taker have always been steeped in a purpose more meaningful than mere acquisition. With an honest conscience, and a mind unclouded by prejudice, you will see how much sense it has made to do what I have done. Taking from those one knows is easy, from those one adores easier yet, in many ways more desirable, more evocative. What my friends and relatives once owned, what was precious to them, was so available to me as to almost force me into possessing it. In the act of taking possession I was transformed, and whatever had been the relationship between me and that person was transformed, too. We were brought closer by the absence of their treasured object. By taking Lydia's ring or Grandfather's watch I had created an opening, a gap through which I might better have access to their hearts. What time was it? "Seven thirty-three, Grampa." It never failed to bring a gentle smile to his lips, and up into his lap I would go, and my dear grandfather would praise me, and my grandmother would say, "You're a fine young boy."

Theft, in other words, has always been for me an act of love.

When my grandfather passed on—this was how we had to put it in our family, "passed on," like there was somewhere to go—it was everything I could do to keep from giving in to the idea that the poor man ought to be buried with his fob watch. He never found it, and he'd looked long and hard. It was the first time I ever considered giving back something I had taken. Being well advanced in my ways—no one in my immediate family and few among my friends hadn't given up something to my growing hoard—it was a disconcerting moment, a moment of, as they say, "truth." I was twenty when he died, and still living in his house as I had done ever since the death of my parents.

My parents died on their way to a family gathering, all dressed up in the wreckage, Christmas presents strewn everywhere so cheery and colorful that I, who was six at the time, couldn't resist opening one of them while I waited in the backseat of the car for the men to finish sawing through the cold, crimped metal to set me free. I have an intense and perfect memory of the wrapping paper on the box. A plum-cheeked, mirthful Santa, working in his shop. A ledger that listed who was naughty and nice on his cluttered desk. The blue snow falling outside his windows, casting light through the room full of toys. Above all, that bag of his, by the door, brimming with presents he was going to give to children around the world. The good children, that is. And I was a good child, I didn't cry when they finally got me out. I hugged the baby doll I'd found in the box tight to my chest and made sure it was warm, too, when they put a blanket over my shoulders. Glass was being broken behind me, and the saw was singing again. The man wouldn't let me look.

I had moved in with my grandparents after the accident, and they were good to me. My grandfather continued to work past the age when most men retire, to help support me and send me through school; to make sure I was dressed as well as anyone and could partake of those activities in which boys, as they got older, liked to involve themselves. I saw movies, I owned a rifle and went out into the woods with friends and shot small game—squirrels, snapping turtles, snakes. After I took my grandfather's watch it was I, as I've said, who would tell him what time it was. My grandmother was always after him to buy another, but he refused because he kept thinking he had mislaid it somewhere in the house. "It'll turn up," he said. As right as my grandfather was about so many things in life, he was not right about that.

I announced one morning, having had some of the brandy Grandmother kept in a breakfront for special occasions, my intentions to leave school, and to leave the country. I wanted to wander. I knew that in March of the next year I would have access to my inheritance. I packed my belongings, withdrew what savings I had in the bank, and kissed my grandmother goodbye. Grandfather's fob watch came with me.

Lydia and I met in Rimini, on an Adriatic summer afternoon— but I'd been overcome with an odd expectancy, as I walked through Paris earlier in the spring, that someone important was near me. I remember thinking this, when the police swept through the crowd of May Day rioters, clubs and shields above and before them. As I was running toward the cathedral, carried by the anger and panic of the mob, I swear I saw Lydia as someone caught her by the shoulder and pulled her down right in front of me. I tripped over her and her assailant.

She has since said that nothing of the sort happened to her. Still, I wonder; when I later showed Lydia the scarf I'd snatched from this woman's neck during the melee—not, of course, revealing how I'd come to possess it—Lydia said, "That's strange." Turns out it was identical to a scarf she once owned, this scarf I'd fondled in the darkness of Notre Dame, where so many of us lingered until the fires outside were extinguished and the island was restored to calm.

Now, the Tempio Malatestiano—without a doubt the greatest work of architecture to be found in the seaside town of

Rimini—is cloaked in marble stolen from another cathedral on the same coast. Sigismondo Malatesta's masons, in need of materials to sheath the brick facades, and having no access to Tuscan quarries, sailed up the coast to the Byzantine port of Classe where they raided the Sant'Apollinaire for all its clean exterior stone. Half a millennium later, the Sant'Apollinaire still stands naked on the sand flats north of Ravenna, and the Tempio still wears its stolen emperor's clothes. Quiet sarcophagi, circled by harmless, lazy bees, line the temple's length outside, sheltered from the rain under its crumbling eaves.

She told me the story about the building's maker, did Lydia, standing under those very eaves. To her it was a parable of "greed and madness." It was "a rape still unavenged." I suggested that, to me, this was an appropriation, an example of Renaissance expediency in its purest form, and was not surprised when she stared at me with one of those quizzical looks I adored, and asked what was I talking about?

Was my ensuing silence too a kind of expediency? Or was I just being lazy like those black and yellow bees that one by one alighted to sleep on the warm marble lids of those ships of death that flanked us where we conversed? What was I to say when, goaded by this silence, she launched into a diatribe about the evil souls of thieves? "I think we should bring back the punishments they used to have for burglars, where they cut off the hands of men who steal." Who was I to disagree?

We were married in March the next year. A day so overcast that a sky spangled with a hundred suns could not have pierced the green and black clouds that stretched out across the earth. (Green for her eyes, black for mine?) March had been the month I was born, March will be the month I'll die. Aptly named, old March, the month of deliberate movement, marching into whatever might be ahead.

Our wedding night was drunken, affectionate. The wind

that wrapped its damp arms around the room, once more in Rimini, in the very hotel we'd stayed at before, didn't dampen our spirits. It only invited us to wrap ourselves tighter in one another's arms, and we obliged, and I took nothing from Lydia that night but her intimacy.

The things I have stolen over the course of the years have always been, of necessity as well as of preference, small in size. Because I've hoarded the things I've taken, it has been practical that they not occupy much space. Until recently, my life was not burdened by their secret presence in it. I have never so much as kept them under lock and key. My custodianship would, I knew, inevitably come to an end sometime. I'm not so sober a man that the theft of my cache would fail to strike an ironic note. The thief, robbed; who wouldn't find comic justice in it? I mean to say, I am aware of the tenuousness of ownership—I know we cannot ultimately *own*. We're just caretakers in this life, isn't that the euphemism?—death being the only real landlord, the real holder of the *real* estate. If someone took my talismans away from me, I had always thought until recently, "So be it"; the purpose, as I have said, was satisfied in their original removal.

Why, then, did I decide to do what I have done tonight? My answer: I was following my heart. In my experience, instructions from the heart are far more explicit and far less easy to follow than instructions from the intellect. The intellect can tell us what we ought to do; can speak to us, with our own sham voice, can reason and cajole. The heart doesn't bother with this nonsense. In that sense it collaborates with Death, where language stops cold—where the words "no more" or "not to be" or even "terror" are changed into sound waves that weave forever outward, unheard by ears, not responded to by argumentative voices.

• • •

Though sentimental, perhaps, Lydia was no fool. After the small extravagance of an overseas honeymoon, we settled where I'd grown up. I bought from my aging grandmother her house and furniture and established her in a comfortable room off the kitchen on the first floor. And while I would have been content to live frugally, and idly, on the interest earned by the balance of what my parents had left me, Lydia had grander plans. How animated she was as she described to me and Grandmother her dream of raising a family. Side by side on the front-room couch we two sat as Lydia paced the hook rug, and I would wince whenever my grandmother rolled her silvery balding head forward and clicked her tongue with approval. What all this meant, of course, was that I was sent out to work.

I cannot say I initially resented the responsibilities I'd begun to incur on behalf of Lydia's dream. No; for a while I was content with my decision to be married, and was happy enough to have come back home after those years of wandering. What did worry me was that the novelty of marriage and the imperatives of responsibility began to pervert my own routine. Miss it as I might, it seemed my resolve to steal abated, my deep need—a need we all share, I might add—to be in touch at a spiritual level with our fellowman was thwarted. Days, months, seasons passed without my making a single addition to the hoard, and I believe this began to take its toll on me who realized he had discovered, in the full-blooded impudence of youth, the perfect way to people's hearts. Denied, I felt myself slowly atrophy into an indifferent worker, a resentful spouse, a distant grandson. However stifled I felt, however lethargic, I was not so blind as to remain unaware that my family and friends were treating me differently than they once had. I fought it, this feeling of isolation, and somewhat in desperation made the petty theft of a coffee mug from a fellow employee at the office. Waste of time, she merely brought in another.

In the meantime, Lydia and I failed at having children, and decided to adopt. Daniel was the boy's name. I would never have named him Daniel, for isn't a Daniel one who was meant to be fed to lions? But the choice was not mine.

Daniel became Lydia's universe. His needs were constant stars, his fears comets, and everything Lydia did was drawn now into his orbit. Daniel this, Daniel that, Daniel the other thing. He was a black hole, was Daniel.

Though I loved him and was a good father, my mind strayed. Lydia didn't notice what was happening; there was no way for her to continue to be aware of me in the same way she had been before. I withdrew into a helpless anger: since I hadn't given her a wedding ring—no ring could match that stag—I had no second chance to win my way back into her heart with a second disappearance.

She's been gone a long time now. So has Danny.

I made an experiment. It occurred to me to take things from people I didn't like. A neighbor down the road, a man toward whom I had always felt an unfounded aversion, relinquished to me (on an impulse one night when he was out of town) a brass mantel clock that I knew was a family heirloom. For good measure I selected a velvet blouse with a brilliant row of white buttons from his wife's closet, a blouse I'd seen her wear on special occasions. When I got these home—long after Grandmother had gone to bed—and set them out on the table to enjoy, I realized what folly the exercise had been. I felt nothing. The clock was ugly. I took the blouse to my face, breathed in, and remembered how ravishing my neighbor's wife looked when she wore it. I smelled the trace of perfume, and of perspiration. Exquisite, but none of the pleasure I sought was to be had from it. With disdain I added the objects to the hoard, unfulfilled, but a man who knew himself somewhat better than before.

The hoard. I took to visiting it more often than I had in the past. It was like a photograph album, but better, in that I was free to conjure the pictures as I pleased.

A caracul cap, this was an uncle's. I liked him all right. A pencil sketch of an orchid. A fountain pen, communication. A feather, flight. The carving of a seal, in soapstone, a memento from a friend's journey to Alaska. A rabbit's foot; a Tarot deck. A cigar box tied with string. A shell, a stone, a tooth. A blue ribbon, earned by a friend from grade school, whose face I can picture but whose name I've forgotten, a boy who won the race, but lost to my need to possess the reward of the occasion. A tattered comic book. A mandolin, a hand-blown vase with clovers etched around the rim. A doll that wets when tapped on her back and tilted in a certain way—the first of my possessions. My stuff, my hoard, my booty, my precious trash. I pondered what would it have been like to add to it a clump of sod, from my father's grave. A clump of dirt festering with weeds, their hopeful, stupid shoots nosing toward the sky, their tiny green buds opening like prayerful hands, the fools!

One doesn't give in to such impulses as mine without making, somewhere down the line, a sacrifice.

It is March again. Years later, but not enough to change my way of thinking. There may never be enough Marches to bring me to a change. Sure, I know about remission. I also know about relapse. Remission is a place you visit; relapse is home.

I'd grown interminably tired. Tired of myself, tired of my fond obsession. Once ascetic, almost to a fault, I'd begun to drink. In the late afternoons at first, after work (yes, I kept my

job, just to sustain the human contact) I became a sullen anonymity whose fingers were reflected in the shiny surface of the
bar as they reached for their solace. Later, I would start in the
mornings before work; then continue quietly, furtively,
through the course of the day. If my need to steal, when
satisfied, had often in the past given rise to moments of unspeakable ecstasy, the exhaustion that crept over me, coupled
with a steady depression, brought me out to the field last night.

I had to do something. I was stalled. I found myself unable
so much as to *think* of acquisition—my poor dead hobby—let
alone carry out some meaningful theft. No, that life was over,
gone, and in its place I'd erected a monumental Nothing in
honor of its faded glories. My spirit had grown more numb
than the stolen marble on Malatesta's temple, my flesh more
indolent than the sleepy bees that lolled on its tombs.

What happened was I became paranoid about the hoard.
This was something new. What if, say, when my guard was
down, I let some stranger in on my secret? Not given to
confession I nevertheless became certain I'd slip up at some
moment, if I kept going on like this. And since I saw no
prospect of changing, I realized there was only one way to
protect my past from my future.

The eye steady, the will steady. The rest of last year's cotton
stalks standing dead and needing to be mowed before planting
time. I had driven several hours north to get there. No map,
my headlights directed me. It had begun to rain, and large
mothlike configurations of fog burst into view. All of it, the
whole hoard, I had gathered into my duffel to bring with me,
and when I pulled it out of the trunk the weight of the bundle
surprised me—surely it had grown. I couldn't help but think,
if someone were to see me dragging this impossible burden
deep in the night, how much I must have looked like a murderer intent on burying his victim. Nothing so predictable as

a corpse would they have found if they—phantom crowd of vigilantes, my victims lighting their way with torches—stopped me from making this simple act of relinquishment.

New moon. Mild after a warm winter. The night was black. The field was black. My hands were black. Or maybe it was that my hands had become a part of the field, this field I had visited once before, and that was why I couldn't see them. Who would have guessed they'd be so capable of doing what they did? Who'd have thought it could be so easy to take a lifetime's obsession and bury it, like you might some pumpkin seed, or a casket. Lydia's voice, it was as if I could hear it again, impassioned by the thought of a robber being punished by giving to society his sinning hands: "Go ahead," she said, "at least give us that much back. And stop acting like it's such a big deal." How did she know where I was, I thought, as I looked up into the watery sky. Ghosts, I guess, know these things.

The realms of strife, so often foggy, can sometimes become so crystal clear. I remembered a cousin, the best hunter of us all back when we were boys—I remembered his Bowie knife, and the good times we had after I'd removed it from his pack. Always happy to loan him mine, he and I were boon companions for years. I groped around and found it deep in the duffel, and pulled it out of its sheath. I am sure it would have glinted had there been any light. I ran my finger along its blade, and yes it seemed still to be sharp. I produced a bead of blood, just to see.

"Go ahead," that voice again proposed. "You don't deserve those hands." Lydia had been critical of me sometimes in the past, but never cruel. When I put the knife away, she said, and these were her last words: "You disgust me." Wish though I might to let my hands live in the field with the rest of my harvest, I knew I had never done anything to make myself worthy of such a sacrifice. Lydia, rinsed with rain, melted into a cotton-stalk soldier.

Who knows where to stop? When is not in question; when happens to you, where remains your choice.

There wasn't a house in sight, and the road back was untraveled. Without remorse or farewell, I left the shallow grave, the muddy field, and the silent stretch of road behind. I was tired still, more tired than before. If I'd known my nighttime act, my slap in the face of whenness, would have succeeded in exhausting me even more than I'd been before, I wonder whether I would have gone to all the trouble. My resolution to rid myself of the hoard had come from the simple notion that by having done with the dregs of a bad idea I might be freed to find my way—not forward, necessarily, but somewhere exhaustion could not flourish.

And yet here I was, in the company of these people. Brandy for old time's sake. A game of cards in a corner, laughter behind a curtain. Several men in uniforms, furloughed perhaps. Others at tables, smoking and talking the night away. It was the woman tending bar who attracted my attention, however, young with skin the color of clean muslin, and deep black hair—like mine—and eyes—my own. More unlike Lydia she couldn't have been, except that she too had an uncommon name.

Naděja. It was Czech, a form of Nadja, or Nadia, she told me—almost rhymed with Lydia. She didn't seem to favor any one person in the place, and yet she had a way of making everyone feel special. This I admired. A real gift, to empathize like that. I realized my hands were dirty, and washed them, and when I returned, I asked her what Naděja meant, and she said that the Russian form was Nadezhda, from the word meaning hope, "and hope is a virtue," she added, with a tender note of cynicism.

I stayed until everyone else had left. I had no idea what time it was, nor even where I was, or where I would pass the night. All I knew was that when Nadĕja removed her bracelet to wash the glasses, continuing to talk about where she grew up, her sisters and brothers, and the prominent events in her life, yes, the future once more became bright. As I listened to Nadĕja, the room—so simple, so homey—began to teem anew with life, and already I could feel the delicate warmth of her dearest treasure, brave against my palm.

For
Dear
Life

RUTH
RENDELL

A great many things that other people did all the time she had never done. These were the ordinary things from which she had been protected by her money and her ill-health. She had never used an iron or threaded a needle, been on a bus or cooked a meal for other people, earned money, got up early because she had to, waited to see the doctor or stood in a queue.

Her great-grandmother had never dressed herself without the help of a lady's maid, but times had changed since then.

Places had not changed much and the family still lived at Temple Stephen in Derbyshire. They still spent Christmas quietly and had a big house party for the New Year. They played games as they always had, Consequences and Kim's Game and a game her brother had invented called Kissing the Gunner's Daughter. Sometimes they took bets on the heights or depths of things and the location of things and the number of things.

One of the guests asked the others to bet on how many metro systems there were in the world. They asked him if he knew the answer, for if he did not how would they ever find out? He said of course he did, he would not have suggested it otherwise.

She said, "What's a metro system?"

"An underground railway. A tube."

"Well, how many are there?"

"That's what I'm asking. You name the number of your choice and put ten pounds in the kitty."

"In the *world?*" she said.

"In the world."

She had no idea. She said twenty, thinking that must be far too many. Someone said sixty, someone else said twelve. The man who had proposed the wager was smiling and seeing his smile, their sister said a hundred, her brother-in-law ninety.

He won and got the kitty. The answer was eighty-nine.

"One for every year of the century," someone said, as if it was appropriate.

"I've never been in the tube," she said.

At first no one believed her. She was twenty-five and she had never been in the tube. It was quite true. She mostly lived in the country and she was rich. Also she was not strong, there was a little something wrong with her heart, a murmur, a valve that functioned less than perfectly. The older people called her "delicate." She had been told that having children might present problems, but nothing that could not be managed. She might want children one day but not yet.

It made her lazy, it made her rather self-indulgent. For instance, she never felt guilty about lying down after lunch. She liked having people about to look after her. It had never occurred to her to get any sort of job.

Since she was seventeen she had had her own car and when she came to London, a fleet of private hire cars at her disposal, not to mention the taxis that swept round the Mayfair corners. She had been married and divorced, had had fifteen lovers, give or take a little, had been to the United States seventeen times, to Africa twice, explored from a car or at a leisurely pace the capitals of Europe, twice circled the world, done the "sophisticated" things but left undone so many ordinary things. And she had never been in the London Underground.

She had no intention of going into it. You heard such stories! Rapes, assaults, gangs, fires, trains halted through suicides, the rush hour.

Her brother, who was also her twin, said when they were back in London, "I shouldn't bother. Who cares whether you have or not? I've never been in St. Paul's Cathedral. I hate it, I'd like to raze it to the ground."

"What, St. Paul's?"

"The tube. I'd like to raze it and plow over the site like the Romans did with Carthage."

She laughed. "You can't raze something that's already underground."

"It runs under my flat. I can't stand it, I hear it in the early hours."

"Move, then," she said idly. "Why don't you move?"

She rested after lunch and then a taxi took her up to Hampstead and a shop that sold a certain kind of ethnic clothes not available elsewhere. The shop was round the corner in Back Lane. She bought a dress made for a Peruvian bride, high-necked, tight-waisted, with big sleeves and a big floor-length skirt, white as a white rose, with white satin ribbons and white lace. They said they would send it, they got so far as taking her address, but she changed her mind, she wanted to wear it that night.

There was no shortage of taxis going down Heath Street and Fitzjohn's Avenue. She let them pass, came to Hampstead tube station and thought what an adventure it would be to go home in a train. Buying the dress had altered her mind. She was possessed by a reckless excitement.

This she knew to have its pathetic side. What would they say to her if they knew, these people who were obliged to use this means of transport day in, day out? The thought of their contempt, their disgust and envy, drove her in.

Some minutes were occupied in the buying of a ticket. She did not know what to ask for at the ticket window so she essayed the machine. It was a triumphant moment when the yellow ticket fell into the space behind the small window, bringing her change with it. She watched what other people did, showing their tickets to the man in the booth, and she did the same.

There was a staircase. A notice informed the public that this was the deepest Underground station in London, three hundred stairs to the bottom. Passengers were advised to take the lift. The gates of the lift closed as she approached it. If she waited, surely another would come. It was then that she re-flected how complicated a process it was, this traveling by tube. She thought of herself as intelligent and had been called so. How was it then that all these *ordinary* people seemed to manage it with effortless ease?

The lift came and she got into it fearfully. She was alone in the lift. Would she have to operate it herself and, if so, how? It was a relief when others came, others who took no notice of her but, if they thought of her at all, must think her as seasoned a traveler as they. An illuminated indicator told them to stand clear of the doors and then they closed. The lift went down of its own accord.

Down there in the depths, and she was very aware of how deep it was, a sign pointing ahead and then to the left said TRAINS. Some people, instead of going ahead, turned directly left, thus indicating their sophistication, their experience, their refusal to be balked of a shortcut by officialdom. On the plat-form she was not at all sure that she was in the right place. She might find herself, not being carried down to London but spirited away to distant unknown suburbs such as Hendon and Colindale.

The train coming in made a a noise that was fearful and seemed dangerous. All her energies were devoted to appearing in the eyes of others as nonchalant. At the same time she watched them to see what they did. It seemed that she might sit anywhere she chose, that there were no rules to obey. She had never been very obedient in other areas of her life but in the tube she was a child again, learning, wary, and without that presence which had always been there in her childhood.

She sat in a seat near the doors. To be near the doors seemed safest. She had forgotten this was supposed to be an adventure, an experience her life lacked. It had become an endurance test. The train started and she breathed deeply, with hands folded in her lap, artificially composed into an attitude of relaxation, she took long slow breaths. Her fear was that it would stop in the tunnel. She understood that she did not like tunnels, though this was something she had previously been unaware of. She did not have claustrophobia in small rooms or lifts. It was possible she had never been in a tunnel before, except perhaps in a car going quickly through some underpass.

But she was surviving. She was all right. The train came into Belsize Park and she looked curiously out at the station. This one and the next, Chalk Farm, were tiled in white and buff, reminding her of the servants' bathrooms at Temple Stephen. She occupied herself with studying a map on the opposite wall because she knew she would have to change trains at some point. Tottenham Court Road must be that point, an interchange from the black line to the red. This train would take her there, was bearing her there rapidly now, and at the station she would follow the signs, for signs there must be, to the Central Line going westward.

They had reached Camden Town, blue and cream, another shabby bathroom.

It was unpleasant, what happened next. Such things happen in bad dreams, dreams of the recurring kind from which one awakens in panic and fear, though she had never dreamed anything like this. How could she, never before having been in the tube?

The next station should have been Mornington Crescent but it was not. It was King's Cross. It took her quite a long time to understand what had occurred and what she had done wrong. The map explained, once she understood how to use the map. By this time she was trembling.

The train she was in was one bound for South London as perhaps all were, but it would reach there via the Bank instead of Tottenham Court Road, describing a loop through the City to do so. She had got into the wrong train.

All this time she had scarcely noticed there were other people in the car with her. Now she did. They did not look like the kind of people she usually associated with but seemed inimical, common, even savage, and with truculent peevish faces. She told herself to be calm. Nothing irreversible had taken place. She could change at Bank and take the Central Line, the red line, from there.

At King's Cross a large number of people got in. This was the station where the fire had been, she had read about it and seen it on television. Her husband—she had still been married then—told her not to look.

"Don't get involved. There's no one you're likely to know."

She could see nothing out of the window to show there had been a fire. By the time the train moved off she could see nothing at all out of the window, she could scarcely see the window, so many people were squeezed between her and it. She sat very still, making herself small, the bag with the dress in it crammed behind her legs, telling herself it was a privilege to have a seat. There were people, thousands if not millions of people, who did this every day.

One thing to be thankful for was that no more could get in. She had to revise this at Angel and again at Old Street. Perhaps a point was never reached where no more could get in, but they would be pushed and crushed until they died or the sides of the car burst with the pressure of them. She thought of a tired analogy she had often heard, people in a crowded train compared to sardines in a tin. If things go wrong inside a tin, gases build up and the contents swell and the whole thing explodes . . .

After Moorgate she had to think how she would get out at the next station.

She watched what others did. She found it was not possible even to get up out of her seat without shoving people, elbowing her way, pushing past them. The doors had come open and

there was a voice on a public address system shouting something. If she could not get out the train would carry her on to
the next station, to London Bridge, it would carry her on *under
the river*. That was what that band on the map was, that zone
of blue bending up and back like a water pipe, the river.

Others got out and she was carried along with them. It
would have been hard at that point not to be ejected from the
train. She felt tumbled out, pushed and pummeled. On the
platform the thick sour air seemed fresh after the atmosphere
inside the car. She breathed deeply. Now she must find the red
line, the Central Line.

The strange thing was that it did not occur to her then to
follow the WAY OUT signs, leave the station and go out into the
street where a taxi could be found. It occurred to her later,
when she was in the westbound Central Line train, but not
then, not when she was trying to find her way to the interchange. All her concentration and all her thought were bent
on finding where to go, on doing it right. The bag with the
dress in it was crushed, her pale shoes were covered with black
scuff marks. She felt soiled.

Once she went wrong. She waited for some minutes on a
platform, a train came and she would have got into it if that
had been possible. She could not have brought herself to do as
some did, step in and squash her body against the bodies of
those who formed the dense wad of people which already
bulged from the open doors. The doors ground to a close.
Looking up at the illuminated sign overhead, she was glad she
had not attempted to push her way in. The train was going
eastward, bound for a place called Hainault she had never
heard of.

She made the transfer to the right platform. A great many
people were waiting. A train came in, going to another place
she had never heard of, Hanger Lane. She knew the direction

was right, it would stop at Bond Street where she wanted to be. She began to feel that if she did this a few more times she would get the hang of it. For all that, once would be enough for her.

Entering the train was not so bad as entering the eastbound one would have been. It was possible to walk in without pushing or being pushed, though there was no question of finding a seat. Others stood, so she could too, it would not be for long. What she should have done was obey the voice that told her to pass right along the car. Instead, she stayed between the doors, holding on as best she could to an upright rail, the bag with the dress in it clutched in her other hand.

A man, quite young, was sitting in the seat nearest to the door. Of course he would get up and offer her his seat. She waited for this to happen. All her life men had given up their seats to her, at point-to-points and tennis matches, their window seats in aircraft, their centrally positioned armchairs in balconies overlooking royal routes. This man stayed where he was and read *The Star*. She held on to the rail and to her bag.

At St. Paul's a great throng crammed the platform. She saw a sea of faces, each stamped with a kind of purposeful, hungry urgency, a determination to get into this train. As before, when she was on the Northern Line, she thought there must be some rule, some operating law, that would stop more than a limited controlled number getting in. Authority would appear and stop it.

But authority did not appear, not even in the form of a disembodied voice, and the people came on in, on and on, more and more of them, a marching army, a shoving, crushing battering ram of men and women. She could not see if the platform emptied because she could not see the platform. A man, pushing past her, swept the dress bag out of her hand, carrying it along with him in his thrusting progress. She could see it still, made an ineffectual grab at it, seized only a girl's skirt instead and, relinquishing it with a gasp, saw its wearer's face loom close to hers, as distressed as her own must be.

The bag was bundled and squeezed, stretched and squashed, between the legs of the stumbling mass. There was no possibility of her reaching it. She did not dare let go but hung on to the rail, where another four hands also hung on, for dear life. Faces were closer to hers than faces had ever been, except those of lovers in the act of love. The back of a head pushed one of them aside and pressed so close into her face that hair came into her mouth, she could smell the less than clean hair, and see the beads of dandruff. She turned her face, twisted her neck, found her eyes meeting a man's eyes, their eyes close and gazing, as if they were about to kiss. His eyes were dead, purposely glazed over, blinded to deny contact.

And then, as the doors groaned shut and the train moved, the fidgeting, the adjusting of positions, the shifting of hands, ceased and all became still. Everyone froze into stillness like people playing the statues game when the music stops. She knew why. If the heaving had continued, if there had been continuous restless movement, existence inside the train would have been impossible. People would begin to scream. People would begin to beat each other in their frenzy at something so intolerable imposed upon them.

They were still. Some held their chins high, stretching necks, their expressions agonized, like martyrs in paintings. Others hung their heads in meek submission. It was worst for the very short, like the fat girl she could see between face and face and back of head, standing with nothing to hold on to, supported by those who surrounded her, her head under the men's elbows, a woman's handbag, clutched under an arm, driving its hard corners into her throat.

By now she had lost sight of the dress bag. Acquiring its contents had been the purpose of her outing, but she no longer cared about it. She cared about surviving, about remaining very still and suffering, enduring, holding on until the train reached Chancery Lane. There she would get out of the train and the system. She should have got out of the system at Bank, she knew that now. To lose the dress, the white Peruvian wedding dress, was a small price to pay for escape.

When the train stopped she thought they were there. She wondered why the doors were not opening. Outside the windows all was darkness and she understood they had stopped in the tunnel. Whether this ever happened without dangerous cause, whether it often happened, what it signified, of all this she had no idea. She would have liked to ask, speak into the face of the man whose breath, rich with garlic, fanned hotly into her nostrils. Her throat had dried. She had no voice. She was aware, more strongly now than before, of all the human bodies pressed against her, the elbows and breasts and stomachs and buttocks and shoulders, and of the hard glass panel against which her own side was crushed.

The heat began to increase. She had not especially noticed the heat before but now she did as droplets of sweat formed themselves on her forehead and her upper lip, as sweat in a single long drop rolled very cold and insinuating down between her breasts. Of that icy coldness she was very aware, but not as relief, rather as pain, rather as shock.

It grew hotter. The train gave a lurch, a kind of belch, and she held on, held her breath, waiting for it to start. It sighed and sank once more into immobility. The man close to her grunted. His face had gone very red and looked as if sprayed with water. A drop of sweat ran down her forehead and into her eye. It stung her eye and she asked herself why this should happen. Why should salt tears not sting while salt sweat did?

While she was wondering this, holding on to the rail with a wet slippery hand, feeling the heat rise and thicken, the train belched again and this movement, much more powerful than before, shifted and heaved the people around her to enclose her in a kind of human tide. Her face now against a tweed back, she fought for breath, struggled and pushed, moaning as another icy drop flowed down her body and set off the pain.

It *seemed* to set it off, to trigger it, for as it slipped along her skin like a bead of ice, a huge pain took hold of her left arm as if an iron claw had grasped it. She arched her back, tried to stretch her neck above assorted flesh and hair and smell. The train started, moved forward on a smooth glide, and as it did so the iron claws embraced her, like the appendages of a monster.

They embraced her and dragged her down, through shoulders and arms and hips and legs, to a conglomeration of dirty, trodden-on shoes. The train ran on smoothly toward Chancery Lane. The last thing she saw, as her heart that had the little something wrong with it collapsed, was the bag with the dress in it, stuck between a pair of trousered legs.

There was no room in the train. Not one more passenger could have squeezed in. Yet as she sank to the floor and died, they fell back, they shrank back and made the space for her she had needed for life. For dear life.

At Chancery Lane the train was cleared and the body removed. Remaining in the car was a large dress-shop bag, made of thick strong paper with some kind of dark blue lacquer coating and a picture of a woman in unidentifiable national costume. They were apprehensive about opening it and sent for the Bomb Squad.

Eventually, much later, a wedding dress was found inside. A receipted bill with it gave the address of the purchaser. It was sent to her home and came at last to her family.

---

Excerpt from *King Solomon's Carpet*

# Rigor
# Beach

EMMA
TENNANT

Friday, 6 P.M.

Ingrid did the last things, awaiting this unknown man, to ensure his comfort, even his surprise. Little fronds of jasmine sprouted in a glass. On the round table were bottles of wine and champagne. I LOVE YOU she had lipsticked on the mirror, which shone, now evening had come and the lights outside in the boulevard were lit, like neon in a room otherwise comfortable and dusty. This is it, she said aloud, for she regretted her age and that there had been so many. And, This will be a holiday to remember, she added. A pâté the size of a fist was laid out ready. Toast when he had come. She went to the window and looked out suddenly tired at the strolling crowds and the shops in the arcades like bright boxes and the strip of static sea beyond. The bell sounded. As much as she could do, after the energy and expectation of the day, to go and pull it open.

7 P.M.

And so I grew up in Paris, Ingrid explained to the stranger. That's why I love the Coast. We came here for our holidays always. And you?

The man, who was fair-haired—and this was a secret disappointment to Ingrid—smiled and nodded and held out his glass for more. Constraint remained between them although the bottle of champagne was nearly emptied and the gold paper at its neck frayed, showing the wire beneath. He was handsome certainly, but spoke little. A toast crumb clung to the smooth skin above his upper lip. There was no violence in him—Ingrid had seldom felt so unafraid. She had become more of a man in his presence perhaps, for when he failed to answer she strode about the room half-dancing and would laugh at the sound of carnival music in the street, wishing, although she would not wish herself anywhere else on earth, for a moment the wearer of a monstrous nose or Humpty-Dumpty head. She must alert him somehow. And he had seen the lipsticked mirror and stayed quiet. He sat a little too forward yet his legs, crossed in green velvet trousers, were elegant. She paused, pretending for the first time to observe his hands.

8 P.M.

The man and Ingrid sat together on the settee. Which faced the open French windows, a smell of cheap scent and salt air blowing in. Because of the nearness of the sea the upholstery in the apartment was sticky and clung for longer than was normal to bare flesh. Ingrid's legs were glued there, the man's hands playing over them like moths; as if the furniture had trapped her and made her quiet at last and the man still free to come and go as he pleased. Now he was so close, signs of fatigue were visible about his eyes, which were blue and slanted and hung suspended like flies in the surrounding spiderwebs of vein and tissue.

Are we falling in love? Ingrid asked him. She felt all at once sad, and imagined this must be the cause. The man smiled, as if resigned to her talk.

9 P.M.

In the bedroom, two doors down the gray-painted landing, Ingrid and the man stripped to the skin and climbed between sheets that were cold and dank. In the dark pool they lay for a moment stunned, then swam for each other. Ingrid knew her own smell and fought to recognize his, but it was nothing she had known yet, it was faint, might even be repulsive, and there was a lotion on the hair which made her see, suddenly in the blackness ringed with magenta circles from her eyes, a day at the seaside long ago when her father had carried her across rocks to a hidden beach. The skin of his face was fine, like sand running through an hourglass when it touched hers. The chest was concave and hesitant, the hips narrow. There was no desire yet—outrage even from his body that it should burn and rise up and exhaust itself.

10 P.M.

Ingrid's tongue probed the man's penis and it shrank and floated away at first like a sea anemone underwater before thickening and beginning to throb. He turned to lie on her again, for in the intervening hour he had lain spreadeagled on her twice, each time retreating cold at the entrance to what she saw now as a monstrous cave, hot and overhung with lichens, filled with an inner sea. Then he was there, uncertain. Ingrid saw there were slippery steps descending, and he was afraid to miss the handrail and plunge perilously. He came and went, going always as if he might never return. The hair tore a little, giving way. She lay entranced, on her own clock of these things time passed slowly. Deep underwater, she felt the hulls of great boats as they went above her on the surface, obscuring the sun. She lost something of herself, joined to his body, and when she came it was with a sense of loss, seeing their white bones, long forgotten, scattered on the ocean bed. The man slept. Only to wake and find her hands cupping him, curving round his penis like hands protecting a candle from the wind.

Saturday, 1 A.M.

Ingrid rode astride the man, her head higher than it could usually be and the wall in front of her like a dim screen where patterns from her eyes flickered among faint moving shadows of light from the street outside. She galloped across a marsh. There was no breath in the air, the man lay still under her.

Bunches of reed poked up out of the wet clay. He shrank, but not before sending a shower of red stars up into her. Triumphant, Ingrid said: We'll go to the beach tomorrow. What a holiday we'll have! Already, as she climbed down from him, she planned with swift strokes the picnic box and the checkered tablecloth spread out over the sand. The man's sand-colored hair she would garland with the wild lilies that grew there. She breathed in deeply, expecting salt and the stench of seaweed which bobbed like knotted fingers in the pools. But he smelled of wet flannel, and she told him, although she knew he would laugh at her for this, that she felt she might grow a crop of mustard and cress on his body. She lay beside him, caressing his shoulders. He turned his head to one side and slept.

8 A.M.

When the man made to go, Ingrid held him down and stared intensely into his face. Her mother was there, loveless. The tides receded, leaving an empty expanse where the pale, half-cloudy sky was reflected. Her entrails went, and she saw herself in the bare day ahead as square and white as the walls of her apartment. Nothing was contained in her. He was tired, for he sighed as she held him and made only a slight move of resistance. She rose with a leap, went to the cupboard, and pulled out bright scarves and straw hats in her search. The room was soon littered with holiday wear, as if something exciting were about to happen and the silks and red cottons must be agitated by the preparations. The butt of the pistol came hard into her hand. The man looked only a little surprised, his eyebrows going up in semicircles, like a clown. The bullet hole in the side of his head was perfectly small and round.

## Noon

Ingrid ransacked the apartment, pulling from the backs of musty shelves the plastic cocktail sticks and frilly serviettes and miniature Japanese umbrellas with which she had adorned her previous parties. She went in to the man, he was stiff now, and she knelt beside him, she on the floor so that her eyes were level with his body. With wads of face tissue she propped up his penis, stiff too though she felt no regret. Jeweled hatpins, imitation rubies, made eyes at the top of the phallus, like the beam of light from a watchtower sweeping the sea. Along the smooth plain of his chest and abdomen, where a few hairs grew, bent double as if flattened by the wind she planted her holiday resort: the gay paper umbrellas shading little tables and chairs of red and blue plastic; a lacy napkin laid out as picnic cloth. Armpits and arms were undulating dunes and these she filled and covered with shells, which were dry and brittle, long since removed from the beach. His face she painted blue from her pot of eye shadow, and made foam-specked waves of cold cream along the ridges of cheekbone and jaw. So that the neck, a thin peninsula of golden sand, ran to an unmoving, glistening sea. She had no idea of his name, but she wished to name him. J, she scratched with nail scissors along a thigh as biscuit-colored and striated as a cliff. The initial she had chosen stood out a pale red, like lettering on seaside rock, and she put her mouth there, sucking at the flesh.

## Sunday, 6 P.M.

It had been hot all day, and Ingrid had paced the apartment, going every few minutes to the French windows to look out at the crowd of holidaymakers below. Down the landing, in the room where the sun never penetrated, the body had begun to bloat and leak. At first she had shored it up, pressing face tissue and beach towels against the oozing apertures. But she was tired now, and went less often to kiss the legs and arms, kneel by the beach with her eyes, like pools of trapped water, just beyond the sand dunes. It was growing dark and she threw on her shawl, went to promenade with the rest in the crowded arcades. She knew, by the time she returned, there would be the smell of the sea in the apartment, the rotting weed.

# The
# Smell

PATRICK
McGRATH

There is a room in my house that for reasons of my own I have always kept locked. It is a downstairs room and was once, I imagine, a dining room, though I use it now to store boxes containing items pertaining to my work. It has a large fireplace and windows facing the wall that surrounds my property. These windows are kept shuttered, and the few pieces of furniture in the room are covered with sheets. Every few months I light a fire in the grate, but not this year, for the winter was mild. We observed Christmas with the solemnity appropriate to the holiday, and my wife prepared a festive meal. I do not permit decorations as they tend in my opinion to trivialize the occasion, though I do allow the exchanging of gifts as this nurtures selflessness, provided of course that the gifts are either useful or educational, good books for example.

For I have a family, I have a wife and children. There's also my wife's younger sister living in the house, rather a disorganized young woman I'm afraid. I support these people through my work at the museum, work that demands my utter concentration, and this is why I insist on silence in the house during the early hours of the evening (five to seven). The children are permitted to make conversation at the dinner table provided that it's of a serious nature, and the same applies to my wife (and her sister). A stern regime, you may think, but I point out to you that such was the climate of my father's house, and I have not suffered as a result, the reverse in fact. You will understand my recent consternation, then, when having refused to allow the children to keep a stray dog they'd found and begun to care for, several of them expressed feelings of resentment. What's more, my wife supported them, and so, apparently, did her sister!

I punished them of course. And having punished them I explained to them why I had punished them, though whether they appreciated this I cannot say. And it was a few days after this that I first detected the smell.

Now what is so curious about all this is that the work I do is the sort that appeals to scholarly, even pedantic minds, and requires little in the way of imagination. In my field an inexhaustible passion for small detail is of much greater value than imagination per se, for it is with fragments that I work, incomplete pieces of ancient figures that must be identified and catalogued. Given, then, that this is the type of mind I have, does it not strike you as peculiar that I and I alone should have detected the odor?

Actually it began less as a smell, more a sort of ineffable vague suggestion of sweetness in the air. I suspected at first some uncleanness in the kitchen, and had my wife's sister thoroughly scour the floors, ovens, cupboards, and pantry with carbolic. To no avail. It grew stronger. I had my wife's sister then scrub out all of the downstairs rooms, with the exception of course of the one I keep locked at all times (for reasons of my own), for who could have entered that room, shuttered as it is and I in sole possession of the key? I began, when this scouring failed to eliminate the corruption, to suspect that she herself might be responsible for the smell, in retaliation, perhaps, for what she perceived as the injustice of my position regarding the stray dog; and I interviewed her in my room. She did not respond to my inquiries with candor, and I punished her again. *And the smell grew worse!*

The smell grew worse. It made me think of fruit, ripe fruit—a bowl of plums all gone soft and rotten and turning to slime. Was it any wonder that I began to spend so much time at the museum? Of course I did, I couldn't be in the house with that smell, though what really disturbed me was this: the rest of them pretended it wasn't there. They stared at me blankly when I referred to it. They affected concern, or perplexity, or impatience or boredom or fear, but they pretended it wasn't there. And refer to it I certainly did, how could I not, how could I ignore it, and here's something else that disturbed me, that it came and went, and how do you explain that, its coming and going like that?

My authority began to crumble. The children were not openly insubordinate, rather there was a subtle hesitation in their manner that I found deeply impertinent. One night I heard them on the roof, and they know they're not allowed on the roof, though when I went out into the garden I couldn't see anyone up there. With my wife it was the same, and with her sister: in fact, my wife's sister grew so bold, one day I discovered her rattling the doorknob of the room I keep locked! If you think the smell's coming from in there, I told her tartly, you're wrong. She gave me a saucy look and walked off.

She would have to be punished. I would have to make an example of her. Behavior like this could not be tolerated, not in a man's own house, not from her, not from any of them. You do see that, don't you? You do see that I had to do it, even though they were my own family and I loved them? You see that love must at times be cruel if it is to rise above the merely sentimental? Is it a loving father who fails to guide and instruct his family, who fails to teach them self-control, who permits them to flaunt his authority with impunity?

I decided to begin with my wife's sister. I asked her to join me in that certain room after dinner. This gave me ample opportunity to prepare for her visit. The day passed with excruciating slowness. I could not concentrate on my work, and left the museum earlier than usual. After dinner, as I rose from my chair, I glanced at her, meaningfully, and went out of the room. A moment later she followed me. I crossed the hall, extracting from my trouser pocket the key. I unlocked the door and ushered her in, and at that moment, to my unutterable

horror, I discovered that the foulness that had been so torment-
ing my senses did originate in the locked room after all: it *stank*
in there, my God it stank, such a sick, sweet stink that I felt
my gorge rise and a wave of nausea almost overwhelmed me.
I mastered myself, with some difficulty—and then became
aware of something else in the room, some new abomination.
It was liquid, dripping liquid, there was a sweet and viscous
liquid dripping into the fireplace.

Oh, viscosity! She turned to me and asked why I'd brought
her here. She appeared *not to smell the smell.* A light, cold
prickle of sweat broke out on my skin and I was barely able
to control the impulse to retch though I did control it, I did.
She asked me again why I'd brought me here, and again I
could not answer, for I'd clapped my hands to my mouth to
keep from vomiting.

I stared wildly about me. Boxes of fragments, sheeted chairs,
shuttered windows, all swam before my eyes. I told her to go,
and as she left the room she barely troubled to conceal her
contempt. I managed to lock the door from the inside, and then
with no little trepidation I approached the fireplace. I was
trembling I remember, and damp with perspiration. I knelt
down on the hearth, and careful to avoid the puddle of sticky
liquid in the grate leaned forward into the fireplace, turning
my head so as to gaze up the chimney. I found only blackness,
but the smell was bad, oh, it was very bad indeed, and there
was little doubt in my mind that I had discovered the source:
somewhere up this chimney, somewhere not far above my
head, was the thing that dripped and stank.

In a sudden frenzy of rage and frustration I seized up a
broomhandle, intending to dislodge the foulness. But broom-
handles are stiff, and as the flue sloped backward at an angle
just above the fireplace I was unable to get it to go up. I
introduced instead a length of wire, and with this succeeded

in negotiating the slope, and then thrust upward forcefully a number of times. All that came down was a shower of dead leaves and soot. I waited a few moments and then tried again. I inserted the wire and pushed and thrust with great violence, but again my efforts availed me nothing but chimney rubbish and coal dust.

I spent the next hours in the room. I paced the floor, pondering the events of the evening. And what I couldn't get out of my mind was the way my wife's sister had looked at me, the way she'd spoken to me—it infuriated me, the picture of her flouncing out like that, with a sneer on her lips. That sneer—! But it wasn't only her, they were all in on it, every single one of them, and I knew that I couldn't delay it much longer, for the situation was rapidly getting out of hand.

They were alarmed now. They knew they'd gone too far. My wife was most agitated when I sent for her, she stood before me fidgeting with great unease and was completely unable to meet my eye. I was not easy on her, I was not easy on any of them, why should I be, after what they'd put me through? But despite my anger I didn't raise a finger, I didn't even raise my voice. I spoke, rather, in cool, quiet tones, I told them what I knew, and saw them grow shifty and afraid, for they had thought me a fool, this was clear now, they'd taken me for a fool.

Dead of night, punishment time. I left my room. I listened to the house. Silence. I am a small-boned, agile man, slightly built, simian in fact. I padded quickly and quietly up the stairs, two at a time, and came to the door of my wife's sister's bedroom. I put my ear to the door. I could hear nothing. I crossed the landing and entered another bedroom. A sleeping child sprawled on the bed with sheet and blanket tangled about its limbs. Then I heard coughing, and I went down the passage to a room where two of the younger children slept. I would start here. I went in and closed the door behind me. I was feeling an immense sadness: oh, that it should come to this—two sleeping children—little fragments, delicate, unfinished things, but no less guilty for that. Then the anger came and I experienced the familiar sensation, the *milky* feeling—how else to describe it?—the sudden loss of clarity, the rapid shift into a sort of pale sunless liquid mist, the numbness, watching the horror from somewhere outside one's own body, and when it had passed, when it was over, finding myself once more out in the passage and *again* the sadness, again the intense, almost overwhelming sense of sorrow, though something had changed, for now there was something that was stronger even than the sorrow.

Even from upstairs I could tell it had grown worse, much, much worse. I knew then I *had* to have done with it, that I could wait no longer: more punishment later, I thought, though in an odd way it was no longer me thinking, no longer me in control, for I was drawn to the smell like a moth to a flame, it was *pulling me in*. Rapidly I descended the stairs and unlocked the room—and almost gagged, it was so strong, the wave of foulness that hit me, but in I came, and covering nose and mouth with my arm stumbled to the fireplace and this time ducked my head under the mantelpiece and stood upright in the foul sooty blackness, *I couldn't help myself!* Above my head bricks projected every three feet, it was stepped, so grasping a brick I began blindly to clamber up the inside of the fireplace to the sloping section. There it became more difficult, for the opening was narrow, but I managed to squeeze myself up and along on my front until I reached the passage of the chimney proper, where I somehow turned myself over in the foetid blackness so I could press my back against the one wall of the chimney, get the soles of my shoes hard against the other, legs bent double, and wedged tight like this start poking upward with the wire. But to my horror I'd wedged myself so tight I couldn't move!

I couldn't move. Slowly the blind hysterical compulsion that had seized me faded, slowly I began to understand where I was, and what I'd done. The effort, then, to suppress panic, and terror, and the nausea born of an almost overwhelming stench of putrefying flesh, as a voice inside my own brain whispered, You're suffocating, you're going to die. You're going to die. You're going to die in this putrid chimney. And *then* the thought, So is it *me?* Is it me who makes the smell? Am I the thing that drips and stinks?

Suddenly in my mind's eye I saw my wife's sister, I saw her as she flounced out of my presence, flung out of the room with her eyes flashing and her little chin lifted, like a little white vessel buoyed and swept forward on the current of her own indignation. And then did I hear her laughing? She was outside the door, laughing at me, and at last I saw it, at last I saw the ghastly gallows humor of it all. For I was indeed the source, I the smell, I the thing that dripped and stank. Behind the locked door I could still hear her laughing, while I slowly suffocated, stuffed up my chimney like a dirty cork in a bottle of rancid milk.

# The
# Kingdom
# of
# Heaven

PETER
STRAUB

*The Kingdom of Heaven*
*Is like a man who wished to assassinate a noble.*
*He drew his sword at home, and struck it*
  *against the wall,*
*To test whether his hand were strong enough.*
*Then he went out, and killed the noble.*


The seven members of the body squad were serving out their remaining time in Vietnam. All of them had been in regular units for at least most of a year, and most of them had re-upped so that they could spend another year in the field. They were not ordinary people—they were not even ordinary combat vets, because the regiment had slam-dunked them into the body squad to get them out of their units. They were foul balls, neither psychopaths nor actual criminals, not so destructive they belonged in the stockade, but people from whom something necessary and sociable had been removed either at birth or through circumstance. They disliked each other, and they detested me.

Their names were Scoot, Hollyday, de Maestro, Picklock, Ratman, Attica, and Pirate. They had a generic likeness, at least to a new arrival, being unshaven, hairy—even Ratman, who was prematurely bald, was hairy—unclean, missing a crucial tooth or two. They looked like people you'd move to the edge of the sidewalk, if not actually cross the street, to avoid. Scoot, Pirate, and de Maestro wore tattoos (*Born to Die, Dealers in Death*, and a blue rose suspended over an umber pyramid, respectively). None of them ever wore an entire uniform. For the whole of my first day, they did not speak to me, and went about the business of carrying the heavy body bags from the helicopter to the truck and from the truck to the "morgue" in a frosty, insulted silence.

The next day, after Captain McCue told me that my orders still had not come through and that I should return to the body squad, he asked me how I was getting on with my fellow workers. That was what he called them, my "fellow workers."

"They're full of stories," I said. "I'm learning a lot."

"That's not all they're full of, the way I hear it," he said, showing two rows of square brown peglike teeth that made his big pink cheeks look as if his character were being eroded from within. He must have seen that I had just decided I preferred the company of Ratman, Attica, and the rest to his own, because he told me that I would be working with the body squad until my orders came through.

My new comrades in arms seemed mildly disappointed to see me again, but the intensity of their disdain had relaxed, and on the second day they began to talk. Which is to say, they resumed the unfinishable dialogue I had interrupted.

So began what I thought was my education about the real Vietnam.

Either because of what they had endured in the field or because their job made them handle bodies all day, their stories were always about death. Because they were from different units, they did not have to stick to a literal accuracy; and because my company had been forced on them, their stories were as fearsome as they could make them.

"We're pounding the boonies," Ratman said, shoving another wrapped corpse into the back of our truck. "Twenty days. You listening, Underdog?"

I had a new name.

"Twenty days. You know what that's like out there, Underdog?"

Pirate spat a thick yellow curd onto the ground.

"Like forty days in hell. In hell you're already dead, but out in the boonies everybody's trying to kill you. Means you never sleep right. Means you *see* things."

Pirate snorted and tossed another body onto the truck. "Fuckin' right."

"You see your old girlfriend fuckin' some numbnuts *fuck*, you see your fuckin' friends get *killed*, you see the fuckin' *trees* move, you see stuff that never happened and never will, man."

" 'Cept here," Pirate said.

"Twenty days," Ratman said. The back of the truck was now filled with bodies in bags, and Ratman swung up and locked the rear panel. He leaned against it on stiff arms, shaking his drooping head. His fingertips were bulbous, the size of golf balls, and each came to a pointed tip at the spot where his fingerprints would have been centered. I found out later that he had earned his name by eating two live rats in a tunnel where his platoon had found more than a thousand kilos of rice. "Too fat for speed," he was supposed to have said.

"The way you smell—you smell like the whole country, you understand? This is normal. Smell like a fuckin' *swamp*. And you can't smell it yourself, dig? Every sense you got is *out* there, man, you hear a mouse move—"

"Hear rats move," de Maestro said, slapping the side of the truck as if to wake up the bodies in the green bags.

"—hear the dew jumpin' out of the leaves, hear the insects moving in the *bark*. Hear your own fingernails grow. Hear that thing in the ground, man."

"Thing in the ground?" Pirate asked.

"Shit," said Ratman. "You don't know? You know how when you lie down on the trail you hear all kinds of shit, all them damn bugs and monkeys, the birds, the people moving way up ahead of you—"

"Better be sure they're not coming your direction," de Maestro said from the front of the truck. "You takin' notes, Underdog?"

"—*all* kinds of shit, right? But then you hear the *rest*. You hear what's happenin' underneath all them other noises. It's some kind of like a hum, like a humming noise. Like some big generator's running way far away *underneath* you."

"Oh, that thing in the ground," Pirate said.

"It *is* the ground," said Ratman. He stepped back from the truck and gave Pirate a fierce, wild-eyed glare. "Fuckin' ground makes the fuckin' noise by *itself.* You hear me? An' that engine's always on. It never sleeps."

"Okay, let's move," de Maestro said. He climbed up behind the wheel. Hollyday, Scoot, and Attica crowded into the seat beside him. Ratman scrambled up behind the cab, and Picklock and Pirate and I followed him. The truck jolted down the field toward the main body of the camp, and the helicopter pilot and some of the ground crew turned to watch us go. We were like garbagemen, I thought. It was like working on a garbage truck.

"On top of which," Ratman said, "people are seriously trying to interfere with your existence."

Picklock laughed, but instantly composed himself again. So far, neither he nor Pirate had actually looked at me.

"Which can fuck you up all by itself, at least until you get used to it," Ratman said. "Twenty-day mission. I been on longer, but I never went on any worse. The lieutenant went down. The radio man, he went down. My best friends at that time, they went down."

"Where is this?" Pirate asked.

"This is Darlac Province," said Ratman. "Not too damn far away."

"Right next door," said Pirate.

"Twentieth day," said Pirate. "We're out there. We're after some damn cadre. We didn't get orders say any different. Hardly any food left, and our pickup is in forty-eight hours. This target keeps *moving,* they go from ville to ville, collecting food and money, do a few executions, they're your basic Robin Hood–type cadre." Ratman shook his head. The truck hit a low point in the road on the outskirts of the base, and one of the bags slithered down the pile and landed softly at Ratman's feet. He kicked it almost gently. We passed a group of soldiers who looked up at us, then looked away.

Garbagemen.

"This guy, this friend of mine, name of Bobby Swett, he was right ahead of me, five feet ahead of me. We hear some kind of crazy noise, a sort of a whoop, and everybody freezes for a second, and then this big red and yellow bird flashes past us, big as a turkey, man, wings like fuckin' *propellers,* man, and I'm thinkin', okay, what woke this mother *up?* And Bobby Swett turns around to look at me, and he's grinnin'. And his grin is the last thing I see for about ten minutes. And then when I come to I remember seeing Bobby Swett come apart all at once, like something inside him exploded, but—you get it?— I'm remembering something I don't remember seeing. I think I'm dead. I fucking *know* I'm dead. I'm covered in blood and this brownskin little girl is bending over me. Black hair and black eyes. So now I know. There are angels, and angels got black hair and black eyes, hot shit."

A brown wooden fence hid the long low shed we called the morgue, and when we had passed the stenciled DISPOSITIONS sign, Ratman vaulted neatly off the back of the truck and ran to open the storage bay while de Maestro backed the truck around. We had four hours turnaround time, and today there were a lot of bodies.

De Maestro backed the truck up into the bay, and we started hauling the long bags into the interior of the shed.

"Long nose?" asked Pirate.

"Long nose, shit yes."

"A Yard."

"Sure, but what did I know? She was a Rhade—most of the Yards in Darlac Province, of which they got about two thousand, are Rhade. The Rhade loved the *French,* man. Some of them Rhade Yards got names like Michel and Row-bear. 'I died,' I say to this girl, still figuring she's a angel, and she coos something back at me. It seems to me that I can remember this big flash of light—I mean, that was something I actually *saw.* "

"Fucking Bobby Swett stepped on a mine," said Pirate.

I was getting to like Pirate. Pirate knew I was the real subject of this story, and he was selfless enough to keep things rolling with little interjections and explanations. Pirate was slightly less contemptuous of me than the rest of the body squad. I also liked the way he looked, raffish without being as *ratlike* as Ratman. Like me, Pirate tended toward the hulking. He seldom wore a shirt in the daytime, and always had a bandanna tied around his head or his neck. When I had been out in the field for a time I found myself imitating these mannerisms, except for when the mosquitos got bad.

"You think I don't know that? What I'm saying is—" Ratman shoved another dead soldier in a zippered bag into the darkness of the shed "—what I'm *saying* is, I was dead too. For a minute, maybe longer."

"Of what?"

"Shock," Ratman said simply. "That's the reason I never saw Bobby Swett get blown apart. Didn't you ever hear about this? I heard about it. Lotsa guys I met, it either happened to them or someone they knew."

"Is that true?" I asked.

Ratman scowled at me. For a second, he looked wrathful. I had challenged some essential aspect of his system of belief, and I was a person who knew nothing.

Pirate came to my rescue. "How come you could remember seeing this guy get wasted, if you didn't see it in the first place?"

"I was out of my body. A million things happened all in a

second. I was covered in blood and this little Yard was leaning over me. And I say 'I died,' like, so what happens now I'm out of my body?"

"God damn it, Underdog," said Picklock, and grabbed the handle of the heavy bag I had nearly dropped. "What the fuck is the matter with you?" Single-handedly, he tossed the bag into the cool shed behind us. Picklock did not look at me once during this operation: he did not approve of Ratman's garrulity in front of a virgin like me.

"Underdog, never drop the fucking bags," said de Maestro, and deliberately dropped a bag onto the concrete. Whatever was inside it gurgled and splatted.

For a moment or two we continued to unload the bodies into the shed.

Then Ratman said, "Anyhow, about a second later I found out I was still alive."

"What makes you think you're alive?" asked Attica.

"On top of everything else, this guy shoves his face into mine, and for sure he ain't no angel. I can see the goddamned canopy above his head. The birds start screeching again. The first thing I know for sure is Bobby Swett is gone, man—I'm *wearing* whatever's left of him. And this guy says to me, 'Get on your feet, soldier.' I can just about make out what he's saying through the ringing in my ears, but you know this asshole is used to obedience. I let out a groan when I try to move, because everything hurts, man, every square inch of me feels like hamburger."

"Ah," say Picklock and Attica, nearly in unison. Then Attica said, "You're a lucky son of a bitch."

"Bobby Swett didn't even make it into one a these bags," said Ratman. "That fucker turned into *vapor.*" He sullenly grabbed the handles of another bag, inspected it for a second, said, "No tag," and shoved it on top of the others in the shed.

"Oh, goody," said Attica. Attica had a smoothly shaven brown head and a flaring mustache and his biceps jumped in his arms when he lifted the bags. He pulled a Magic Marker from his fatigues and made a neat check on the end of the bag. As he turned back to the truck he grinned at me, stretching lips without opening his mouth, and I wondered what was coming.

"Finally I got up, like in a kinda daze," Ratman said. "I still couldn't hear hardly nothing. This guy is standing in front of me, and I see he's totally crazy, but not like *we* go crazy. This mother's crazy in some absolutely new kinda way. I'm still so fucked up I can't tell what's so different about him, but he's got these eyes which they are not human eyes." He paused, remembering. "Everybody else in my platoon is sort of standing around watching. There's the little Yard mascot in these real loose fatigues, and there's this big blond guy in front of me on the trail with the sun behind his head. I mean this dude is in command. He *is* the show. Even the lieutenant, who is a fucking ramrod, is just standing there. *Well, shit,* I think, *he just saw this guy raise me from the dead, what else is he gonna do?* The big blond guy is still checking me out—he's scoping me. He's got these eyes, like some animal in a pit that just killed all the animals that were down there with him."

"He looked like Attica," said de Maestro.

"Damn straight he did," Attica said. "I'm a warrior, I ain't like you losers, I'm a fucking god of war."

"And then I see what's really funny about this guy," said Ratman. "He's got this long-sleeve T-shirt and tan pants and there's a little black briefcase on the ground next to him."

"Uh oh," said de Maestro.

"This is after *twenty days.* Bobby Swett gets turned into—into *red fog* right in front of me. I get killed or *something* like that, and nobody's moving because of this guy with the brief-case. 'I've been hearing about you,' this guy says to me. But he's really talking to all of us, he's just checking me out to see how bad I got hurt.

"And then I look down at my hands and I see they're this funny color—sort of purple. Even under Bobby's blood, I can see my skin is turning this purple color. And I push up my sleeve and my whole damn *arm* is purple. And it's swelling up, fast.

" 'This fool's a walking bruise,' says the guy. Then he gives me a disgusted look and turns around and gives the whole platoon the same look. We're a bunch of damn fools. Which just got proved by one of our guys stepping on a mine. We're in his part of the world now, by God, and we better know it. For two weeks we been fucking up his action, scaring his people, getting in his way, and he wants us out. He's asking us politely, and we're on the same side, after all, which is worth remembering, but if we don't get outa his share of the country-side, our luck might take a turn for the worse. He just kind of smiles at us, and the Montagnard girl is standing right up next to him, and she's got an M-16, and *he's* got some kind of fancy machine I never saw before or since but I think was some kind of *Swedish* piece, and I got to thinkin' about what's in the briefcase, and then I got it. All at once."

"Got what?" I asked, and everyone in the body squad looked down, or at the stack of bodies in the shed, and then they unloaded the last two bodies. We went into the shed to begin the next part of the job. Nobody spoke until de Maestro looked at the tag taped to the bag closest to him, and started checking the names.

"So you got out of there," he said.

"The lieutenant used the guy's radio, and even before the argument was over, we was on our way toward the LZ. When we got back to the base, we got our showers, we got real food, we got blasted every possible way, but afterward I never felt the same. That fuckin' briefcase, man. And the little Yard chick. You know what? He was havin' a ball. He was throwin' a party."

"I thought civvies went out after '62," said Scoot. Scoot had been in Vietnam for five or six years, and these words were the first I had heard him speak. Unlike most members of the body squad, he was waiting to get back into the field—I don't think he believed that the United States really existed anymore, at least not in any way that actually mattered. He had adapted for good. Scoot was a short, skinny man with deep-set eyes, a ponytail, and a huge knife that dangled from his waistband on a dried, crinkly leather thong that looked like a body part. He could lift twice his own weight, and like a weightlifter he existed in some densely private space of his own. He must have been something like the mysterious figure Ratman had encountered on the trail in Darlac Province.

"They more or less got their own war," said Attica. "It kind of runs alongside the one the rest of us got, but it's got a whole different agenda."

"Green Berets are cool with me," said Scoot, and then I understood part of it.

"Some of them were on my flight," I said. "They—"

"Can't we get some work done around here?" asked de Maestro, and for a time we checked the dog tags against our lists.

Then Pirate said, "Ratman, what was the payoff?"

Ratman looked up from beside a body bag and said, "Five days after we got back to camp, we heard about three hundred Rhade Yards took out about a *thousand* VC. They went through all these hamlets in the middle of the night. 'Course, the way I heard it, some a those thousand VC were little babies and such, but CIDG did itself a power of good that night."

"CIDG?" I asked.

"Village Defense League," Pirate supplied. He too would not look at me.

"I heard of fifty, sixty guys, First Air Cav, offed by friendly fire," Scoot said. "Shit happens."

"Friendly fire?" I said.

"Comes in all shapes and sizes," Scoot said, smiling in a way I did not understand until later.

Ratman uttered a sound halfway between a snarl and a laugh. "And the rest was, I puffed up about two times my size. Felt like a goddamned football. Even my *eyelids* were swole up, man. They finally put me in the base hospital and packed me in ice—but not a bone broken, man. Not a bone broken."

"Now, I wonder what shape this boy is in," said Attica, patting the body without a tag. Nearly all the bags that came to us had been named by the time they got to us, and it was our task to ensure that all had names by the time they left. Field units sent in the names of the deceased along with the body bags, and we made sure they matched up. Now and then, someone exhausted, someone in a hurry, mixed up the tags, and we were supposed to correct these errors. We had to unzip the bags and compare the name on the tag taped to the body bag with the name on the tag either inserted into the dead man's mouth or taped to his body. Sometimes it took a long time to find the extra tag on or in whatever was left of the soldier; sometimes the tags had been blown away or destroyed, and then we had to match up the bodies to the handwritten list provided at the scene by the field officer, which was supplemented by a printed list supplied by the division office. Variants of spelling, changes of nationality, shifts in religion, race, origin, all of these were frequent. *Schmidt* became *Smith* or *Smit*; *Harris* became *Herrus* or *Hairs*; *Lebenthal* mutated to *Liebowitz* to *Lieber* or even *Lee*. We replaced the colorful documents prepared by the field officer with our own list—this demanded an inordinate amount of time, until the body squad learned about my typing—which accompanied the bodies to Tan Son Nhut or some other airfield, where a battalion clerk prepared a final list. This document included last known address and name and address of the next of kin. From Vietnam the bodies went back to America, where the army decanted them into wooden coffins and sent them home, along with an NCO and a lieutenant. The lieutenant carried a Bible and a flag folded into a tricorn. He presented these objects to the dead soldier's wife or parents. None of the conventional phrases uttered by the young lieutenant, none of his banal, heartfelt but hollow phrases, were the sort of thing likely to be said by Pirate or Picklock or Scoot.

"Your turn, Underdog," said Attica. "Your hands ain't dirty yet, are they? You check this mother out."

"Don't puke, you fuckin' knothead," said Picklock.

"You puke, I'll stomp your guts out," said de Maestro, and surprised me by laughing. I had not heard de Maestro laugh before. It was a creaky, humorless bray that might have come from one of the bags lined up before us.

"Just don't puke on the unit," said Pirate. "That really messes 'em up. You puke on the unit, *I'll* stomp your guts out."

Attica had intended me to open the bag and find the dead soldier's tag from the moment he had noticed that the matching tag was missing. "You're new boy," he said. "This the new boy's job."

I moved around the rows of bags toward Attica and the bag with the check. For the first time I wondered what the members of the body squad had done to be taken from their units. If you thought about it, they could not have done anything really bad: they had a responsible job.

For a moment I suspected that they had arranged a gruesome practical joke—when I unzipped the bag, some hideous creature would jump out at me, drenched in blood like Ratman after Bobby Swett has disintegrated in front of him. *Because that was why he told the story!* They wanted me to scream and faint. They wanted my hair to turn white. They were depraved criminals, and that was why they had this job. After I vomited, they'd take turns stomping my guts out. It was their version of friendly fire.

They looked like giant, perverted dwarves because that was what they were.

I had not entirely left my old self behind on the tarmac at Tan Son Nhut, after all.

Scoot was regarding me with real curiosity, and Ratman shook his head. "It's the new boy's *job,*" Attica repeated, and I guessed that although the term was ridiculous when applied to him, that he had been the new boy before me.

I bent over the long green bag. There were fabric handles on each end, and the wide black zipper ran from one to the other. A plastic pouch would hold the typed list of names, one circled.

I grasped the zipper and promised myself that I would not close my eyes. Behind me, the men took a collective breath. I pulled the zipper across the bag.

And I almost did vomit, not because of what I saw but because of the dead boy's stench, which moved like a huge black dog out of the opening in the bag. For a second I did have to close my eyes. A greasy web had fastened itself over my face. The gray ruined face inside the bag stared upward with open eyes. My stomach lurched. This was what they had been waiting for, I knew, and I held my breath and yanked the zipper another twelve inches down the bag.

The dead boy's mud-colored face was gone, shot away, from his left cheek down. His upper teeth closed on nothing but the black rear of his neck, where a few loose teeth had lodged. The other tag was not in the cavity. The uniform shirt was stiff and black with blood, and the blast that had taken away the boy's lower jaw had also removed his throat. The small, delicate bones of the top vertebrae were fouled with blood.

"There's no tag on this guy," I said, though what I wanted to do was scream.

De Maestro said, "You ain't finished yet."

I looked up at him. A big fuzzy belly drooped over his pants, and four or five days' growth of beard began just under his rapacious eyes. He looked like a fat goat.

"Who cleans these people up?" I asked before I realized that the answer might be that the new guy does.

"They hose 'em down at the field and make 'em presentable in San Francisco." De Maestro grinned and crossed his arms over his chest. "San Francisco's where you get your flag-wrapped coffins." The tattoo of a blue rose floated over a brown pyramid on his right forearm. It looked more like a symbol than a tattoo. Millhaven, *my* Millhaven was now present all about me, the frame houses with peeling brickface crowded together, the vacant lots and chain-link fences. I saw my sister's face.

"If you can't find the tag inside the shirt, sometimes they put 'em in the pockets or the boots." De Maestro turned away. The others had already lost interest.

I struggled with the top button of the stiffened shirt, trying not to touch the ragged edges of flesh around the collar. The odor poured up at me. My eyes misted. The soldier had limp brown hair and an arched forehead. He had not looked anything like de Maestro or Ratman. He might have been someone I had seen at Berkeley, carrying a capuccino on a book-laden tray out onto a sunny terrace.

The button finally squeezed through the hole, but the collar refused to separate. I pulled it open. Dried blood crackled like breakfast cereal. His throat had been opened like in a surgical diagram. A few more teeth were embedded in the softening flesh. I knew that what I was seeing I would see for the rest of my life—the ropes of flesh, the open cavity that should have been filled with speech. Lost teeth.

The tag was nowhere inside his neck.

I unbuttoned the next two buttons, and found only a pale bloodied chest.

Then I had to turn away to breathe, and saw the rest of the body squad going efficiently down the rows of bodies, dipping into the unzipped bags, making sure the names matched. When they were done, they made a little *X* on the side of the bag, like a customs official's sign. Two contradictory things occurred to me: one, that they were calmly doing pretty much the same sort of thing that I found so distressing; and two, that I was completely alone in a world of unspeakable horror. I turned back to my anonymous corpse and began fighting with a shirt pocket.

The button finally passed through the buttonhole, and I pushed my fingers into the opening, cracking it open like the pocket of a stiffly starched shirt. A thin hard edge of metal caught beneath my fingernail. The tag came away from the cloth with a series of dry little pops. "Okay," I said.

De Maestro said, "Attica used to shake down these unknown units in five seconds flat."

"Two seconds," Attica said, not bothering to look up.

I got away from the gaping body in the bag and held out the unreadable tag.

"Underdog's a pearl diver," de Maestro announced. "Now wash it off."

The stained, crusty sink stood beside a spattered toilet. I held the tag beneath the trickle of hot water. The stench of the body still clung to me, as gummy on my hands and face as the film of fat from ham hocks. Flakes of blood fell off the tag and dissolved to red in the water. I dropped the tag on the bottom of the sink and scrubbed my hands and face with Phisohex until the greasy feeling was gone. The body squad was cracking up behind me. I rubbed my face with the limp musty rag that hung between the sink and the toilet.

"Looking forward to the field?" Ratman asked.

"The unit's name," I said, picking the tag out of the pink water at the bottom of the sink, "is Andrew T. Majors."

"That's right," said de Maestro. "Now tape it to the bag and help us with the rest of them."

"You knew his name?" I was too startled to be angry. Then I remembered that he had the field officer's list, and Andrew T. Majors was the only name on it not also found on a tag.

"You'll get used to it," de Maestro said, not unkindly.

I never did, though.

Excerpt from *Throat*

# Fever

JOHN
EDGAR
WIDEMAN

*To Matthew Carey, Esq., who fled Philadelphia in its
hour of need and upon his return published a libelous
account of the behavior of black nurses and
undertakers, thereby injuring all people of my race
and especially those without whose unselfish,
courageous labours the city could not have survived
the late calamity.*

*. . . Consider Philadelphia from its centrical
situation, the extent of its commerce, the number of
its artificers, manufacturers and other
circumstances, to be to the United States what the
heart is to the human body in circulating the blood.*
                              *—Robert Morris, 1777.*

He stood staring through a tall window at the last days of
November. The trees were barren women starved for love and
they'd stripped off all their clothes, but nobody cared. And not
one of them gave a fuck about him, sifting among them,
weightless and naked, knowing just as well as they did, no
hands would come to touch them, warm them, pick leaves off
the frozen ground and stick them back in place. Before he'd
gone to bed a flutter of insects had stirred in the dark outside
his study. Motion worrying the corner of his eye till he turned
and focused where light pooled on the deck, a cone in which
he could trap slants of snow so they materialized into wet, gray
feathers that blotted against the glass, the planks of the deck.
If he stood seven hours, dark would come again. At some point
his reflection would hang in the glass, a ship from the other side
of the world, docked in the ether. Days were shorter now. A
whole one spent wondering what goes wrong would fly away,
fly in the blink of an eye.

Perhaps, *perhaps it may be acceptable to the reader to know how*

*we found the sick affected by the sickness; our opportunities of
hearing and seeing them have been very great. They were taken
with a chill, a headache, a sick stomach, with pains in the limbs
and back, this was the way the sickness in general began, but all
were not affected alike, some appeared but slightly affected with
some of these symptoms, what confirmed us in the opinion of a
person being smitten was the colour of their eyes.*

Victims in this low-lying city perished every year, and some
years were worse than others, but the worst by far was the long
hot dry summer of '93 when the dead and dying wrested
control of the city from the living. Most who were able, fled.
The rich to their rural retreats, others to relatives and friends
in the countryside or neighboring towns. Some simply left,
with no fixed destination, the prospect of privation or starvation on the road preferable to cowering in their homes awaiting the fever's fatal scratching at their door. Busy streets
deserted, commerce halted, members of families shunning one
another, the sick abandoned to suffer and die alone. Fear ruled.
From August when the first cases of fever appeared below
Water Street, to November when merciful frosts ended the
infestation, the city slowly deteriorated, as if it too could suffer
the terrible progress of the disease: fever, enfeeblement, violent
vomiting and diarrhea, helplessness, delirium, settled dejection
when patients *concluded they must go, (so the phrase for dying
was) and therefore in a kind of fixed determined state of mind went
off.*

*In some it raged more furiously than in others—some have
languished for seven and ten days, and appeared to get better the
day, or some hours before they died, while others were cut off in two
or three days, but their complaints were familiar. Some lost their
reason and raged with all the fury madness could produce, and died
in strong convulsions. Others retained their reason to the last and
seemed rather to fall asleep than die.*

Yellow Fever: an acute infectious disease of subtropical and tropical New World areas, caused by a filterable virus transmitted by a mosquito of the genus *Aëdes* and characterized by jaundice and dark-colored vomit resulting from hemorrhages. Also called *yellow jack*.

Dengue: an infectious, virulent tropical and subtropical disease transmitted by mosquitoes and characterized by fever, rash, and severe pains in the joints. Also called *breakbone fever, dandy*. [Spanish, of African origin, akin to Swahili *kindinga*.]

Curled in the black hold of the ship he wonders why his life on solid green earth had to end, why the gods had chosen this new habitation for him, floating, chained to other captives, no air, no light, the wooden walls shuddering, battered, as if some madman is determined to destroy even this last pitiful refuge where he skids in foul puddles of waste, bumping other bodies, skinning himself on splintery beams and planks, always moving, shaken and spilled like palm nuts in the diviner's fist, and Esu casts his fate, constant motion, tethered to an iron ring.

In the darkness he can't see her, barely feels her light touch on his fevered skin. Sweat thick as oil but she doesn't mind, straddles him, settles down to do her work. She enters him and draws his blood up into her belly. When she's full, she pauses, dreamy, heavy. He could kill her then; she wouldn't care. But he doesn't. Listens to the whine of her wings lifting her till the whimper is lost in the roar and crash of waves, creaking wood, prisoners groaning. If she returns tomorrow and carries away another drop of him, and the next day and the next, a drop each day, enough days, he'll be gone. Shrink to nothing, slip out of this iron noose and disappear.

*Aëdes aegypti:* a mosquito of the family *Culicidae*, genus *Aëdes* in which the female is distinguished by a long proboscis for sucking blood. This winged insect is a vector (an organism that carries pathogens from one host to another) of yellow fever and dengue. [New Latin *Aëdes,* from Greek aedes, unpleasant: *a-,* not + *edos,* pleasant . . .]

All things arrive in the waters and waters carry all things away. So there is no beginning nor end, only the waters' flow, ebb, flood, trickle, tides emptying and returning, salt seas and rivers and rain and mist and blood, the sun drowning in an ocean of night, wet sheen of dawn washing darkness from our eyes. This city is held in the waters' palm. A captive as surely as I am captive. Long fingers of river, Schuylkill, Delaware, the rest of the hand invisible; underground streams and channels feed the soggy flesh of marsh, clay pit, sink, gutter, stagnant pool. What's not seen is heard in the suck of footsteps through spring mud of unpaved streets. Noxious vapors that sting your eyes, cause you to gag, spit, and wince are evidence of a presence, the dead hand cupping his city, the poisons that circulate through it, the sweat on its rotting flesh.

No one has asked my opinion. No one will. Yet I have seen this fever before, and though I can prescribe no cure, I could tell stories of other visitations, how it came and stayed and left us, the progress of disaster, its several stages, its horrors and mitigations. My words would not save one life, but those mortally affrighted by the fever, by the prospect of universal doom, might find solace in knowing there are limits to the power of this scourge that has befallen us, that some, yea, most will survive, that this condition is temporary, a season, that the fever must disappear with the first deep frosts and its disappearance is as certain as the fact it will come again.

They say the rat's-nest ships from Santo Domingo brought the fever. Frenchmen and their black slaves fleeing black insurrection. Those who've seen Barbados distemper say our fever is its twin in the tropical climate of the hellish Indies. I know better. I hear the drum, the forest's heartbeat, pulse of the sea that chains the moon's wandering, the spirit's journey. Its throb is source and promise of all things being connected, a mirror storing everything, forgetting nothing. To explain the fever we need no boatloads of refugees, ragged and wracked with killing fevers, bringing death to our shores. We have bred the affliction without our breasts. Each solitary heart contains all the world's tribes, and its precarious dance echoes the drum's thunder. We are our ancestors and our children, neighbors and strangers to ourselves. Fever descends when the waters that connect us are clogged with filth. When our seas are garbage. The waters cannot come and go when we are shut off one from the other, each in his frock coat, wig, bonnet, apron, shop, shoes, skin, behind locks, doors, sealed faces, our blood grows thick and sluggish. Our bodies void infected fluids. Then we are dry and cracked as a desert country, vital parts wither, all dust and dry bones inside. Fever is a drought consuming us from within. Discolored skin caves in upon itself, we burn, expire.

I regret there is so little comfort in this explanation. It takes into account neither climatists nor contagionists, flies in the face of logic and reason, the good Doctors of the College of Physicians who would bleed us, purge us, quarantine, plunge us in icy baths, starve us, feed us elixirs of bark and wine, sprinkle us with gunpowder, drown us in vinegar according to the dictates of their various healing sciences. Who, then, is this foolish, old man who receives his wisdom from pagan drums in pagan forests? Are these the delusions of one whose brain the fever has already begun to gnaw? Not quite. True, I have survived other visitations of the fever, but while it prowls this city, I'm in jeopardy again as you are, because I claim no immunity, no magic. The messenger who bears the news of my death will reach me precisely at the stroke determined when it was determined I should tumble from the void and taste air the first time. Nothing is an accident. Fever grows in the secret places of our hearts, planted there when one of us decided to sell one of us to another. The drum must pound ten thousand thousand years to drive that evil away.

Fires burn on street corners. Gunshots explode inside wooden houses. Behind him a carter's breath, expelled in low, labored pants, warns him to edge closer to housefronts forming one wall of a dark, narrow, twisting lane. Thick wheels furrow the unpaved street. In the fireglow the cart stirs a shimmer of dust, faint as a halo, a breath smear on a mirror. Had the man locked in the traces of the cart cursed him or was it just a wheeze of exertion, a complaint addressed to the unforgiving weight of his burden? Creaking wheels, groaning wood, plodding foot-steps, the cough of dust, bulky silhouette blackened as it lurch-es into brightness at the block's end. All gone in a moment. Sounds, motion, sight extinguished. What remained, as if trapped by a lid clamped over the lane, was the stench of dead bodies. A stench cutting through the ubiquitous pall of vinegar and gunpowder. Two, three, four corpses being hauled to Potter's Field, trailed by the unmistakable wake of decaying flesh. He'd heard they raced their carts to the burial ground. Two or three entering Potter's Field from different directions would acknowledge one another with challenges, raised fists, gather their strength for a last dash to the open trenches where they tip their cargoes. Their brethren would wager, cheer, toast the victor with tots of rum. He could hear the rumble of coffins crashing into a common grave, see the comical chariots bouncing, the men's legs pumping, faces contorted by fires that blazed all night at the burial ground. Shouting and curses would hang in the torpid night air, one more nightmare trou-bling the city's sleep.

He knew this warren of streets as well as anyone. Night or day he could negotiate the twists and turnings, avoid cul-de-sacs, find the river even if his vision was obscured in tunnel-like alleys. He anticipated when to duck a jutting signpost, knew how to find doorways where he was welcome, wooden steps down to a cobbled terrace overlooking the water where his shod foot must never trespass. Once beyond the grand houses lining one end of Water Street, in this quarter of hovels, beneath these wooden sheds leaning shoulder to shoulder were cellars and caves dug into the earth, poorer men's dwellings under these houses of the poor, an invisible region where his people burrow, pull earth like blanket and quilt round themselves to shut out cold and dampness, sleeping multitudes to a room, stacked and cross-hatched and spoonfashion, themselves the only fuel, heat of one body passed to others and passed back from all to one. Can he blame the lucky ones who are strong enough to pull the death carts, who celebrate and leap and roar all night around the bonfires? Why should they return here? Where living and dead, sick and well must lie face to face, shivering or sweltering on the same dank floor.

Below Water Street the alleys proliferate. Named and nameless. He knows where he's going but the fever has transformed even the familiar. He'd been waiting in Dr. Rush's entrance hall. An English mirror, oval framed in scalloped brass, drew him. He watched himself glide closer, a shadow, a blur, then the shape of his face materialized from silken depths. A mask he did not recognize. He took the thing he saw and murmured to it. Had he once been in control? Could he tame it again? Like a garden ruined overnight, pillaged, overgrown, trampled by marauding beasts. He stares at the chaos until he can recall familiar contours of earth, seasons of planting, harvesting, green shoots, nodding blossoms; scraping, digging, watering. Once upon a time he'd cultivated this thing, this plot of flesh and blood and bone, but what had it become? Who owned it now? He'd stepped away. His eyes constructed another face and set it there, between him and the wizened old man in the glass. He'd aged twenty years in a glance and the fever possessed the same power to alter suddenly what it touched. This city had grown ancient and fallen into ruin in two months since early August when the first cases of fever appeared. Something in the bricks, mortar, beams, and stones had gone soft, had lost its permanence. When he entered sickrooms, walls fluttered, floors buckled. He could feel roofs pressing down. Putrid heat expanding. In the bodies of victims. In rooms, buildings, streets, neighborhoods. Membranes that preserved the integrity of substances and shapes, kept each in its proper place, were worn thin. He could poke his finger through yellowed skin. A stone wall. The eggshell of his skull. What should be separated was running together. Threatened to burst. Nothing contained the way it was supposed to be. No clear lines of demarcation. A mongrel city. Traffic where there shouldn't be traffic. An awful void opening around him, preparing itself to hold explosions of bile, vomit, gushing bowels, ooze, sludge, seepage.

Earlier in the summer, on a July afternoon, he'd tried to escape the heat by walking along the Delaware. The water was unnaturally calm, isolated into stagnant pools by outcroppings of wharf and jetty. A shelf of rotting matter paralleled the riveredge. As if someone had attempted to sweep what was unclean and dead from the water. Bones, skins, entrails, torn carcasses, unrecognizable tatters and remnants broomed into a neat ridge. No sigh of the breeze he'd sought, yet fumes from the rim of garbage battered him in nauseating waves, a palpable medium intimate as wind. Beyond the tidal line of refuse, a pale margin lapped clean by receding waters. Then the iron river itself, flat, dark, speckled by sores of foam that puckered and swirled, worrying the stillness with a life of their own.

*Spilled. Spoiled.* Those words repeated themselves endlessly as he made his rounds. Dr. Rush had written out his portion, his day's share from the list of dead and dying. He'd purged, bled, comforted, and buried victims of the fever. In and out of homes that had become tombs, prisons, charnel houses. Dazed children wandering the streets, searching for their parents. How can he explain to a girl, barely more than an infant, that the father and mother she sobs for are gone from this earth? Departed. Expired. They are resting, child. Asleep forever. In a far, far better place, my sweet, dear, suffering one. In God's bosom. Wrapped in His incorruptible arms. A dead mother with a dead baby at her breast. Piteous cries of the helpless offering all they own for a drink of water. How does he console the delirious boy who pummels him, fastens himself on his leg because he's put the boy's mother in a box and now must nail shut the lid?

Though light-headed from exhaustion, he's determined to spend a few hours here, among his own people. But were these lost ones really his people? The doors of his church were open to them, yet these were the ones who stayed away, wasting their lives in vicious pastimes of the idle, the unsaved, the ignorant. His benighted brethren who'd struggled to reach this city of refuge and then, once inside the gates, had fallen, prisoners again, trapped by chains of dissolute living as they'd formerly been snared in the bonds of slavery. He'd come here and preached to them. Thieves, beggars, loose women, debtors, fugitives, drunkards, gamblers, the weak, crippled, and outcast with nowhere else to go. They spurned his church so he'd brought church to them, preaching in gin mills, whoring dens, on street corners. He'd been jeered and hooted, spat upon, clods of unnamable filth had spattered his coat. But a love for them, as deep and unfathomable as his sorrow, his pity, brought him back again and again, exhorting them, setting the gospel before them so they might partake of its bounty, the infinite goodness, blessed sustenance therein. Jesus had toiled among the wretched, the outcast, that flotsam and jetsam deposited like a ledge of filth on the banks of the city. He understood what had brought the dark faces of his brethren north, to the Quaker promise of this town, this cradle and capital of a New World, knew the misery they were fleeing, the bright star in the Gourd's handle that guided them, the joy leaping in their hearts when at last, at last the opportunity to be viewed as men instead of things was theirs. He'd dreamed such dreams himself, oh yes, and prayed that the light of hope would never be extinguished. He'd been praying for deliverance, for peace and understanding when God had granted him a vision, hordes of sable bondsmen throwing off their chains, marching, singing, a path opening in the sea, the sea shaking its shaggy shoulders, resplendent with light and power. A radiance sparkling in this walkway through the water, pearls, diamonds, spears of light. This was the glistening way home. Waters parting, glory blinking and winking. Too intense to stare at, a promise shimmering, a rainbow arching over the end of the path. A hand tapped him. He'd waited for it to blend into the vision, for its meaning to shine forth in the language neither word nor thought God was speaking in His visitation. Tapping became a grip. Someone was shoving him. He was being pushed off his knees, hauled to his feet. Someone was snatching him from the honeyed dream of salvation. When his eyes popped open he knew the name of each church elder manhandling him. He knew without looking the names of the men whose hands touched him gently, steering, coaxing, and those whose hands dug into his flesh, the impatient, imperious, rough hands that shunned any contact with him except as overseer or master.

Allen, Allen. Do you hear me? You and your people must not kneel at the front of the gallery. On your feet. Come. Come. Now. On your feet.

Behind the last row of pews. There ye may fall down on your knees and give praise.

And so we built our African house of worship. But its walls could not imprison the Lord's word. Go forth. Go forth. And he did so. To this sinful quarter. Tunnels, cellars, and caves. Where no sunlight penetrates. Where wind off the river cuts like a knife. Chill of icy spray channeled here from the ocean's wintry depths. Where each summer the brackish sea that is mouth and maw and bowel deposits its waste in puddles stinking to high heaven.

Water Street becomes what it's named, rises round his ankles, soaks his boots, threatens to drag him down. Patrolling these murky depths he's predator, scavenger, the prey of some dagger-toothed creature whose shadow closes over him like a net.

When the first settlers arrived here they'd scratched caves into the soft earth of the riverbank. Like ants. Rats. Gradually they'd pushed inland, laying out a geometrical grid of streets, perpendicular, true-angled and straight-edged, the mirror of their rectitude. Black Quaker coats and dour visages were remembrances of mud, darkness, the place of their lying-in, cocooned like worms, propagating dreams of a holy city. The latest corners must always start here, on this dotted line, in this riot of alleys, lanes, tunnels. Wave after wave of immigrants unloaded here, winnowed here, dying in these shanties, grieving in strange languages. But white faces move on, bury their dead, bear their children, negotiate the invisible reef between this broken place and the foursquare town. Learn enough of their new tongue to say to the blacks they've left behind, *thou shalt not pass.*

I watched him bring the scalding liquid to his lips and thought to myself that's where his color comes from. The black brew he drinks every morning. Coloring him, changing him. A hue

I had not considered until that instant as other than absence, something nonwhite and therefore its opposite, what light would be if extinguished, sky or sea drained of the color blue when the sun disappears, the blackness of cinders. As he sips, steam rises. I peer into the cup that's become mine, at the moon in its center, waxing, waning. A light burning in another part of the room caught there, as my face would be if I leaned over the cup's hot mouth. But I have no wish to see my face. His is what I study as I stare into my cup and see not absence, but the presence of wood darkly stained, wet plowed earth, a boulder rising from a lake, blackly glistening as it sheds crowns and beards and necklaces of water. His color neither neglect nor abstention, nor mystery, but a swelling tide in his skin of this bitter morning beverage it is my habit to imbibe.

We were losing, clearly losing the fight. One day in mid-September, fifty-seven were buried before noon.

He'd begun with no preamble. Our conversation taken up again directly as if the months since our last meeting were no more than a cobweb his first words lightly brush away. I say conversation but a better word would be soliloquy because I was only a listener, a witness learning his story, a story buried so deeply he couldn't recall it, but dreamed pieces, a conversation with himself, a reverie with the power to sink us both into its unreality. So his first words did not begin the story where I remembered him ending it in our last session, but picked up midstream the ceaseless play of voices only he heard, always, summoning him, possessing him, enabling him to speak, to be.

Despair was in my heart. The fiction of our immunity had been exposed for the vicious lie it was, a not-so-subtle device for wresting us from our homes, our loved ones, the afflicted among us, and sending us to aid strangers. First they blamed us, called the sickness Barbados fever, a contagion from those blood-soaked islands, brought to these shores by refugees from

the fighting in Santo Domingo. We were not welcome anywhere. A dark skin was seen not only as a badge of shame for
its wearer. Now we were evil incarnate, the mask of long
agony and violent death. Black servants were discharged. The
draymen, carters, barbers, caterers, oyster sellers, street ven-
dors could find no custom. It mattered not that some of us were
born here and spoke no language but the English language,
second-, even third-generation African Americans who knew
no other country, who laughed at the antics of newly landed
immigrants, Dutchmen, Welshmen, Scots, Irish, Frenchmen
who had turned our marketplaces into Babel, stomping along
in their clodhopper shoes, strange costumes, haughty airs, low-
lander gibberish that sounded like men coughing or dogs bark-
ing. My fellow countrymen searching everywhere but in their
own hearts, the foulness upon which this city is erected, to lay
blame on others for the killing fever, pointed their fingers at
foreigners and called it Palatine fever, a pestilence imported
from those low countries in Europe where, I have been told,
war for control of the sea lanes, the human cargoes transported
thereupon, has raged for a hundred years.

But I am losing the thread, the ironical knot I wished to
untangle for you. How the knife was plunged in our hearts,
then cruelly twisted. We were proclaimed carriers of the fever
and treated as pariahs, but when it became expedient to command our services to nurse the sick and bury the dead, the
previous allegations were no longer mentioned. Urged on by
desperate counselors, the mayor granted us a blessed immunity. We were ordered to save the city.

I swear to you, and the bills of mortality, published by the
otherwise unreliable Mr. Carey, support my contention, that
the fever dealt with us severely. Among the city's poor and
destitute the fever's ravages were most deadly and we are
always the poorest of the poor. If an ordinance forbidding

ringing of bells to mourn the dead had not been passed, that awful tolling would have marked our days, the watches of the night in our African-American community, as it did in those environs of the city we were forbidden to inhabit. Every morning before I commenced my labors for the sick and dying, I would hear moaning, screams of pain, fearful cries and supplications, a chorus of lamentations scarring daybreak, my people awakening to a nightmare that was devouring their will to live.

The small strength I was able to muster each morning was sorely tried the moment my eyes and ears opened upon the sufferings of my people, the reality that gave the lie to the fiction of our immunity. When my duties among the whites were concluded, how many nights did I return and struggle till dawn with victims here, my friends, parishioners, wandering sons of Africa whose faces I could not look upon without seeing my own. I was commandeered to rise and go forth to the general task of saving the city, forced to leave this neighborhood where my skills were sorely needed. I cared for those who hated me, deserted the ones I loved, who loved me.

I recite the story many, many times to myself, let many voices speak to me till one begins to sound like the sea or rain or my feet those mornings shuffling through thick dust.

We arrived at Bush Hill early. To spare ourselves a long trek in the oppressive heat of day. Yellow haze hung over the city. Plumes of smoke from blazes in Potter's Field, from fires on street corners curled above the rooftops, lending the dismal aspect of a town sacked and burned. I've listened to the Santo Domingans tell of the burning of Cap François. How the capital city was engulfed by fires set in cane fields by the rebelling slaves. Horizon in flames all night as they huddled offshore in ships, terrified, wondering where next they'd go, if any port would permit them to land, empty-handed slaves, masters whose only wealth now was naked black bodies locked in the hold, wide-eyed witnesses of an empire's downfall, chanting, moaning, uncertain as the sea rocked them, whether or not anything on earth could survive the fearful conflagration consuming the great city of Cap François.

Dawn breaking on a smoldering landscape, writhing columns of smoke, a general cloud of haze the color of a fever victim's eyes. I turn and stare at it a moment, then fall in again with my brother's footsteps trudging through untended fields girding Bush Hill.

From a prisoner-of-war ship in New York Harbor where the British had interned him he'd seen that city shed its grave-clothes of fog. Morning after morning it would paint itself damp and gray, a flat sketch on the canvas of sky, a tentative, shivering screen of housefronts, sheds, sprawling warehouses floating above the river. Then shadows and hollows darkened. A jumble of masts, spars, sails began to sway, little boats plied lanes between ships, tiny figures inched along wharves and docks, doors opened, windows slid up or down, lending an illusion of depth and animation to the portrait. This city infinitely beyond his reach, this charade other men staged to mock him, to mark the distance he could not travel, the shore he'd never reach, the city, so to speak, came to life and with its birth each morning dropped the palpable weight of his despair. His loneliness and exile. Moored in pewter water, on an island that never stopped moving but never arrived anywhere. The city a mirage of light and air, chimera of paint, brush, and paper, mattered naught except that it was denied him. It shimmered. Tolled. Unsettled the watery place where he was sentenced to dwell. Conveyed to him each morning the same doleful tidings: *the dead are legion, the living a froth on dark, layered depths. But you are neither, and less than both.* Each night he dreamed it burning, razed the city till nothing remained but a dry, black crust, crackling, crunching under his boots as he strides, king of the nothing he surveys.

We passed holes dug into the earth where the sick are interred. Some died in these shallow pits, awash in their own vomited and voided filth, before a bed in the hospital could be made ready for them. Others believed they were being buried alive and unable to crawl out howled till reason or strength deserted them. A few, past caring, slept soundly in these ditches, resisted the attendants sent to rouse them and transport them inside once they realized they were being resurrected to do battle again with the fever. I'd watched the red-bearded French doctor from Santo Domingo with his charts and assistants inspecting this zone, his *salle d'attente* he called it, greeting and reassuring new arrivals, interrogating them, nodding and bowing, hurrying from pit to pit, peering down at his invisible patients like a gardener tending his seeds.

An introduction to the grave, a way into the hospital that prefigured the way most would leave it. That's what this bizarre rite of admission had seemed at first. But through this and other peculiar stratagems, Deveze with his French practice had transformed Bush Hill from lazarium to a clinic where victims of the fever, if not too weak upon arrival, stood a chance of surviving.

The cartman employed by Bush Hill had suddenly fallen sick. Faithful Wilcox had never missed a day, ferrying back and forth from town to hospital, hospital to Potter's Field. Bush Hill had its own cemetery now. Daily rations of dead could be disposed of less conspicuously in a plot on the grounds of the estate, screened from the horror-struck eyes of the city. No one had trusted the hospital. Tales of bloody chaos reigning there had filtered back to the city. Citizens believed it was a place where the doomed were stored until they died. Fever victims would have to be dragged from their beds into Bush Hill's cart. They'd struggle and scream, pitch themselves from the rolling cart, beg for help when the cart passed a rare pedestrian daring or foolish enough to be abroad in the deadly streets.

I wondered for the thousandth time why some were stricken, some not. Dr. Rush and this Deveze dipped their hands into the entrails of corpses, stirred the black, corrupted blood, breathed infected vapors exhaled from mortified remains. I'd observed both men steeped in noxious fluids expelled by their patients, yet neither had fallen prey to the fever. Stolid, dim Wilcox maintained daily concourse with the sick and buried the dead for two months before he was infected. They say a woman, undiscovered until boiling stench drove her neighbors into the street crying for aid, was the cause of Wilcox's downfall. A large woman, bloated into an even more cumbersome package by gases and liquids seething inside her body, had slipped from his grasp as he and another had hoisted her up into the cart. Catching against a rail, her body had slammed down and burst, spraying Wilcox like a fountain. Wilcox did not pride himself on being the tidiest of men, nor did his job demand one who was overfastidious, but the reeking stench from that accident was too much even for him and he departed in a huff to change his polluted garments. He never returned. So there I was at Bush Hill where Rush had assigned me with my brother, to bury the flow of dead that did not ebb just because the Charon who was their familiar could no longer attend them.

The doctors believe they can find the secret of the fever in the victims' dead bodies. They cut, saw, extract, weigh, measure.

The dead are carved into smaller and smaller bits and the butchered parts studied but they do not speak. What I know of the fever I've learned from the lips of those I've treated, the stories of the living, that are ignored by the good doctors. When lancet and fleam bleed the victims, they offer up stories like prayers.

It was a jaunty day. We served our white guests and after they'd eaten, they served us at the long, linen-draped tables. A sumptuous feast in the oak grove prepared by many and willing hands. All the world's eyes seemed to be watching us. The city's leading men, black and white, were in attendance to celebrate laying the cornerstone of St. Thomas Episcopal African Church. In spite of the heat and clouds of mettlesome insects, spirits were high. A gathering of whites and blacks in good Christian fashion to commemorate the fruit of shared labor. Perhaps a new day was dawning. The picnic occurred in July. In less than a month the fever burst upon us.

When you open the dead, black or white, you find: The dura matter covering the brain is white and fibrous in appearance. The leptomeninges covering the brain are clear and without opacifications. The brain weighs 1,450 grams and is formed symmetrically. Cut sections of the cerebral hemispheres reveal normal-appearing gray matter throughout. The white matter of the corpus callosum is intact and bears no lesions. The basal ganglia are in their normal locations and grossly appear to be without lesions. The ventricles are symmetrical and filled with crystal-clear cerebrospinal fluid.

The cerebellum is formed symmetrically. The nuclei of the cerebellum are unremarkable. Multiple sections through the pons, medulla oblongata, and upper brain stem reveal normal gross anatomy. The cranial nerves are in their normal locations and unremarkable.

The muscles of the neck are in their normal locations. The cartilages of the larynx and the hyoid bone are intact. The thyroid and parathyroid glands are normal on their external surface. The mucosa of the larynx is shiny, smooth, and without lesions. The vocal cords are unremarkable. A small amount of bloody material is present in the upper trachea.

The heart weighs 380 grams. The epicardial surface is smooth, glistening, and without lesions. The myocardium of the left ventricle and septum are of a uniformly meaty-red, firm appearance. The endocardial surfaces are smooth, glistening, and without lesions. The auricular appendages are free from thrombi. The valve leaflets are thin and delicate, and show no evidence of vegetation.

The right lung weighs 400 grams. The left lung 510 grams. The pleural surface of the lungs is smooth and glistening.

The esophageal mucosa is glistening, white, and folded. The stomach contains a large amount of black, noxious bile. A vermiform appendix is present. The ascending transverse and descending colon reveal hemorrhaging, striations, disturbance of normal mucosa patterns throughout. A small amount of bloody, liquid feces is present in the ano-rectal canal.

The liver weighs 172 grams. The spleen weighs 150 grams. The right kidney weighs 190 grams. The left kidney weighs 180 grams. The testes show a glistening white tunica albuginea. Sections are unremarkable.

Dr. Rush and his assistants examined as many corpses as possible in spite of the hurry and tumult of neverending attendance on the sick. Rush hoped to prove his remedy, his analysis of the cause and course of the fever correct. Attacked on all sides by his medical brethren for purging and bleeding patients already in a drastically weakened state, Rush lashed back at his detractors, wrote pamphlets, broadsides, brandished the stinking evidence of his postmortems to demonstrate conclusively

how the sick drowned in their own poisoned fluids. The putre-
faction, the black excess, he proclaimed, must be drained away,
else the victim inevitably succumbs.

Dearest:

I shall not return home again until this business of the fever is
terminated. I fear bringing the dread contagion into our home. My
life is in the hands of God and as long as He sees fit to spare me I
will persist in my labors on behalf of the sick, dying, and dead. We
are losing the battle. Eighty-eight were buried this past Thursday. I
tremble for your safety. Wish the lie of immunity were true. Please
let me know by way of a note sent to the residence of Dr. Rush that
you and our dear Martha are well. I pray every hour that God will
preserve you both. As difficult as it is to rise each morning and go
with Thomas to perform our duties, the task would be unbearable if
I did not hold in my heart a vision of these horrors ending, a blessed
shining day when I return to you and drop this weary head upon
your sweet bosom.

Allen, Allen, he called to me. Observe how even after death,
the body rejects this bloody matter from nose and bowel and
mouth. Verily, the patient who had expired at least an hour
before, continued to stain the cloth I'd wrapped round him.
We'd searched the rooms of a regal mansion, discovering six
members of a family, patriarch, son, son's wife and three children, either dead or in the last frightful stages of the disease.
Upon the advice of one of Dr. Rush's most outspoken critics,
they had refused mercury purges and bleeding until now,
when it was too late for any earthly remedy to preserve them.
In the rich furnishings of this opulent mansion, attended by
one remaining servant whom fear had not driven away, three
generations had withered simultaneously, this proud family's
link to past and future cut off absolutely, the great circle bro-

ken. In the first bedroom we'd entered we'd found William
Spurgeon, merchant, son and father, present manager of the
family fortune, so weak he could not speak, except with pained
blinks of his terrible golden eyes. Did he welcome us? Was he
apologizing to good Dr. Rush for doubting his cure? Did he
fear the dark faces of my brother and myself? Quick, too
quickly, he was gone. Answering no questions. Revealing
nothing of his state of mind. A savaged face frozen above the
blanket. Ancient beyond years. Jaundiced eyes not fooled by
our busy ministrations, but staring through us, fixed on the
eternal stillness soon to come. And I believe I learned in that
yellow cast of his eyes, the exact hue of the sky, if sky it should
be called, hanging over the next world where we abide.

Allen, Allen. He lasted only moments and then I wrapped
him in a sheet from the chest at the foot of his canopied bed.
We lifted him into a humbler litter, crudely nailed together,
the lumber still green. Allen, look. Stench from the coffin cut
through the oppressive odors permeating this doomed household. See. Like an infant the master of the house had soiled his
swaddling clothes. Seepage formed a dark river and dripped
between roughly jointed boards. We found his wife where
she'd fallen, naked, yellow above the waist, black below. As
always the smell presaged what we'd discover behind a closed
door. This woman had possessed closets of finery, slaves who
dressed, fed, bathed, and painted her, and yet here she lay, no
one to cover her modesty, to lift her from the floor. Dr. Rush
guessed from the discoloration she'd been dead two days, a
guess confirmed by the loyal black maid, sick herself, who'd
elected to stay when all others had deserted her masters. The
demands of the living too much for her. She'd simply shut the
door on her dead mistress. No breath, no heartbeat, Sir. I could
not rouse her, Sir. I intended to return, Sir, but I was too weak
to move her, too exhausted by my labors, Sir. Tears rolled

down her creased black face and I wondered in my heart how
this abused and despised old creature in her filthy apron and
turban, this frail, worn woman, had survived the general calamity while the strong and pampered toppled round her.

I wanted to demand of her why she did not fly out the door
now, finally freed of her burden, her lifelong enslavement to
the whims of white people. Yet I asked her nothing. Considered instead myself, a man who'd worked years to purchase his
wife's freedom, then his own, a so-called freeman, and here I
was following in the train of Rush and his assistants, a func-
tionary, a lackey, insulted daily by those I risked my life to heal.

Why did I not fly? Why was I not dancing in the streets,
celebrating God's judgment on this wicked city? Fever made
me freer than I'd ever been. Municipal government had collapsed. Anarchy ruled. As long as fever did not strike me I
could come and go anywhere I pleased. Fortunes could be
amassed in the streets. I could sell myself to the highest bidder,
as nurse or undertaker, as surgeon trained by the famous Dr.
Rush to apply his lifesaving cure. Anyone who would enter
houses where fever was abroad could demand outrageous sums
for negligible services. To be spared the fever was a chance for
anyone, black or white, to be a king.

So why do you follow him like a loyal puppy, you con-
founded black fool? He wagged his finger. *You . . . His finger
a gaunt, swollen-jointed, cracked-bone, chewed thing. Like the nose
on his face. The nose I'd thought looked more like finger than nose.
Fool. Fool.* Finger wagging then the cackle. The barnyard
braying. Berserk chickens cackling in his skinny, goiter-
knobbed throat. You are a fool, you black son of Ham. You
slack-witted, Nubian ape. You progeny of peeping toms and
orangutans. Who forces you to accompany that madman Rush
on his murderous tours? He kills a hundred for every one he
helps with his lame-brain, nonsensical, unnatural, Sangrado

cures. Why do you tuck your monkey tail between your legs and skip after that butcher? Are you his shadow, a mindless, spineless black puddle of slime with no will of its own?

You are a good man, Allen. You worry about the souls of your people in this soulless wilderness. You love your family and your God. You are a beacon and steadfast. Your fatal flaw is narrowness of vision. You cannot see beyond these shores. The river, that stinking gutter into which the city shovels its shit and extracts its drinking water, that long suffering string of spittle winds to an ocean. A hundred miles downstream the foamy mouth of the land sucks on the Atlantic's teat, trade winds saunter, and a whole wide world awaits the voyager. I know, Allen. I've been everywhere. Buying and selling everywhere.

If you would dare be Moses to your people and lead them out of this land, you'd find fair fields for your talent. Not lapdogging or doggy-trotting behind or fetch doggy or lie doggy or doggy open your legs or doggy stay still while I beat you. Follow the wound that is a river back to the sea. Be gone, be gone. While there's still time. If there is time, *mon frère.* If the pestilence has not settled in you already, breathed from my foul guts into yours, even as we speak.

Here's a master for you. A real master, Allen. The fever that's supping on my innards. I am more slave than you've ever been. I do its bidding absolutely. Cough up my lungs. Shit hunks of my bowel. When I die, they say my skin will turn as black as yours Allen.

Return to your family. Do not leave them again. Whatever the Rushes promise, whatever they threaten.

Once, ten thousand years ago I had a wife and children. I was like you, Allen, proud, innocent, forward looking, well spoken, well mannered, a beacon and steadfast. I began to believe the whispered promise that I could have more. More of what, I didn't ask. Didn't know, but I took my eyes off what I loved in order to obtain this more. Left my wife and children and when I returned they were gone. Forever lost to me. The details are not significant. Suffice to say the circumstances of my leaving were much like yours. Very much like yours, Allen. And I lost everything. Became a wanderer among men. Bad news people see coming from miles away. A pariah. A joke. I'm not black like you, Allen. But I will be soon. Sooner than you'll be white. And if you're ever white, you'll be as dead as I'll be when I'm black.

Why do you desert your loved ones? What impels you to do what you find so painful, so unjust? Are you not a man? And free?

Her sleepy eyes, your lips on her warm cheek, each time may be the last meeting on this earth. The circumstances are similar, my brother. My shadow. My dirty face.

The dead are legion, the living a froth on dark, layered depths.

*Master Abraham. There's a gentleman to see you, Sir.* The golden-haired lad bound to me for seven years was carted across the seas, like you, Allen, in the bowels of a leaky tub. A son to replace my son his fathers had clubbed to death when they razed the ghetto of Antwerp. But I could not tame the inveterate hate, his aversion and contempt for me. From my aerie, at my desk secluded among barrels, bolts, crates, and trunks of the shop's attic, I watched him steal, drink, fornicate. I overheard him denounce me to a delegate sent round to collect a tithe during the emergency. 'Tis well known in the old country that Jews bring the fever. Palatine fever that slays whole cities. They carry it under dirty fingernails, in the wimples of lizardy private parts. Pass it on with the evil eye. That's why we hound them from our towns, exterminate them. Beware of Master Abraham's glare. And the black-coated vulture listened intently. I could see him totting up the account in his small brain. Kill the Jew. Gain a shop and sturdy prentice, too. But I survived till fever laid me low and the cart brought me here to Bush Hill. For years he robbed and betrayed me and all my revenge was to treat him better. Allow him to pilfer, lie, embezzle. Let him grow fat and careless as I knew he would. With a father's boundless kindness I destroyed him. The last sorry laugh coming when I learned he died in agony, fever-shriven, following by a day his Water Street French whore my indulgence allowed him to keep.

In Amsterdam I sold diamonds, Allen. In Barcelona they plucked hairs from my beard to fashion charms that brought ill fortune to their enemies. There were nights in dungeons when the mantle of my suffering was all I possessed to wrap round me and keep off mortal cold. I cursed God for choosing me, choosing my people to cuckold and slaughter. Have you heard of the Lamed-Vov, the Thirty Just Men set apart to suffer the reality humankind cannot bear? Saviors. But not Gods like your Christ. Not magicians, not sorcerers with bags of tricks, Allen. No divine immunities. Flesh and blood saviors. Men like we are, Allen. If man you are beneath your sable hide. Men who cough and scratch their sores and bleed and stink. Whose teeth rot. Whose wives and children are torn from them. Who wander the earth unable to die, but men always, men till God plucks them up and returns them to his side where they must thaw ten centuries to melt the crust of earthly grief and misery they've taken upon themselves. Ice men. Snow men. I thought for many years I might be one of them. In my vanity. My self-pity. My foolishness. But no. One lifetime of sorrow's enough for me. I'm just another customer.

One more in the crowd lined up at his stall to purchase his wares.

You do know, don't you, Allen, that God is a bookseller? He publishes one book—the text of suffering—over and over again. He disguises it between new boards, in different shapes and sizes, prints on varying papers, in many fonts, adds prefaces and postscripts to deceive the buyer, but it's always the same book.

You say you do not return to your family because you don't want to infect them. Perhaps your fear is well founded. But perhaps it also masks a greater fear. Can you imagine yourself, Allen, as other than you are? A free man with no charlatan Rush to blame? The weight of your life in your hands?

You've told me tales of citizens paralyzed by fear, of slaves on shipboard who turn to stone in their chains, their eyes boiled in the sun. Is it not possible that you suffer the converse of this immobility? You Sir, unable to stop an endless round of duty and obligation. Turning pages as if the next one or the next will let you finish the story and return to your life.

Your life, man. Tell me what sacred destiny, what nigger errand keeps you standing here at my filthy pallet? Fly, fly, fly away home. Your house is on fire, your children burning.

I have lived to see the slaves free. My people frolic in the streets. Black and white. The ones who believe they are either or both or neither. I am too old for dancing. Too old for foolishness. But this full moon makes me wish for two good legs. For three. Straddled a broomstick when I was a boy. Giddyup, Giddyup. Galloping M'Lord, M'Lady, around the yard I should be sweeping. Dust in my wake. Chickens squawking. My eyes everywhere at once so I would not be caught out by mistress or master in the sin of idleness. Of dreaming. Of following a child's inclination. My broom steed snatched away. Become a rod across my back. Ever cautious. Dreaming with one eye open. The eye I am now, old and gimpy-limbed, watching while my people celebrate the rumor of Old Pharaoh's capitulation.

I've shed this city like a skin, wiggling out of it tenscore and more years, by miles and ells, fretting, twisting. Many days I did not know whether I'd wrenched freer or crawled deeper into the sinuous pit. Somewhere a child stood, someplace green, keeping track, waiting for me. Hoping I'd meet him again, hoping my struggle was not in vain. I search that child's face for clues to my blurred features. Flesh drifted and banked, eroded by wind and water, the landscape of this city fitting me like a skin. Pray for me, child. For my unborn parents I carry in this orphan's pot belly. For this ancient face that slips like water through my fingers.

Night now. Bitter cold night. Fires in the hearths of lucky ones. Many of us still abide in dark cellars, caves dug into the earth below poor men's houses. For we are poorer still, burrow there, pull earth like blanket and quilt round us to shut out cold, sleep multitudes to a room, stacked and cross-hatched and spoonfashion, ourselves the fuel, heat of one body passed to others and passed back from all to one. No wonder then the celebration does not end as a blazing chill sweeps off the Delaware. Those who leap and roar round the bonfires are better off where they are. They have no place else to go.

Given the derivation of the words, you could call the deadly, winged visitors an *unpleasantness from Egypt.*

Putrid stink rattled in his nostrils. He must stoop to enter the cellar. No answer as he shouts his name, his mission of mercy. Earthen floor, ceiling and walls buttressed by occasional beams, slabs of wood. Faint bobbing glow from his lantern. He sees himself looming and shivering on the walls, a shadowy presence with more substance than he feels he possesses at this late hour. After a long day of visits, this hovel his last stop before returning to his brother's house for a few hours of rest. He has learned that exhaustion is a swamp he can wade through and on the far side another region where a thin trembling version of himself toils while he observes, bemused, slipping in and out of sleep, amazed at the likeness, the skill with which that other mounts and sustains him. Mimicry. Puppetry. Whatever controls this other, he allows the impostor to continue, depends upon it to work when he no longer can. After days in the city proper with Rush, he returns to these twisting streets beside the river that are infected veins and arteries he must bleed.

At the rear of the cave, so deep in shadow he stumbles against it before he sees it, is a mound of rags. When he leans over it, speaking down into the darkness, he knows instantly this is the source of the terrible smell, that something once alive is rotting under the rags. He thinks of autumn leaves blown into mountainous, crisp heaps, the north wind cleansing itself and the city of summer. He thinks of anything, any image that will rescue him momentarily from the nauseating stench, postpone what he must do next. He screams no, no to himself as he blinks away his wife's face, the face of his daughter. There is no rhyme or reason in whom the fever takes, whom it spares, but he's in the city every day, exposed to its victims, breathing fetid air, touching corrupted flesh. Surely if someone in his family must die, it will be him. His clothes are drenched in vinegar, he sniffs the nostrum of gunpowder, bark, and asafetida in a bag pinned to his coat. He's prepared to purge and bleed himself, he's also ready and quite willing to forgo these precautions and cures if he thought surrendering his life might save theirs. He thinks and unthinks a picture of her hair, soft against his cheek, the wet warmth of his daughter's backside in the crook of his arm as he carries her to her mother's side where she'll be changed and fed. No. Like a choking mist, the smell of decaying flesh stifles him, forces him to turn away, once, twice, before he watches himself bend down into the brunt of it and uncover the sleepers.

Two Santo Domingan refugees, slave or free, no one knew for sure, inhabited this cellar. They had moved in less than a week before, the mother huge with child, man and woman both wracked by fear. No one knows how long the couple's been unattended. There was shame in the eyes and voices of the few from whom he'd gleaned bits and pieces of the Santo Domingans' history. Since no one really knew them and few nearby spoke their language, no one was willing to risk, etc. Except for screams one night, no one had seen or heard signs of life. If he'd been told nothing about them, his nose would have led him here.

He winces when he sees the dead man and woman, husband and wife, not entwined as in some ballad of love eternal, but turned back to back, distance between them, as if the horror were too visible, too great to bear, doubled in the other's eyes. What had they seen before they flung away from each other? If he could, he would rearrange them, spare the undertakers this vision.

Rat feet and rat squeak in the shadows. He'd stomped his feet, shooed them before he entered, hollered as he threw back the covers, but already they were accustomed to his presence, back at work. They'd bite indiscriminately, dead flesh, his flesh. He curses and flails his staff against the rags, strikes the earthen floor to keep the scavengers at bay. Those sounds are what precipitate the high-pitched cries that first frighten him, then shame him, then propel him to a tall packing crate turned on its end, atop which another crate is balanced. Inside the second wicker container which had imported some item from some distant place into this land, twin brown babies hoot and wail.

We are passing over the Dismal Swamp. On the right is the Appalachian range, some of the oldest mountains on earth. Once there were steep ridges and valleys all through here but erosion off the mountains created landfill several miles deep in places. This accounts for the rich loamy soil of the region. Over the centuries several southern states were formed from this gradual erosion. The cash crops of cotton and tobacco so vital to Southern prosperity were ideally suited to the fertile soil.

Yeah, I nurse these old funky motherfuckers, all right. White people, specially old white people, lemme tell you, boy, them peckerwoods stink. Stone dead fishy wet stink. Talking all the time bout niggers got BO. Well, white folks got the stink and gone, man. Don't be putting my hands on them, neither. Never. Huh uh. If I touch them, be wit gloves. They some nasty people, boy. And they don't be paying me enough to take no chances wit my health. Matter of fact they ain't paying me enough to really be expecting me to work. Yeah. Starvation wages. So I ain't hardly touching them. Or doing much else either. Got to smoke a cigarette to get close to some of them. Piss and shit theyselves like babies. They don't need much taking care anyway. Most of them three quarters dead already. Ones that ain't is crazy. Nobody don't want them round, that's why they here. Talking to theyselves. Acting like they speaking to a roomful of people and not one soul in the ward paying attention. There's one old black dude, must be a hundred, he be muttering away to hisself nonstop every day. Pitiful, man. Hope I don't never get that old. Shoot me, bro, if I start to getting old and fucked up in body and mind like them. Don't want no fools like me hanging over me when I can't do nothing no more for my ownself. Shit. They ain't paying me nothing so that's what I do. Nothing. Least I don't punch em or tease em or steal they shit like some the staff. And I don't pretend I'm God like these so-called professionals and doctors flittin round here drawing down that long bread. Naw. I just mind my own business, do my time. Cop a little TV, sneak me a joint when nobody's around. It ain't all that bad, really. Long as I ain't got no old lady and crumb crushers. Don't know how the married cats make it on the little bit of chump change they pay us. But me, I'm free. It ain't that bad, really.

By the time his brother brought him the news of their deaths . . .

Almost an afterthought. The worst, he believed, had been overcome. Only a handful of deaths the last weeks of November. The city was recovering. Commerce thriving. Philadelphia must be revictualed, refueled, rebuilt, reconnected to the countryside, to markets foreign and domestic, to products, pleasures, and appetites denied during the quarantine months of the fever. A new century would soon be dawning. We must forget the horrors. The mayor proclaims a new day. Says let's put the past behind us. Of the eleven who died in the fire he said extreme measures were necessary as we cleansed ourselves of disruptive influences. The cost could have been much greater he said I regret the loss of life, especially the half-dozen kids, but I commend all city officials, all volunteers who helped return the city to the arc of glory that is its proper destiny.

When they cut him open, the one who decided to stay, to be a beacon and steadfast, they will find: liver (172 grams), spleen (150 grams), right kidney (190 grams), left kidney (180 grams), brain (1,450 grams), heart (380 grams), and right next to his heart, the miniature hand of a child, frozen in a grasping gesture, fingers like hard tongues of flame, still reaching for the marvel of the beating heart, fascinated still, though the heart is cold, beats not, the hand as curious about this infinite stillness as it was about thump and heat and quickness.

J

---

KATHY
ACKER

THIS STORY ISN'T WRITTEN FOR FEMALES: *MY* DAUGHTERS, *MY* SISTERS, *MY* MOTHER, *MY* WIFE, ETC. THIS STORY ISN'T WRITTEN FOR THEM FOR ANY DAUGHTERS SISTERS MOTHERS WIVES. THIS STORY IS PENNED FOR MY BROTHERS.

I AM AWARE THAT ANYONE, MALE OR FEMALE, WHO LOVES BEAUTY (AND ART) EXPOSES HIMSELF OR HERSELF TO THE MASSES' HATRED. IN OTHER WORDS, I'M WRITING THIS ESSENTIALLY USE-LESS AND VERY INNOCENT STORY ONLY TO DIVERT MYSELF AND TO EXERCISE MY PASSION FOR TROUBLE.

THOUGH THE MAN WHO WROTE THESE WORDS LIVED IN THE NINETEENTH CENTURY AND IN PARIS, I'M GOING TO TELL ABOUT PART OF HIS LIFE AS IF HE'S LIVING NOW AND IN NEW YORK CITY. THOUGH HE HAD SYPHILIS, THEN A PLAGUE, I'M SAYING THAT HE HAS AIDS.

OTHERWISE THIS TALE IS TRUE. ACCORDING TO SOME BIOGRA-PHERS.

I'M ACTUALLY TELLING THE STORY OF HIS GIRLFRIEND ABOUT WHOM NOTHING IS KNOWN EXCEPT WHAT HE SAID ABOUT HER AND THAT SHE WAS MULATTO.

. . . For a long time now I've wanted to stick my fingers, fearfully, into your thick, heavy hairs.

Though I've been wounded in former love affairs, I want to put my head into that tomb: your skirts filled by your cunt smell. Because then I can smell the sweetness of my own sperm. As if it's a withered flower. Because I don't want to be alive as most people are alive. Because I want to be in a sleep as deep and spermlike as death so I can with no guilt lick my tongue across your mulatto body.

Only the abyss in your bed is going to destroy these sexual wounds, my flesh; only your tongue can lap away my memo-ries; only your nipples spurt out the liquids I need, the deaths of all but sensation.

I'm going to do what I have to, as if what I have to do is pleasure. I'm going to bury myself in your cunt. As if I've a choice. I'll be a martyr to my Fate, the liquids dried on your hairs. I'm the innocent prisoner who's about to be executed: I can do whatever I want. From now on, my need for pleasure will increase my pain.

And in order to get rid of any ambiguity, if there is any, I'll suck more and more poisoned milk, every kind of sexuality, out of your pointed nipples which have never been loved.

You, hairs.

Curling all over the place because you don't give a shit about anyone or rules. Your lawlessness is ecstasy to me.

Because my memories hide in you.

This night, in order to resurrect all memories and make them deathless, I'm going to wave you, hairs, as if you're banners, in front of people's faces.

I want to make all that is obscure and obscurity the normal world.

Languorous, demented Asia who slowly burns everything and everyone inside her, the climatic regions of the North in which no man dare live, and all that's primitive or cannot be mutilated (which our government hates most of all) reside in you, forest. Impassable. Just as some people claim that certain kinds of music open up the higher realms of perception, your stink leads me to . . .

I'm going to voyage to where soil and air are so hot that all who are living pass out.

Cunt hairs, you're going to be the waves who carry me there.

You cast long shadows that form an ebony sea. Here is found the dream of pirates, sails, and fires:

*The Port of Echoes* in which sailors, lonely, and exiles gulp down cheap gin like your juices. A murderer will tell my real fortune: no story or future; just color smell and sensation.

*J*

Smell's metaphysical. In this harbor, ships, slipping through
the watered silk, spread their legs as far as they can be spread
in order to hold on to a sky in which eternal heat is shuddering.    305

I've perceived you never stop coming.

Then I'll drown my head which has been migraining with
need and drunkenness in the black ocean. Otherness hides in
the black ocean. There I'll find luxury and timelessness, the
source of creation. You are the stinking liquid in which creativ-
ity is found.

Midnight hairs, pavilions of tenebral memories, returned the
sky's space to me. The smells of coconut oil mixed with sperm
urine and cunt juice have made me permanently drunk. I
promise that I'll keep giving you money so that I can keep
sniffing you and so that you'll keep doing what I want.

Hairs, aren't you the spaces in which I can begin to dream?
Aren't you always wet? Aren't you the nipples from which I
suck memories' liquors?

B WASN'T SURE OF J'S NAME, THOUGH HE KNEW SHE WAS MU-
LATTO.

IT'S NOT KNOWN WHEN OR WHERE J AND B MET. IN AN UN-
DATED LETTER TO HIS MOTHER, B REVEALED THAT HE WAS
DEEPLY BOUND TO A GIRL WHO WAS WORKING IN THE *PANTHEON*
THEATER. HE DIDN'T REVEAL THAT THE *PANTHEON* WAS A COMBO
PEEP SHOW AND STRIP JOINT ON 43RD STREET.

A WEEK AFTER HE HAD WRITTEN THIS LETTER TO HIS MOTHER,
B RENTED AN APARTMENT FOR J SO THAT SHE COULD STOP DIS-
PLAYING HER BODY TO MEN FOR MONEY.

ACCORDING TO THE BIOGRAPHERS, FACTS ARE KNOWN ABOUT
B'S LIFE. HE HAD AIDS. IT IS NOT KNOWN WHETHER OR NOT
AIDS WAS CONGENITAL. HE EITHER WOULDN'T OR COULDN'T
GET IT UP THOUGH HE WAS PAYING FOR J. ACCORDING TO HIM,
J WAS SEXUALLY INSATIABLE.

B SAID TO J:

"Do you remember what we saw on that beautiful summer morning when the sun was as white as my sperm?

"Just as the street across from Forbidden Planet took that sharp turn, we saw rotting meat. A hooker, her legs up in the air as if lubricating. Her mattress was holes and garbage.

"The lubrications were steaming poison and someone had nonchalantly opened up the stomach. Blobs of gas were bloating up the flesh that was left.

"The sun beat down on the rotting meat as if it wanted to cook it to a T or else return to Mother Nature as fast as possible Her creation.

"To the passionate sky this carcass became a flower opening in full bloom its vulnerability in full bloom. The inner parts' reeks eradicated the smells of the homeless' urine. Flies buzzed over the stomach while battalions of maggots in waves of viscosity so thick what was left of the flesh was resurrected emerged from the gut.

"All of this rose up and down like a wave and then orgasmed and transformed the hooker into a woman having a baby. We live in a world of transformation. The sounds of the birth process were natural, like brooks running through iced grass at the sides of steep mountains or winds howling while they roam through mists on mists.

"Then all of what I was seeing faded, became nothing more than a dream, not even a dream but what is waiting to be expressed and can't be on paper that's forgotten which the writer can find only by means of memory.

"The city disappeared.

"Behind one of the tenement staircases, a woman who had one all-white eye and that eye hated us, was waiting for when the corpse would be alone so that she could eat what meat was left. I saw two sisters.

"You are the stars that my eyes see and you are the only sun that has ever burned inside me. You're going to die. You're going to become shit. Since I'm bound to you who're my only joy, you're my disease. You're the passion I can know. This is what you're going to be, this hooker, after you die.

"Then, when you're sinking under whatever's beneath a graveyard's fake turf, maybe herbs and the richest efflorescence, and moldering among bones, for the first time you'll be able to speak and you'll tell the worms who're eating you the way I hate eating you that I protected and immortalized my decomposed love."

J DIDN'T REPLY.

J "carried her dark head . . . proudly and simply; her queenly step, full of savage grace, was that of a goddess or beast."

B MUST HAVE GOTTEN IT UP FOR HER ONE TIME BECAUSE HE MADE HER SICK.

SHE CONTRACTED SMALLPOX. "Under the dreadful crust of smallpox, her beauty vanished." SINCE SHE WAS NO LONGER DESIRABLE TO MEN, SHE WAS NO LONGER ABLE TO SECURE THE FUNDS NECESSARY FOR EXISTENCE.

IN J, B SAW HIS DISEASE AND HIMSELF. THAT CHANCE OR HIS FATE HAD EXILED HIM TO A COUNTRY NAMED *TOMB: SADNESS* WHICH WAS A GRAY LAND INHABITED SOLELY BY NIGHT WHO, DUE TO A MISERABLE CHILDHOOD, HAD NEVER LEARNED ANY MANNERS AND WAS A WORSE-THAN-NOTHING FUCK.

"Night," B SAID, "I'm just a painter whom God the Father or My Fate has condemned to draw, not upon canvas, but on nothingness. To paint by eating myself so everyone can eat me.

"Poe said that if an artist ever expressed the truth, society would go up in flames.

"One time love appeared to me, I knew it was love, and, as is her nature, grew larger, richer, more baroque, dreamier and

African, or else opened up to me all the unknown regions. Until she became my world. Then I was able to name my visitor.

"After that, dream equaled childhood equaled actuality. This was all I had ever wanted: an abyss or the loss of the world and simultaneously the only light I had ever known.

"What was this memory that she awoke? The land of memory that's neither past nor future but present burning joy? What is this memory that I now refuse to remember?

"Night . . .

"Night, I want to journey to your lands which I now can't reach.

"I can only travel there by means of smell. For smell is the one perceptual mode that, uniting body and mind, disappears and so reveals the realms that are unknown. Smell's the sense that leads to experience that's as real as death but not death.

"This is what I want.

"Through the odors of religious musks and sweatings, no longer as if all roads are closed, I'm going to go where only sensations are present. This is J's body: her elastic and heavy hairs are a living sachet of all the savage and wild musks. Her clothes were full of her vaginal and anal emissions which always stunk like fur."

ACCORDING TO B, ALL J HAD WANTED WAS TO FUCK AND BE FUCKED. AGAIN AND AGAIN. NO HUMAN KILLS ANOTHER HUMAN, FOR EVERY HUMAN MUST DIE. BY INFECTING HER, B HAD DECIMATED HER LIVING BODY WHILE SHE WAS LIVING. SINCE THE BODY IS SEXUALITY, CRIMES AGAINST SEXUALITY ARE THE ONLY CRIMES AGAINST HUMANS THAT EXIST.

THESE CRIMES B NAMED *BOREDOM.*

WHEN YOU'RE BORED OR WITHOUT HOPE, THERE'S NO COMMUNICATION IN THIS WORLD.

"Under a heavy sky, you don't know anything about shattered dreams. You've always been bored, but now disease, like a pothole cover, sits on the multiplication of you and boredom, sexlessness.

"Go back to the beginning: the days at the end of punk and after punk prior to the onset of the plague. The horizon that embraced the whole had made a black day sadder than any night. Lives turned into death-in-life.

"At the same time, the culture was becoming a mausoleum for any joy. These are what facts are. Myths. For everyone who had, prior to these days, believed in sex and drugs and rock-n-roll (in Joy or Hope), Hope, now a dying bat, with timid labial wings threw herself against building walls and thrust her head through the rotting ceilings.

"I am a city. The city of THE CRIME OF SEXUALITY or New York's descending. The ruin's tiny brown spiders who're spreading their nets in the bottoms of people's brains.

"New Yorkers refuse to see reality: spiders are eating up their brains. And now the screams, including cries about AIDS homeless crack gentrification and recession, that have to be their brains, explode in the air, gone mad, like church bells and lance the sky with their howlings and hideousness so that the pain never ends and simultaneously all those who are homeless and exiled are beginning to urinate like dogs.

"The mourners for all these dead are sitting in the hearses traveling down the arteries untwisting in my heart: THERE IS NO MORE LANGUAGE.

"Since there's no freedom from this plague, HOPE conquered lies silent while endless ANGUISH, tyrant, is sticking his black banner into my bowed head."

THIS ISN'T A STORY ABOUT B, BUT ABOUT NEW YORK CITY.

·  ·  ·

"Moved by J's long sufferings," B said, "gazing on the ineffaceable stigmata on that body that I used to adore, from now on this disease is going to be part of my happiness. Not only pity or sympathy, but actual physical pleasure."

B MADE HIS DECISION.

BECAUSE HE HAD GIVEN J THE DISEASE, B CARED FOR HER FOR THE REST OF HIS LIFE. AS IF HE LOVED HER OR HE GREW TO LOVE HER.

B, AT THE END OF HIS LIFE, WROTE AGAIN ABOUT J:

"She's a beautiful woman who pours wine over her cunt hairs. Desire's claws broke as soon as they attacked her. She laughed at Death and mocked Sin—those two monsters whose hands're always scratching and bending. Even these destroyers had to respect the erect, strong, and primitive majesty of her body.

"She's a goddess. She believes only in pleasure; her eyes summon every living being to stroke her clit. This woman, not fertile but necessary to the continuance of the world, knew that the body is a gift that extracts pardon for every sin.

"She ignores Purgatory and Hell, and when the hour will come to enter Black Night, she'll look without hatred, remorse, or fear at the face of Death."

The
Grave
of
Lost
Stories

---

WILLIAM T.
VOLLMANN

In the Grave of Lost Stories there is neither day nor night, but a stupendous blackness shot through with corpuscles of fluorescence, like droplets of oil in water—an inalienable fact, of which the vulgar minds around him could not conceive. They were too busy writing anonymous articles about him (he knew that Griswold was behind most of it, but not all; there were so many envious scoundrels!) to ever comprehend that the light and dark of Plato's cave might, indeed *must* mingle at the bottom of the universe, as they could see for themselves if they'd but look through a telescope whose power penetrated into the depths of the earth, beyond the graves that honey-combed the clay like the shafts of mines, so far beyond them as to leave them seeming shallow indeed; and the deeper shot the beams of that telescope, the more violently surged the gloom-rays through the eye-piece, staining the world black like bad old memories; but if it were possible to see through these swirling atoms, and the cosmos of Ether under them, then at last the darkness would seem to thicken and narrow into a gorge whose cliffs and stones were darkness coagulated into obsidian. Into this chasm no telescope could pierce. This was the center of the majestic circle of planets and suns—so extreme its gravitational attraction that light was swallowed in it forever. There was a stifling horror about the place, about which hovered the most vile and pestilential fumes; somewhere in this pit was Death itself unfolded. But in what form it revealed itself was unknown, because the gulf was roofed with the foliage of night-trees that leaned toward each other on all sides, gripping each other's soft and flabby trunks with branches that terminated in claws, so that every tree gashed every tree to the heart, growing deeper and deeper into each other's wounds until their agony could never end; from their pallid mushroom flesh bled drops of black sap that rained down into the darkness below, and their velvety leaves vibrated in pain, with a sound like a cloud of midges. —A narrow Path of Dead Tales passed through an arch of these leaves and branches, and then spiraled downward into the pit. At first the moistly disagreeable presence of the charnel vegetation polluted every breath, and icy droplets of tree-blood plashed down upon hands and shoulders, but then the descent steepened, so that it was necessary to hug the wall of the pit and feel one's way sideways, and in the course of many downward revolutions the air became ever cooler and drier, like the stale atmosphere of mummy-caves. Meanwhile, however, the smell of mortality had increased, according to the cube of proximity to that concentrated vortex of corruption, the Grave of Lost Stories. —How pitiably foolish he had been, to imagine that his victims would have been reduced to marble-white skulls, to tibiae as clean as tusk-ivory, to ribs like bleached harps! —No, that would hardly be the Demon's modus operandi. —So be it. He had looked upon such sights before. —Still, the *foulness* . . . which is why he concluded in his final poem that matter was a means, not an end. At that time he was working feverishly by lamplight, intoxicated with the solution of ciphers that unlocked his pages of darkness with great clicks, so that he did not have to think about how everything he had written would disgust him the next morning; and he went out to the dark black garden to walk to and fro, wearing a deep and narrow path in the snow as he worked out precisely how deep the Grave would have to be to hold those millions and millions of Stories whose white souls had risen upward like a snowstorm of dreamy unhappiness; well, of course the volume of the bodies would flatten with decomposition; therefore the required depth must be the quotient, but the *full* quotient, not the square root of the quotient; as to how tightly they could be packed into that death-house, their structure had to be considered; it was distinctly stated by all the authorities that Stories have skeletons, except for the very early embryos and abortions from those times when you wail in the night knowing that something has just been lost forever but not what; you will never know what, because it is gone. Let us conceive these skeletons, then, to be composed of variegated vertebrae the hue and sheen of black crystal, almost like gaming pieces as he had thought when Mrs. Osgood was moved by his white-skinned sadness and said ah, Mr. Poe, this country affords no arena for those who live to dream and he said do you dream? I mean sleeping dream? and she smiled and said oh yes Mr. Poe I am a perfect Joseph at dreaming, except that my dreams are of the Unknown and *Spiritual* and he said I knew it; I knew it by your eyes and for the first time he embraced her and she held his hand in hers so tenderly but all at once it seemed to him as if something black, steely—cold, cutting, had closed around his wrist and were pinching it to the bone, the frozen ache of it poisoned him, and the veins stood out on his white wrist; as his phalanges and metacarpi shattered into chessmen he uttered a cry of agony so that she pulled her hand away and said you are *ill*, are you not, Mr. Poe? at which she became so beautiful to him, and he fell on his knees before her saying is the idea fixed in your head to leave me? as his little wife sat by obediently. Later he was seized with inspiration, and sat down hastily to write, but before he had gotten any farther than that weirdly metallic phrase *the Grave of Lost Stories,* it had already left him, and he sat groaning. Somewhere the Story was struggling desperately to breathe; she was smothering, and he could do nothing. In his life he had committed so many murders . . . Maybe he could save her. He wrote very quickly *there is no day or night* and heard the Story draw in a deep gasp of breath and begin sobbing with hysteria and weariness.

He threw down his pen and knelt upon the floor, wringing his hands. —I call on you to live! he cried. Are you going to vanish like everything else? I wouldn't wrong you if I could help it! Please—I—but the shadow is already there on your throat . . .

The Demon came in, chilling his forehead with an ache like ice. He arose at once. The Demon came in smiling.

I *see* that you smile, he said to this enemy, with quick and bitter sensitivity. Well, everyone is out to ruin me. It really doesn't matter that you smile. But what delegation sent you?

Whoever they are, said the Demon, they are very collected in their resolve. Of that you may be sure.

He heard someone struggling for breath.

*Live!* he shouted hoarsely. *You beautify the earth—live!* Tears streamed down his face.

He sat listening, knowing that the Demon smiled behind him. He heard the Story begin gasping for breath again, choking and weeping. Trembling, he wrote *lost, Stories, whose shrouds are—are* . . . He scarcely knew what he wrote; one word, one line, might prolong her life a little longer, until he could think, until he could save her . . .

Oh, very few Stories die of their own accord, the Demon said. They are like us; they want to live, no matter how badly they are treated . . . And yet there are some who know . . .

*Help me!* she screamed. For a dozen eternities her ragged gasps of breathing tortured him; then he heard her say very faintly *oh,* there's someone sitting on my heart . . .

He kept expecting some miracle to happen. He kept expecting her not to come sobbing to him saying I'm dead.

He wrote *there is neither day nor night* and desperately crossed it out and wrote *neither night nor day can be found in the country beyond this Vault, which I so call for lack of any better name* and crossed it out and wrote *in this place, which is hideously exempt from the laws of day and night, the horror of one's situation can scarcely be described* and he heard her sweet breathing (yes! she was breathing still!) and he wrote *there they seized me with mildewed hands and held me fast beyond my power to struggle. Then I fell into a darkness that was not yet darkness—oh, would that it were!—for it prickled with globules of magnetism like—like—* he would not write *the Grave of Lost Stories* in this unlucky context; he gnawed at his pen, forgetting the Demon and even her for the moment; he crossed out the last two lines and wrote *I fell into a darkness whose teeming shadow-tides rushed over me, whose waves poured down upon me with soundless weight, pressing down upon me with a force as steady and interminable as my own unsought-for return to consciousness. My thoughts were ticking like death-beetles, like antique watches. As yet, I had not opened my eyes. I would not; I would not—and then suddenly terror shot through me like a galvanizing current, for I felt weight and narrowness and stifling compression all around me; I smelled fresh pine-wood; I . . .*

Too late, laughed the Demon, and departed.

Where she had been was silence. As always, the Demon was correct. He knew that there would be circular excoriations about her throat, and the black marks of his own fingers. He had strangled her. The arms would be outstretched as usual, the fingers clenched so tightly that blood was oozing from the palms. Blood must be trickling from the opened mouth; the head thrown back, the protruding tongue ghastly blue.

What a young and beautiful Story you were! he screamed. I—I—I—

Eddie? his wife called timidly from the other room.

Instantly he was beside her. —Are you warm enough, little Sis? he said.

She nodded. The cat purred on her breast. He stooped down and kissed her forehead.

I was . . .

Yes? he said.

I was—worried about you. I heard you shouting . . .

You've coughed none at all today, he said. I'm really in excellent spirits about that. You can't imagine how I—

He felt the familiar *Vulpine Presence* behind him, breathing icy stinking breath into his ear. He must not let it get near her. —Good night, Sissy, he said, rushing out and slamming the door behind him.

So, he said to himself, bringing pencil to paper:—the skeletons of my lost Stories, being for all practical purposes incompressible, must enforce a minimum volume upon this Tomb (the *Vulpine Presence* snapped its teeth together in his ear)—but still more so the coffins. Were *I* the Architect, I would have quarried deep in the slag of subterraneous fires to get those glassy black building-stones, and then I would have laid out the work in *very definite* proportions. —Which proportions? The question was perplexing, like that of the ratio of infinite lines, and yet not insoluble; for in architecture the Vault, or Cavern, or Cloister with its many tiers of catacombs, must surely obey the primordial law of *Grandness*. That this did not constitute proof he admitted, of course; he could not be *certain* of it, but no other possibility could be seriously entertained. Therefore it would be an oblong room of great dimensions—*and here once again* he wrote *let me suggest that, in fact, we have still been speaking of comparative trifles. The distance of the planet Neptune from the sun has been stated; it is 28 hundred millions of miles*—no doubt it was carpeted with crimson silk of imperishable virtue, through which meandered blue veins. Because the influence of death would be at its maximum here, he expected it to be as cold in his tomb as the blackness of space. The walls must be of marble, of course. They would rise like cliffs, tunneled through with crypts in as much profusion as the caves where sea swallows make their nests; and indeed the twitterings that came from them were birdlike, but they were tormented cries of the dead Stories in the coffins, and the deep square openings went up the wall as far as could be seen, some glowing with green or yellow light, the rest abandoned to their own blackness; thus the walls rose until they were lost in the luminescence of those sluggish globules that swarm in the air like glowworms. Surely, then, he must take account of the coffins, and the spacing between them . . . He wrote: *Behind this portal I saw with unquiet eye the black arch of darkness that led to the vaults—but it was a most peculiar and uncanny sort of arch, for not only did the edges of the ceiling curve downward, but the edges of the floor sloped* upward *as well until they too met the marble wall; thus it seemed to me as I hurried ahead of my echoing footsteps into that darkness that I was at the bottom of a vast bowl. My disorientation was increased by the glittering whitish pillars that had been set into both floor and ceiling; these towered above my head, or grew downward like stalactites; they were as close together as the pipes of a church organ, except for a narrow space or channel at the center of the floor, where it was lowest, through which I could barely pass my body.* In the margin he wrote: *Not only is the foregoing mathematically accurate; but it also rings true to all the harmonies of my soul.* He sat at his desk almost until dawn, calculating the dimensions on blue paper. His mother-in-law (or mother as she had really become) sat knitting and dozing beside him, and every now and then he would read out the results of his calculations to her and say: Do you understand, Muddie? Am I correct in this? and she said how you *do* read out those figures so cleverly, Eddie! and brought him a mug of fresh hot coffee and pulled in a stitch and her head sank down upon her shoulder; he heard her snoring; he heard his wife coughing in her sleep; the ticking of the clock was almost insufferable to his ears. Thank God for Muddie! She never went to bed before he did, out of consideration for his horror of being alone.

Early the following afternoon, as he pretended to sleep, he heard Muddie talking about him in the kitchen with her dear friend Mrs. Phelps, and Mrs. Phelps was saying how could you *think* such a thing Muddie when I can see the *depth* of his love for her! and Muddie said with a sad laugh God knows Eddie loves my Virginia that is not what I meant and Mrs. Phelps said in that tone he hated Mrs. Clemm it is *certainly* not my place to pry and Muddie said oh no no I need to open my heart to someone and he said to himself *faugh!* and Mrs. Phelps said well then what do you mean? and Muddie said Eddie is a very dear boy, and Virginia idolizes him; since she is so sick I think it is a great mercy for them both that he is not a man in the full sense of the word and as I say he does love her fondly and faithfully as I do and Mrs. Phelps said something in a voice that was drowned out by the beating of his heart and Muddie said I honestly fear for his reason if Virginia should pass away; he is so devoted to her and he heard her crying and Mrs. Phelps was saying sssh dearie sssh.

He dressed and went out silently, trying in his mind to gather the Grave of Lost Stories into visibility so that he could go down to it and harrow it of its agonized souls; if this proposition proved tenable, he could even—ah, to the Devil with it! He went to the theater with his friend J. B. Booth, and the usher said gentlemen, where are your tickets? and J. B. Booth took a ticket out of his breast pocket and the usher bowed and turned to Eddie and said and you, sir? to which he replied for your stupidity I cannot hold you responsible because you were born that way, but your ignorance is an affront: I am a member of the Press. Kindly trouble me no further, do you understand me?

*You* a member of the Press? said the usher scornfully. You—a drunkard in a shabby black suit! Will you leave quietly or shall I be forced to expel you?

He pulled himself rigidly upright. He looked the usher in the eye. He said very quietly: May God have mercy on your soul.

Oh, Eddie, don't be such a character, said J.B. I'll spring for your ticket, and later we'll have a glass, eh? Eddie! Where are you going, Eddie?

Later that night, it was raining heavily, and somebody saw him standing under an awning in that frock coat of his, glaring at something and muttering to himself, for all the world as if he were repeating the occasion when he wrote "The Bells" with Mrs. Shew and started talking to unseen white-shrouded girls until he fell into a swoon and when they had laid him on the bed the doctor fished a massive gold watch from the depths of his waistcoat and took the pulse and said to Mrs. Shew this man has heart disease and will die early in life and although the bystander had an umbrella, something other than unkindness, as he later put it, prevented him from offering it to this crazed emperor of disasters, whom, as it proved, he was gazing upon for the last time. The bystander went home and to bed.

What a dreary dismal rain!

When he felt the familiar breath of corruption in his ear, when he heard the shrill voice of the *Vulpine Presence* (whose parchmentlike forehead he could not bear to see), he realized that he had almost been expecting it. How exceedingly it disliked him he measured by the snapping of its jaws.

Overhead, the moon was shooting its meteor-stones from every volcano. He could hear the whizzing fires . . .

It was at that time, as he dated it, that the *Vulpine Presence* began following in his every footstep. When he sat down at his desk to write, it stood behind him, elongating itself and bending over him to whisper odiously in his ear. If he fled into the garden, it pursued him there, striding alongside him with its arm about his waist. Even into Virginia's room it came with him, aping his every movement, so that when he bent down to kiss her lips it did the same, breathing into her nostrils until she whispered that terrible smell, Eddie and he said I I I and she choked with nausea and began to cough, until he rushed back to his desk and struggled not to hear it clacking its teeth in laughter. Every day it grew more distinct, until he knew its hateful visage better than his own face: that ghastly yellow forehead, whose skin was stretched to drumlike tautness over the bones, the oval pits of the eyes, that sank like twin wells into the skull, the hunched white shoulders, the sunken cheeks, whose deep concavities enhanced the effect of abnormal protrusion in the chin, the shrunken lips that split open like a fissure to display to his gaze every one of those vicious little teeth . . . just as it had been a decade before, when he was writing "Berenice," and because he could not write the next word *instantly* Berenice was already clawing at her breast trying to get air and he heard the delicate rustle of her garments as she sank to her knees and her last breath was rattling in her throat when the *Vulpine Presence* appeared and grinned at him so that he could see nothing but its vicious rows of teeth, like a shark and he exclaimed in horror and closed his eyes but he could not stop thinking about *the teeth* and he wrote *the white and ghastly spectrum of the teeth* and he heard Berenice begin to sob on the floor as his Stories did, feebly, hysterically, when they had been saved; and he sprang up, forgetting the *Vulpine Presence* entirely, and shouted to her would to *God* you had died!

The Demon appeared and said to him: No, it is *you* who should have died. Write it.

I *will not!* he shouted.

She lives, does she not? Shall I return with the Black Cat? Shall we wall her up together?

Slowly, he set pen to paper and wrote *and in a smile of changed meaning, the* teeth *of the changed Berenice disclosed themselves to my view. Would to God that I had never beheld them, or that, having done so, I had died!*

Good, said the Demon behind his shoulder. Very good.

The *Vulpine Presence* worked its mouth into a little O and gibbered in delight.

But she lives, he thought to himself. At least she lives.

Virginia died in the last week of January. Her death-agony was very protracted; in the end she smothered. For a keepsake of her, the ladies painted a watercolor of her dead face to give him; and he knelt sobbing and kissing that cold white forehead until her mother put aside her own grief to comfort him and he said I can't forget the *horror* when her eyes closed forever and Muddie rocked him in her arms like a baby and later, shaking and shaking because he still saw how those sad eyes had suddenly become hateful, lusterless, he went to his desk and wrote *the vortical in-drawing of the orbs* . . . But after that, though he turned his pen round and round in his fingers, there was nothing to do with the anguish save endure it. (Twenty-eight years later, when he himself was dead and the cemetery was destroyed, her remains were rescued by his biographer Gill and stored in a box under his bed. Sometimes other gentlemen would come to visit Gill and they'd sit on the bed together, talking in low whispers because the landlady was a dragon, and Gill would say how about a spot of sherry? And Gill would say can I refill your glass? and Gill would say it feels rather warm in here and Gill would say so we finished off that d——d bottle! and Gill would dig the other in the ribs, breathing heavily, and say well *I* know why you're here you old rounder you! and Gill would say well do you want to see them or don't you? and Gill would say all right then! and he'd reach under the bed and set the box on his lap and undo the black ribbon with a flourish and crow yessir, here they are: the bones of Annabel Lee!)

It was a dark and snowy afternoon, and he sat listlessly at his desk turning over the leaves of his books. Muddie had gone out with her begging basket again; there was nothing to eat. In the margin of his Livy he penciled *I believe that Hannibal passed into Italy over the Pennine Alps; and if Livy were living now, I could demonstrate this fact even to him.* In his Bridgewater he wrote *The plots of God are perfect. The universe is a Plot of God.*

What if Virginia had not been dead when he bore her to the tomb? What if she had only swooned, and were coming to life at this very moment in the nailed coffin, shrieking inside her shroud, struggling for life and breath . . . ? He groaned.

On his first interview with Mrs. Whitman in the cemetery, he professed his love, and when it came out that their birthdays were the same, she was sure that the Stars had called them together; later he held her hand; he would have fallen at her feet but for fear of wounding her, as he wrote to her, telling her how he felt the touch of her hand even when she laid it on the back of his chair; she for her part thinking what a chalky clammy forehead that gentlemen has!

Helen, he said, my Helen.

But later that night, when he returned to the tombs alone to see them by moonlight, he saw a marble vault incised with the name MORELLA and he fell to his knees in the snow, weeping as he remembered the panicked scratching of his pen twelve years before as the word-tails grew down below the ruled lines like the alphabet-roots of those night-trees in the cleft where the dead Stories went; and she had shimmered in the air like milk in water and then slowly took shape; and now he could hear nothing but her anguished panting as his pen raced to save her and the *Vulpine Presence* pursed its black lips and blew upon the paper so that it fluttered like an ocean and he could scarcely see the words and lines; and Morella was gasping with asphyxia; and the sweat of terror for her leaped in beads upon his forehead and he felt his heart curdle in him even as he wrote frantically *fate bound us together at the altar; and I never spoke of passion, nor thought of love* and he heard her desperate rasping breaths and he wrote *the notion of that identity* which at death is or is not lost forever, *was to me—at all times, a consideration of intense interest* and Morella made a little clicking noise in her throat and thrust back her neck until the skin was unbearably taut and sank to the floor as the triumphant Demon appeared with the shroud, but he wrote *a consideration of intense interest; not more from the perplexing and exciting nature of its consequences* and Morella opened her eyes *than from the marked and agitated manner in which Morella mentioned them* and she sought to rise but the Demon seized her shoulders and thrust her back down upon the floor, hissing you may not be dead yet, child, but you are dying; then Morella gazed at him with her melancholy eyes and replied: I am dying, yet I shall live.

Yes! he shouted joyously, writing *I am dying, yet I shall live* on the blue sheet of paper that Virginia would later attach to the others in the roll, using the *almost negligible* proportion of gum tragacanth powder that he had taught her, so that when Mrs. Osgood accepted her invitation to visit she could laughingly unroll the pasted sheets across the floor as *he* behaved shyly and sweetly and waywardly in front of these two women whom he loved; but for now he was suddenly cast into a well of bitter grief when Morella arose and caressed his cheek with her icy fingers, asking him: But *why* did you make me live, when you feel nothing for me?

and he said I I I

and she said does the Demon love me?

He *does not!* Poe shouted. The oppression of his soul now stifled him so much at these words of hers that he wanted nothing more than that the black and sluggish waters should close over his eyes and mouth. —But Morella only smiled faintly and with one pale hand brushed back the lush, blue-black ringlets from her forehead. Her eyes gleamed; her little white teeth glittered. —Tell me, husband, have I sisters?

Yes, he said in a low voice.

And whom ought I to love best?

Well, he said, Berenice was born just before you, so she is the nearest to you in age, but you must be careful when you play with her, as she is sickly and not likely to live long.

And when she dies, where will she go?

To the Grave of Lost Stories.

Oh, that will be the day of days for her, said Morella. Does the Demon live there?

I cannot say. I do not know where he lives. I have never been down to that place.

And Virginia—how about her? she said to him, singing the name like a bitter mockingbird.

He flew into a rage and said: You have no right—you—to mention *her* to me! You are never to mention her, or I shall throw these pages into the fire—do you hear me?

She said nothing.

He bowed his head over the blue paper and wrote *But thy days shall be days of sorrow.* A moment later, his heart softened, and he wanted to call her to him, but she was gone. How to write it? She was gone like narrowing passages of dead stories dwindling into hollow veins in which silence beat instead of blood.

And now, here was her tomb.

Then he saw her pallid figure hurrying toward him in the

darkness, and he was chilled with dread. What if she touched him and the droplets of brightness came oozing out of her fingers . . . ? (He had thought that he wanted to go down deeper, but now he knew himself to be as paltry as a shallow grave.)

He found himself at his desk, writing "Sepuleth," writing *a terrible disorder beat in my veins,* writing *I shrieked aloud,* but the Demon said this time, you drunkard, you won't be able to pull it off and the *Vulpine Presence* blew a whistling wind from its mouth that swept the papers off his desk, and in a twinkling he heard Sepuleth's heart-rending catchings of breath, the lovely Lady Sepuleth *with whom,* he bent down to write, *I would have dwelled in happiness, among all the flowers and brooks of Arnheim* . . . but it was too late; he knew that it was too late; he covered his ears so as not to hear her awful expiring sounds and Muddie said Poor Eddie do you have a headache? and he said yes, Muddie and she said shall I rub your forehead for you? and he said I was thinking of—of—and she said I know, Eddie; and he closed his eyes for weariness and instantly saw Sepuleth's head lolled against her shoulder, with her long blond locks streaming down her black dress like rays of the sun, and her elbow was drawn in against her breast, like the wing of a sleeping bird;—it was only the extreme angle of the neck that appeared unnatural.

He had proven in his tale "Of One Hans Pfaall" that some sort of atmosphere must extend from the sun to the orbit of Venus and perhaps indefinitely beyond; if not, as he had written there, *I can see no reason, therefore, why life could not be sustained even in a vacuum* . . . But now he admitted that he had deceived himself.

I cannot bear this anymore, he said. Berenice, Morella, Ligeia, Lenore, Ulalume, I call on you to mourn for her and for me. I am going to the Antarctic moon.

Are you going out, Eddie? Muddie said.

Just to her grave, he said.

A fine rain was falling. The air was very thick and impure.
The river was blackish gray; the reflections of lights gleamed
in it like eyes. He wandered through the streets of the city,
where the Conqueror Worm reigned in all the theaters, per-
forming its terrible deeds behind stage-curtains the color of
puddled blood, and the senile old Man of the Crowd rushed by
him like a whirligig and vanished in the fog beyond the gas-
lights and then appeared again to wink at him knowingly
because they shared the same panic and the same bottle and his
breath was the same as that of the *Vulpine Presence* and then he
was gone. Dark-windowed houses of palish brick walled the
fog in. He saw a woman running into a narrow lighted arch-
way and the door closed behind her. He saw white pillars
glittering in the dark porticoes of building-fronts; grand white
sepulchers shone against the blackness of the river. A literary
lady called to him from her carriage good evening to you, my
Raven! and he lifted his hat unthinkingly; his eyes had already
fixed themselves in the glare of death. His doubles bowed
ironically to him from every alley, wearing the gentlemen's
suits that he had never had the funds to wear since his guardian
cast him off. They said *Mr. Poe, Mr. Poe, whooh-whoosh!* He
trembled to look at them, but when they greeted him with
condescension he was filled with rage, and quoted himself to
these selves, shouting: For the love of *God*, Montresor! at
which they blanched and fled, knowing that if he but had them
in his power he would wall them up alive, and the Demon and
the Black Cat would help him. —The streets were slimy with
rain. He felt a swelling ache in his chest, and knew that the Red
Death was already inside him, speckling his blackened organs
with carmine and scarlet. It was unbearable; he needed a drink.
His hands searched eagerly in his pocket and found a penny;
he went into a tavern and had a glass of wine, and his face

flushed and he determined to seek out the Grave of Lost Stories and set those poor souls free; for he *knew* where it was, and though the task scarcely be safe or easy, he thought that he had sufficient boldness to undertake it.

Undoubtedly this Tomb lay in a difficult and eccentric direction. The foolish and superficial cosmographers (to whom he had to confess a glacial coolness, in respect of the unwarranted praise that they had received), would surely choose to locate it at the center of the earth, as if it were the cavern of Avernus—a distance precisely equal to the earth's radius. But this said nothing about where the actual *vortex* was. To repeat: he knew where it was. His prospects now seemed unbounded. —In other words, the attraction of the Vault must be increasing in an exponential ratio.

He followed the Auber River past the red cliffs of Circassy, and sunset came, and he descended into the Valley of Unrest where the lilies bowed over a grave—he did not know whose; he refused to know; and now it was dark at last, and he was in the ghoul-haunted woodland of Weir; and the water of the Auber was a mottled silver that showed him his own reflection. Psyche met him at the bank and he was glad to see her, but as he wrote *Our talk had been serious and sober, but our thoughts they were palsied and sere* and truthfully her unfocused eyes with the glittering whites and the pupils like green marbles disturbed him far more than the barkings of the ghoul-packs who ravaged the churchyards in the misty darkness behind them; and suddenly a star-ball of blowing gases descended through the trees and Psyche said I fear the pallor of that Star but he showed his teeth in a laugh and said don't be afraid Sis I assure you that a star as bright as that can only light our way but she said no Eddie I don't want to. —*Then* certainly he pacified his sweet Psyche; he had to; I am entitled as a reader to say that he kissed her, still thinking of the crystalline light

of that Star that maddened and exalted him; but Psyche still
sniveled and trailed her little wings in the dust, so to distract
her from her scruples and gloom he asked her what do you
think happens to the dead Stories? and she said oh Eddie
they're not as unhappy as you think because I see them all
around me so brittle and sparkling, blowing everywhere like
dandelion seeds, so *many* of them, even here in this horrid dark
place that they're around me in constellations of stars! but
saying this, she remembered the evil Star that drew them both
on, and her happy face fell again, so to keep her from dwelling
on her fear he said but aren't these dead Stories restless? and
she said yes, but they try to be patient because someday someone will write them again and they'll be reborn as new living
girls and brides so healthy and happy and she also said Eddie
you should not destroy the paper of the dead Stories because
that hurts them as they walked deeper down the cypress ways
in the direction that the Star was pulling them, and the ghouls
had fallen silent, and Psyche said please Eddie don't make me
go on with you anymore and her plumes were dragging in the
dust again but he put his arm around her and said what makes
your dead Stories happiest? and she said when a child thinks
of them have you ever heard children tell each other Stories?
and he said no and she said poor Eddie and he said but you do
grant that they remain bound to their bodies? and she said yes
and he said triumphantly well then that's why we go to the
graves of our dead women, because their skeletons are lying
there for us to love and treasure beneath the marble slabs!
Don't you admit that a grave and corpse are more real than a
memory and a lock of hair? and she said I never thought you
such a materialist, Eddie and he laughed and they went on into
the suffocating gloom and the Star set slowly over the black
valley which his reasoning powers in combination with his
accurate knowledge had enabled him to predict in bold relief,

and as the Star set it cast a last beam down through the night-trees that occluded the gulf, and tenderly brushed the pure darkness below, like the hem of a skirt brushing his lips; and Psyche said let's go home now Eddie please! but he kissed her so many times and fell on his knees and entreated her and made her laugh by telling her how her cat Catarina had chased her tail and how Muddie had been so astounded, until again he quenched her tears; and so hand in hand they walked among the sad-scented night-trees and descended into that gorge of coagulated darkness, and on the opposite wall he saw that a face had been carved—a titanic face, whose mouth could have swallowed armies; and he stiffened like a galvanized corpse to see that it was the face of the *Vulpine Presence*! Its jaws champed and it ground its black stone teeth together. Its eyeballs were the size of millstones, and they rolled to and fro with a sullen thundering sound. But he would not let poor little Sissy see it. So he talked and talked to her ever more rapidly and gaily like his pen speeding so desperately across the paper to save the dying Stories; and Psyche was smiling again through her tears and saying oh you're so funny Eddie and so they descended hand in hand into that sweet-sulphur stench of concentrated mortality. They were in a narrow valley of bones and smoldering fumes, made still narrower by the ledges that projected overhead, comprised of a pinkish mineral such as chalcedony, into which were set white nodules of a cuspid shape; from these little drops of moisture unpleasantly dripped. She continued to grasp his hand, and he was so happy to be with her even though her face was so ghastly pale and there was black mold around her eyes and lips; and the yellowish greenish smoke that swirled around her made her hair smell singed and he felt the mold growing cold and clammy on his eyebrows and the taste of death was in his mouth and so they came to a gigantic door of tarnished iron. He said Sissy what does it say on the door? And she leaned forward to spell out the letters with her fingers (for in truth the dark air was so thick that despite the globules of light that writhed in the atmosphere like maggots it was very difficult to see); and she said *U* and she said *L* and a sudden agony of terror made his heart beat so loudly that he could not hear what she said and he cried yes? yes? with his haunted face uplifted and she said *ULALUME!* and his heart became as ashen and brittle and brown as a dead leaf. —I *killed* her, he said in a kind of choked wonder. He remembered now how the suffocation had been consummated. —Psyche had begun to walk away. A chilly and rigid magnificence issued from her. She called back over her shoulder: —Yes, she is dead, but *she is waiting for you inside!*

Please don't leave me, he said in a very small voice, as if to himself.

Remember, laughed Psyche from far away (she was almost out of sight), they're all waiting for you!

A key was in the lock, high above that name carved in weeping letters. The lock was thickly overgrown with fungi, and condensation from the reeking mists all about him had scored the iron with a thousand little channels like tear trails, now choked with rusts and lichens. From the crack where that massive block of iron had been fitted into the doorway of the tomb, a sickening exhalation issued, and he thought to himself it was *thus* in the place where we buried Madame Usher! —Immediately there came to him a vision of those thousands of wives and daughters of his who waited within, their white bodies puffing outward with the gases of decomposition; which convinced him, by right of the Grave's position as universal vortex, that these horrible vapors might indeed become the *vaporous rings* of the outer planets. —He rose from his desk and rushed outside to look for Saturn. It was a clear night; Mrs. Shew had very kindly lent him her pocket telescope. —Yes,

yes!—Indeed, since all the planets were no more than globular condensations of these ring forms, the conclusion was inescapable (despite the laughable ignorance of the astronomers), that the universe was composed of nothing other than this miasma. And in consequence, since the law of gravitation was nothing but the fact of inexorable collapse, one could expect, after untold millions of epochs, all matter to congeal into that jet-black, obsidianlike form of which the Valley of the Grave was comprised! Some might call this rash speculation; as for him, he could not but smile at the numbskulls who thought to confute him.

Standing on tiptoe, he was just barely able to get the tips of his fingers around the key. It would not move. He leaped up and hung from the key with all his weight; he raised his body halfway above it and locked his elbows; he braced his feet against the door; his face glowed with the fiercely radiant joy of self-destruction. He strained and strained to turn the key in the lock, but it would not move. In his anxiety and frustration he began kicking the door, which resounded with sullen hollow boomings like an immense drum; at last he placed one hand over the other, and then, squeezing until the veins stood out on his forehead, he wrenched the key clockwise with all his strength. There came a great squeaking and grinding. Flakes of rust showered him like bloody sparks. Now the key turned with ease. He let himself down to the ground and took hold of it again; the revolution of the circle was completed, and he heard a click. The massive door swung slowly inward. A foul wind rushed out from that dark place. Now he would discover the corpses. Now the tomb would open for him like a vagina. With a cry of joy, he ran inside. Too late, he saw that the interior was a wedge-shaped *cul-de-sac* lined with spikes. In horror and dismay, he wheeled around to escape, but long before he reached it, the door had slammed shut with a malignant boom; an instant later, the wall-jaws closed upon him.

Poe's "final poem" is, of course, *Eureka* (1848). While I have breathed deeply of its dreamily logical atmosphere, I have also felt free to distort or ignore its arguments. Poe himself would not agree with the hypotheses that I attribute to him. The conversation between Poe and Mrs. Osgood is excerpted from an entry in the diary of Elizabeth Oakes Smith for 1845. Poe's hopeless cries to the first of the dying stories are partly based on a letter of his (I believe the last) to Mrs. Shew. The sentence in italics about the planet Neptune comes from *Eureka*. (The phrase "the vortical in-drawing of the orbs" also comes from *Eureka* in an astronomical context.) The conversation between Mrs. Clemm and Mrs. Phelps is reconstructed from a brief mention by Mrs. Phelps's daughter. The anecdote about Poe's biographer keeping Virginia's remains under his bed is given in Hervey Allen's *Israfel: The Life and Times of Edgar Allan Poe* (New York: Farrar and Rhinehart, 1934, p. 581 fn). The marginal note on Livy is given in Poe's "Marginalia" (November 1844). The lines in italics attributed to "Berenice" do in fact come from that story (1835). Ditto for "Morella" (1835). Ditto for "Hans Pfaal" (1835). Ditto for "Ulalume" ("Our talk had been serious and sober . . .") (I have slightly abridged some of the excerpts.) "Sepuleth," however, being one of the Lost Stories, is of course imaginary. For some of the Psyche's views on dead stories I am indebted to Miss Moira Brown, who lost her life-work of paintings in a fire.

# Contributors

KATHY ACKER's books include *Great Expectations, Blood and Guts in High School, Don Quixote, Empire of the Senseless,* and *Literal Madness.*

MARTIN AMIS has written, among other books, *Money, Other People: A Mystery Story, Success, Dead Babies, The Rachel Papers,* and *London Fields.*

SCOTT BRADFIELD is the author of *The History of Luminous Motion* and *Dream of the Wolf.*

ANGELA CARTER's books of fiction and nonfiction include *Nights at the Circus, The Bloody Chamber, Heroes and Villains, The Sadeian Woman,* and *The Passion of New Eve.*

ROBERT COOVER's books include *The Origin of the Brunists, Pricksongs & Descants, The Public Burning, Gerald's Party,* and most recently, *Pinocchio in Venice.*

JANICE GALLOWAY is the author of *The Trick Is to Keep Breathing* and *Blood,* a story collection.

JOHN HAWKES has written some thirteen novels, among them *The Blood Oranges, Second Skin, Travesty, The Passion Artist, Adventures in the Alaskan Skin Trade,* and *Whistlejacket.*

JAMAICA KINCAID is the author of *Annie John, At the Bottom of the River, A Small Place,* and *Lucy.*

PATRICK MCGRATH's books are *Blood and Water and Other Tales, The Grotesque,* and *Spider.*

BRADFORD MORROW is the author of the novels *Come Sunday* and *The Almanac Branch.* He edits the literary journal *Conjunctions.*

YANNICK MURPHY's first book is *Stories in Another Language.*

JOYCE CAROL OATES is the author of numerous books of fiction including *You Must Remember This, Them, Raven's Wing, Bellefleur,* and *Because It Is Bitter, and Because It Is My Heart.*

RUTH RENDELL, under her own name and the pseudonym Barbara Vine, has published many books including *The Lake of Darkness, Live Flesh, The Tree of Hands, The House of Stairs,* and *A Fatal Inversion.*

ANNE RICE's most recent novel is *The Witching Hour.* She is also the author of *Interview with the Vampire, The Vampire Lestat, The Mummy,* and *The Queen of the Damned.*

PETER STRAUB's novels include *Julia, If You Could See Me Now, Ghost Story, Shadowland, Floating Dragon, Koko,* and, in collaboration with Stephen King, *The Talisman.* His most recent book is a collection of stories, *Houses Without Doors.*

Among EMMA TENNANT's novels are *The Last of the Country House Murders, Hotel de Dream, The Bad Sister,* and *Wild Nights.*

LYNNE TILLMAN's books are *Haunted Houses, Motion Sickness,* and *Absence Makes the Heart.*

WILLIAM T. VOLLMANN is the author of *You Bright and Risen Angels, The Rainbow Stories,* and *The Ice-Shirt.*

PAUL WEST's numerous books of fiction and nonfiction include *Words for a Deaf Daughter, The Very Rich Hours of Count von Stauffenberg, Rat Man of Paris, Lord Byron's Doctor,* and *The Women of Whitechapel and Jack the Ripper.*

Among JOHN EDGAR WIDEMAN's many works of fiction are *Sent for You Yesterday, Hiding Place, Damballah, Fever,* and *Philadelphia Fire.*

JEANETTE WINTERSON's books include *The Passion, Sexing the Cherry,* and *Oranges Are Not the Only Fruit.*

## About the Editors

BRADFORD MORROW is the author of two novels, *Come Sunday* and *The Almanac Branch*, as well as *A Bestiary*, a book of thirty-six animal prose poems. Founder and editor of the literary journal *Conjunctions*, he is a Bard Center Fellow, and currently teaches at Bard College. He lives in New York, where he is working on his next novel.

PATRICK MCGRATH has written the story collection *Blood and Water and Other Tales*, and the novels *The Grotesque* and *Spider*. He is at work on his next novel.